Praise for Linwood Barclay

'Barclay's winning second comic caper . . . includes both long-term set-ups and well-hidden surprises'

Publishers Weekly

'Mr Barclay is the master of what might be dubbed the Barclay Effect: that point in a column or novel when a reader, shanghaied by a well-planted gag, is forced to laugh out loud'

Wall Street Journal

'Delightful characters and a clever plot created with thoughtful and skilled writing'

Washington Times

'Though written with a light touch, the novel is gripping when it counts, and includes a very nicely handled twist ending . . . *Bad Guys* makes for a good time. More Zack Walker would be welcomed'

The Strand Magazine

'Humour, realistic characters, a jaunty first-person narration, and fast pacing make for an enjoyable read'

Booklist

'Some days, all you really want is for someone to tell you a wicked-good story. Linwood Barclay answers the reader's perpetual prayer'

New York Times

Linwood B......... .... copy international bestselling author of many critically acclaimed novels, including the Richard & Judy Summer Read winner and number one bestseller *No Time for Goodbye*. He lives near Toronto with his wife where they raised two children and is a former columnist for the *Toronto Star*.

To find out more about Linwood and his books, follow him on Twitter @linwood_barclay or Facebook f/linwoodbarclay/ or visit his website www.linwoodbarclay.com

Also by Linwood Barclay

THE ZACK WALKER MYSTERIES

Bad Guys

LINWOOD BARCLAY

An Orion paperback

First published in the USA in 2005
First published in Great Britain in 2017
by Orion Books
an imprint of The Orion Publishing Group Ltd,
Carmelite House, 50 Victoria Embankment
London EC4Y 0DZ

An Hachette UK company

1 3 5 7 9 10 8 6 4 2

A CIP catalogue record for this book
is available from the British Library.

ISBN 978 0 7528 8314 4

Printed and bound in Great Britain by Clays Ltd, St Ives plc

Typeset by Born Group

MIX
Paper from
responsible sources
FSC
www.fsc.org   FSC® C104740

www.orionbooks.co.uk

For my wife, Neetha, and children, Spencer and Paige

INTRODUCTION

Back in 2008, when *No Time for Goodbye* was a Richard and Judy Summer Read and at the top of the bestseller lists, a lot of readers said, 'Not bad for a first novel.'

Except *No Time for Goodbye* was not my first novel. It was my fifth. Before Terry and Cynthia Archer had their adventure, Zack Walker had four, which were published between 2004 and 2007 by Bantam Books in the United States.

Now, for the first time, they are officially being published in the United Kingdom and Ireland. I hope you think they were worth the wait, because I loved writing the Zack books, and I think they stand right alongside the best of my other thrillers.

But they are different.

The Zack books are lighter and funnier than *No Time for Goodbye* and the books that I've written since. Zack, an ex-reporter and the author of some unsuccessful science-fiction novels, is a quirky guy. He is an anal retentive, obsessive compulsive, anxiety-riddled individual, and I hate to tell you who he's based on. He is, essentially, me unchecked. I threw all my fears and eccentricities into Zack, then multiplied them by about a hundred.

Zack is something of a safety nut. He changes the smoke detector batteries before they start to beep. He locks the doors before he goes to bed at night. He gets the oil changed in the Honda right on time. The problem is, Zack's wife and two children are somewhat less obsessed about these issues than he is, and on occasion, Zack has gone to unusual lengths with them to drive home his point. What one might call 'instructive theatrics' which have a tendency to backfire rather spectacularly.

Given his fearful nature, Zack is the most poorly equipped person on the planet to go up against bad guys. And yet, that's exactly what happens, starting with *Bad Move*. It's in this debut novel that Zack moves his family from the city to the suburbs, believing they'll be safer there. But it's just possible Zack has delivered them into more danger than anyone could have imagined.

Zack learned a few lessons about curbing his behavioral excesses by the time his second adventure, *Bad Guys*, gets underway. But he's as anxious as ever. (You may, at this point, be noticing a pattern with the titles . . .).

In *Bad Luck* (original US title: *Lone Wolf*) Zack finds himself pitted against his most formidable foe yet, and in *Bad News* (original US title: *Stone Rain*) Zack comes to the rescue of his neighbor in book one, Trixie Snelling, whose unconventional occupation and mysterious past have landed her in some very deep trouble.

Given that the first Zack book was written more than fifteen years ago, there's a noticeable absence of texting and mobile phone photography, and getting all the clues off the internet. It was a simpler time.

Well, maybe not for Zack. It was nothing but BAD times for him.

Linwood Barclay

ONE

'So, what are you asking me?' Harley said. 'Are you asking me for drugs? If you want drugs, there are drugs. There's alprazolam – that's your Xanax generic – or lorazepam; you've got your diazepam and—'

'Diaza-what?'

'Diazepam. It's not a cooking spray. It's Valium. There's a huge list of anti-anxiety prescriptions out there, some better than others, some downright dangerous. We don't use barbiturates anymore, too addictive, sometimes fatal. There's various herbal remedies, if you're into that sort of thing. Or, I don't know whether you've considered something like this before, but you could just lighten the fuck up.'

Harley's not your average doctor. He's more of a friend, with a medical degree, and a successful practice, and an examining room, which I happened to be sitting in at this moment, somewhat under duress. Harley and I were buddies back in high school, then lost touch a bit while I went to college for an English degree and he went off to medical school. 'Hey,' I would say to him when we occasionally ran into one another, 'just what kind of job do you expect to get with a medical degree?'

Years later, he became my doctor.

This appointment hadn't been my idea. It had been my wife Sarah's. And 'idea' is probably the wrong word. 'Ultimatum' would probably be a better one. 'Go see Harley,' she said, 'or I'm going to call a divorce lawyer. Or smother you in your sleep.'

The threat about the divorce lawyer didn't worry me that much. Sarah has a low opinion of the legal profession, and would probably choose sticking with me over engaging the services of one of its members. But the smothering-me-in-my-sleep thing, that seemed within her range of capabilities.

'The thing is,' Harley continued, leaning up against the paper-covered examining bed, 'there's a lot of shit to deal with in life, and sometimes that's just what you have to do. Deal with it. You're not the only one with a teenage daughter, you know. Mine's twenty-two now, seems to finally have her head on straight, but two years ago she was too busy boffing some out-there art student to study for her midterms. The guy did a show of sculptures made from raw meat. You had to go early.'

'I can't seem to help it,' I said. 'I worry. I worry all the time. It's the way I'm hardwired. Sometimes I've let it get the better of me.'

'I know,' Harley said. 'I watch the news.'

'And I've been trying to do better, honest to God, but this thing with Angie . . .'

'How old is she now?'

'Eighteen.'

Harley's eyes rolled, remembering. 'And what did you do, exactly?'

'She'd promised to be home by one in the morning. She was going out with some guy from where she worked for the summer, at the pool store. She sold

2

chlorine and algaecide and tested water samples, and there was this guy who worked there, young kid, who went around the neighborhood maintaining people's pools for them.'

'Yeah.'

'So she started going out with Pool Boy.'

'This is what you called him. Pool Boy.'

'Not to his face, or to Angie. It was just a name I had for him, is all. Anyway, she was out with him one night, and I was already awake around midnight, and sometimes if I'm up that late, I'll stay up to make sure she gets home okay. I'll read. But if I read in bed, it keeps Sarah up, with the light on, so I went down to the living room, stretched out on the front couch right by the front door, so I'd be right there when Angie got home. Even if I nodded off, I'd hear her when she got in.'

'Go on.'

'Well, I guess I did doze off, and when I woke up, it was two-thirty in the morning, which meant Angie was way past curfew, way past when she said she'd be home. So I got up, went into the kitchen and called her cell, but couldn't get an answer.'

'So, knowing you, you did what you do best,' Harley said. 'You panicked.'

'I did not panic,' I said. 'I went out looking for her. I knew where Pool Boy lived – he lives with his parents – and what kind of car he drove, so I drove over there, and the whole house is dark, except for one light in the basement.'

'Not a good sign,' Harley said, nodding slightly.

'Yeah, well, I got out of my car, looked around his, then went up to the house.'

3

'You knocked on the door at, what, nearly three in the morning?'

'No, I kind of didn't want to do that unless I knew for sure Angie was there, since I was probably going to be waking up Pool Boy's mom and dad, so I thought I'd just have a look in the basement window. I had to get down on my knees – they're these shallow windows, only come up about a foot from ground level.'

Harley sighed, closed his eyes.

'There was a bit of a gap in the curtains, and I could see it was your basic rec room, wood paneling on the walls, old couch.'

'And who was on the couch, I'm afraid to ask,' Harley said.

'No one,' I said. 'Look, you need to understand, I don't want to violate Angie's privacy, I know what kids are up to today, but it's a safety thing, okay? I just needed to know that she was okay.'

'So you didn't see her in the window,' Harley said. 'Was Pool Boy there?'

'Not inside,' I said. 'But when I got up from looking in the window, I noticed that he was standing next to me.'

'Awkward,' said Harley

'And his dad was next to him. I guess the dad heard the car, his son was still up, they came out to investigate.'

'Was this before or after they called the cops?'

'After. But by the time they arrived, we'd sorted it out. I mean, they realized who I was. Pool Boy said he'd dropped off Angie around twelve-thirty, and asked if I'd checked her bedroom before I'd come to his place.'

'Which you hadn't.'

'I was sure I'd hear her when she came in. But she says she tiptoed, didn't want to wake me.'

'How long ago was this?'

'About a month. Before school started up again. Angie's still hardly speaking to me. And the thing is, now I think she's got some sort of stalker.'

Harley dropped into the other chair in the small examining room. He was looking pretty exhausted. I seem to have that effect on people at times. 'A stalker.'

'Not the Pool Boy. I think they've broken up.'

'There's a surprise,' Harley said.

'Is this part of the new medicine?' I asked. 'Crack wise while your patients open up to you?'

'Of course not. Go ahead. I shall remain nonjudgmental.'

'She calls him a stalker, but you know how kids talk. Anyone who's interested in them they don't like is categorized a stalker. But he calls her a lot, shows up unexpectedly wherever she is. I'm just worried this guy may be some kind of a nutcase. But I'm kind of in a bad spot now, what with the Pool Boy incident being so fresh in everyone's mind, that anything I say or do looks like some kind of hysterical overreaction.'

'Just because a guy calls her a few times and shows up where your daughter hangs out doesn't make him a serial killer.'

'I know that. But I get, jeez, I get this knot in my chest, worrying about my family. It's not like we haven't had some problems in the past.'

'That was then. That was an isolated incident.' Harley leaned forward a bit in his chair, like he wanted our conversation to be more intimate. 'Zack,' he said slowly, 'I don't want to put you on anything unless you feel it's absolutely necessary. It's better to work out your problems without medications.'

'I totally agree,' I said. 'I'm not asking for a prescription. It's not like I'm a hypochondriac or something, although, if you did diagnose something, I'd have to conclude it was fatal.'

'Maybe you need to focus your attention on work, get your mind off what's happening at home. What you're going through isn't any different than what every other parent goes through. We all worry about our kids, but we have to let them live their own lives, you know.'

'Sure.'

'So, when you're writing, doing your work, doesn't that help get your mind off other things? Isn't that a good way to reduce your anxiety level?'

I nodded. 'For the most part.'

'So, what are you working on now? Another book?'

'Well, I'm back with a paper now, *The Metropolitan*, doing features. You can't exactly make a living writing books.'

'I liked that one you did, about the guy goes back in time to kill the inventor of those hot-air hand dryers in men's rooms before he's born. That wasn't a bestseller?'

'No,' I said.

Harley looked surprised. I continued, 'I'm doing a feature right now on this private eye, and the last few nights, I've been with him on this, like, well, a stakeout I guess you'd call it, hoping to catch some gang that's been smashing into high-end men's shops, making off with hundreds of thousands of dollars' worth of stuff.'

'Sounds interesting,' Harley said. 'But I trust it's not the sort of thing where you're exposing yourself to any real risk. You've had enough of that.'

I smiled tiredly. 'Don't worry. From now on, I just write about stuff, I don't get personally involved.'

'That's good,' he said. 'And what about the pharmaceutical option? You want a scrip for anything?'

I shook my head. 'Naw, unless there's anything else you can recommend.'

Harley got up, opened one of the stainless steel cabinets that held cotton balls and gauze and tongue depressors and bandages, rooted around in there and came out with a bottle of what appeared to be very expensive Scotch. He set it on the table next to him, found two small paper cups, and poured a couple of fingers' worth into each.

'I find this works well,' he said.

7

TWO

'I'm bored,' I said.

Lawrence Jones ignored me. We'd been sitting curb-side in his rusting ten-year-old Buick for nearly three hours now, on Garvin Avenue, half a block down from Brentwood's, the expensive men's shop owned by Arnett Brentwood, who had pooled his resources with some other proprietors to hire Lawrence and some other detectives to find out who was busting into their places of business at night and making off with their inventory. This was not some 'lame-ass security gig,' Lawrence had assured me. Arnett Brentwood and his fellow clothiers not only wanted to stop these guys, but find out who they were and get their merchandise back.

Lawrence sat behind the wheel, rarely taking his eyes off the storefront. It was probably the third or fourth time I'd suggested I was not being sufficiently entertained, and he was learning quickly that the best way to deal with me was to pretend I wasn't there.

He was an ex-cop in his late thirties, black, fit and trim, slightly over six feet, and gay, which I thought explained why he was a much better dresser than I. After a couple of minutes of dead silence, he said, 'Sorry.'

'Hmm?'

'Sorry this isn't more exciting for you. If I could have, I'd have called these guys, told them to rob this place sooner, that you had to go to bed early.'

'I appreciate the thought.'

We'd been watching the traffic, paying close attention to any vehicles that slowed down as they went past Brentwood's. We were still in the city proper, but beyond the downtown. Few of the buildings around here got above two or three stories. Brentwood's took up two floors, with an apartment on the third. Brentwood didn't live there. He was doing too well to live above his shop and had a nice house in the Heights.

'So, are we looking for any particular kind of car?' I asked.

Lawrence did half a shrug. 'Not sure. Probably a truck, something big like that. Middle of the night, they drive up, ram through the front window and into the store. You can't do that in Civic. Guys run in and grab armloads of suits off the rack, run back into the truck, and they're gone. Usually do the whole thing in under a minute.'

'Neat. Maybe it's a pit crew, those guys who can gas up a car and change the tires in ten seconds.'

'Well, there's a driver, at least two more guys running in and out, that would be my guess. Brentwood got hit once before, about three months ago, and his security cameras picked up some blurry images of guys all dressed in black with black ski masks, looked like a bunch of commandos. Some of the other places around the city, didn't even have any cameras, but sounds like the same bunch. Cops promise drive-bys, but they're not going to solve this unless they stumble onto some warehouse and find the suits by accident.'

Lawrence's cell rang inside his jacket. 'Yeah?' he said. 'Nothing happening here either. Yeah, right, at least I got company.' He cast a sideways glance my way. 'I'll check in with you in half an hour.'

He slipped the phone back into his jacket. 'That was Miles.'

'Miles?'

'Miles Diamond. I work with him a lot, pass stuff his way. He's watching Maxwell's. They haven't been hit yet, but they're just the kind of place these guys like. High-end stuff, Italian suits, right on the street, big window that goes right down to the sidewalk. Perfect.'

'Miles Diamond,' I said. 'Now, there's a name for a detective.'

'It helps make up for the fact he's this little bald white dude. He's good on surveillance, 'cause you can hardly see him behind the steering wheel.'

'You meet him when you were on the force?'

'Miles is too little to ever make it as a cop. He's always been private. And he's got this gorgeous wife, she must be five-ten, spectacularly engineered. Saw them out dancing one time, he's got his head nestled in between them there, looking very contented. Not my kind of thing, but hey, he's happy.'

'So, if it's quiet at Maxwell's, maybe our guys are going to hit here tonight?' I suggested, ever hopeful. This wasn't going to be much of a feature on the life of a private detective if all we ever did was shoot the breeze in a rusted-out Buick.

'I should've got a coffee,' I added. 'Tomorrow night, we get coffee.'

'Just makes you piss,' Lawrence said.

I made a few notes in my reporter's notebook, some color, how the street looked so late at night. Hardly any cars passing by—

'Hold on,' said Lawrence. 'Big black pickup ahead.'

I looked up from my notes. It was one of those Dodge Durangos, with that front grill as big as a barn door. But it didn't slow as it passed Brentwood's, and there was no one inside but the driver.

'Stand down,' Lawrence said.

We were quiet for a while. When I felt it was time to attempt a bit of conversation, I said, 'What do you do for anxiety?'

'Anxiety?'

'Yeah. You've got a stressful job, things to worry about, you make a living tracking down not-very-nice people. So how do you deal with that?'

Lawrence thought for a moment. 'Jazz,' he said.

'Jazz?'

'I go home, I put some Oscar Peterson, some Nina Simone, maybe some Billie Holiday or Erroll Garner on the stereo. Sit and listen to it.'

'Jazz,' I said. 'So you don't actually take anything. You listen to music.'

'You're not paying attention. Not just music. *Jazz*. And no, I don't take anything. What the fuck would I take?'

I felt on the defensive. 'I don't know. Xanax? Herbal remedies?'

Lawrence smiled. 'Yeah, herbal remedies. That's me.' He glanced at his watch, 'Time to check in.'

Lawrence got out his cell again and punched in what I presumed was Miles Diamond's number. He put the phone to his ear and waited. 'Come on, Miles, pick up.' There must have been time for a good eight rings. Lawrence gave up, held the phone in his hand, which he rested on the bottom of the steering wheel.

'What's going on?' I said.

'I don't know.' His cheek bulged out as he moved his tongue around. 'Sometimes you just can't answer your phone. I'll give him another minute.'

We didn't say anything for the next sixty seconds. Lawrence entered Miles Diamond's number again, put the phone to his ear.

The phone probably rang only twice. 'Hey,' said Lawrence, and then something happened to his face. His eyes narrowed, grew sharper.

'Who is this?' Lawrence said. 'No, why don't you tell me who you are, and then maybe I'll tell you who I am.'

I could hear, faintly, someone at the other end.

'Fuck,' said Lawrence. 'It's me, Steve. It's Lawrence. What the hell's happened to Miles?'

He listened quietly, then said, 'I'll be there in ten.'

He put the phone away, turned the ignition, and the Buick rattled to life. I just looked at him, waiting.

'Nothing's going to happen here tonight,' he said to me. 'But Miles got a little action.'

Lawrence put the car into drive, swung the car across Garvin so we were headed in the other direction, and drove a lot faster than that car had any business going.

We rounded the corner onto Emmett, a short but trendy street with several ritzy stores, including a jeweller's, a shoe store, a place that sold rare art books, a couple of high-end ladies'-wear places, and one storefront that was nothing but shattered glass and splintered wood. Above what used to be the window was the name Maxwell's.

There were three black-and-white police cars, and a couple more unmarked cruisers with their trademark tiny hubcaps, plus an ambulance, but the attendants weren't doing any rushing around. Most of the attention seemed to be focused on something in the middle of the street.

Lawrence pulled the Buick up onto the sidewalk about a hundred feet back, and we both got out. A uniformed officer approached Lawrence, raising his hand up flat to press against his chest and keep him away from the scene, but before he could touch him Lawrence said, with some authority, 'Where's Steve Trimble?'

'Over there,' the cop said, lowering his hand and using it to point.

A tall white guy with short dark hair, glasses and a pencil-thin mustache, who was kneeling over the face-down body of a man a few steps away from the curb, glanced our way and got to his feet. He and Lawrence approached each other with an uncomfortable familiarity, like they knew each other but weren't friends. Still, I thought maybe Lawrence would extend a hand, but he didn't, and this Trimble guy didn't either.

'When he got hit,' Trimble said, 'at least it didn't break his cell phone. When we heard it ringing inside his jacket, I grabbed it. What was he doing here?'

Lawrence looked over at the dead body of Miles Diamond. 'He and I were watching different stores, thinking they might get hit. I guess his did.'

Trimble pursed his lips, nodded. 'You friends?'

'We each threw each other a bit of work. He was a good guy. He's got a wife.'

'I've seen her,' Trimble said, grinning. 'He was a lucky guy till now. Who's this?' he asked, tilting his head towards me.

'Zack Walker. He writes for *The Metropolitan*.'

'Hi,' I said. Trimble glared at me briefly, then said to Lawrence, 'What's he doing, a piece on guys who couldn't hack it on the force?'

Lawrence ran his hand over his mouth, like he was going to have to physically keep his comments to himself. He slipped his hand into his pocket and said, 'Do you know what happened here, Steve?'

'Mr Diamond appears to be the victim of a hit-and-run. We got a witness, guy walking his dog, about a block away, said this black SUV was backing out of Maxwell's here after taking out the front of the store, and squashed our guy here. He must have got out of his car – that's it parked over there – I don't know, but he woulda been better off staying put.'

'So they ran him down,' Lawrence said. A vein I'd not noticed before was pulsing at the side of his head.

Trimble shook his head slowly. 'Not sure. The dog walker, he said Miles was behind the SUV, one of those big tall ones, you know, and he was so short, they just might not have seen him when they were backing up. These SUVs, they should all go beep-beep when they back up, like trucks, you know?'

THREE

My daughter Angie was at the kitchen table, ignoring the buttered toast I'd put in front of her and fiddling with one of her nails instead, when her cell phone started chirping. She dug it out of her purse, looked at the display, and said, 'Shit, my stalker.'

I made some coffee. I really needed some coffee. It had been nearly five o'clock when I'd fallen into bed, and even then I'd had a hard time sleeping. I'd nodded off around six, and now it was eight, and I'd been up half an hour, so do the math. I was hoping coffee would help, but was not particularly hopeful.

All I wanted to do was crawl back into bed, but it had been my plan originally to head into the paper with Sarah when she went in, and this particular week that happened to be around eight-thirty.

'I can't believe he's calling me this early,' Angie said. 'Bad enough having a stalker. I have to get an early-bird stalker.' The phone had rung six, seven times now, but I'd lost track, since I was counting out eight spoonfuls of fine-grind Colombian into the coffeemaker. Finally, the ringing stopped. 'Now he'll leave me a message,' she sighed, brushing back some of the blond locks that had fallen across her face.

Her brother Paul, who at sixteen is two years younger

than Angie, had his back to her as he looked into the fridge, but he'd been listening. 'Five bucks says he phones the house next,' he said as he struggled to get a yogurt from the back of the fridge without moving the milk and pickles and orange juice that blocked the way.

Angie took one bite of her cold toast. 'Last night he phoned me five times. I never did answer it. So then I have to listen to all his creepy messages. "How are you? I was just thinking about you. Why don't you give me a call? Do you want to get together?" Uh, I don't think so.'

Paul, his head still in the fridge, said, 'You're so hard on everybody.'

I spilled the last spoonful of coffee before I could get it into the filter, and scooped it to the edge of the counter and into my other hand. I went to toss it into the wastebasket we keep under the sink, when I noticed a glass bottle sitting on top. It was an empty Snapple bottle that earlier, according to the label, had had apple juice in it. 'Hey,' I said. 'Who's tossing Snapple bottles in the regular garbage?'

Angie was still shaking her head over her unwanted phone call and Paul was peeling off the top of the yogurt container. I glared at him. He was the one who liked apple juice.

'We have a recycling box,' I reminded everyone, taking out the Snapple bottle, which had its metal cap screwed back on it. 'Glass bottles, tin cans, plastic – that all goes into the box, not into the garbage. Are we interested in saving the planet or not?'

'I could go either way,' Angie said.

'Is there, like, some Most Irritated Dad contest going on we don't know about?' Paul asked.

'I didn't get home till five,' I said.

Paul, putting on his concerned face and adopting his mock-parent voice, said, 'Maybe if you got to bed in good time, you wouldn't be so grumpy in the morning.'

I ignored that and walked through the kitchen to the small alcove by the back door, where we keep the blue plastic baskets that hold glass and cans and newspapers for the recycling pickup. I dropped the Snapple container into the one reserved for bottles and cans, making it the only item there.

Sarah was coming into the kitchen as I returned, and Paul was bringing her up to speed. 'Angie has a stalker.'

Sarah said, 'Huh?'

'The thing is,' Paul said, 'I think Angie actually likes him. He's mysterious.'

'Fuck you,' Angie said to her brother.

'Hey,' I said. 'Come on.'

Sarah let out a breath. 'You got coffee going?' she asked me. I pointed.

Paul said, 'And Dad's in training for the Irritable Olympics. Those are our main headlines this morning.'

'Two days ago,' Angie said, 'I run into him at Starbucks. I'm there with my friends, we're getting ready to go, and he walks in, like he's my best friend, and he's Mr Oh-So-Perfect Gentleman, helping me on with my coat, handing me my purse.'

'Who are we talking about?' Sarah asked. Good question, I thought. I might have gotten around to it eventually. A trained journalist, that's me.

'Trevor Wylie,' she said. The name didn't register with me immediately. Switching gears, Angie said, 'Am I going to be able to get a car tonight?'

After waiting in line behind Sarah, I poured myself a cup of coffee, added some cream, spooned in two sugars. Sarah already had that morning's *Metropolitan* in her hand and was scanning the front-page headlines, looking to see whether any of the stories she'd promoted at the newsroom's budget meeting the night before had made it to the front page.

'I don't believe it,' she said. 'They didn't put the dead skateboarder on front. How many sixty-year-old skateboarders are there? He was *sixty*. That's what makes it news. Assholes.'

'Hello?' Angie said. 'I need a car tonight? Is anyone there?'

Sarah looked over her paper at me, and I looked at her. Without actually saying anything, we had entered consultation mode. We were asking each other, *Do you need a car? And are we going to let her have a car?*

'Why do you need a car?' Sarah asked.

Angie sighed, the I-told-you-this-before sigh, and said, 'Remember, I've got all these evening lectures, and it's a lot easier, and safer, coming home if I've got the car instead of taking the subway.'

'Oh yeah,' said Sarah.

'I mean, you're the ones who freak out about me taking the subway at night, so if you don't want me to get raped, you should let me have the car.'

No pressure there.

Our kitchen phone rang. 'That'll be him,' Paul said. 'Betcha anything. He figures your cell is off or something.'

'Don't answer it . . .' Angie said.

Paul looked over at our wall-mounted phone so he could read the call display. How he could see it from

18

where he stood, without binoculars, was beyond me. 'Shit, nope. I was wrong.'

Now that Paul was satisfied this call was not Angie's stalker, he made no moves to actually answer the phone.

'So who is it?' Sarah snapped.

'Paper,' Paul said.

'Could you *get* it?' Sarah said, considering that Paul was two steps away while his mother was on the other side of the kitchen.

I took a long sip of coffee, let the warmth run down my throat. Caffeine, do your thing.

Paul grabbed the receiver. 'Yeah? Sec.' He handed the phone to his mother – 'I told you it was for you,' he said – as she strode across the hardwood kitchen floor, the newspaper scrunched into one hand.

'I was sure it was going to be him,' Angie said, her body relaxing as though she'd dodged a bullet.

'Who is this guy again?' I asked her. 'Who's phoning you?'

'I just told you.'

'Tell me again. I wasn't taking notes earlier.'

'Trevor Wylie.'

'Isn't that Paul's old friend? The one with the zits?'

'You gotta be kidding me,' Sarah said into the receiver. 'I filled in for him last night. He's still sick?'

'You're thinking of Trey Wilson,' Paul said defensively. 'He's the one with a face looked like a pizza. Trevor Wylie's got a very pretty face, doesn't he, Angie?'

'Shut up. He wouldn't even know me if he wasn't running errands for you.'

'What errands?' I asked.

'He showed up at our high school end of last year,' Paul said, ignoring the question. 'He's this total loner kid, with the long trenchcoat, thinks he's Keanu Reeves from *The Matrix*. Even wears the shades. Speaks in two-word sentences. Must have flunked a couple of times, like, he must be twenty. Moved from out west or something, don't even think he has any parents. Like, out here. And he's a total computer nut, and he's helped me totally reformat my computer.'

'He's twenty and still at high school?'

'Last year. If he goes to college next year, maybe he'll pick Mackenzie, and he and Angie can commute together.'

Angie gave him her best death stare.

'And why didn't they use the skateboarder on page one? Who's idiotic call was that?' Sarah wanted to know.

'So, is he dangerous, this guy?' I said, sipping some more coffee. I was trying to be casual about it, working to keep the panic out of my voice.

'He's fine,' Angie said.

'I mean, I don't think he's going to shoot up the school or anything,' Paul said, thinking that I'd find that reassuring. 'But he really is a computer genius. I think he spends his spare time inventing viruses. You know when the Hong Kong stock market or something crashed? I think he did that. And the MyDoom virus? I'm betting that was him. His dad's some software king, makes bazillions of dollars, but now that Trevor's living on his own, I'm guessing this is his way to get back at his old man, to cripple the Internet or something.'

'Where do you get this information?' I asked.

Paul shrugged. 'I don't know.'

Sarah hung up. 'I have to stay late again tonight. I've got to run the meeting again. Bailey's still gone.' Bailey was her boss, the city editor. 'I was hoping to get tonight off, since they've got me going to this retreat later in the week.'

'Retreat?' I said.

'Maybe I should write everything down for you,' Sarah said. 'You know, department heads, other management types from circulation and advertising, we all get together off-site and brainstorm about how to make the paper better and how we can all work as a team, improve employee relations, make everyone feel part of the process, and we draft some list of goals, then come back to the paper and forget it ever happened.'

'Does that mean I can't get the car?' Angie said. 'I have to have a car.'

We only had the one, an aging Toyota Camry. Before we moved back into the city, from Oakwood, we had a second car. Out in the suburbs, where there were no subways or decent bus lines, you couldn't survive with just one vehicle. But our Honda Civic came to a grisly end one night (Sarah and I very nearly did as well, but that's a long story, and I've already told it), and we opted not to replace it once we'd sold our house and returned to our old neighborhood.

We bought a house a few doors down from our former one, on Crandall, a couple of blocks from the subway and connecting streetcars, and we'd been managing with one car for some time now. Paul's high school was within walking distance, but in the last few weeks Angie had started college, in town, and, as she'd just reminded us, a few of her classes were in the evening. That meant a walk of several blocks in the dark to catch the subway home, and Sarah was almost as paranoid as I on this issue. We wanted Angie walking alone at night as little as possible.

'What time do you finish?' Sarah asked.

Angie thought. 'Eight? Eight-thirty?'

Sarah said, 'You take the car, swing by the paper on the way home and pick me up.'

'Then I can't hang out with anyone after,' Angie said. 'I was thinking of getting a coffee with someone after the lecture.'

'Who?'

'Someone. I don't know.' She got all sullen. 'Anybody.'

Which of course meant someone in particular. Sarah said, 'You want a car, you pick me up.'

'Jeez, fine, I'll pick you up. I just won't make any friends at college at all. I'll go to school, come home, leave it to the people who live on campus to have lives.'

I wanted to steer the conversation in another direction, not only because I hated family arguments, but because my head was pounding. 'What's the class tonight?' I asked.

'Some psych-sociology male/female studies thing,' she said. 'I have to do some research paper for, like, ten days from now. About why men are so weird.'

'Interview your father,' Sarah offered.

'And I need five dollars for parking,' Angie said.

Sarah sidled up to me as she put in some toast. I said to her, quietly, 'Maybe it's time to think about getting another car.'

'I can't have this discussion now,' she said.

'We're having these kinds of problems every day,' I said.

I squeezed out of the way as she got some strawberry jam out of the fridge. This kitchen was about half the size of the one in our house out in the suburbs, and quarters were close. 'We can't afford another car now,' Sarah said. 'We've got Angie's tuition, a mortgage—'

The phone rang again. I grabbed it instinctively, not thinking to look at who the caller was, and already had the receiver in my hand when Angie started to shout 'Don't answer it . . .'

But she cut herself off as I brought the phone to my ear, the mouthpiece exposed. Angie mouthed to me, 'I'm not here . . .'

'Hello?' I said. At this point, I looked at the call display and saw 'Unknown name/Unknown number.'

'Hi. Is Angie there?' Very cool. You could almost tell, over the phone, that he had to be wearing sunglasses.

'Can I take a message?' I said.

'Is she there?'

'Can I take a message?' I repeated.

A pause at the other end. 'Who's this?'

Now I paused. 'This is her father.'

Angie raised her hands up, rolled her eyes, mouthed, 'Jeez . . .'

'Oh,' he said. 'You wrote that book.'

That caught me off guard. 'Yeah, I did. I wrote a few.'

'SF stuff.'

'That's right.'

'About the missionaries.'

'Yeah,' I said.

'I like that kind of shit. You see *The Matrix* movies?'

'Yes,' I said.

'First one was great, the other two sucked ass.'

I said, 'Do you want to leave a message for Angie?'

Angie, in a loud, angry whisper: 'I. Am. Not. Here . . .'

'Tell her Trevor called.' And he hung up.

'God,' I said, taken aback by the abrupt end to our conversation. 'What an asshole.'

'What did he want?' Angie said. 'What were you talking about?'

'He was asking if I'd seen *The Matrix*, and if I was the guy who wrote that book, about missionaries.'

'Did he say anything about me?'

'Just wanted me to tell you he called. You think he read my book?'

Paul, finishing his yogurt, said to Angie, 'I think he wants to enter your matrix.'

Angie gave him the finger. On her way out of the kitchen she said again that she needed five dollars to pay for parking at Mackenzie that evening. Sarah dug a bill out of her purse and handed it over.

The kitchen emptied out. Paul left for high school, Sarah went up to our room to finish getting ready for work. Angie, who didn't have a class until midmorning, was in her room, probably fuming about what it was like to live with Third World parents who only had one car.

Sarah and I got into the car, I rode shotgun. We worked out a quick plan, that I'd drive the car home later in the day so that Angie, who was going to return home by way of public transit after her midday class, would have a car for going back to school in the evening. Every day, it was like planning the raid on Entebbe.

As was usually the case when Sarah was behind the wheel, we were attracting the finger from a cross section of motorists as she moved from lane to lane, tailgated, failed to signal. Sarah was what you might call an aggressive driver. The people in the other cars might be more likely to call her a maniac.

'They call it *rush* hour for a reason,' Sarah said, shaking her head as she got past those slowpokes and got some more in her sights. 'How'd it go last night?'

I told her.

Her jaw dropped and she looked over at me. 'This other detective, he's *dead*? These guys, the ones you and this Lawrence Jones character were waiting for, they killed him?'

'It may just have been because he was short. They might not have seen him when they were backing up.'

'Fuck. Did you call the desk?'

The city desk. 'Yes,' I said. 'They said they'd call Cheese Dick and send a photog.' Dick Colby, *The Metropolitan*'s police reporter, who smelled like old havarti. The paper's editors might trust me to write a profile of Lawrence Jones, but a breaking news story, you couldn't leave that to some writer from the features team. The desk would want the story covered by someone who could turn it in in under a week.

'So this thing, it really will turn into a decent feature,' Sarah said. The editor in her had taken over. Sooner or later, it might occur to her that if these guys could kill one detective, they could just as easily kill another, particularly one I was hanging out with.

'Wait a minute,' she said. 'What if they'd shown up at the store you guys were staking out?'

'I'm sure we'd have been fine,' I said. 'Lawrence seems to know what he's doing.'

'So they killed this Miles Diamond,' Sarah said. 'Did they also rob the store?'

'Pretty much cleaned it out of Hugo Boss and Versace and—'

'It's a *ch* sound. It doesn't rhyme with "face."'

'Okay, so I'm not familiar. It's not the Gap.'

Sarah, in the middle of cutting off a Mustang, said, 'Yeah, well, you haven't even seen the inside of a Gap in years. You could use some sprucing up, some new clothes.'

'I sure won't be buying them at Brentwood's. It's very expensive Italian suits, designer stuff, silk ties, you get the picture.'

'You're right. That doesn't sound like your kind of place.'

'It's Lawrence's, though. Nice dresser. Why do gay guys always dress better?'

Sarah scowled, 'You might be surprised to learn that there are heterosexual men who know how to look good in clothes. Does he never go by Larry?'

'No. It's Lawrence Jones, Private Eye.' I used my TV announcer voice.

'So, you got enough to write this piece? You've got color, there was the incident last night.'

'You promised me a week. I'm going back out with him tonight, this'll be night three.'

Now Sarah looked apprehensive. 'You've probably got enough already.'

'Look, don't worry, I'm perfectly safe.'

At which point Sarah swerved from the middle to the inside lane to avoid a green Cutlass. 'Jesus,' she said. 'Was he going slow or what?'

Now Sarah was taking the off-ramp that would lead us down to the *Metropolitan* building. The ramp was designed as a single lane, but Sarah was trying to squeeze along the inside, so close to a Mazda that if she put her window down she could hand the guy a coffee. I kept jamming my right foot into the floorboards,

26

figuring if I shoved hard enough I could stop the car. There were a lot of things that made me feel anxious.

I said, 'Do we have any jazz CDs?'

'I hate jazz,' Sarah said. There wasn't a CD player in the Toyota; it was too old to have come equipped with one. But at home, she often slipped a disc into the stereo. Rock, lots of seventies stuff, Neil Young, Creedence Clearwater Revival. 'Why you asking about jazz?'

'No reason.'

This was a new wrinkle to our relationship, this business of having Sarah as my boss. Well, one of my bosses. At a newspaper, you had so many, it was hard to keep track. This was my first experience working for the same person with whom I slept. I had been back working at a newspaper for almost a year now, after spending a few years writing commercially unsuccessful science fiction novels. Okay, the first one did reasonably well, which had given me the confidence to quit a salaried job and write fiction full-time. But as most people who write fiction understand, unless they happen to be Tom Clancy, or a former president penning his memoirs, you can't support a family and pay a mortgage without a regular job. And I was back at one.

The Metropolitan offered me a feature-writing position. Given my experience, coupled with the fact I'd written four novels, the editors in charge seemed to feel I had graduated beyond the level of general assignment. To my surprise, and Sarah's, they put me among the stable of city feature writers who reported to her. Although she wouldn't admit this to me, I'd heard through the newsroom grapevine that she'd fired off a memo to the managing editor, Bertrand Magnuson, expressing some concern, something along the lines of

'I can't get him to do anything I say at home, so what makes you think I can do it here?'

The problem was, the newsroom has a long history of people who sleep together – spouses, and non-spouses, and a few spouses with non-spouses – being thrown into the mix together, and Sarah's superior probably wrote her back with a note consisting of three letters – 'DWI' – which in the *Metropolitan* newsroom meant 'deal with it.'

Moving on, I said, 'You know about this Trevor Wylie kid?'

Sarah thought a moment. 'The one calling Angie? Not much. He the one had a face like a pizza?'

'No.'

'Then I don't know anything.'

'I just don't like the sounds of this guy.'

'Has he done anything?'

'He's calling Angie all the time, shows up where she is, like maybe he's following her.'

'You mean, like when you were interested in me?'

'I just don't like him. You should talk to Angie, find out more about this guy, tell her to be careful.'

'You talk to her.'

'I think she's still mad at me, over the Pool Boy incident.'

'Yeah, well, who can blame her. I can't believe Harley didn't give you a prescription. You ask me, you need to be on something.'

FOUR

The phone rang as I sat down at my desk. 'Zack Walker,' I said.

'Lawrence here. You get any sleep?'

'Not much. You?'

'No. I ended up going back to the scene, talking to Trimble a bit more, trying for more information, but there wasn't much to get.'

'What's the deal with you two? I didn't sense a whole lot of mutual admiration there.'

'We used to be partners. When I was still on the force.'

'Partners? You were partners?'

'Yeah, well, maybe sometime I'll tell you all about it. We still on for tonight?'

'Of course. I was afraid, after what happened to Miles, maybe you wouldn't let me tag along.'

'No, it's okay. Meet me at ten, doughnut shop around the corner from Brentwood's. Still too much traffic that time of night for anyone to try anything. Anything happens, it'll be later.'

'You think they'll come out, the night after they hit a store and ended up killing a guy?'

'Honestly, no.'

'I hate to ask, but you go anywhere near Crandall on your way?' If he wasn't able to pick me up at home, I'd have to grab a cab, what with Angie needing the car.

Lawrence said nothing for a moment. He was probably consulting one of several mental maps he kept upstairs. 'Yeah, sure, why?'

'No car tonight. But if it's out of your way, I can get a cab, bill the paper—'

'No, no, that's fine. Give me your address.' I did. 'See you round nine forty-five.'

We were parked in the same place we'd been the night before, on Garvin, half a block down from Brentwood's.

Although we'd not had to meet at the doughnut shop, Lawrence and I still pulled in there. He still had the old Buick, what Lawrence called his 'business' car, at least the one he used when the business involved surveillance. When he wanted to make a better impression, he drove a Beemer or Jaguar or some other type of high-end yuppiemobile that he kept back at his apartment.

'Don't get coffee,' Lawrence warned me. 'You'll be having to take a leak every twenty minutes.'

I ignored him and got an extra-large, triple cream with two low-cal sweetener packets, and half a dozen doughnuts.

'That makes sense,' Lawrence said. 'Why don't you get one more sweetener, and then you can get two more doughnuts.'

But later, sitting in the car, he said, 'You got a double chocolate in there?'

'Aren't you the one who mocked me for buying these?'

'You got one or not?'

I fished around, found a chocolate doughnut with chocolate icing slathered on top, and handed it to him with a napkin. Then I reached down for my coffee, tucked down in the cup holder, and had a sip. 'Ohhh, my thanks to whoever invented coffee,' I said. 'This is the only thing that will get me through this.'

'Yeah, well, when your bladder's ready to burst, don't think that you're using my emergency kit,' Lawrence said, nodding his head in the direction of the backseat, where he kept a plastic juice bottle with a screw top.

The juice container was, as Lawrence had explained to me on our first night out, a key part of his surveillance kit. When you're on a stakeout, and expecting your subject to be on the move at any moment, and you've got to take a leak, you can't strike off searching for the nearest men's room or slip into the nearest alley.

Lawrence fiddled with the radio, located a jazz station, someone playing piano. 'That's Enroll Gamer. This is from *Concert by the Sea*.' He kept the volume down, but loud enough that he could tap his finger on the steering wheel.

I thanked him for picking me up at home. 'We're having a bit of car trouble.'

'Oh yeah? What kind?'

'We need another one.' I filled him in on the daily negotiations to try to get everyone where they had to be, and Sarah's concerns about spending the money for a second vehicle.

'Interesting that this problem of yours should crop up now,' Lawrence said. 'What are you doing tomorrow?'

'Usual.'

'There's a government auction tomorrow, out Oakwood way. Where they sell off cars and other merchandise seized from drug dealers and other lowlifes, unclaimed stolen property – people already got their insurance payment, they don't come looking for what they lost.'

'Okay, so?'

'I got my Jaguar at one of those for a song. You could probably pick up something reasonable, not much money. I know the people there, there's a guy, Eddie Mayhew, knows what cars look good and what cars don't. I was talking to him the other day, he said they're selling off a bunch of merchandise that used to belong to Lenny Indigo.'

'I know that name.'

'He just got fifteen to twenty. Joint operation, local cops working with the feds, got him on trafficking, racketeering, half a dozen other things. They seized a few million in cocaine and took his cars and other toys at the same time. Indigo had his finger into everything in this town from drugs to table dancers and prostitution to robbery. Thing is, his organization is still around, some bozo's trying to keep it together while he's inside, but Indigo's still trying to run the thing from the inside. Anyway, if you're looking for a car with an interesting history, I know where you could get one.'

I shrugged. 'Sounds worth going. Even to get a feature out of it. But I don't think I'm in the market to buy anything. Sarah was pretty adamant this morning. It's just not in the budget.'

'Let's just go, then. I've been, even when I wasn't looking for a car, bought one, sold it a week later for five thou more. It's just after lunch. I'll pick you up.'

We sat for a few minutes quietly, watching cars go past Brentwood's in both directions. The store window lights had been dimmed by half, casting soft shadows on half a dozen headless mannequins decked out in expensive menswear. 'That where you get your stuff?' I asked. Lawrence was dressed in a pair of black slacks, a dark silk shirt, and a black sports jacket that I guessed cost more than everything I had in my closet at home.

'Sometimes. Brentwood promised me a new suit if I find out who's been hitting his store, but now, after last night, I don't know. It's hard to feel we've been doing our job very well.'

'You got anyone else helping you, now that Miles is . . .' I hesitated, 'gone?'

'No. Thing is, they're not going to be hitting Maxwell's now. Next most likely target is here.'

'Why aren't the cops out here, too? After what happened last night?'

'They promised to take a run by, step up patrols. Speak of the devil.' A city police car approached, slowed as it went past Brentwood's, then kept going. 'But they haven't got enough people to stake out every place that *might* get hit. So that's why you and I are sitting here.'

Moments after the police car had disappeared, a red, lowered Honda Accord coupe with a set of flashy after-market wheels slowed as it drove by the store. The windows were tinted, making it impossible to make out who or how many were inside. 'Anything?' I said.

Lawrence looked thoughtful. 'I don't know. Maybe. But we're really looking for a truck or SUV. Maybe this guy's a lookout, cases the place, then calls his buds. Can't even see with the dark windows.' The

Accord moved on. 'Looked like just one guy, but I couldn't be sure. It's easy enough to remember, with the chrome rims, so if we see it again, might be worth checking out.' He had a notepad on his lap and scribbled something down.

'What's that?' I asked.

'The Honda's license plate,' he said. The guy was quick. I hadn't even thought to look at the plate.

That reminded me to dig out my own reporter's notepad, make a few notes. I scribbled 'red Honda' and 'waiting' and 'doughnuts.'

'So, you were a cop,' I said.

Lawrence nodded. 'Went on my own about three years ago, still have plenty of friends on the force. They send work my way, help me out when I need a license plate ID, that kind of thing, which I'll be asking them for in the morning.'

'Why'd you leave?'

Lawrence kept looking out through the windshield, chewing on a bit of double chocolate, never taking his eyes off the scene in front of Brentwood's. 'Oh, I don't know. Differences of opinion, I guess.' He paused. 'Hello.'

A big black SUV rolled past us. The windows were even darker than those on the Honda, and looked as black as the doors and fenders.

'That's one of those whaddya-call-thems,' I said.

'An Annihilator,' Lawrence said. 'They used them in the army, then regular folk wanted to get them. So they gussied them up with power steering, CD players, air bags, and now soccer moms can drop their kids off in something that could be used to launch surface-to-air missiles. Fucking ridiculous.'

The Annihilator slowed as it passed on the opposite side of the street, in front of Brentwood's. Lawrence's entire body seemed to tense. He turned off Enroll and wrapped his fingers around the steering wheel. I felt a tingle work its way through me, like I'd put a toe into ice water.

The towering sport utility vehicle inched ahead a bit more, then the brake lights went off, and the Annihilator continued up the street.

'Interesting,' said Lawrence.

'I thought you said they wouldn't come back tonight,' I said.

'I might have made a mistake. It was bound to happen eventually.'

Suddenly I thought of the license plate. 'Did you get the plate number?' I asked.

'It had one of those opaque covers over it,' Lawrence said. 'Couldn't make it out. Maybe, if it comes around again.'

I had a sip of my coffee, made a couple more notes. 'Red Honda,' Lawrence said. 'Coming this way. Can't see the wheels, not sure whether it's the same one. Come here.'

'Huh?' I said.

'Just come here,' he said, pulling me toward him and slipping his arms around me in an embrace. His cheek was pressed up against mine, his lips just to the side of my own. He felt warm, and there was a scent of aftershave. Hesitantly at first, I raised my right arm and slipped it around his shoulder.

As the Honda drove by, Lawrence casually moved his head around to give it a better look. Even with Lawrence's head pressed up against mine, I could see that this car had simple hubcaps.

'Not our car,' Lawrence said, freeing me from his embrace and leaning back up against his window. 'Sorry. Didn't mean to get fresh. I was afraid, had it been the same car, he was going to make us. Two guys sitting in a car at night, that's a surveillance. Two guys going at it, well, that's something else. And congratulations on not freaking out.'

'I'm fine,' I said.

'Not to worry,' he said. 'You're not my type anyway.'

I gave that a moment. 'What do you mean, I'm not your type?'

Lawrence glanced over. 'I'm just saying, if you were gay, you wouldn't be the kind of guy I'd go for.'

'Oh,' I said.

'Nothing personal,' Lawrence said.

'Of course not,' I said. As if it could be anything but.

'You could dress a little better,' he said.

We were both quiet for a moment. There was no traffic on the street. 'So, let me try again,' I said. 'Why'd you leave the force?'

Lawrence breathed out, sounded tired. 'This isn't for your feature.'

I slipped my pen through the metal spiral at the top of my notepad. 'Go ahead.'

'I'd made detective about eight, nine years ago, I guess, and towards the end, last year or so, I was partnered with this guy, Steve Trimble, the guy you met last night. Okay guy, knew him back when we were both in uniform. Married, had a kid who must be in college by now. Didn't seem to have any hang-ups working with a guy who was not only black, but gay.'

'The rest of the department, they knew?'

'I'm not keeping any secrets, man. This is who I am. You don't like it, you can kiss my ass. Trimble seemed okay with it, we got along well, I got to know his wife, I'd go over to his place sometimes, hang out.

'We got a call one night. We're plainclothes now, detectives, and we're working some case, can't remember what, but a call comes over, some sounds of gunfire in the west end, the warehouse district. We were a block away, I guess, so I thought maybe we should just take a stroll by, and Steve thinks okay, why not. So we turn off from this street of row houses, which is probably where the call came from, someone hearing shots, and we're driving nice and slow, windows down, looking and listening for anything suspicious. And the thing is, it could be nothing, you know? Some old lady, hears a car backfire, she calls 911.

'We're driving down between these two big industrial buildings when suddenly this car comes screaming around the corner ahead of us, one of these low-slung rice machine jobs with the dark-tinted windows, and Steve slides a flashing red light onto the roof, pulls across the street to block his way. Might be nothing, right, but it is suspicious, so few cars down there, this one appearing out of nowhere.

'So we try to flag him down, and he veers, going right up on the sidewalk and around, and by this time we're out of the car, both of us, guns drawn, and Steve takes a shot, at the tires, because with the windows tinted you don't know how many people are in the car, it's just too risky. He doesn't hit the car, but the driver's losing control and hits a telephone pole a hundred yards up or so. The door opens and this white kid bails, starts running away from us, and Steve's after him on foot and I go back for the car, turning it around and radioing in at the same time, looking for backup, and I catch a glimpse of Steve turning down this alleyway, elbow bent, gun drawn.'

Lawrence licked his lips, like his mouth had gone dry. 'What we didn't know, till later, was that this kid had just come from a deal gone bad, well, not from his point of view until we showed up. He'd gone to make a buy, and rather than hand over the money, shot his supplier. Gets his coke, keeps his cash. I try to head the kid off, so I drive around the block, and he's coming out the other end of the alley when I get there. Steve comes right out after him.

'I end up cornering him up against the wall with the car. The car's not actually touching him, I'm back a good thirty feet, but I've got the lights on him, and he's got nowhere to go, and Steve moves into the frame. We're both yelling at the kid, that we're cops, to drop his gun.

'I'm getting out of the car, and with the headlights on, we've both got a good look at this kid, and we can see he's got a gun held down at his side. And I still don't have mine drawn, I just got out of the car, and the kid decides he's going to shoot it out with us, I guess, and he raises his weapon to take a shot at me, and I figure, okay, this could be it, but Steve's already got him in his sights. And then the kid fires.'

'At you.'

'Yeah. He gets off a shot, which hits the window frame of the car door. A chance in a million he doesn't hit me. What I did next happened so fast, but it's like slow motion when I replay it in my head. I draw my gun and take aim and drop him, one shot right in the chest.'

'He died.'

'He died.'

'And you're wondering why it was you that had to bring him down. Because your partner must have had him in his sights, and didn't fire.'

'It did kind of occur to me.'

'What did Trimble have to say for himself?'

'Comes over, says he was just about to shoot, but I beat him to it.' Lawrence shook his head, about an eighth of an inch in either direction.

'You didn't buy it,' I said.

'He froze. The fucker froze. And I nearly bought it. And I had to kill that kid.'

'Who was he?'

'His name was Antoine Mercer, and he was seventeen, and he was a gofer, if you can believe it, for Lenny Indigo back then. And after that, I started thinking that maybe I didn't like being in a job where you had to depend on others to watch your back. Figured I was better off looking out for myself.'

'What was the fallout?'

'Ah well, there was the usual lynching in the press. Cop kills kid. Your paper played a leading role.'

I felt my cheeks go hot.

'But that died down. Steve and I were still partnered together, but I couldn't work with the guy. Couldn't trust him to be there for me. And I started wondering whether I could trust any of them. Decided the only one I could trust to cover my ass was myself, and that's when I decided to go it alone.'

'You quit.'

'I quit. I was good at being a cop, for the most part. Liked solving things, figuring stuff out, doing what's right. But I figured I was better working alone.'

'Thanks for telling me.'

A shrug. 'Well, you asked, and I don't know. I don't talk about it all that often. You seem a bit of an asshole, but you're a likeable asshole, so what the hell? It's a long night out here without something to talk about. Speaking of which, black Annihilator up ahead, doing more reconnaissance.'

The SUV, with its lofty military stance and blacked-out windows, looked every bit the predator as it rolled down the street, its headlights, set high amidst a massive network of metal crisscrosses that looked more like a set of shark's teeth than a grill, shining towards us. Again, in front of Brentwood's, it slowed.

'They like what they see. They're getting ready, I guarantee it.'

And then, from the other direction, that same city police car, doing another sweep. No lights or siren, just heading down the street, doing a regular patrol. As the cop car came into range, the driver of the SUV gave the oversized vehicle some gas, pulling away from the men's shop.

'He got spooked,' Lawrence said as the SUV rolled past us. 'He might come around again, but I doubt it. Not tonight.'

He turned his ignition key.

'What are we doing?' I asked. I had an open coffee in my hand.

Lawrence was already cranking the wheel, swinging across the street.

'We're leaving our stakeout?' I said. 'What if it's not them, and somebody else hits the store while we're gone?'

'Oh, that's them,' Lawrence said, straightening out and hitting the gas so he could keep the Annihilator in sight. 'As long as we know where he is, I don't think we'll miss seeing the store get hit.'

I felt an adrenaline rush. My heart was starting to pound. We were in a chase. Suddenly my feature was getting a whole lot more interesting.

'Where's the lid for my coffee?' I said, glancing down at the console and down around my feet. 'Fuck it,' I said, and tossed it out the open window. Who needed caffeine to stay awake now?

FIVE

The driver of the Annihilator must not have suspected anyone was following him, because he wasn't booting it up Garvin Avenue. Lawrence Jones hung several car lengths back as we traveled along behind the big, hulking vehicle. The SUV's brake lights came on and it slowed, turning right onto Belvenia.

'He didn't signal,' I said. 'Can't you get him for that? Then we don't even have to worry about Brentwood's.'

Lawrence ignored me. He swung the wheel hard to the right as we turned the corner. The SUV drove up Belvenia, then took a left, again without signaling.

'He's going on to Wilson,' Lawrence said. 'I'm hoping maybe he's decided to call it a night, will head home, we can get some idea where he's come from, who he is. You got your notepad there?'

'Yeah.'

'Can you make out that plate at all?'

I squinted. It was impossible. 'No.'

The Annihilator hung another right, then a left two blocks on. 'Oh dear oh dear oh dear,' Lawrence said softly. There was an almost cheerful lilt to his voice, but I had a feeling it was masking some concern.

'What?'

'I think he's onto us. He's just driving around randomly,

watching to see whether we go where he goes. What we need is another car, two guys with phones, trade off following him so he doesn't get so suspicious. Fuck.'

'Maybe he hasn't made us. Maybe he's just killing time, waiting to go back to Brentwood's.'

As the Annihilator passed under some bright street-lights, Lawrence peered intently at the vehicle. 'Trying to see past that tinting, get some idea how many people might be in there.'

'Those windows are pretty dark,' I said. 'You can't see— Hold on, he's pulling over to the curb.'

The Annihilator slowed and eased over to the right.

'I'm just gonna have to drive on by,' Lawrence said. 'Don't look over or do anything suspicious.'

'What if I mooned them?'

Lawrence guided the old Buick past the black SUV, which was now fully up against the curb, lights extinguished. It would have been nice to slow down and see how many people got out, but it was clear Lawrence didn't want us drawing attention to ourselves that way.

Once we were a couple of car lengths past it, I glanced back. No doors were opening, no one was getting out. The Annihilator's lights came back on, and the truck slipped back into the lane behind us.

I was still turned in my seat, taking in our new situation, when Lawrence barked at me, 'Eyes front . . . Don't look . . .'

I shifted back, tried to get a glimpse of the SUV in the mirror on the passenger door.

'This is not a good thing,' Lawrence said. 'Not a good thing at all. I hate it when I get made. Absolutely fucking sloppy. You want to know what they're doing right now?'

'What?'

'They're taking down *my* license plate, that's what they're doing right now.'

'That's bad, right?'

'Normally, it would be, but I've got bogus plates on this car, so it's not that big a problem.'

'Uh, isn't that illegal, Lawrence?'

He had only a moment to glance at me and grin. 'Which Hardy Boy are you? Frank or Joe?'

I decided not to respond to that, but go on the attack myself. 'So what's your plan now, Sherlock?'

'We just drive along, like we don't know who he is and don't care, and maybe he starts thinking that maybe he was wrong, that we weren't following him.'

As the Annihilator gained on us, its raised headlights shone through the back windows of the Buick, reflecting off the rearview mirror and nearly blinding Lawrence. 'Fucking SUVs,' he muttered. He was on edge, and it had to be taking every bit of resolve he had not to tromp on the accelerator and leave that lumbering vehicle in our dust.

'We'll just keep going straight up Wilson,' he said quietly. And so we did, driving at the speed limit, a couple of guys out for a cruise around the town. The Annihilator kept pace behind us, barely a car length, those annoying lights illuminating everything inside the Buick.

'Okay, moment-of-truth time,' Lawrence said, put on his blinker, and turned right down a side street, nice and proper, like he was delivering, instead of me, his grandmother back to the nursing home.

The SUV stayed with us, rounding the corner without slowing down. I didn't want to admit this to

Lawrence, but I was starting to feel just a tad apprehensive. And by apprehensive, I mean scared.

There was a deep throaty roar behind us, and the lights from the Annihilator grew more massive. The vehicle was only inches behind our bumper. Then there was the sound of a horn, a deep, resonating blast like a ship pulling into the harbor, that I could feel in my bones.

'The guy's out of his fucking mind,' Lawrence said. He hit the gas and we pulled away from the truck. We heard another roar as our pursuer gunned his engine.

'I think he wants to drive right over us,' I said.

'If he gets a chance, he will,' Lawrence said. 'Hang on.'

He yanked the wheel hard to the right, sending us down a side street. The car lurched wildly and all four tires skidded across the pavement, but we made the turn and barreled our way up the street. The SUV, with its high center of gravity, couldn't navigate the turn at such a high speed, but this didn't seem to trouble the driver all that much, who steered the beast over someone's lawn, plowing through a row of hedges and a small fence, and flattening a bicycle that had been left out on a driveway.

'If you had a chance to pull over anywhere,' I said, 'you could just let me out.'

And then I heard a popping noise. *Pop-pop-pop.*

Lawrence said nothing, just kept both hands gripped on the wheel, swinging hard to the right, then to the left, glancing for split seconds at his rearview mirror.

Pop. Pop.

'Lawrence,' I said, somewhat hesitantly, as the Annihilator, half a dozen car lengths back, caught the back half of a parked motorcycle and sent it flying across a sidewalk.

'Yeah?'

'I hate to ask, but what are those popping noises I keep hearing?'

Rather than answer my question directly, Lawrence told me to open the glove compartment. 'There's something in there we need. You'll know it when you see it.'

I took out a customized auto-club map detailing the route to Florida. 'Triptik?'

'Keep looking.'

Behind several maps, tissue packets, a roll of masking tape, and ownership papers, I came across a small handgun.

'Actually,' said Lawrence, 'given that I'm driving, it might be better if you used it.'

This was not a good idea. The last time I'd had a gun in my hand, I'd fatally shot a desk. 'This really isn't my area of expertise, Lawrence,' I said. 'I'm not particularly adept where guns are concerned. Plus, there's the nature of my role here. I'm really more of an observer, not a participant, so—'

And then the back window of the Buick blew out.

'Jesus . . .' Lawrence said, turning so hard this time the g-forces jammed me against my door. 'Hand me the fucking gun . . .'

I handed it over. He was still steering with both hands, but there was little more than the thumb of his right hand around the wheel, his fingers gripped around the gun.

'You ever hear about how to get away from a crocodile?' he asked. He was shouting now. With the back window gone, it was a lot noisier in the car, especially with the Annihilator bearing down on us.

'No,' I said.

'Well, they're bigger and stronger and faster than people, but they can't corner worth shit. So if you've got one coming after you, you keep running in circles. They can't navigate the turns. Right now, we're being followed by a crocodile, and we're coming up on the perfect place to lead him in circles.'

Up ahead, a sign for the Midtown Center. The largest mall in this part of the city. As the mall's west-end anchor store, a Sears, came into view, so did the massive, entirely empty, parking lot.

Our Buick screeched around the entrance into the lot. Again, the black Annihilator missed the turn, but rode right up over the curbs, its fat wheels rolling over them like they were Kit Kat bars. 'Here comes the fun part,' Lawrence said, using the wide-open spaces of the mall lot to do huge circles. 'What I'm gonna do,' he shouted, 'is come up around behind him, and then well give him a taste of his own medicine.'

'What do you mean, own medicine?'

'He took a few shots at us, now we'll return the favor.'

'How are you going to shoot and drive at the same time?'

'If you can't handle a gun, surely you can handle a fucking steering wheel.'

'You gotta be kidding.'

'Does steering compromise your journalistic integrity, too?'

So I leaned over in the seat, ready to grip the wheel whenever Lawrence wanted me to.

The Annihilator was trying hard to keep up with us, but the SUV was leaning precariously. I wondered if maybe this was Lawrence's real plan, to trick our pursuer into flipping his own vehicle over. If it was, I approved.

But the driver seemed to know what he was doing. He wasn't pushing the truck to extremes. I glanced back and saw a leather-jacketed arm hanging out the window. The hand was clutching a weapon that looked a lot bigger than the gun I'd handed to Lawrence.

The Buick lurched and its tires squealed. A hubcap went flying off, spinning across the pavement towards the Sears. But Lawrence seemed to know what he was doing, too. We were now actually coming up around behind the Annihilator.

'Okay,' he said. 'Hold the wheel.'

I gripped it like I was holding on for dear life, allowing Lawrence to switch the gun to his left hand, get his arm and shoulder out the window, and start firing.

He got off two shots, but the Annihilator was bearing to the right, so he wrested the wheel back from me and changed course.

'Again . . .' he said, and I grabbed the wheel as he leaned out the window, firing the gun twice more. 'Shit . . .' he shouted, wind blowing into his face.

'Did you hit him?' I asked as he took control of the steering wheel again.

'I don't think so. And even if I did, the thing's a fucking elephant.'

Ahead, the Annihilator abruptly turned, but where it was headed didn't make any sense. The SUV was speeding to the far end of the lot where the ground sloped steeply upward to a road that was actually a ramp that led from a city street that circled the mall, and on to the highway.

'What's he doing?' I said. 'He's got nowhere to go.'

The Annihilator's brake lights came on only briefly, as if the driver had lightly tapped the pedal, and then the truck drove off the end of the parking lot and up the embankment, all four tires kicking up sod and dirt, its headlight beams dancing in the night sky like a searchlight. The vehicle bucked and jerked as it climbed, the embankment clearly a challenge even for an Annihilator.

'He's going for the highway,' Lawrence said. 'He's creating his own shortcut, the son of a bitch.'

The Annihilator crested the embankment and hung a right onto the ramp, then, with another roar of its massive engine, sped off in the direction of the highway. There was no way Lawrence's old, two-wheel-drive Buick could even begin to scale the hill. And by the time we'd wound our way out of the mall lot, onto the street, and found that ramp, our friends in the Annihilator would be home, tucked into their beds.

Lawrence brought the car to a stop, and neither of us spoke for a moment as we listened to the motor idle and tick, as though trying to catch its breath.

'Fuck me,' said Lawrence.

'I take it that's not an actual invitation,' I said.

SIX

I got home around three in the morning, and rather than try to sneak into our bedroom without disturbing Sarah, I turned on the lights, plopped myself down on the bed next to her, and said, 'You won't believe what happened . . . We started following them, and then they were following us, and things were getting smashed, and then they started shooting, and we lured them into the parking lot at Midtown, and we came up around behind them, and that's when Lawrence tried to shoot out their tires, and then they drove right up the side of a hill and took off and I can't fucking believe it happened . . .'

Sarah sat up in bed, bleary-eyed. 'Huh?'

I told it all to her again, more slowly this time. She asked a couple of clarifying questions, and then, once I was finished, said, 'Are you out of your goddamn mind?'

'I was fine, really, Lawrence knew what he was doing. He's a professional.'

'You are. You are out of your goddamn mind.'

I shrugged, then realized she might be onto something, and suddenly felt that I was going to lose my coffee and doughnuts, because car chases laced with gunplay are not typical activities for former-science-fiction-authors-turned-newspaper-feature-writers. I was breathing pretty rapidly, and Sarah let me fall into her arms. It's possible that I was, perhaps very slightly, shaking.

'You are a stupid, stupid man,' she said quietly. 'You're not cut out for a life of adventure. You're not Indiana Jones. If you tried to be, instead of carrying a whip tucked into your belt, you'd have a bottle of Maalox.'

'We're going back out there tomorrow night,' I whispered into her hair, and she shoved me away abruptly.

'You really have lost your mind,' she said, suddenly looking angry enough to slug me.

I held up my hands, as much to protest as to defend myself. 'We're going into it with our eyes open this time. And Lawrence will be talking to the cops, and it's not going to be the same kind of thing at all. We know what we're up against.'

'So what does that mean? You're taking a bazooka next time? Something big enough to bag an SUV?'

Seriously, I said, 'I let Lawrence make the firepower decisions. It's really not my area.'

She got up, stormed into the bathroom, and closed the door behind her. From inside, she shouted, 'You're done. This assignment is terminated. Write what you've got, it'll be a fine feature.'

Whoa. Wait a minute.

'Who's that in the bathroom?' I asked. 'Is that my wife in there, or is it my editor?'

Sarah opened the door abruptly, a fierce expression on her face. 'Take your pick.'

'Is that what you'd tell Cheese Dick Colby? If he was on this assignment, would you pull him off it, just when it was getting good, because he might hurt himself?'

'I don't know. I don't sleep with Colby.'

'I don't even know how he sleeps with himself. You gotten close to him?'

She went back into the bathroom and closed the door. I shook my head, then unbuttoned my shirt and slipped off my pants. What was I supposed to do? Apologize? Had I done something wrong?

Maybe. Maybe not. But if there's one thing I've learned from twenty years of marriage, it's that you don't have to be wrong to apologize.

It was awfully quiet in the bathroom, so I went up to the door and quietly rapped on it. 'Listen,' I said. 'I—'

And the door swung open and Sarah, tears running down her cheeks, threw her arms around me and buried her face in my chest. 'I'm sorry,' she said. 'I just don't want anything to happen to you. Nearly losing you once was enough.'

Neither of us slept much during the three hours that were left before sunrise, which meant this was the second night in a row where I'd hardly had any sleep. Sarah, alternately staring at the ceiling and then spooning into me under the covers, said she was going to cancel going on her management retreat.

'Don't do that,' I said. 'Really, everything's fine.'

'Maybe it's got nothing to do with you. Maybe I just don't want to go on the retreat.'

'Sure you do. No matter how bad it is, you're out of the office for a couple of days, and that's got to be worth something. Plus, there'll be snacks.'

'That's true,' she said quietly. 'They will have to feed us.'

We were down in the kitchen as the sun came up. I heard the morning's *Metropolitan* hit the front door and saw our delivery man working his way down the street when I stooped over to pick it up.

'The thing is,' I said, scanning the front page as I wandered back into the kitchen, 'if no one heard those shots being fired at the mall last night, and there's no police report, there's no sense writing anything about it now. In fact, if I did, it would give things away to whoever those guys in the Annihilator are. Assuming, of course, that they subscribe to *The Metropolitan*. They'd know who, exactly, had been watching them, and then they'd never come back.'

'Wouldn't that be a good thing?' Sarah asked.

'Now, that's my wife talking, not my editor. Of course we want them to come back. We want this story to have some sort of ending, a resolution.'

'Here's your coffee,' she said, handing me a mug. 'I'll talk to Magnuson. This is the sort of thing you have to let the managing editor know about. If a member of his newsroom is engaging in shootouts, even if he's not the one actually pulling the trigger, well, he might want to have some input. I think he likes his reporters to maintain some distance.'

'Magnuson,' I said, shaking my head. Bertrand Magnuson, a fixture in the newsroom for thirty years, a veteran of every major world combat and scandal through the sixties and seventies, was a fierce, take-no-prisoners kind of editor. He had these black eyes that you could almost feel boring right through you. 'So you'll talk to him on my behalf?'

Sarah glared. 'If Magnuson wants to talk to you, he won't settle for talking to anyone else, believe me.

53

I sat down at the kitchen table, leafed through the first section of *The Metropolitan*, and my eyes landed on a car ad. 'Oh. Nearly forgot.' I told her Lawrence and I still intended to attend a government auction later in the day where it might be possible to pick up a car for a song. He was going to pick me up from the house before lunch.

'We had this discussion yesterday,' Sarah said, putting in some toast. 'We don't have money for a new car. And I don't want us to throw money away on some old clunker. That doesn't make any sense.'

'If we absolutely had to get one, what could we afford?'

'I don't know. Seven, eight thousand, maybe? But there's no point in even having this conversation.'

Paul, strolling into the kitchen, had evidently heard at least some of what we'd been talking about. 'A government auction?' he said. 'I've heard you can get cars for like nothing at those. Get a Beemer.'

Paul had his learner's permit. I didn't even want to think of the damage he could do to an expensive German sports car. 'And get a standard. Only pussies drive automatics.'

I didn't see any need to get dragged into a debate over transmissions for a car that I was not even going to buy. I put my nose back into the paper, my eye catching a headline next to the car ad. It was an Associated Press item, out of California, about a teenage boy who'd shot several of his classmates, supposedly his friends, at a neighborhood park.

'Color's not important,' Paul said. 'Unless it's like some bright yellow or something, but I don't think BMW makes cars in bright yellow. Their little convertibles, maybe, but not the 5 series or 3 series. You get something too bright, the cops are just going to pull you over all the time for speeding tickets. If they're auctioning off cars that belonged to drug dealers, there should be lots of Beemers. Drug dealers love Beemers.'

It said in the story that this boy, who was seventeen, spent most of his time parked in front of a computer in his bedroom, hacking into places he shouldn't be sticking his nose into, checking out websites that told you how to make your own bomb, how to kill people with nothing but a pencil, that kind of thing.

'We're not getting a Beemer,' Sarah said. 'We're not even getting a car. We can't afford another car.'

'What if Dad's last book gets made into a movie?' Paul asked.

Sarah made a dismissive noise. 'Your father's book did not do well enough to get made into a movie, Paul.'

I glanced up from my paper, decided to let it go. Angie wandered into the kitchen, dressed, but her hair wrapped in a towel.

'What's this about a car?' she asked.

Paul brought her up to speed.

'Get a Hummer,' Angie advised. In my head, I could see the headlights of the Annihilator, like eyes on a dragon, filling the Buick with cold, cold light.

'If there's one thing I won't be getting, ever,' I said, 'it's a Hummer, or a Suburban, or an Annihilator. They run over other people's cars, pollute the atmosphere, get a mile to the gallon, you can't see around the damn things, they—'

'Okay, Dad, we hear ya,' said Paul. 'SUVs, bad. Little cars, good.'

According to the AP story, this boy in California was pretty reclusive. A loner. Obsessed with counterculture, not particularly good at making friends. Liked to take pictures of people without their knowing it, post them on a website. He'd had a crush on some girl, but she'd rebuffed him, and something snapped. He finds his dad's revolver in a drawer, takes it to the park one night where he knew his classmates went to make out, drink underage, and smoke a few joints, and shoots three kids from his class.

Everyone interviewed had said that yeah, he was kind of weird, they weren't totally surprised by what he'd done, but no one had reported his behavior to anyone. No one thought it worth mentioning. Not until after he'd killed three of them.

I said, interrupting the conversation at whatever point it happened to be in, 'Has this Trevor guy called you anymore?'

Angie glanced over at me, deciding, I guess, whether she was speaking to me these days, other than to tell me not to answer the phone. The Pool Boy incident was several weeks old now.

'A couple times. Five times last night my cell rang in one hour. I was hanging out at Deb's? And it's going off in my purse every ten minutes. And I have to check it every time, because it might be—'

She stopped herself.

'Might be who?' Sarah asked.

'Just anybody. It could be somebody I actually want to talk to, and not him. But he's got this thing, so his number doesn't show, so I don't answer any calls unless I see an actual number. So I guess he figures this out, and he goes to a pay phone, I don't know, and calls me, and this time I see an actual number, so I answered.'

'I hope you weren't mean to him,' I said, scanning the rest of the story.

Angie sighed. 'I was . . . pleasant. So he asks me where I am, and before I can think up a good story, I tell him I'm at Deb's house, and he says Deb Chenoweth? And I go yeah, and he goes, oh I know her, have we been friends a long time? That kind of thing. So, I tell him I have to go, and Deb and I decide to go over to Jennifer's, and we go outside and there's Trevor walking along the street.'

She paused and we all waited.

'You don't get it?' she said. 'Deb's place is like, nowhere near here, or where he lives, but it's only been a minute since he hung up, so he had to know that I was already there. He must have followed me. Deb lives just around the corner from the 7-Eleven, where there's a pay phone, and we figure he must have called from there.'

Paul said, ever so casually, 'He's psycho.' He shrugged. 'I heard he boiled a live rabbit once, like that woman in the movie?'

'That's bullshit,' Angie said. 'You made that up.'

'Okay, maybe. But I bet he's the kind of guy who would boil a rabbit. Did you ever see that movie? Where Michael Douglas does that woman, right in the kitchen?'

Sarah shot our son a glance. It was just as well that Norman Rockwell was no longer with us. He would never have done this family's portrait.

Paul continued, 'But he is strange. Maybe that's why he likes *you*.'

'Knock it off,' I said.

'You should consider yourself lucky,' Paul said. 'Lots of girls think he's really hot. They're into this whole mysterious loner thing he's got going. And he is kind of hot. I'm speaking strictly hetero here.'

'He's not my type,' Angie said. 'Maybe he's more your type, Paul. You seem to like him enough to let him get things for you.'

'What are we talking about here?' I said.

'Nothing,' said Paul. 'Shut up, Angie. I don't go ratting you out.'

'What are you talking about?' I said again, trying to force some authority into my voice.

'It's nothing, forget about it,' Angie said. 'I'm just joking.'

Deciding to let this part go for now, I returned to the issue of Trevor Wylie and security. I said, 'Maybe I should speak to him.'

I can't begin to tell you how wrong that comment was.

It was as if Angie exploded. A grenade went off inside her head.

'Great idea . . .' she shouted at me. 'Brilliant . . . Just like you did with Irwin . . .'

That was it . . . The Pool Boy's name was Irwin.

'Just a fucking brilliant idea . . .' And with that, she stormed out of the kitchen.

It was very quiet in the kitchen for a few moments after that, until Paul said, 'Actually, it would be kind of funny if you did.'

I gave him a look that strongly suggested he should move on, which he did.

Sarah was ready to go, so I walked her to the door. 'Nice going in there,' she said.

I ignored that. 'If I see a car I think would be good for us, I'll give you a call.'

'Where is this thing, anyway?'

'Out past Oakwood,' I said.

'Maybe you should drop in on Trixie,' Sarah said, smiling slyly. 'Might be an education for Lawrence.'

Trixie Snelling lived two doors down from the house we'd had in the suburbs, and just as I had when I lived out there, she ran her business from home. And while she didn't write science fiction novels, her occupation would make an interesting subject for a book. She was a stay-at-home dominatrix, with a basement decorated in early Marquis de Sade.

Trixie and I'd become friends while I still thought she was an accountant. One night, after a series of circumstances led me to discover what she actually did for a living, she came to my aid, and we'd remained friends, even if we didn't see each other every day or get together for coffee.

'Somehow, I think we'll give Trixie a wave,' I said.

'You know,' Sarah said, looking a bit sheepish, 'if you did see something cute, and if it was really a good deal . . .'

'I don't believe you,' I said.

'Or maybe a little convertible. That might be fun.'

'You tell me we can't afford a second car, but you want a ragtop.'

'Fine, forget I just said that. Leave your checkbook at home. Come back with a feature and nothing else.'

I opened the door of the Camry for her. 'Let me ask you something,' I said. Sarah looked at me and waited. 'If you were gay, would you still find me attractive?'

She paused. Sarah's been with me long enough now to know that it's simpler to just answer the question than figure out what's behind it.

'Well, let's see, if I were gay, that would make me a lesbian, so I would have to say, no, you would not be my type.'

'No no, if you were a male gay person, would you find me attractive? Would I be your type?'

'So, if I find you attractive as a straight female, would I find you attractive as a gay male?'

'Something like that.'

She pretended to give it some thought. 'No,' she said.

I must have looked hurt. 'Okay, *yes,*' she said. 'Hot, very hot. I'd throw you over the hood of this car in an instant.' She thought a moment. 'Face down, I guess.'

'No, hang on,' I said. 'Let's go with your first instinct. You said no.'

'Well, the thing is, I think gay men put a greater emphasis on, I don't know, sartorial matters.'

'It's how I dress.'

'You are a bit rumpled, and you know, if you ever decide to update your wardrobe, I'd be happy to assist you. But for now, as a rabidly heterosexual female, I have decided to regard your lack of fashion sense as endearing. I'd love to talk about this more, but I have to get going. I've got a bunch of stuff to do at the office before I leave on this stupid retreat. Give me a kiss, you disheveled beast.'

I did as I was told. And she got in the car, backed down the narrow driveway, and disappeared down Crandall.

SEVEN

Sometimes, I blame my father.

He worried about everything, and I imagine he still does. We don't talk all that much since my mother died more than a decade ago, and he lives up in the mountains now, renting out a few lakeside cabins to fishermen, and presumably he moved up there because there would be less to worry about.

His obsessive nitpicking and general sense of impending doom were his gift to me, and from all accounts they are what led my mother to leave the family home for nearly six months when I was in my early teens.

We were the only family I knew of that had fire extinguishers on every floor, an escape route in case of fire taped to the back of bedroom doors. Dad had to be the one, every night, to make sure the doors were locked. You always ran cold water in the shower first, then added hot, to ensure against scalding. You put away as much money as you could every week because for sure you'd be fired the next.

We never had a fire. We never got burned in the shower. Dad was never laid off. He'd be the first to tell you his strategy has paid off.

And now I am the worrier. There is no stuff too small to sweat. My obsession with personal safety issues and protecting the members of my family has been a problem for a while, and has even backfired rather spectacularly. You might have heard about that.

It was the memories of my father that persuaded me to listen to Sarah and pay a visit to Harley, my smartass doctor, in a bid to get a handle on this aspect of my personality. But the thing was, the more I tried not to worry about things, the more things there were, landing on my doorstep, to worry about.

Only hours before, I had been in a car that was being pursued by men with guns. I'd looked down the barrel of a gun before, but I'd never been shot at, nor had I ever been in a car that was being shot at. If that guy hanging out the window of the Annihilator had had a little better aim, Lawrence and I might have been sharing space down at the funeral home with Miles Diamond.

Standing in the kitchen, I found myself almost short of breath, and took a seat at the table. I pushed *The Metropolitan*, with its story about the deranged, gun-toting teen, out of sight, and wrapped both hands around my coffee mug to keep them from shaking.

It wasn't just my night with Lawrence that had me on edge. There was this whole thing with Angie and Trevor Wylie. All I could picture was Keanu Reeves, decked out in shades and long black coat, a machine gun in each hand, spraying bullets every which way. All while doing that leaning-back doing-the-limbo thing he did.

I'd yet to meet Trevor Wylie, but I was betting he couldn't do that.

Maybe if it hadn't been for that story in the paper, about that withdrawn kid blowing away his friends in the park, I wouldn't have been so obsessed with this. But it was the kind of story you come upon more and more in the news. Postal workers, it seemed, had taken a break from shooting their fellow employees so that dysfunctional teens could have a piece of the action. It was a modern-day cliché: the quiet kid, the one no one believed was an actual threat, the one no one could ever remember causing any trouble, suddenly going off like a bomb. Computer nerd turns mass killer.

Did that describe Trevor? Probably not. Angie's characterization of him as a 'stalker' was teenage hyperbole. A stalker was anyone whose attentions you didn't welcome.

It was pretty clear Angie didn't want me interfering, talking to him. Angie probably didn't want me to talk to any of her friends ever again.

I reached for the paper that I'd pushed to the far corner of the table, glanced again at the article. 'Police said that while the boy had been ostracized by his peers on occasion, no one thought him capable of bringing a gun from home and executing youngsters he'd sat with in school.'

I tossed the paper aside a second time. It was a curse to have an imagination that allowed you to envision worst-case scenarios so vividly.

It was time to think about something else. Like women in leather.

I had Trixie's number in an address book in our study. I got it out, found the number, and dialed. She had two phone lines, one personal, another for work. I called the former.

'Hello,' she said cheerfully. This was definitely her personal line. I'd called her business line once, by mistake, and it's a bit like getting Eartha Kitt. Your whole body temp goes up a degree or three.

'It's Zack.'

'Hi . . . Long time no hear . . . How've you been?'

'Good, pretty good. You?'

'Can't complain.'

'Business good?'

'I think I'm recession proof. No matter how bad the economy gets, there are guys who need to be tied up and spanked. You called the wrong line if you want to book a session.'

'No, this is personal.'

'You think spanking isn't personal?'

'Point taken.'

Trixie and I don't exactly occupy the same worlds, and I don't mean that to sound judgmental. She's in a line of work my kids would call 'sketchy' and maybe even a little bit dangerous, not to mention very possibly illegal. But her straightforwardness, honesty and will-ingness to help me when I was in trouble once, made her a friend.

'Listen,' I said, 'I haven't touched base with you in a while, and thought I'd call. It was nice, when you were next door, we could have a coffee now and then.'

'Usually when you were having some sort of crisis,' Trixie said. 'Does that mean you're having one now?'

'I guess you could say I'm a bit stressed.'

'Nothing like when you lived next door, I hope.'

'I'm not trying to duck a murder charge, if that's what you mean.' I told her about the night before, with Lawrence.

'How does a normal guy like you find so much trouble?' Trixie asked.

'It's a gift. And then there's this thing with my daughter.'

'My mind's gone blank. Your daughter . . .'

'An—'

'Angie . . . Yes. How's she? Still interested in photography?'

'Not enough that we've put a darkroom into the house, like we did when we lived in Oakwood. She's pretty busy, anyway. This is her first year in college. With all the studying and assignments, there's not that much time for hobbies. She's living at home, heading downtown for her classes, taking a mix of things, but kind of leaning toward psychology, I think. She's got a couple of psych courses.'

Trixie said, 'Maybe, if she takes enough of them, she'll be able to figure out what's wrong with you.' I smiled. She went on, 'So, what's up with her?'

I told her about Trevor Wylie.

'I think you're making a big thing out of nothing. So there's a guy who likes her, she's not interested. Eventually, he'll get the message.'

'You're probably right. But showing up at her friend's place, out of nowhere. Sounds like he had to be following her, don't you think?'

'Look, Angie's a smart kid, right?'

'Yeah, sure.'

'She knows how to take care of herself. If she thinks there's a real problem, she'll tell you.'

'Maybe,' I said, not with much conviction.

'Listen, she'll be okay. How's Paul? Still gardening?'

'Not quite as much as before we moved. He still gets his hands dirty now and then, but he spends a lot of time in front of the computer now. And he's working on getting his driver's license.'

'Next time you're out this way, let me know. We'll get caught up.'

'I'm actually headed out that way today, around lunch, with my detective friend, to go to a government auction.'

'Lunch today won't work. My first client's coming around then. Which reminds me, I've got to iron my Girl Scout troop leader outfit, and dig out my matching stilettos.'

'Girl Scout leaders wear stilettos?'

'This one's going to be. Oh shit, that reminds me, I hope I still have some of their cookies around. I put a box in the freezer. . . .' She was on the cordless and I could hear her walking around the house. 'Here we go, yeah, I've got them. Gotta give them time to defrost.'

'Your client likes to eat Girl Scout cookies?'

'Well, let's just say they help complete the scene for him.'

'I should let you go,' I said. 'Thanks for listening.'

I puttered around the house for the next three hours, until I heard a car pull into the driveway. I stepped out onto the front porch and saw a blue four-door Jaguar sedan. Lawrence was easing himself out the front door.

'The Buicks in the shop, getting a new rear window,' he explained. I locked up the house, got into the Jag, buckled up, and ran my hand over the leather upholstery, the walnut inlays in the dash.

'Nice,' I said.

'Used to belong to a Jamaican guy ran the drug trade in the north end. Agents busted him, seized pretty much everything he owned, and I got it when they auctioned it off. You looking for a Jag?'

'I don't know that I'm looking for anything, but if I were it wouldn't be a Jag. Head office says we can't afford one at the moment.'

'Head office?'

'Sarah.'

'Okay.'

'I didn't even bring my checkbook, in case I get tempted.'

'Yeah, well, if you change your mind, let me know. I've got mine, you could pay me back after.'

'I don't know. Sarah was sort of weakening towards the end there, talking about a convertible, but I think she was briefly delusional. She really doesn't want me to spend the money.'

'This is one of those times when it pays to be gay. I don't get pussy-whipped,' Lawrence said.

'No significant other?' I asked.

'I'm seeing a guy, name's Kent. Runs a restaurant, Blaine's, on the east side. He's thirty-six, a white guy.'

'Really.'

Lawrence smiled. 'I met him before I quit the force, but didn't really hook up with him till recently. Might work into something, never know.'

On the highway heading out to Oakwood, I said to Lawrence, 'Okay, here's a hypothetical. Someone you know might, and it's just might, be being stalked by someone. She thinks this guy has been following her, he shows up wherever she is, and it kind of freaks her out, but he hasn't done anything dangerous, or threatened her, nothing like that.'

Lawrence listened.

'And she's not really making a big deal of it. She says the guy's just a pest, nothing to worry about.'

'Okay,' Lawrence said. 'But it seems like a big deal to you. What do we know about this guy?'

'Well, he's twenty or so, I gather, seems to be living on his own, his parents are out west or something, kind of a computer geek, into the whole *Matrix* look, the sunglasses and long coat, not bad-looking according to those who've seen him, but a loner.'

'And how long has he been following your daughter?'

I was about to remind him that this was a 'hypothetical' case, then figured what the hell. 'Doesn't sound like a long time. Couple weeks, maybe. Calls her cell phone quite a few times every day, calls the house. He called at breakfast yesterday morning, I had to field it because Angie didn't want to talk to him. Angie, she's going to college now, and I think he's—'

'He got a name?'

'Wylie. Trevor Wylie.'

'Okay.'

'And he's shown up, just the other night, outside of one of her friend's houses, like it was just a coincidence, but this was clear across town.'

'So he would have had to follow her there, that's your thinking?'

'I guess.'

'He's got a car?'

I shrugged. 'I'm guessing yes, but I don't know.'

'What's she said to him? Your daughter. Angie, right?'

'Yeah. I don't think she's told him to drop dead or anything. She's not like that. But she's probably given him the brush-off, bordered on rude. When she thinks it's him calling her cell, she doesn't answer. Anyone with an ounce of sense would have gotten the message by now.'

68

'Some people often don't read the signals very well.'

I looked out the window. We were approaching the Oakwood exit, and from the highway you could see the hundreds of new suburban homes, each one barely distinguishable from the next.

'What would you do if you were me?'

'Well, you could do nothing. Chances are he's harmless and this whole thing will work itself out.' Lawrence put on his blinker.

'Or?'

'Or you could check him out. Find out a bit more about this kid. Which might put your mind at ease, or tell you that you've got reason to be concerned.'

'And how am I going to do that? Start tailing him?'

'Hey,' said Lawrence, 'you're not exactly learning from the master. I blew that tail last night in the first mile. What you could do, though, is follow Angie.'

'Huh?'

'Well, what you want to know is, is he following your daughter around? You follow her, you'll find out whether he is, too.'

I shook my head. 'That's crazy. I couldn't follow my own daughter.' But even as I dismissed the idea, I was working out the logistics in my head. Would I wear a disguise? Rubber nose and glasses? And if Angie was using our car for the evening, and Trevor was following her in his car, then how was I going to follow him following her if we didn't have a second car? Well, we didn't have a second car yet, but—

Enough, I told myself. This is crazy talk.

What kind of father would consider, for even a moment, actually tailing his own daughter around town? And what would his wife do to him if she found out he'd been doing such a thing?

'No, no, I could never do that,' I said quietly.

'Hey, I'm only talking out loud,' Lawrence said. 'Your other option is, let someone else check the kid out.' He paused, considering. 'I'll do it if you want.'

'No, no, that's okay. I don't think Sarah and I really have money in the budget for hiring a private eye. No offense. I mean, if we were ever going to hire somebody, you'd be the guy.'

Lawrence smiled. 'Don't worry about it. When you finally do your story about hanging out with a private eye, I'm gonna be getting lots of business.'

'I can't accept services in return for editorial coverage,' I protested, but not, I have to admit, very strenuously.

'We didn't even have this conversation,' Lawrence said.

He was quiet for a few more blocks, then said, 'The thing is, Zack, where your own family is concerned, you have to trust your instincts. If your gut tells you something's wrong, it probably means something's wrong. Read the signals. If a guy thinks, just because his wife is coming home late from work every night, closing the door when she gets a phone call, and dressing a lot hotter than usual, that maybe she's having an affair, odds are she's having an affair. If your gut says this kid is weird, he's probably weird.'

'But weird doesn't always mean dangerous.'

'No,' Lawrence said, 'it doesn't. You'll have to listen to what your gut has to say about that. And let me tell you something else, pal. Don't ever let anyone hurt someone who's important to you. Don't hesitate. Don't second-guess yourself.'

'I hear ya,' I said.

'And don't miss your moment.'

'What do you mean by that?'

'Years ago, I was a cop, but off duty, didn't have my weapon, and I walked into a drugstore right in the middle of a holdup, guy has a sawed-off pointed at the cashier, screaming at her to empty the till.'

'Jesus.'

'So I freeze, and the guy knows I'm there, tells me to back off, but he's doing this thing with his nose, sniffing, you know? It's ragweed season, and he's doing these funny little intakes of breath, and not only has he asked the cashier for money, but a box of anti-histamine on the counter behind her. The guy's very jumpy, like he wants to use the gun even if he gets everything he's asking for, and it's clear he's got a sneeze on the way, and I'm guessing that when it comes, it's gonna be a doozy. So I wait for my moment.'

'The sneeze.'

'We're in the windup, each intake a bit bigger than the one before, and it's just about to happen, and I figure, this is the moment, there will never be a better opportunity to deal with this situation, and then he blows. Nearly blew out a window with this sneeze, and I tackle him the millisecond before it happens, because when you sneeze that big, you close your eyes. He never saw me coming.' He smiled to himself.

'How do you know,' I asked, 'if it's *the* moment?'

'If you don't know,' Lawrence said, 'then it's not the moment.'

He brought the car to a stop outside a bureaucratic-looking red brick building that fronted the street and was flanked by a ten-foot-high chain-link fence, and beyond that, hundreds and hundreds of vehicles. Lawrence took the key out of the ignition. 'Let's go look at all the shiny cars. Maybe we can find one with a few million in coke still in the trunk, you and I can both retire.'

EIGHT

'We gotta find Eddie,' Lawrence said. 'He's not the actual auctioneer, but he oversees this whole operation. He'll tell you everything you want to know, but don't be afraid to make a run for it if he starts to drive you crazy.' Lawrence asked around inside the office and was told we could find Eddie out in the compound.

He was peering through the windshield of a Cadillac, double-checking the vehicle identification number against a sheet attached to the clipboard in his hand, when Lawrence called to him. He was a slight man, about five-six, probably late forties, bookish in appearance with his oversize black-framed glasses and half a dozen pens clipped to his shirt pocket. His hair was short, curly and greasy looking, like maybe he hadn't stood under a shower for a number of days.

'Hey, hey, Lawrence, how are ya, how are ya?' he said. Even with the big glasses on, he was squinting through them at us.

'Good, Eddie. How's life treatin' ya?'

Eddie Mayhew shrugged. 'Oh, you know, busy, busy, all the time, busy. The stuff's always coming in, you know, always coming in.'

'How's the missus?'

I looked at Lawrence. Missus?

Eddie made a face, like he'd caught a whiff of something that smelled bad. 'Oh, you know, still talk talk talking, wants me to drive her out to see her sister in the spring, out in Milwaukee. Both of them, talk talk talk, for a whole week.'

'They got a lot of beer there,' Lawrence said, trying to offer Eddie a glimmer of hope.

'Yeah, beer, yeah, that's good. What I really need, really need, is something to put me out for the drive out, so I won't have to listen, won't have to listen, to my wife.'

'That's kind of difficult if you're the one doing the driving.'

'Yeah, yeah, I know, I know. Can't win.' But then, oddly, a look of calm came over him. 'Oh well, oh well. Maybe it won't be so bad, so bad after all. A lot could change by the spring, yeah.'

'I'd like you to meet my friend here, Eddie,' Lawrence said, allowing me to step forward. 'This is Zack Walker. He's a writer for *The Metropolitan*, he's going to do a feature on the auction, have someone take a few pictures.'

'Oh sure, yeah, sure, that's fine. Good paper, *The Metro*, I read that. Read that all the time.'

'Thanks,' I said.

I explained that I was doing a color piece on what it was like to buy a car at a government auction. Eddie said he could spare some time to answer my questions, and Lawrence excused himself to register and check out what vehicles were available.

'We've got boats, motorcycles, furniture, high-end stereo equipment, oh yeah, we got everything,' Mayhew said. 'Sometimes we have people submit written bids, whoever bids highest wins.'

'Like those silent auctions my son's high school does sometimes for fundraisers,' I offered.

'Well, sort of, I don't know, I don't have any kids, never had any kids, but the stuff they're auctioning off at your kid's school probably didn't all belong, at one time, to drug dealers and smugglers, am I right? Huh?'

'That's probably true.'

'But today, okay, today we're auctioning off some big stuff, and we're doing it the way you're probably more familiar with, with an auctioneer, right? Mostly cars, SUVs, couple of boats, good stuff, really really good stuff. Come on, we'll go out into the paddock, out in the paddock, I'll show you.'

We wandered out into what looked like a used-car lot, with the odd boat, motorcycle and RV tossed into the mix.

'So, who'd this stuff used to belong to?' I asked, scribbling into my notebook.

'We've got goods here that belonged to biker gangs, mean ones, you know, mean bikers, and drug smugglers, big-timers who got away with it for a long time, and small-timers who thought they could make it big but were a bit too stupid to do this kind of thing without getting caught. Even some CEO types, stock fraud guys, get their fancy Beemers and boats seized. I know the history of everything out here. Make it my business to. It's interesting, you know? You got your whole crime microcosm here, wrapped up in these cars.'

'I'll bet,' I said.

'Ask me anything,' Eddie said. 'Go ahead, go ahead, ask me anything about anything you see. Go on.'

'Uh, okay,' I said. I pointed to a shiny red Mustang. 'What's the story there?'

'Wait a minute, wait a minute, okay, okay, I know,' he said quickly. Eddie seemed to be running on premium unleaded. 'Bobby Minor, twenty-four, bought the thing from money he made dealing crack on the north side, it's got a V8 under the hood, barely 15,000 miles on it. Go ahead, check the odometer, go on, check it, see if I'm right.'

With some reluctance, I opened the door and glanced at the dash. The car had 14,943 miles on it.

'Pretty good,' I said.

'Ask me another,' he said. 'Go on, ask me.'

I didn't know how long I wanted to play this game, but figured I could go another couple of rounds.

'All right,' I said. 'That one.' I indicated a motorcycle.

Eddie, cocky behind the Coke rims, circled the bike. 'Harley-Davidson, belonged to a member of the Snake Eyes gang, yeah, that's right, loosely affiliated with the Hell's Angels, those Hell's Angels, ran prostitution, table dancers, that's what they did. This bike belonged to Buzz Crawley. They called him Nut Crusher.' Eddie giggled. 'Guess why? Go on, guess.'

'I think I have an idea.'

'You know why? He'd go visit guys, guys who owed the gang money, grab their boys with a set of pliers, drag 'em around the parking lot that way. Oooh, that would hurt, wouldn't it? Wouldn't that hurt?' He was smiling big-time now.

'That would hurt.' I had stopped taking notes.

'You see that Land Rover? That got taken away from the Jamaicans; that little silver car, that was in Lenny Indigo's driveway before they put him away; that one, that green Winnebago there, that was—'

'You really know your stuff, Eddie, no doubt about

it. I think what I'm going to do is, talk to some of the people who're planning to bid on something, get a bit of color for my story.'

'Oh, good idea. But you need anything else, I'm always here.'

'Don't you ever go home?' I asked.

He grinned, leaned in towards me. 'You knew my wife, you'd know why I'm here all the time. Like to avoid going home as long as possible, you know? You married?'

'Yeah.'

'Then you know what I'm talking about, right? You know what I'm talking about, oh yeah, I can see it.'

'Well, thanks again,' I said, and broke away.

I'd called *The Metropolitan*'s photo desk ahead of time to arrange for a photographer to meet me here. I'd been a reporter-photographer myself on another paper a few years back – what they called a two-way – but my new employer was content to limit my skills to writing.

I spotted Stan Wannaker, one of the paper's most distinguished shooters, who you'd be more likely to run into in Afghanistan or Pakistan or one of the other 'stans' where people are always shooting each other and blowing up things because they don't have access to cable. He was evidently slumming it to be covering something as mundane as a police auction alongside a lowly reporter like me.

'Hey, Stan,' I said, interrupting him as he snapped a couple of frames of a guy inspecting a Lexus.

He glanced away from the viewfinder. 'Hey, uh, Zack, right?' He reached into his pocket where he'd stuffed a folded blue assignment sheet, opened it up and confirmed that I was the reporter he was supposed to meet. I was still relatively new on staff, and this was the first time I'd linked up with Stan. Given that I'm not exactly a foreign-correspondent type, what with my aversion to getting sand in my shoes or visiting nations where intense heat is likely to cause me a rash, our paths had not crossed.

'How come they've got you doing stuff like this?' I asked.

'I'm in town for a while, catching my breath,' he said. 'Until all hell breaks loose someplace else, which shouldn't be long.' Stan's in his early forties, unmarried, lives in a tiny apartment someplace in the city, and isn't saddled with the kinds of obligations that might keep the rest of us from leaving at a moment's notice for the North Pole or Taiwan or the Falkland Islands. His jeans and multipocketed jacket hung loosely on his thin frame.

'So, what kind of shots you looking for?'

I shrugged. 'I just got here. I'm gonna talk to people, see what they're looking for.'

'Well, give me a shout if you need me. I'll wander.'

I found Lawrence checking out a Saab convertible, then looking it up on the sheet he'd been given listing the items available for sale.

'Interested?' I asked.

'Not really.'

'I'm going to talk to some people,' I said.

'Knock yourself out. Auction doesn't start for another half hour.'

I meandered with my notebook open, pen in hand, chatted people up. Some were civil servants of one stripe or another – cops or firefighters or clerical workers

– who had an inside line on when these kinds of auctions were held and made a point of attending them. And there were general members of the public who were on mailing lists, or signed up at Internet sites that, for a fee, let one know when and where these types of sales were going to be held.

One guy, an accountant, told me he thought it was cool that his current car, a Lexus, was once owned by some notorious cocaine dealer. 'Gives me something to tell my lady friends, gives me a little cachet,' he said. Sort of like being a badass by association, which struck me as pitiful.

Even though a lot of these cars were going to go for rock-bottom prices, I didn't see much in my price range. Most of the vehicles were listed with a suggested opening bid, and maybe a loaded 7-series BMW at $25,000 was a good deal, but it was still a lot more than I could spend.

I'd just finished talking to a guy who planned to bid on a 1998 Land Rover that had sustained a lot of damage in a police chase and was going for next to nothing ('I can rebuild anything,' he said) when I spotted the silver compact four-door that Eddie Mayhew had pointed to earlier. Nice flowing lines, but not too flashy. Bucket seats, a sunroof, reasonably roomy back seat.

A couple of other potential bidders were checking it out as well. A woman I guessed to be in her early sixties, and a short, balding guy built like a fire hydrant. He brushed past me as he rounded the car, and I noticed he was dressed in an expensive suit that didn't fit him worth a damn. You spend that much money on clothes, you figure you could spend a few more bucks on alterations. He coughed, took a swig of juice from a glass bottle in his right hand, coughed again. There was a jingling noise coming from his left hand, which turned out to be a full set of keys hanging from his index finger. I guessed they must have been a set belonging to his wife or daughter. You don't see that many guys with a two-inch Barbie doll hanging from their key ring.

'Nice, huh?' the woman said, noticing that we were both admiring the same car. 'The Virtue is such a cute car. It's perfect for my daughter.'

Hmmm. It might be perfect for mine, too, if the price was right.

The guy in the ill-fitting suit kicked the car's tires, coughed again, took another sip, and shot me a look as I made a closer inspection of the car's interior. I looked at the dash, the layout of the gauges, which were placed in the center of the dash and angled towards the driver. There were several buttons I couldn't figure out the purpose of, then realized they controlled the CD player. A CD player . . .

I found Lawrence and asked him for the auction list. 'What's a Virtue?' I asked. 'I think I've seen some ads.'

'One of the big Japanese companies makes it. It's one of those hybrid cars.'

'A who?'

'A hybrid. Has like two engines. A gas one and an electric one. The electric one keeps the gas one from working so hard. When you're stopped at a light, electric motor kicks in so you don't have to waste gas; light changes, you hit the accelerator, gas motor kicks in. Like that. Great gas mileage, hardly pollutes the environment.'

'Okay' I said, remembering what I'd read about hybrids in the paper's weekly automotive section. 'Is this the one, the electric engine is always recharging its own batteries?'

'Yeah, and it's got a lot of them. They got one of those here?'

'I guess it belonged to a drug dealer who was environmentally conscious,' I said. 'There's a little good in everybody.'

'Yeah. Wasn't Hitler nice to his dog?'

'Come and have a look at it.'

Lawrence followed me over. 'Looks in pretty good shape,' he said. He opened the door, checked the odometer. 'Not all that many miles on it. And I hear they have a pretty good reliability record.'

'And the suggested opening bid,' I said, finding the car again on the list and holding my thumb there for future reference, 'is kind of reasonable.' I slipped in behind the wheel. 'I like it,' I said.

I checked out everything. The size of the glove box, the map pockets on the door, more storage pockets on the back of the seats, the interior trunk release, the sunroof buttons. 'Seems pretty well equipped. And you know what else I like?'

'Tell me,' said Lawrence. 'What else do you like?'

'The statement it makes. Says you care about the planet, that you want to do your part to preserve the ecosystem.'

'Yeah,' said Lawrence. 'Chicks love that.'

'Some might.'

'So, you gonna bid on it?'

I was nervous. I'm always this way when I consider spending a lot of money. I get short of breath and my mouth goes dry.

'I think maybe it's worth a shot.' I paused. 'You know what? Let me give Sarah a quick call.' I dug my cell phone out of my jacket and called her at her desk at *The Metropolitan.*

'City,' she said.

'Me. I'm at the auction. I think maybe I found us a car.'

'Uh-oh.'

'No, just listen. It's perfect. Good on gas, perfect for Angie commuting to school, an excellent repair record according to Lawrence.'

'Is it a convertible?' Sarah sounded tentatively hopeful.

'No, it's not a convertible.'

'Oh. Okay.'

'You're something else, you know that?'

'I didn't say it had to be a convertible, I was just asking. What color is it?'

'Silver,' I said.

'I'm not crazy about silver, but I can live with it. What kind of money?'

I told her the minimum bid was $8,000, and I could almost feel her intake of breath. 'Listen, you said that was sort of in the ballpark of what we could manage. If I have to go way over, then I'll just walk away.'

'You promise.'

'I promise.'

'And don't do something dumb like pull on your ear. They have all these signals. You could end up buying it and not even know it.'

'I'm not in a Dick Van Dyke episode,' I told her. 'I just have to – Oh shit.'

'What?'

'I didn't bring my checkbook. I figured there was no way I'd buy anything. No, wait, Lawrence said he could buy it for me, I could pay him back after. That way—'

'Don't fucking take my picture, man . . .'

I whirled around. Stan Wannaker was being shoved up against a Ford Explorer by the short guy with the bad cough and the Barbie keys. 'Call you back,' I said, and slipped the phone back into my jacket.

'Fuck you . . .' Stan shouted back, the two cameras hanging down on his chest suddenly flinging about like enormous necklaces.

'Give me your film . . .' the man demanded.

'Fuck you . . .' Stan said again. He'd dealt with bad guys all over the world, in countries a lot scarier than this one, and he wasn't about to surrender his film to some short asshole with a bad attitude in an ill-fitting suit.

'I wasn't even taking your picture,' Stan told the man. 'I was just doing an overall shot. Take a pill or something.'

The short guy was in Stan's face now, as best he could, being about six inches shorter. He set his bottle of juice on the hood of the Explorer so he could poke a stubby finger into Stan's chest. 'You gonna hand over—' and he coughed '—that film?'

Stan backed up an inch to avoid any incoming phlegm. 'Listen, dickwad, I'm here for *The Metropolitan* and if you want my film you better call our fucking lawyers and take it up with them. And if you touch me with that finger again, I'm gonna snap it the fuck off.'

The short guy was a bomb about to go off. His face went flush red, his shoulders tensed, and even Stan, as fearless as he'd been a moment earlier, looked like he was getting ready to move sideways in a hurry if he had to.

But then Stan's attacker began to notice that he was getting a lot of attention. People had stopped looking at cars and boats and motorcycles and turned their heads in the direction of the commotion, not sure whether to intercede, watch, or move on. The guy glanced around, his lips pressed firmly together, breathing in and out in short bursts through his flat, wide nose. He gave Stan a final shove up against the SUV and strode off in the direction of the paddock exit.

'You okay?' I said once I'd reached Stan.

He was unruffled, just checking his cameras for any damage. 'Fucking little Nazi,' he said. 'Thought I was at an Afghan checkpoint there for a minute.'

'He was crazy,' I said. 'I thought he was going to explode there for a second.'

'A suicide bomber without the dynamite,' Stan said flippantly. 'Anyway, good thing he decided to take a hike.' He smiled, nodding his head toward the crowd. 'Too many witnesses around. I'll have to watch myself in dark alleys for a while.'

Once I was sure Stan was fine, I rejoined Lawrence.

'Let's bid on the Virtue,' I said. 'But I don't want to go over eight-five. Eight-six, maybe. But that's it. Maybe eight-nine.' I'd started sweating again.

Lawrence said, 'You're grace under pressure, aren't you?'

NINE

The older woman who'd been eyeing the Virtue the same time I was bailed out at $8,800. And I managed to go through the bidding process without tugging my ear or nodding my head in such a way as to end up with a $100,000 yacht by mistake.

There was some paperwork to deal with, forms to fill out, and then the car was ours. And not just any car. But a fuel-conserving, environment-saving, socially responsible automobile. And yet, I had a feeling, once I got home with it, I was going to be made to feel like Charlie Brown after he came back with the spindly Christmas tree.

Actually, it wasn't quite mine yet. Lawrence wrote the check, and once I'd repaid him by the end of the day, he'd transfer the ownership to me.

We split up outside the government auction headquarters. Lawrence left in his Jag, and I had the Virtue. I decided that its first adventure would be a drive down to the newspaper. The car's mileage was relatively low, and it had cleaned up nicely. The ashtray didn't even appear to have ever been used for anything but candy wrappers, and the coils on the lighter weren't smudged with ash. What were the odds, a drug dealer who didn't even smoke? Lawrence's theory was that it had been a drug dealer's wife's or daughter's car. How else to account for its pristine condition?

It was roughly the same size as our old Civic. Sleeker looking, too, but not necessarily peppier. I floored it as I got onto the highway and merged with traffic, and it felt a tad, well, anemic. But it hadn't been my intention to buy a sports car. This vehicle was going to do just fine, and when you figured that I got it for about half the price of a new one, it was a hell of a good deal. There were times when I wasn't even sure the car was still on. Sitting at red lights, when the electric motor took over to conserve fuel, the car was practically noiseless, like a golf cart. It wasn't until the light changed, and I tapped the accelerator and moved, that I was certain the car was still in the game.

I found a metered spot on a side street around the corner from the *Metropolitan* building, walked past the huge bay doors where the papers rolled down off the presses, were bundled, and loaded into dozens of waiting trucks. I took the stairs up to the second-floor cafeteria and grabbed a coffee on my way to the fourth-floor newsroom.

I set my paper cup down next to my 'work station,' part of a cluster of four desks separated by chest-high partitions, and pressed a button on my computer to bring it to life. I dug my notebook out of my sports jacket and flipped it open as I slipped down into my chair. I was typing a possible first sentence for the auction feature when I sensed a presence over my left shoulder.

I whirled around in the chair, catching one of my fingers on the edge of my notebook. It was Sarah. 'Hey,' I said, glancing at the side of my index finger where a slender red line was developing.

'Hey yourself. What the hell happened when I was talking to you on the phone? Why didn't you call me back? If you're trying to give me a heart attack, your plan's working perfectly.'

For a moment, I couldn't remember ending our conversation so abruptly. 'Oh yeah. Some nutjob went ballistic on Stan. No biggie. He's dealt with worse.'

'How am I supposed to know that if you don't call me back?'

I didn't see Sarah's other staffers getting chewed out like this. 'Could we just move on?' I asked.

She took a breath, let it out slowly. 'What are you doing now?'

'I'm gonna knock off this auction feature, Metro can use it any time they want with the pics Stan took.' I sucked on the side of my index finger. It was stinging like hell.

'Okay. How long?'

'Twenty inches or so.'

'Let it run. There's a lot of big holes in the section tomorrow.'

Welcome to the newspaper biz. No one cares what's in your feature, just so long as it will fill the space.

'And this feature on Larry? Is it—'

'Lawrence.'

'Right. Lawrence. Is that thing going to be done soon, because I was telling the M.E. about it, that things got a bit hairy last night.'

'Did you really have to do that?'

'Zack, there was no way I could not tell the managing editor about that. If Magnuson finds out about it from someone else, then comes to me and asks why I didn't let him know, I'm toast around here.'

'Okay, I get it. But you explained it, right? That it just happened? It wasn't like I planned to be in a shootout.'

'Uh, pretty much. But he wants to see you.'

My stomach did a flip. 'You're not serious.'

'He said, "Would you be good enough to have Mr Walker come by and see me?" And I said of course. He seemed a bit uncomfortable with the idea of you riding around in a car that's taking shots at people. He also found it a bit hard to picture.'

'What does that mean?' I sucked on my finger again, winced.

'I don't think he sees you as one of our more gung-ho staffers, risking his life to get a story.' She smiled and laid a hand on my shoulder. 'Of course, he doesn't know you the way I do. What have you done to your finger?'

'Paper cut,' I said. 'Hurts like the devil. You got any Band-Aids in your office?'

Sarah sighed. 'It would help, what with you being summoned to see Magnuson, if we had something to show him, some sort of progress on the Lawrence feature.'

'We're going out at least one more night, tonight. Things could easily come to a head, then I can wrap the whole thing up.'

'Couldn't you write it up now? Surely you've got enough. I mean, you've got a major robbery, a guy left dead in the street, what more do you want? It's not like you have to solve these clothing store robberies. That's Lawrence's job, and if it takes him another month, I can't afford to lose you for that long.'

'You just don't want me to go. That's what this is about.'

'That's not true. I'm speaking totally as your editor here.'

'You're lying. I can tell. You're getting that flushed look at the base of your neck there.'

'Stop looking at the base of my neck.' She looked off into a far corner of the newsroom. 'You know, I'm not sure this is working.'

'What? Our marriage?'

'No, you idiot. Our marriage is fine. You working for me, that's the problem. Reporting to me. I hate it.'

'Do you find me a difficult employee? Because, if you're considering giving me a poor performance review, I think we might be able to come to some sort of an arrangement.' I gave her my best 'come hither' look.

'Oh, shut up,' she said.

'I have to admit, though, there are times when it is a bit distracting. For example, when I'm talking to anyone else in the newsroom, I'm not thinking about what color underwear they might be wearing.'

'Not even Sylvia, in sports?'

I paused, perhaps for too long. Sylvia, who keyed in late-night scores, possessed an amazing superstructure. 'No,' I said. 'Not even Sylvia.'

'Then you're the only one,' Sarah said. 'I swear, those have to be implants. I have two things to say to you. One, this kind of talk is the kind of thing that could get you in trouble with the paper's sexual harassment police. And two, what color underwear do you think I'm wearing now?'

I studied her blouse. It was dark blue. That made it tough. Plus, Sarah was standing with her arms crossed.

'I'm betting the black one, with the clasp in the front,' I said.

Sarah mulled my answer.

'So, am I right?'

'You'll never know,' she said. She started to walk away, then turned on her heel. 'I nearly forgot to ask. What happened at the auction?'

I steeled myself. 'We have a new car.'

Sarah looked wary, afraid to ask. 'How much?'

'It's perfect,' I said. 'Not only that, it's something we can be proud to own.'

Sarah's eyebrows went up. 'Oh my God. You went and bought a Beemer.'

'No no, not that kind of proud. That's showy. I'm talking proud in a civic-minded kind of way.'

Sarah continued to look suspicious. 'God, just tell me.'

'A Virtue.'

'A who?'

I explained the whole hybrid concept, as best as I was able.

'An electric car,' she said dubiously.

'Only half electric.'

'So, you got us a car that needs an extension cord? And you still haven't told me what this cost us.'

'Not that much,' I said.

Sarah was starting to glower. 'How much?'

'Just a little over eight thousand.'

She swallowed. 'How much over eight thousand?'

'Nine hundred.'

'Nine hundred? So the car was nine thousand? Dollars?'

'No, just $8,900.'

Sarah shook her head. 'There goes the budget for the next six months.'

'It'll be okay. We'll be saving hundreds on gas. Just wait and see. It's a good deal.'

Sarah shook her head. 'I think life was simpler when I only had to put up with you at home,' she said, and turned to make the trek back across the newsroom to her office.

I turned back to my computer screen and started typing. A moment later, I felt a pair of hands on my shoulder, then noticed the familiar scent of Sarah as she leaned down and put her mouth close to my ear.

'You were right about one thing,' she whispered.

'About what?' I said, eyes on my screen.

'Black, front clasp.' And she strode off. I would have spun around in my seat to say something, but I had responded, involuntarily, to her comment, and felt that keeping a good part of me under the desk was prudent for the next couple of minutes.

Stan poked his head from behind the partition. 'That was a good guess on the clasp thing,' he said, startling me. 'I wasn't even sure she was wearing one at all.'

'You probably know, Stan, that Sarah's my wife,' I said.

He nodded. 'I had a feeling you'd met her before.' He came around the partition, dropped a contact sheet on my desk. 'There's the auction stuff. There's another copy with the desk, whenever they want it.'

I glanced at the negative-size shots. Stan could take something as mundane as a lot full of cars and, with the right angles and lighting, turn it into something special.

'Great,' I said. Stan didn't acknowledge the compliment. He'd been praised by people a lot more important than I. One of the frames caught my eye. 'That the guy?'

Stan squinted. 'What?'

'The one who wanted your film? That him there?'

The angry short man was off to the left side of the frame, not doing anything in particular. Stan's focus had been a pair of guys looking under the hood of a Pontiac. 'I think so. I wasn't even shooting him. Asshole.'

'Hey, Walker,' someone on the other side of me said.

I looked around. It was Cheese Dick Colby, the paper's star police reporter, a heavyset man in his mid-fifties. A police search of his medicine cabinet would be unlikely to turn up any deodorant.

'Hey, Dick,' I said.

'Thanks for the call the other night, about the hit-run outside the men's shop. Just so you understand, I do the breaking stuff, you can do the puff pieces.'

'Sure, Dick. I just hope someday I'm trusted to handle the big stories like you.'

Colby, evidently oblivious to sarcasm, said, 'What you working on?'

'A feature.'

'This still the same thing you were working on the other night, hanging out with the detective?' He was leaning over my desk, forcing me to hold my breath, and looking at the contact sheet Stan had presented to me.

'Whoa, the fuck is this?' Colby asked. 'That's Barbie Bullock there.'

'Who?' I said, leaning in close to the pictures, not only to see them better but to put as much distance as possible between my nose and Colby's armpit.

Colby pointed to the guy who'd roughed up Stan and demanded his film.

'Him. His actual name is Willy Bullock, but everyone refers to him as Barbie Bullock. He's been attempting to run Lenny Indigo's organization ever since Lenny got sent away for everything from dealing to robbery.'

'That name's popping up everywhere,' I said.

'Lenny's number two guy, Donny Leppard, he got sent up, too, but he's going to be out in less than a year. Barbie here's under a lot of pressure to do well while Donny's gone a few months. He does a good job, Indigo's likely to make him his number two guy instead of Donny.'

'So why do they call this clown Barbie?' Stan asked.

'He collects them. Barbies. Got hundreds of them, they say. All sorts of rare ones, plus accessories.'

'His key chain,' I said. 'It was a like a mini-Barbie. I figured it was his wife's or something. Doesn't a guy who collects Barbies run the risk of being made fun of?'

Colby paused. 'Last guy who made fun of Barbie Bullock had his face shoved into the running propeller of an Evinrude. You doing something on Bullock?' Colby eyed me warily, like I was trying to work his side of the street.

Stan spoke up. 'He just happened to be in the picture. We were there doing something else, Dick, so chill out.'

Colby snorted, and I shifted in case any of it landed on me. After he walked away, I said to Stan, 'So, don't you feel special? Pissing off an important underworld character?'

Stan shrugged. 'Listen, when you've pissed off the Taliban, everything else kind of pales in comparison.'

TEN

I banged off the auction story in under an hour, let the desk know it had been handed in, and popped into Sarah's office. She was at her desk, reading stories on her screen.

'I'm outa here,' I said.

'Okay,' she said.

'Cheese Dick came by to see me.'

Sarah closed her eyes. 'And?'

'He strutted about, then left. Could you put him on some sort of beat that requires bathing? Maybe send him to fashion, writing about skin care.'

'See ya at home. And don't forget to see the managing editor before you leave.'

I hadn't forgotten, but I had been considering pretending to have forgotten. I wandered over to his office, where his secretary was posted outside the door.

'Mr Magnuson wanted to see me?' I said.

His secretary said, 'And you are?'

This is always encouraging, when the secretary to the guy who runs the newsroom where you are employed has no idea who you are.

'Zack Walker?' I said. 'I work here?'

She buzzed him, spoke so quietly into her phone that I could not make out what she was saying, and when she was done, said to me, 'He'll be with you in a moment.'

I cooled my heels for about five minutes, standing around Magnuson's closed door like a kid waiting to see the principal. Finally, it opened, and Magnuson himself gestured for me to come in.

He was a slight man, a bit round-shouldered, thinning gray hair atop his head, immaculately dressed, even with his suit jacket off and hanging over the back of the leather chair behind his broad oak desk.

'Mr Walker, what a pleasure,' he said. 'I don't think we've actually spoken since you joined us.'

'No, Mr Magnuson, I don't think we have.'

'Have a seat.'

I took a chair in front of his desk as he got back into his behind it. He tossed a red binder across the desk at me. There was a sticker on the front that read 'Editorial Policy Manual.'

'Did you get one of these when you were hired?' Magnuson asked.

'Uh, I believe I did.'

'I'm going to have to rewrite it,' he said.

'Really? Why is that, Mr Magnuson?'

'I left something out. I should have thought of this before I had it drafted. I can't believe how neglectful I was.'

I didn't want to ask, but felt it was expected of me. 'What, uh, did you leave out?'

'The part that says *Metropolitan* staffers are not supposed to be involved in shootouts.'

'Mr Magnuson, that's not exactly correct. I was in a car with someone who was doing the shooting, but the only thing I was doing was holding the steering wheel so he could get off a few shots.'

'Oh, I see,' Magnuson said. I didn't get the impression that this made everything okay. 'You used to work for the competition, didn't you?'

'Several years ago, yes. I worked at *The Leader*.'

Magnuson nodded thoughtfully. 'Did the reporters over at *The Leader* get involved in shootouts, Mr Walker?'

'Not regularly, sir, although there was one night when two guys from sports who'd had a bit too much to drink started shooting at each other over a Leafs-Sabres game. I don't know where they got the guns, exactly.'

Magnuson cocked his head, squinted at me. 'Is that an attempt at humor, Mr Walker?'

I swallowed. 'If it was, sir, it was evidently a very weak one.'

Magnuson eased back in his chair. 'I've asked around a bit about you. You know what I hear back?'

'I'm somewhat hesitant to ask, sir.'

'People say you're annoying.'

'You should talk to more people than my wife, Mr Magnuson.' I was hoping that might spark a smile, even a small one. It did not.

'When you were hired there, at *The Leader*, did they give you a notepad, a pen, a tape recorder and a .45?'

'No, sir, they didn't.'

'Because I was thinking, if it was okay for reporters there to do that kind of thing, to ride around in cars shooting off guns, that might explain why you thought it was okay when you got hired here. Maybe no one told you.'

'You see,' I said, swallowing, 'what happened last night was kind of an unusual set of circumstances because—'

'Mr Walker,' Magnuson said, leaning closer to me and pointing his finger, 'we write the news. We try not to create it. It's nice when we can be there as it's happening, but as a rule we don't hold the steering wheel so that others can fire wildly into the night. Do you understand what I'm saying?'

'Yes.'

'That's good. Because if you do, maybe I won't have to rewrite this manual.'

'I don't think that will be necessary.'

'Excellent.' He leaned back in his chair. 'Good day, Mr Walker.'

I understood what that meant, too, so I got up and walked out of the office, and as I headed for the elevator, thought I'd rather take my chances with those guys in the Annihilator than have another run-in with Bertrand Magnuson. The guys in the Annihilator didn't have control over my paycheck, and with a new car and a daughter in college, it was the Magnusons of the world who could really put the screws to you.

ELEVEN

I'd picked a bad time to leave the office. It was rush hour, and it took me the better part of half an hour to get uptown to our place on Crandall.

As I was approaching our house from the south, I saw a blue Jag coming from the north. I scooted into our driveway, pulling far enough ahead to allow Lawrence to pull in behind me.

'Nice timing,' I said, walking up to his car as he got out.

'I wants ma money,' he said. He was leaving the car running, which I took as a signal that he didn't have a lot of time to chat.

'Hang on,' I said, running up the porch steps to the front door. I noticed, sitting in one of the wicker chairs we keep on the porch, a backpack I didn't recognize. I unlocked the door, ran upstairs to my study, where I keep the checks for our line-of-credit account, and went back outside.

'How's the car?' Lawrence asked as I used the hood of his Jag to write him out a check for $8,900.

'So far so good,' I said.

Lawrence was casting his eye across the house and garage. 'Nice place. You've only been here a year or so, right?'

'That's right. We lived on this street once before, then flirted with a house in the suburbs for a couple of years, then moved back. We used to live up there.' I pointed up the street.

As I handed him the check I noticed his eyes narrowing, focusing on something at the far end of the driveway.

'You got a visitor,' he said.

'What?' I said, whirling around.

'Someone's hiding out behind your garage. I just saw somebody sneak in there.'

'Seriously?'

He nodded. We both began walking the length of the drive, past the Virtue, toward the single-door garage. Lawrence pointed for me to go down the right side of the garage while he went down the left. There were only a couple of feet between the back of the garage and a six-foot fence, so there wasn't going to be anyplace for our mysterious stranger to go.

Lawrence and I came around the end of the garage at the same time, and our eyes landed on a man – a young man, probably in his late teens, early twenties – about five-ten, slim, short-cropped dirty-blond hair, black lace-up boots, black jeans, long black jacket, dark sunglasses.

He should have felt embarrassed, trapped and cornered as he was, but he stood there confidently, almost defiantly.

'Can I help you?' he asked.

I recognized the voice. 'You must be Trevor,' I said.

A slight nod of the head. 'You must be Mr Walker,' he said. He stepped forward, and as he did so, I noticed he tried to shove something between some tall weeds. He extended a hand. 'A pleasure to meet you.'

I couldn't think of anything to do but shake, so I did.

'What's that you stepped over?' I asked.

'Hmm?' said Trevor.

'Down there,' I pointed, just behind his feet. Trevor moved forwards a bit, and we could all now see a six-pack of beer. Budweiser, in cans.

'Someone's stashed some beer back here,' Trevor said.

'But not you.'

'No, not me.'

'Then if you're not leaving beer behind my garage, what are you doing, Trevor?' I asked.

He said, as if the answer were obvious and my question bordering on stupid, 'Trying to find my dog.'

'Really. You thought he might be trapped in here, between the garage and the fence?'

He reached up, slowly took off his sunglasses, and looked at me with eyes like cold blue steel. 'Yes.'

'I don't see any dog, Trevor.'

'That's because I haven't found him yet.'

Lawrence finally spoke. 'Where do you live, Trevor?' He wasn't just making conversation. This was his cop voice.

Trevor slowly and warily turned his attention on Lawrence. 'Around. I've got a room over on Ainslie, a block over. My dog wanders over here a lot when he gets loose. But I have this way of tracking him.'

Lawrence again: 'How might that be, Trevor?'

He smiled. 'Satellite.'

Now it was my turn. 'You keep track of your dog by satellite,' I said. Trevor's head lazily turned my way. I had a feeling we were boring him.

'Yeah, satellite. It's a software program, like that thing they have in some of the new cars, you know, where you press the button and you get connected to these people who always know where you are. Your air bag goes off, they know instantly, send an ambulance to your exact location. Not that I would ever have a car like that. You really want General Motors to know where you are every second you're out and about? You think they'd be above selling that kind of information? Who do you think gets loads of government contracts to build military technology? Companies like General Motors, that's who. One hand washes the other, right?'

The theme from *The Twilight Zone* started playing in my head.

'So Trevor, you have this software program in your pocket or what?'

He beckoned us with his finger, leading us around the front of the house and stepped up onto my porch. He grabbed the backpack I noticed in our wicker chair.

He brought it back over by the cars, but when he went to set it, with its various straps and buckles everywhere, on the hood of Lawrence's Jag, Lawrence said, 'Just put it on the drive, pal.'

Trevor complied. There was something about Lawrence's voice that made you do what he asked even if you were a kid who thought he was tough like Trevor.

Trevor glanced up at Lawrence as he opened the flap on the backpack. 'Who are you, may I ask?'

'My name is Mr Jones,' he said.

Trevor glanced at me. 'Is he a friend of yours?' I stared, thinking this kid had a lot of attitude, standing here with two adults who'd just caught him trespassing. 'What do you do, Mr Jones? I'm betting you're a cop.'

'You know a lot of cops, do you, Trevor?'

'No, but I know an authority figure when I see one. It's in the way you carry yourself, your voice like when you tell somebody to do something, you expect them to do it.'

'I was,' Lawrence said. 'Now I'm what you might call an independent.'

'You mean, like a security guard?'

Oh boy. I hoped, when Lawrence decided to kill him, he'd be quick.

Amazingly, Lawrence kept his cool. 'No,' he said icily. 'I'm a private detective.'

Trevor's eyes were wide. 'Ahhh. Interesting. I don't think I've ever met an actual private detective before. Do you have, like, a license or something? I'd love to see it.'

'How'd you like to see your face planted on the sidewalk?'

That didn't seem to faze Trevor. But rather than try to up the attitude, he adopted a reasonable tone. 'I'd merely like to know whether you have some authority to interrogate me like this. Mr Walker here, this is his property, and he's entitled to ask what I'm doing here, and I can understand why he might be troubled, but I'm afraid I don't understand your role here.'

He was good, I had to give him that.

Lawrence eyed Trevor like he was a cobra waiting to strike. Slowly, Lawrence reached into his jacket and extracted a small white business card. 'Here,' he said, handing it carefully to Trevor. 'You can shove this up your ass.'

Trevor glanced at the card, smiled, and slipped it into the pocket of his jeans. 'Thanks,' he said.

'Don't mention it,' Lawrence said coolly. 'Someday, when you want someone to tail your wife because she's having an affair, you can give me a call.'

'Oh,' Trevor said, smiling, 'I don't think that will be necessary. There are so many other ways to find out what people are up to, folks like you will be out of business in a few years.'

'Why don't you just show us what's in the bag,' I said.

Trevor slipped a laptop from inside it, opened it up, where the screen was already up and running.

'Wireless Internet connection,' he said, 'so I can do this sort of thing from anyplace.'

'Amazing,' I said. 'Do what?'

'You see this? This is a map of this quadrant of the city.'

Lawrence and I looked. He was right. There was Crandall and a five-block radius around it. And what looked to be a moving dot that was pulsing.

I pointed to it. 'What's that?'

'That's Morpheus.'

'Morpheus?'

'My dog. His name's Morpheus. It looks like he's moving back this way.' The dot appeared to be traveling from one side of the street to the other. 'He's probably on the trail of a squirrel. Or looking for a place to take a whiz.'

'I don't get it,' I said. 'How can you do this?'

Trevor gave me a no-big-deal shrug. 'There's a tiny transmitter on his collar, and that sends the message to the satellite, and it shows up on here.' Looking at Lawrence, he said, 'I'm sure you must have equipment like this for the kind of work you do.' Saying it like he knew Lawrence didn't. Lawrence said nothing.

I still wasn't buying it, until Trevor, looking up the street, jumped up and shouted, 'Morpheus . . . Here, boy . . .'

And a black knee-high, scruffy-looking thing that was one part bulldog and at least five parts of something else came hurtling down the sidewalk, up our short drive, and threw itself at Trevor and into his arms.

'Hey, Morpheus, I was watching you all the time.' He wrapped his arms around the dog's neck and nuzzled his face into the mutt's, unconcerned about the slobber that was dripping onto his coat. He pointed to a quarter-size disc-like item clipped to the dog's collar.

'That's it there,' he said.

'How do you get this kind of stuff?' I asked.

Trevor stood up. 'My dad. He's in software. He's rich. He puts stuff in the mail for me to play with.'

'You don't live with your parents anymore?' I asked.

Trevor smiled. 'My parents and I reached the conclusion that I was better off on my own.'

'Trevor, why don't you cut the shit,' Lawrence said. 'You're not here looking for your dog.'

He cocked his head slightly to one side. 'That's quite true. I was hoping to run into Angie. I thought she might be interested in all this, and that she might like my dog, too.'

'Angie's not here,' I said, although I could not be certain of that. I'd run in and out of the house pretty quickly, and if she was home, and knew Trevor was outside, she was probably hiding someplace in the basement.

'Well then, I'll just give her a call later.' He slipped the sunglasses back over his eyes, slid the laptop back into the backpack and slung it over his shoulder, and said, 'Come on, Morpheus, let's go.'

Neither Lawrence nor I said anything as he and Morpheus headed up Crandall, the dog walking obediently at his master's side. He was almost to the corner when he stopped and got into an old black Chevy, Morpheus hopping into the backseat. He started the car, turned around in a driveway, and headed back down the street past us. The car was rusted, without hubcaps, and rumbled as it drove by. Trevor didn't glance our way.

Lawrence walked out into the street, studied the car as it trailed away, then walked back up the drive.

'I am definitely running a check on that kid,' Lawrence said. 'Whether you want me to or not.'

I'd just had my first face-to-face encounter with Trevor, and I could honestly say I was not nuts about him. 'I won't try to stop you,' I said.

Lawrence got back into his car. 'I'll give you a call later, set things up for tonight at Brentwood's. I've already talked to the cops. The moment we see anything, *if* we see anything, I call them. No chases tonight.'

'Good.'

He gave me a little salute, backed out of the drive, and sped off.

About the same time, Paul appeared, walking up the street from the south, no sunglasses, no trench coat, a pretty normal-looking kid. He had his own backpack slung over his shoulder and was returning from his day at high school.

'Hey,' he said to me, and then his eyes landed on the Virtue. He stopped dead in his tracks and stared at it. There was no way I was going to let him drive it, not when he didn't have his license yet. I prepared myself for an onslaught of argument.

Instead, he said, 'Tell me this isn't our car.'

I cocked my head. 'Yeah, it is. I got it at the auction today. It's a great car. Is there a problem?'

'I hope you're not expecting me to drive that when I get my license. It's one of those enviro-friendly cars. I'm surprised you were able to get it up the driveway. There's nothing under the hood but gerbils.'

'It's got a sunroof,' I said, but he was already walking past me into the house, snorting and shaking his head in disgust.

It's a terrible burden, being the only one who wants to save the planet.

TWELVE

I bounded into the house after Paul.

'Angie . . .' I called out. I mounted the stairs to the second floor and rapped on her bedroom door. 'Angie, you in there?' When there was no answer, I opened it tentatively. 'Angie, you home?'

The room was empty. I came back downstairs, passed Paul in the kitchen, and poked my head through the door to the basement. 'Angie?'

'She's not home, Dad,' Paul said. I was inclined to agree with him. I put one hand on the kitchen counter, resting. My heart was pounding, and I felt a little winded from running around the house. I was relieved that Angie wasn't home, that Trevor hadn't had a chance to find her here, but then again, where was she?

'What's up?' Paul asked. 'Did you get that car at the auction? Didn't they have any cheap Beemers?'

'Where's your sister?' I asked him.

'She's at class, Dad,' Paul said, looking at me like I was an idiot. 'She's not going to be home now.'

Of course. I was an idiot. 'Right,' I said. 'Where else would she be?' Pulling myself together, I opened the fridge and grabbed a beer.

'Can I have one?' Paul asked.

'No,' I said.

'It's not like I've never had a beer, you know,' he said. 'And I think it would be a lot better, you know, if I had a beer in the open, with my dad, instead of, you know, trying to sneak around to have a beer.'

My mind went back to that six-pack left between the back of the garage and the fence.

'Is that what you do now, sneak booze?'

Paul's face flushed. 'Of course not.'

'Because if you are—'

The phone rang. I grabbed the receiver. 'Hello?' I said.

'Hey, Dad.'

'Angie . . .' I said, perhaps a bit too enthusiastically. 'Hey, we were just talking about you.'

'Who?'

'Paul and I. We were just saying you were probably in a class.'

'That's right, Dad. That's what I do. I'm at college.' Still a bit frosty.

'I know, I know. We were just thinking about you, that's all.'

'Is Mom there by any chance?'

'No, hon, she's at work. What can I do for you?'

There was a hint of a sigh. She would have to deal with me. 'Would I be able to have the car tonight? Because I've got a bunch of things to do, and I need to go to the mall, and then I have to do some research for this essay, and—'

'Guess what. I bought a car today.'

A hesitation. 'Oh my God, are you serious? Like, not to replace the Camry, but a second car?'

'That's right.'

'That's so awesome . . . What did you get?'

'Listen, why don't I drive down and show it to you? I'll give you a lift home.'

'Sure, I guess.'

'Now, I have to warn you, you may not like it. The car has not been unanimously endorsed by members of this household.' I glared at Paul, who had reached into the fridge, grabbed a beer bottle, and was miming the act of opening it, looking at me for approval. I shook my head.

'Oh well, as long as it's got wheels,' she said, and told me to pick her up in front of Galloway Hall at 5:30 p.m., when her last tutorial of the day would be over.

I hung up the phone and barely had time to tell Paul to put the beer back into the fridge when the phone rang again. It was Sarah.

'This retreat thing starts early tomorrow morning,' Sarah said. 'So the paper's paying for a room at the conference center so we can go tonight, be ready to start fresh in the morning, instead of having to get up before dawn and driving an hour and a half.'

'Great,' I said.

'So I'm getting out of here now, gonna come home and throw some stuff in a bag, have a quick bite to eat, and then Bev, you know her? The foreign editor?'

'Yeah.'

'Bev's being sent to this thing, too, so she's going to pick me up around six and we're going to head up.' It was already a little past four.

'If you're here by five,' I said, 'I'll see you, but I've promised Angie I'd pick her up at five-thirty. I'll get some dinner started.'

I had some pork tenderloin in a mushroom gravy going when Sarah got home at four forty-five. She dropped herself into one of the kitchen chairs.

'I saw the car,' she said. 'In the drive.'

I waited.

'It's kind of cute,' she said.

'Seriously?'

'Yeah, it should do us. Although I looked all around it and couldn't find the outlet where you plug it in.'

'That joke's really running out of gas.'

'Hey, that's a good one,' Sarah said. 'I have to say, it's perfect for Angie getting back and forth to school.'

'Paul hates it,' I said.

Sarah shrugged. You reach a point when you stop worrying about what your teenagers hate.

I called Paul to dinner, setting out three plates, and making up a fourth and covering it with plastic wrap for Angie to eat later. I stood and ate by the sink, Paul grabbed his plate and went to the basement, leaving Sarah the only one to actually sit at the kitchen table to eat her meal. But because she had to be ready to leave in a little more than an hour, she shoveled it down like a teenager.

'Guess who was prowling around the backyard when I got home,' I said.

Sarah glanced over, one cheek puffed out with pork tenderloin. 'Urmff?' she said.

'Trevor Wylie.'

'Hmmff?'

'That's right.' I filled her in on the conversation Lawrence and I had had with the boy. The dog named Morpheus. The satellite program, the six-pack in the backyard.

Sarah drank some water to clear all the food from her mouth. 'I don't know,' she said. 'He does sound a bit weird, but lots of kids are like that, they grow out of it. He's probably harmless.'

'You should meet him yourself.'

'Remember when you were first interested in me, and I lived out on Highway 74, and you came around one night, planning to call up to my window, but when you climbed the fence, you snagged your pants—'

'I know the story.'

'— you snagged your pants as you were coming over the other side, and you kept going but your pants got left behind?'

'I don't see—'

'And my dad heard the racket and went out to investigate, and there you were in your Jockeys?'

I suffered a moment with the memory, then said, 'The difference is, you were interested in me, but Angie's not interested in Trevor.'

'Actually, at the time, I wasn't interested in you.'

'You weren't?'

'Not really but you kind of grew on me. And it took a lot of convincing for my dad to accept a guy he'd first found standing in our backyard in his skivvies.'

'I think you have some of the details wrong. I was wearing a tuck-in shirt that had long tails front and back, so you could hardly even see my shorts.'

Sarah nodded. 'I think you're right. You were the picture of dignity.'

'So you're saying finding Trevor in our backyard isn't that big a deal?'

'Did he have his pants on?'

'Yes.'

'Well then, he's one up on you, isn't he?'

I finished the last bite of my dinner, rinsed off the plate in the sink and left it sitting in there. This didn't seem like a good time to tell Sarah about the course of action I was contemplating for after dinner.

'I have to go,' I said. I gave Sarah a kiss. She said she would leave a note on the counter with the details of where she was going to be for the next two days.

'And you can always get me on my cell,' she said, and I ran out the door. Sarah's Camry was parked behind our new Virtue, so I did some driveway car juggling so I could take the new one to show Angie.

Traffic heading back downtown toward the university was light, and I was down there in about fifteen minutes. It was a nice evening, so I opened the sunroof and occasionally raised the fingers of my right hand into the passing breeze.

What I'd forgotten was that to pull up in front of Galloway Hall meant paying a parking entrance fee to enter the system of roads within the university grounds. I protested to the gatekeeper who handed me my ticket.

'I'm just picking someone up,' I said.

He looked at me with dull eyes. He'd heard this lament before. 'If you're back within five minutes, there's no charge.'

Given that I'd shown up ten minutes earlier than Angie had asked me to be there, it looked like I was going to be out the five. Slowly, I drove onto the grounds and past the stately, vine-covered buildings. The Virtue, with its little sewing-machine motor, barely made a sound as I wound my way through the narrow, some of them cobblestone, streets.

I found Galloway Hall and a curbside spot a short ways down from it. Angie wouldn't know what car to look for, so I got up and leaned against our new wheels, keeping an eye on the building's front door.

Fifteen minutes later, Angie appeared. She spotted me, waved, and walked my way. She gave me a somewhat tentative hug and then stood back to look at the car.

'I like it,' she said.

'Tell your brother,' I said.

'Oh, ignore him. So, I can use this for school?'

'Not every day, but probably when you need it.'

'Can I drive it?' She was doing a circle around the car. As I watched her, I felt, as I so rarely do, at ease, relaxed even. She was here, in front of me, safe, far from Trevor, and looking so grown up as she checked out the vehicle.

I tossed her the keys and she got behind the wheel. I settled in next to her. Angie had slipped the key into the ignition and was familiarizing herself with the controls. 'Lights, radio – CD player?'

'Looks like it,' I said.

'And a sunroof . . . I love a sunroof. We've never had a car with a sunroof.'

Angie turned the key, tilted her head, puzzled. 'I don't hear anything,' she said. 'Is it on?'

'It's on, don't worry about it. Just put it in gear and go.'

She put the car in drive and pulled away from the curb. 'It's so quiet,' she said. 'I can't believe how quiet it is.'

'I know,' I said. 'You know they make you pay for parking just to come in here and pick somebody up?'

'Yeah, they're real pricks,' Angie said, her chin up in the air as she looked down the short hood. 'But not to worry.'

'What do you mean?'

'I know another way out.'

'What? What do you mean?'

Angie smiled mischievously, the way she did when she was a little girl and had taken her brother's cookie. It was the smile that said she had secrets, that there were parts of her life I knew nothing about.

'There's this way, you go down the side of Galloway Hall here' – she turned right – 'and just keep your eye open for this kind of alleyway.'

'Guess who was at the house today when I got home.'

'Are you kidding me?'

'He said he was looking for his dog.'

'What kind of dog?'

'This black mangy mutt, I don't know. It looked like, if he was going to have a dog, that would be the dog.'

'You know, it's not like I hate the guy. He's just a little too out there for me. This whole black-jacket-and-boots thing, I'm just not into that. And he's – Wait, here it is.'

She slowed the car, turned into a cobblestone lane that wasn't much wider than the car, and inched forward.

'What are you doing?' I asked. 'Where the hell are you going?'

'I never have to pay for parking. I can almost always get out this way.'

'This isn't even a road . . .' I said. 'It's a walkway . . . And besides, your mom or I always give you money for parking.'

'Hey, if you guys want to give me money for parking, I'm not going to turn it down. I put it towards other educational expenses.'

'Like parties?'

'Of course not,' she said, looking straight ahead. 'Someday they're going to get smart and close this off and then I'll need it anyway.'

'Where does this come out?'

'Edwards Street. There's a little chain at the end, and you just have to unhook it to get out, there's not a lock.'

'You better hope not or you're going to have to be very good at backing up long distances down narrow alleys.'

Like I said, this walkway was only slightly wider than the Virtue, with Galloway Hall on one side and some other building on the other. It wasn't even suitable for service vehicles, with low, vine-covered archways overhead that I could almost reach sticking my arm out the sunroof. I was starting to feel a bit pissed.

'This is wrong,' I said to Angie.

'Dad, you're such a Boy Scout, you worry about everything. I'm a student. You cut costs any way you can.'

'What about the ticket you pick up when you enter the grounds? It never gets checked or validated or whatever. You ever hand it in by mistake some other day and you'll owe hundreds of dollars in parking fees . . .'

Angie reached over and touched my knee. 'Dad, take your medication. And go unhook that chain up there.'

I did as I was told, skulking about like a guilty man, looking over my shoulder for campus security, certain we'd be arrested at any moment. Angie drove through, then I hooked the chain back across and got back into the car.

'You were saying, about Trevor,' Angie said, pulling onto Edwards.

'He had some computer thing he wanted to show you.'

'Any excuse. He's got some new computer thing every other day. He called me this afternoon, says, guess who? Says it's Neo, for crying out loud.'

'Neo?'

'Keep up, Dad. The character, in the movie. God. Just promise me, Dad, that you won't do anything stupid again.'

'You mean, like, with . . .' I struggled to remember the Pool Boy's name again.

'Exactly.'

'I'm sorry about that,' I said. 'I know you've been pissed at me for a long time.'

'No kidding.'

'And I'm sorry if you guys broke up over that.'

Angie shrugged. 'Well, I'm sort of seeing . . .' She stopped herself.

'Sort of seeing?'

'Never mind.' She gave me a small smile. 'I think, from now on, you only get boyfriend information on a need-to-know basis. And right now, you do not need to know.' She gave the car some gas. 'It's cute, but it seems a bit slow.'

Patiently, I again explained the hybrid concept.

'So, it's got, like, batteries in it? Like the TV remote?'

'Not those kind of batteries. Big batteries, which are constantly recharging to run the electric motor, which takes over from the gas motor. Look, it's good for the environment, okay?'

'Maybe we can put our recycling in it,' Angie said.

When we got home, I told her there was a plate of food waiting for her in the kitchen.

'I'm going out,' she said, smiling apologetically. 'I've got to get ready.' And she disappeared up to her room.

Paul, who'd heard us come in, shouted up from the basement, 'Dad . . . Some Lawrence guy called, said you should call him . . .'

I did.

Lawrence said, 'Now that you're a two-car family, can you get yourself out to Brentwood's tonight? I've got a few things to do and might be heading straight to our little stakeout from the other side of town.'

'When do you want me there?'

'How about eleven?' Lawrence said. 'And park around the corner or something, not in front of the store.'

That seemed good. This idea, this plan of action that I'd neglected to mention to Sarah, was forming in my head, and the later I could rendezvous with Lawrence, the better.

'I think this'll be the last night for me,' I said. 'They're getting antsy for the story, and the truth is, Sarah's scared to death, me hanging out with you.'

Lawrence chuckled softly. 'I'm not even optimistic they'll show. Not after last night. Our friends in the SUV may be going for a lower profile. Although I have to admit, I didn't think they'd show last night either.'

'True.'

'Listen,' Lawrence said. 'That Wylie kid. I did a little checking after we had our run-in with him.'

'You're kidding,' I whispered, huddling myself secretively around the receiver, even though neither of the kids was in the room with me. 'What did you find out?'

'I think it'd be better if I told you about it later, when we get together. That'll give me a little more time to check a couple more things.'

'Can't you tell me now?'

'It can wait. Actually, meet me at the doughnut place around ten-thirty. I'll be in the Buick again. They managed to get a new window in it this afternoon.' And he hung up.

Shit. He couldn't tell me now? My daughter's being dogged by some potential nutcase and he wants to tell me the details later?

I considered phoning him back, then held off. He was doing this as a favor, no charge, so I didn't feel I had the right to get pushy. But he had something on the kid, that much was for sure, which only strengthened my resolve to be proactive. By the time I saw Lawrence tonight, I might have a bit of information to share about Trevor Wylie myself.

There wasn't all that much to do to prepare for the job I was about to undertake in the hours before I joined Lawrence at Brentwood's men's store. He'd explained to me that the most important item for any would-be private detective about to go out on a stakeout was a bottle to pee in.

I stepped into the little mudroom we have between the kitchen and the back door, where we keep our two blue recycling boxes: one for bottles and cans and one for newspapers. There was, in the box for bottles and cans, nothing but the glass Snapple apple juice bottle I'd dropped in there the morning before. There was clearly more work to be done to make this family environmentally conscious.

I leaned over and grabbed the bottle. The screw-on cap was still attached, so it would do. I was ready to go on my first stakeout.

THIRTEEN

It was just as well that Sarah had left for her retreat by the time I'd gotten back home with Angie. I don't quite know how I would have explained what I was about to do. Given the recentness of the Pool Boy incident, not very well.

'Where you off to?' Sarah asks.

'Oh, just going to tail Angie wherever she goes, see if that Trevor kid really is stalking her.'

'Well, you just have a nice time, okay?'

The truth is, Sarah would have viewed such a plan as intrusive. An invasion of privacy. Wrongheaded. Difficult to justify, even for concerned parents.

Okay, perhaps.

But that was not what this was about. This was not about finding out what my daughter was up to. This was about finding out what Trevor Wylie was up to. And it made the most sense to follow Angie to find that out. I didn't need to know what Trevor Wylie did every minute of the day. I just wanted to know whether he was targeting Angie.

Of course, I could have been upfront with her. I could have told her my plan. I could have explained to her that she should just go about her business as she normally would, that I didn't care in the least what she was up to.

But being upfront presented a number of problems. Angie, who was now a young woman, might be of the view that having her father trail her cramped her style, and persuading her otherwise might present something of a challenge. The smartest thing, I decided, was to deal with this on my own. See what was going on. And, depending on what transpired, be upfront later if certain decisions had to be made. Like, for one, calling the cops about Trevor Wylie if he proved to be an actual threat.

About half an hour after I'd brought her home, Angie came bounding down the stairs. She'd touched up her make-up, brushed her hair, changed her clothes. She looked, I'd have to say, quite beautiful, and like most fathers, I have mixed feelings about having a beautiful daughter. There's pride, and then there's the business of not being able to sleep at night.

'I'm heading out in a couple of minutes,' she told me. I was in the family room off the kitchen, sitting in the recliner, watching the news, drinking some coffee. Doing my nonchalant thing. Doing it very well.

'Uh, actually, so am I,' I said, sensing the time had come to launch Operation Trevor, and stood up out of the chair. 'I might as well take off now, too.'

I grabbed my jacket from the closet. I'd already tucked the Snapple bottle into a pocket, making it bulge out conspicuously. 'Where you off to?' Angie asked.

'I just got a few things to do, and I'm meeting up with Lawrence, that detective I'm writing about, in a little while.'

'What's in your pocket?' she asked, noticing the huge lump in my jacket.

'Just bringing a bottle of water, something to drink in case I get thirsty,' I said.

Paul appeared in the front hall as I was about to leave. 'Where you going?'

'I just told your sister. I'm doing a couple of things, then meeting up with Lawrence Jones.' The guilt I felt at not being totally honest with my son was offset by the six-pack of beer hidden in the backyard, I suspected, specifically for him. Trevor was doubtless old enough to buy booze, and was probably helping Paul get some.

Paul and I would definitely be having a chat about this. But not now. I had more pressing matters to deal with. I had a job to do. I was heading out into that dark night, a kind of Philip Marlowe, a private eye, going it alone against the forces of—

Enough.

'What if I need a ride tonight?' Paul asked. 'Angie's going out, you're going out, Mom's not here, there's no car.'

I pulled out my wallet and handed him a twenty. Paul looked at it in his hand, not sure whether to believe his eyes. 'If you run into a jam, grab a cab,' I said.

'A cab?' Paul said. 'An actual cab? What if I end up not going out tonight?'

'Then you can give me the twenty back.'

Paul nodded quickly. 'Well, I'm pretty sure I'm going to be going out.'

'Can I have the Virtue?' Angie asked, calling out from the kitchen. I glanced out and saw that it was at the end of the drive, blocking the Camry. I didn't want to take the time to switch cars around.

'I'm taking it tonight,' I said.

'Aww. It's got the sunroof.'

I said goodbye, got in the Virtue, moved the Snapple bottle from my jacket pocket to the cup holder, and slipped the key into the ignition. I turned it forward.

Whir whir.

What the? I turned the key again.

Whir whir.

What the hell was this? My new car didn't want to start? I turned the key a third time, and it proved to be my lucky attempt. The engine turned over. It was, I told myself, just a fluke. I backed down the drive and headed south on Crandall. Once I was out of sight of the house, I tromped on the accelerator, although in a hybrid, that didn't accomplish a lot. The car took its own time getting up to speed, making me anxious about circling the block in time to see Angie pull out.

But I managed to get around the block with a few seconds to spare before the Camry, with Angie at the wheel, backed out onto Crandall and headed south. Good, good, I thought. Everything was going okay. I was pumped. I was getting into it. At one point, I realized I'd been saying 'Hello, shweetheart' under my breath unconsciously. But that was Sam Spade, wasn't it, from *The Maltese Falcon*? Not Philip Marlowe.

I'd have to check that later.

What I didn't know, until Angie reached the end of the street and turned right, was that the left brake light was out on the Camry. Not good, but at the same time, as it got darker, it would make it easier to spot the car as I attempted to maintain some distance between us.

The other thing I quickly realized, not ever having driven behind Angie, was that Angie was not very good at remembering to signal. She'd made a right at the bottom of Crandall without putting on her turn indicator. And a mile or so further along, when she made a left, she forgot again.

I was going to have to talk to her about this. Just as soon as I could figure out how to tell her I'd been in a position to notice. I blamed Sarah for this. Angie's disregard for the rules of the road had to be a genetic thing.

In addition to watching Angie, I was watching all the cars around her, in particular the black Chevy Lawrence that I had seen Trevor Wylie leave in earlier. So far, no sign of him.

The Camry turned onto Elmdale, home to a long block of coffee shops, ethnic restaurants, boutiques catering to the eclectic. I held back as the one Camry brake light came on and Angie began cruising the street slowly, evidently looking for someplace to park. I pulled over into a no-parking zone close to the curb, figuring I could idle there long enough to find out what she planned to do. A Jeep Wagoneer, a Mazda, then one of those new Mini Coopers drove past, and I did a quick study of each of the drivers, on the off chance that Trevor might be behind the wheel of something different. Two women, and an older guy, in the Cooper, trying to cure his midlife crisis.

Angie tried to parallel park at an open curb spot, but even from where I was sitting, it looked like a tight fit. She gave it a couple of tries, then went further up the street, where she found another, larger opening. This time, she slipped right in. Nice parking job, I thought. Way better than when we practiced it together prior to her final driving test.

She came back up the street on the sidewalk, in my direction, and I suddenly realized I needed an exit strategy to avoid being spotted. Could I back up and maneuver around the corner? I'd be trying to back right into traffic. If she got all the way up to the corner, where I was idling, she'd see me for sure.

But she stopped in front of a coffee shop, glancing up at the sign. Then a young man came out the front door, his arms wide in greeting. He was maybe twenty, with thick black hair, about a week's worth of scraggly beard, nearly six feet. Dressed in jeans and a brown leather jacket, trim with a solid upper body, like he played a sport, football maybe, or hockey.

Angie spread her arms as well, and then they had their arms around each other, and Angie angled her head up to his, and he bent his head down and kissed her. But this was not some quick, hey-how-are-you kiss, but a long, lingering embrace. Fifteen, twenty seconds, easy. They pulled apart long enough to look into each other's eyes, and then they kissed again.

Oh man.

I guess I hadn't really considered the implications of following my own daughter. It had never been my intention to witness something like this. I wanted to be able to make myself disappear, to transport myself out of there. Anything to make myself less uncomfortable, less scummy. It was one thing peeking in on your little girl when she was playing with her dolls in her bedroom, and quite another observing her with a member of the opposite sex in a moment of intimacy.

I looked away, at the clock dashboard, at the cars going by, at just about anything but my daughter locking lips with this young man.

Maybe, if I hadn't been overwhelmed with shame and felt the need to look away, I might have missed seeing Trevor Wylie drive past my car in his black Chevrolet.

FOURTEEN

Angie and her boyfriend disentangled themselves from each other – it seemed to take some effort, I thought – and slipped into the coffee shop as Trevor Wylie's black Chevy drove past. The car continued slowly up the street, rumbling a bit, exhaust spewing from the tailpipe.

'You little bastard,' I muttered under my breath. I pulled away from the curb and fell in behind Trevor.

He turned right at the next stop sign, then three more rights, and we were going past the coffee shop again. The Camry was still parked on the street. We did that loop, Trevor and I, three times, until finally a large enough spot opened up for Trevor to back his long Chevy into it. I waited for him to get fully into the spot, then drove by, trying very hard not to look over. Now I did another loop of the block on my own, and when I came around again, Trevor was still in the car, looking half a block ahead at the coffee shop.

I weighed my options.

My first instinct was to pull up alongside Trevor, box him in, get out of my car and haul him out of his car and beat the shit out of him.

Then I considered whether to pull up alongside Trevor, box him in, put down the window and strike up a conversation. 'Hey, Trevor, what brings you down here?' See what he had to say for himself. See whether he could, on the spot, come up with some convincing lie.

Possibly.

But suppose he denied following Angie down here? What was I going to do, exactly? And what if, in the middle of this confrontation, Angie and this leather-jacketed player from the tonsil hockey league emerged from the coffee shop and witnessed this exchange? And who'd have a lot of explaining to do then?

So I drove by Trevor and did another slow turn around the block. This time, another spot had opened up, this one close to the corner, half a dozen cars behind Trevor, which was perfect. I could park here, keep an eye on both Trevor and the front door of the coffee shop. I slipped into the spot. It was fully dark now, and I felt fairly anonymous sitting in the car, watching people stroll by on the sidewalk.

Okay, how about this, I thought. I walk up, open the passenger door of Trevor Wylie's car, slip in, close the door. Have a frank and open exchange of ideas.

It was a plan with some merit. It might put a little fear into him, even though Trevor didn't act like a kid who was easily intimidated. But to be caught on his little stakeout, by the father of the girl he was stalking, well, wouldn't that mess up his shorts a bit? If the roles were reversed, I knew it would scare the living shit out of me.

It must have taken me close to twenty minutes to decide this was the way to go, and I had my hand on the door handle and was just about to pull it when Angie and this guy – who, even without knowing a great deal about him I could tell was not right for her – come back out of the coffee shop.

They chatted for a while on the sidewalk. Angie rested her hand on his elbow, and her head was nodding up and down enthusiastically, and then he reached up and brushed some of Angie's hair back over her shoulder, and I could see her head lean, ever so slightly into his hand, beckoning it.

I felt sort of, I don't know . . . what's the word I'm looking for here? Slimy? Yes, that will do. And a bit queasy, too.

'Just say goodbye, come on, let's get this show on the road,' I said.

They kissed again, not quite as long this time, thank God, and stood back from each other, and Angie slung the strap of her purse up over her shoulder, made a small waving gesture, and so did the guy, and then he turned and started walking up the street in my direction, and Angie headed back the other way, toward the Camry.

Ahead, I could make out the edge of the Chevy's tail lights, and could see that Trevor had his foot on the brake as he turned the ignition and put the car into gear. I did the same, engaging the Virtue's oh-so-quiet motor, slipped the car into drive, and held my foot on the brake, waiting for this convoy to get under way.

Even further ahead, I saw Angie get into her car, and about a minute later, she had her blinker on (good girl . . .) to indicate that she was pulling back into traffic. Then Trevor pulled out, and I brought up the rear. So far, I was the only one who had any idea how ridiculous this all looked.

Angie was heading crosstown along one of the main thoroughfares. Four lanes, lots of traffic lights. I wasn't always able to keep the Camry in sight, although the burned-out brake light helped. But when I couldn't spot Angie, I looked for Trevor, since he was closer and every bit as eager to keep Angie in his sights as I was.

I had a hunch where we were going. If we stayed on this route, we'd be at the Midtown Center, the site of Lawrence's and my shootout with the black Annihilator. The mall sign came into view, and Angie, and then Trevor, moved over into the right-turn lane as they approached the entrance.

Angie swung into the mall parking lot without signaling, trolled up and down the aisles looking for a spot. It didn't look much like it had the night before, when Lawrence's Buick and the SUV did doughnuts chasing each other, not another car to be seen anyplace.

Angie found an opening, pulled into it, and Trevor's Chevy rumbled past behind her. I needed to find something fast, before I lost her going into the mall. About twenty spaces further away from the mall entrance I found a spot flanked by a massive Ford Expedition and a small sports car. I slipped in, hopped out, locked the car, and started running in the direction of the mall. Under the lights of the entrance, I could see Angie heading inside. About sixty feet behind her, I could see the back of a young white male in a long black coat. I was pretty sure was Trevor.

I could guess what he was up to. Another 'accidental' meeting. He'd bump into her near the food court, be amazed that they'd run into each other, suggest they grab a coffee or something to eat. I could already imagine Angie's discomfort.

Following someone in a car was one thing, but trailing someone – two people, actually – on foot was going to be something different altogether. What now, Marlowe? I hadn't trained long enough with Lawrence to know how to handle this one.

By the time I reached the mall doors, I saw Angie rounding the corner of a jewelry store to enter into the main part of the mall. Not too far ahead of me, a boot-clad Trevor walked by briskly.

My breathing became shallow and rapid. I hadn't counted on doing anything like this at all. I thought all I needed for this kind of work was a car and a Snapple bottle. Now, I needed a disguise. A fake face, like everyone wears in *Mission: Impossible*, would be good. Or, a hat. Something I could pull down over my eyes.

Angie wandered into a Banana Republic. There was no need to follow her inside. There was only one way in or out, which Trevor must have figured out, too, since he was hanging back, positioning himself on the opposite side of the mallway, in front of an electronics store that sold CDs and DVDs. He pretended to check out the new releases set just inside the door. I parked myself behind a two-sided mall directory sign that offered sufficient cover while I kept watch on both the Banana Republic and the electronics store.

I figured I'd be in this spot for a while. Angie, like her mother, never went into a fashion store and walked right back out again. Whenever I happened to accompany either of the women in my household to the mall, even on a supposedly short errand to go into a drugstore to buy a lipstick, I always allowed an hour.

I usually killed time in a bookstore or grabbed a coffee. Sometimes I left the mall altogether, ran some other errand, maybe trekked over to some hobby shop that carried sci-fi models, and came back in sixty minutes. But this time, I was staying put. The only comforting thing was, this would be as much torture for Trevor as it was for me. Maybe trailing after Angie in a mall would be enough to cure him of stalking.

I was still standing behind the directory sign, one eye peeking around the side, when I realized a small girl in a puffy-sleeved dress, no more than five years old, was standing a few feet away and had been watching me for several minutes.

'What are you doing, mister?' she asked.

Terrific. Shirley Temple had blown my cover.

'Go away,' I said. I was about to say something else when I spotted Angie coming out of Banana Republic, store bag in hand. She headed in the direction of the Sears, the anchor store at the far end. Trevor picked up the trail, keeping to the opposite side of the mall walkway. She ducked into a Gap right next to the food court, so I walked over to a coffee stand that still afforded me a view of the front of that store.

I bought a large coffee, shifted over to where they had the cream and sugar and stir sticks, found a lid that fit, and when I looked up, there was Angie, standing right in front of me.

'Dad? What are you doing here?' she said, her head cocked quizzically to one side. Her question didn't sound accusatory. The truth was, she seemed very happy to see me.

I was so rattled I was having a hard time speaking, let alone coming up with an answer.

'You? At the mall? Without Mom? This is totally unbelievable.'

Think. Think. Think. Was it almost our anniversary? No, no, that was months away. If I said that, she'd never believe it. Her mother's birthday? I'd had a habit of keeping track of that one, but no, I was pretty sure we'd celebrated that only four or five months ago. Valentine's Day had long since past, Christmas was still a couple of months off, and—

'I'm looking for clothes,' I blurted.

'Clothes?' Angie said. '*You're* looking for *clothes*?' Then she looked upward, as if there was no roof there and she was looking into the heavens.

'What are you doing?' I asked.

'Looking for flying pigs,' Angie said.

I attempted to look indignant. 'I can't shop for clothes?'

'Doesn't Mom buy all your clothes?'

'Not all of them. I do know how to buy clothes on my own.'

She smiled. 'Since when? You're totally hopeless. You're telling me you've come out here, on your own, to buy a new wardrobe.'

'I don't know why that's so incredible. I just had to have a coffee to fortify myself before starting.'

'I don't think it's incredible,' Angie said. 'I think it's wonderful. Because, let's be honest, you could use a bit of sprucing up.'

'You think so?' My eyes were darting about, trying to find Trevor.

'I mean, you always wear the same sort of thing. You've got your blue jeans, but then, once in a while, if you really want to dress up, you wear your black jeans. And these pullover shirts you wear, I mean, what is it with these?' She was plucking at my top with her fingers.

'The thing is,' I said, 'it's been pointed out to me in the last couple of days, as recently as last night, in fact, that my fashion sense leaves a lot to be desired. An opinion that was not contradicted by your mother. So I thought, while she was out of town on this retreat thing, I'd pick out a few new things.'

'That is so terrific,' Angie said. 'You know what?' She glanced at her watch. 'I've got a bit of time. I'll help you. Since we haven't got five gay guys here to give you a makeover, it might as well be my job.'

'No, no, that's okay, you've got stuff to do.'

'No, really, this'll be fun. Let's hit the Gap. It's sharp, but not too flashy. Finish that coffee and we'll go over.'

I didn't see Trevor anywhere. Maybe seeing Angie hook up with her father had scared him off. I drank my coffee as quickly as I could, but it was still pretty hot, and it took me a couple of minutes. Finally, I pitched the paper cup into the trash and allowed Angie to drag me over to the Gap, wondering whether Joe Mannix had ever been dragged off a stakeout to pick out new pants.

'Okay,' she said, taking me first to a display of shirts. 'I think you'd look good in something like this.' She held up, against my chest, a plaid, button-up-the-front shirt. 'What are you?'

'What do you mean, what am I?' I was waiting for an insult.

Angie rolled her eyes. 'Size? Are you large, extra-large? I'm guessing you'd take a large.'

'Uh, yeah, I think so,' I said.

A salesperson wearing a 'Gary' name tag approached. 'May I help you with anything?'

Angie said, 'My dad wants to get some pants, maybe some khakis?'

'Sure, they're over here, if you want to follow me.'

Angie motioned for me to come along. Gary of the Gap said, 'He'd prefer loose fit, you think?'

Angie nodded. 'Oh yeah, no kidding.'

And I thought, Hello? I'm here, *too*. You can ask *me* questions.

Angie loaded me down with three pairs of pants, half a dozen shirts. 'Go try these on,' she ordered.

'Honestly,' I said. 'I think I'll just get the shirts. I don't have to try them on. They'll be fine. But the pants, it's a lot of trouble.'

Angie looked at me sternly.

I was directed into a changing room. I slipped off my shoes, pulled off my pants. I pulled on a pair of navy blue khakis first, and one of the checked shirts Angie had handed me. I tucked in the shirt, slipped my shoes back on, and grabbed the wallet from my pants. This has long been a fear of mine, that my wallet will be stolen while trying on new clothes.

When I stepped back into the main store, Angie was there with Gary.

'Oh my God,' she said. 'You look terrific.'

'I want to take another look at some shirts up at the front,' I said.

'Oh sure . . .' Angie said and then, glancing at Gary, said to me, 'I'll be right here.' She and Gary were chatting, and it didn't sound like the subject was fashion. Didn't she already have a boyfriend?

I walked to the front, not to look at shirts, but to scan the mall. There were dozens of people walking past, but at a glance, I didn't see anyone who resembled Trevor.

I returned to the back of the store, told Angie I hadn't seen anything else I cared for. But by the time we got to the counter, I had five shirts, three pairs of slacks, a new belt and five pairs of socks.

While Gary was removing all the tags and scanning the items, I said to Angie, 'So, what have you been doing tonight? Did you come straight to the mall?'

'No,' she said. 'I met a friend for coffee first.'

'Oh yeah,' I said, trying not to act too interested. 'Anyone I know?'

'No.'

'A good friend, someone from school?'

'Just a friend,' she said. She spotted a rack of boxers. 'You know what, you should get some of those, too.'

'I'm not sure it's appropriate for my daughter to be buying me boxers. That has to cross a line somewhere.'

'If I have to see you walking around the house in them, I should have the right to pick them. Here,' she said, grabbing three pairs and tossing them onto the counter just before Gary rang up the sale.

'Okay,' said Gary. 'That comes to $576.42.'

'What?' I said.

Gary repeated the amount for me. 'Will that be on your Visa, sir?'

I handed over my plastic and Gary ran it through. As I walked out of the store, loaded down with three bags, Angie said, 'That's the most fun I've had shopping in months.'

I wasn't sure I was cut out for this whole surveillance thing. I didn't think I could afford it.

FIFTEEN

As we came out of the Gap, Angie stopped, maneuvered herself between the bags I had in both hands, and hugged me. 'We should do that more often,' she said, giving me a quick peck on the cheek. I let the bags slip from my hands and hugged her back.

'Thanks for letting me do that for you.'

'Thank *you*,' I said. 'I hope I didn't take up too much of your time.'

Angie glanced at her watch. 'Well, I do have to get going now, but I'm not going to be late or anything.'

'Where you off to?' I asked.

'Just doing some research for an essay I've got to do. I'm getting together with a friend.'

'Same friend you got together with earlier?' I asked.

'Nope, different,' she said, giving me another quick peck on the cheek. 'Gotta go, Daddy.'

I felt my throat thicken. I could not remember her calling me that in years, not since she was little. It was as though, with one word, she had emerged from a period when it was not cool to show that you loved your dad.

As we walked out of the mall together, I kept scanning, looking for Trevor. My guess was he'd packed it in. We came out into the night air. 'Where you parked?'

Angie asked. I pointed in the general direction, but said I would walk her to her car before going to mine.

'How is it so far?' Angie asked, referring to our new wheels.

'Pretty good, although I might get it checked out. It wouldn't start for me right away when I left the house. Had to try it three times before it would turn over.'

'Lemon city,' Angie said.

'I'm sure it was just a one-time thing.'

'Hey,' Angie said, looking puzzled, 'you left the house long before I did. What did you do before you went to the mall?' Her question made sense, given that when she did find me at the Midtown Center, I had yet to do any shopping.

'Hobby shop,' I said. I was losing track of the number of times I'd lied to my own children this evening. 'There was a new version of the *Enterprise* ship, from the *Star Trek* movies, the early ones, with the original crew?'

Angie sighed. 'You're such a dork. At least you won't be quite as nerdy in your new clothes.'

I was about to laugh when I spotted a black Chevy, lights on, engine presumably running, parked alongside the sidewalk that went around the mall's perimeter. I could see one head silhouetted behind the wheel. It was hard to tell whether it was Trevor, because he appeared to be holding something in front of his face. Binoculars, maybe, or a camera.

'What is it?' Angie asked. 'You see something?'

'No, nothing.'

We got to the Camry, and Angie got in, dropping her Banana Republic package in the passenger seat. I told her not to be too late, waved goodbye, and then, once I was sure I was out of sight of her rear-view mirror, sprinted back to the Virtue. Trevor, with his car in position and the engine running, was going to have the jump on me if I didn't get out of my spot quickly. I'd end up losing both of them.

When I'd left my car, there had been a small compact car on one side of me and a massive Ford Expedition on the other. The compact had left and been replaced by some other kind of SUV, some General Motors variety. It was as though I'd parked the Virtue at the bottom of a canyon. This was the thing about these vehicles: you couldn't see around them at intersections, you couldn't see around them in parking lots, you couldn't—

There really wasn't time to work up a satisfying rant about SUVs. I had to get moving. I got into the Virtue, threw the Gap bags down in front of the passenger seat, and got my key into the ignition. The engine, much to my relief, turned over right away this time. 'Yes . . .' I said, put the car into reverse, and turned around to see my way out of the spot.

I was looking into walls of steel – massive doors and fenders – on both sides. The only view I had of the outside world was directly behind me, across the aisle to the tail ends of some cars on the other side.

So I began to creep out. Surely, if someone saw me backing out, they would stop and let me—

Someone laid on their horn. I slammed on the brake as a car shot past. Okay, maybe not everyone was as polite as I would have hoped. I began inching out again, just a little bit, just a little bit more.

Another horn. I hit the brake again, and this time a car roared by from the other direction, but at least this motorist had the time to roll down his window and respond to me: 'Watch it, asshole . . .'

And I thought: I do not know who you are, but if I had the time, I would get out of my car, walk over, and beat you with a tire iron. Parking lot rage.

After he drove on, I kept on inching. But two more cars went by and their drivers didn't even bother to honk. They just drove past, figuring that I, somehow, deep down in my corridor of steel, could see them.

'Fuck it,' I said, threw the car into park, got out, and walked out into the aisle. A vehicle was driving up, and I held up my hand to stop it.

The driver put down his window. 'Yeah?' he said as I approached.

'You want a spot?' I asked. 'I'm pulling out.'

'Uh, no. I'm picking someone up.'

'Okay, then, just do me a favor. I'm surrounded by those two goddamn SUVs and can't see to back out. You mind blocking everyone here for a second until I can get out?'

It wasn't until that moment I actually noticed that this guy, who was now scowling, was behind the wheel of an SUV.

'I mean,' I said, 'they're great cars and all, super in the snow, right? But when you're driving a little shitbox like I've got, it's hard to see, you know?' He glared at me a moment longer. I did a minor eye roll and said, 'It's my wife's car.'

He shrugged, indicating he would wait.

I ran back to the Virtue, hopped in, screeched out of the spot, and sped toward the exit I figured was the one Angie would most likely have used. I was looking for her car or Trevor's, or both.

I got as far as the exit without seeing either of them. My palms were slipping on the plastic steering wheel, and I could feel sweat forming on my forehead. I was up to the light and had to make a decision whether to head left or right, and as I pondered an impossible decision, someone honked at me from behind to get moving.

'Fuck off . . .' I shouted, even though there was no chance whoever it was would be able to hear me. And then, a couple of hundred yards up the road to the right, I caught a glimpse of a car with only one tail light.

I turned the wheel hard right, hit the accelerator, listened to the motor whine a little harder. I was hoping a major thrust of power would kick in at some point, if not now, maybe by the weekend. Maybe Paul was right. Maybe there was nothing under the hood but gerbils.

Now that I'd spotted what I was sure was Angie's car, I looked for Trevor's, and sure enough, there it was, about five car lengths behind Angie. Now that I had both of them in sight, I could catch my breath, let my heart rate get back to something approaching normal.

Trevor and I followed her, discreetly; all the way to the ramp to the highway that led west out of the city. Angie eased over onto the ramp (no signal, what was I going to do?) and picked up speed as she merged with the traffic.

Where the hell was she going?

You could take the expressway to get from one part of the city to another, of course. It was a great way to bypass dozens of lights. But it became clear after a few miles, no doubt to Trevor as well as to me, that she was headed outside of the city limits. If I didn't know better, I'd think we were headed out to Oakwood.

Why would Angie be headed to Oakwood? Of course, she still had a few friends out there, but not that many. And of course, maybe she wasn't going to Oakwood. There were plenty of other suburban enclaves between the city and our old neighborhood.

I was only a few car lengths behind Trevor. It was night, and there was enough traffic that riding directly behind him wasn't going to raise his suspicions any. Every once in a while another head would pop into view, then disappear. The dog, Morpheus. For a while, he rested his front paws on the top of the rear seat and looked out the rear window. The world's biggest bobbing-head dog.

While he was looking back towards me, it appeared that Trevor was occupied with something. He kept glancing down between the seats, like he was searching for something in the console. His head kept turning, looking down, then back up again to watch the highway. If he kept this up, he was going to have an accident.

Once we were about five minutes out from the city, Trevor's right blinker came on and he was gone at the next exit. I guess he'd had enough, grown tired of the chase. For all he knew, Angie was headed for the coast, and even stalkers had to pack it in at some point.

I was faced with a choice. Follow Trevor. Follow Angie. Follow no one, and go home.

Now that Trevor had given up following Angie, at least for this evening, there wasn't anything else for me to do. It made sense for me to get off at the next exit, turn around, and head back home as well.

Except I couldn't help but wonder where Angie was going.

A few minutes later, Angie turned off at Oakwood.

I took the same exit, hanging far enough back that I wouldn't end up pulling alongside her at the light at the end of the ramp. She made a left, in the direction of our old neighborhood, and I turned left as well so that I could catch the ramp that would put me back onto the highway and into the city.

I'd like to tell you that I don't know what made me drive past the ramp and stay on Angie's tail. But I do.

I wanted to know where she was going. I wanted to know who she was seeing. I'd crossed some line myself here, from following her to make sure she was okay, to following her to find out what she was up to. Because, at some level, I was scared about the choices she might be making, and that if they were choices I didn't approve of, scared by how little influence I might have to stop them.

She guided the Camry into our old neighborhood. And then Angie was turning down our old street. I hung way back, not wanting to get caught in the act by her a second time. It was starting to look, and this didn't make any sense to me at all, as though she was going to turn into the driveway of our old house.

But then she drove past it, slowed, and turned into the driveway two doors down.

She was parking the car at Trixie's house.

Angie was making a stop at the home of the friendly neighborhood dominatrix. During office hours.

Angie got out of the car, locked it, knocked on Trixie's door, and a moment later, was admitted and disappeared.

SIXTEEN

I had a good friend once. Sarah and I would hang out with him and his wife every once in a while, and we'd always have a good time. We'd do dinner, maybe a movie, sometimes just go to each other's houses and have a few drinks. And one night he phoned me, late, after Sarah had gone to bed, and told me he'd been seeing someone else, for more than a year, and that he wasn't sure, but he might be in love with her, and I thought: Why did you tell me this? Did I really need to know?

I was his friend, and he needed to talk, but the honest-to-God truth was, I'd have been much happier being kept in the dark. I didn't want to know that he was cheating on his wife. It shattered some illusions, first of all. I thought everyone was as happy as Sarah and I. (This was, of course, before she became saddled with me as an underling at work.) I dreaded the next time we'd all get together, the four of us, and have to pretend, when I engaged in small talk with his wife, that I did not know what I knew. Because the knowledge seemed to carry with it the burden of responsibility. Should I tell his wife? No, of course not, I told myself. Don't get involved. But knowing something that she did not know, something that intimately affected her, overshadowed every moment of conversation. Part of me resented my friend after that. He'd *implicated* me in his indiscretion. He'd made me a part of his deception.

I think there's an element of this to parenting. There are things you simply do not want to know. Weren't there things I'd done as a teenager that it was better my parents never knew about? Maybe a couple. Perhaps even a lot. And hadn't I turned out okay, so long as you didn't count the paranoid, obsessive-compulsive behavior tics my dad had passed on to me? As long as your kids are okay, as long as they're safe, as long as they're back home in their own bed when the sun comes up, isn't that enough?

I wish I knew.

These were the thoughts bouncing around in my head as I sat in a car just down the street from Trixie Snelling's house. My daughter had paid her a visit. If I had not followed her out here, if I had never known she'd made this trip, I would not have had to wonder what its purpose was.

Only a few hours earlier, I'd been talking to Trixie on the phone, and as we'd caught up on each other's news, she'd struggled to remember Angie's name. Her faulty memory now struck me as forced, as an act, a way to preemptively throw me off the trail. Why would she not want me to know that she and Angie had been in touch?

It wasn't as though Angie and Trixie had been friends when we'd lived out here. For most of the time we'd lived in Oakwood, none of us had known what Trixie did for a living. But by the time we moved away, we were all in on the secret.

Who'd contacted whom? Had Trixie invited Angie out? Had Angie gotten in touch with Trixie?

And if I didn't relieve myself immediately, would I do permanent damage to my bladder?

I'd had a lot of coffee, and it had suddenly caught up with me. I uncapped the Snapple bottle that was in the cup holder between the seats, the one I'd brought along just for this very purpose, and, after unzipping, did what I had to do. It occurred to me that this would be a bad time for a police officer to do a patrol of the neighborhood and find a seemingly respectable reporter for *The Metropolitan* sitting alone in a car while keeping an eye on the home of a dominatrix.

Carefully, I recapped the now-full bottle, giving the cap an extra-tight turn. Rather than put the bottle back in the cup holder, I slipped it, upright, down into the storage pocket on the back of the passenger seat. It was a tight fit, which was a blessing, since there was no chance the bottle would tip or fall out.

I'd been sitting in front of Trixie's house, staring at it and our Camry in the driveway, for nearly fifteen minutes now. I'd considered all the possibilities.

1. Angie was a client. Unthinkable.
2. Angie was an apprentice. Unimaginable.
3. Angie had decided to drop by for a cup of tea. Unbelievable.
4. Angie was getting a gift certificate for me for my birthday. Unlikely.

I happened to glance at the digital clock on the dashboard. It read 10 P.M. Nuts. I was supposed to meet Lawrence Jones at the doughnut shop at 10:30. If I left right now, I might make it in time.

But could I leave Angie out here? And could I leave without knowing why she was here?

I got out my cell phone from my jacket pocket and Lawrence's business card from my wallet. I keyed in the office number from the card. I could ask him whether he was on schedule, and whether I could afford to be a bit late to our rendezvous.

No answer.

So I tried the second number listed, his cell.

No answer.

'Shit,' I said.

Unless I was prepared to get out of the car, knock on Trixie's door, and demand some sort of an explanation from the two of them, there wasn't much to be gained by hanging around. It wasn't like I could, at this hour, pretend to drop by Trixie's, and discover Angie there by accident. All that would accomplish would be to give Angie the idea that I was a customer.

So, riddled with reservation and doubt, I turned the key forwards.

And the car said, *Whirwhirwhir*.

This can't be happening, I thought. I turned the key again.

This time, not even a *whir*. There was no sound at all.

This was not the best place to sit and wait for the auto club to show up. I mentally crossed my fingers and turned the key a third time.

The engine caught.

I put the car into drive and sped out of Valley Forest Estates, got back onto the highway, and broke the speed limit (once I was finally able to coax the Virtue into exceeding it) all the way back into town.

I arrived at the doughnut place around the corner

from Garvin Street about 10:35 P.M. and glanced at all the cars in the lot as I pulled in. I felt a weight lift from my shoulders when I didn't see Lawrence's Buick. At least I hadn't kept him waiting.

I went inside. Now that I had been thoroughly drained of coffee, I felt I could accommodate some more. But, rattled as I already was by the evening's revelations, I opted for a decaf. And an oatmeal muffin.

Some badly mangled, coffee-stained and crumb-covered sections of *The Metropolitan* were piled atop the garbage receptacle, and I grabbed them before I took a seat by the window, looking for a way to take my mind off Trevor and Angie and Trixie.

The inside of the shop was reflected in the glass, but I could still see outside well enough to watch for Lawrence. I glanced at my watch. It was 10:40 P.M.

I thumbed through the front section of my paper, and came upon, once again, the story I'd been reading at breakfast, about the computer nerd who shot and killed his classmates. I tossed it aside and looked at the Arts section.

I read a review of some new George Clooney movie, not really taking any of it in, and a short write-up on a $ 1 million advance that was being paid to some unknown writer for his science fiction thriller, which had already been optioned for a movie even before the book had hit stores. I tried to wash down my envy with the coffee, but it didn't work. And I realized another ten minutes had gone by.

Lawrence was generally pretty punctual, but I decided to give him another five minutes before doing anything about it. I read the editorials, a few letters to the editor. My coffee cup was empty and my muffin was history.

Lawrence was still a no-show.

I dug out his business card again and phoned him. This time, I tried his cell phone first.

It rang five times, then the message kicked in. 'Hi. I can't take your call right now. Leave a message.' Typically cagey Lawrence. Didn't even give his name.

'Hey, it's Zack, it's coming up on eleven, and I'm waiting for you at the doughnut shop. Call me.' And I gave him my cell number, even though I knew he already had it.

I waited another minute. I tried the office number on his business card, which I seemed to recall him mentioning once was also his home number. He lived in a second-story apartment above a shop someplace. His card gave a Montgomery Road address.

Another five rings, and a similar message.

'Hey. Zack here. I already left a message on your cell. I'm here, waiting to go get the bad guys, and get your report on Trevor. I've got some news of my own in that department.'

I considered the possibilities. Lawrence had run into some sort of delay, couldn't answer his phone. Maybe he was in a bad area, under a bridge, where his cell couldn't receive a signal.

I tried the cell again. 'Hi. I can't take your call right now. Leave a message.'

I phoned home. Paul picked up, sounding a bit groggy. 'Hello?'

'Hey, it's me,' I said.

'Yeah?'

'Let me talk to your mom.'

'She's not here. She's gone to that thing. Remember?'

With all that had happened in the last hour or so, I'd completely forgotten about the retreat. 'Okay,' I said. 'Have there been any calls?'

'I guess. I've had a couple.'

'I mean for me.'

'Uh,' Paul said dozily, 'I don't think so.' Paul's words seemed to be running together, ever so slightly.

'Were you asleep?' I asked.

'Nope.'

I paused. 'Lawrence Jones didn't call there by any chance, say he was going to be late?'

'Lawrence who?'

'The detective? The one I've been seeing every night this week? The one who took me to the car auction? The one who called earlier, and you took a message? Paul, what's wrong with you?'

'Nothing. I am perfectly fine.' He worked hard to say 'perfectly' perfectly. And the 'I am' instead of 'I'm' was a bit weird and Data-like. 'Where are you?'

'At the doughnut place, a couple of blocks from Garvin. Listen, if Lawrence calls, have him call my cell.'

'Okay.' Sleepylike. Like maybe he'd had a few beers.

'Paul,' I said, 'did you find what Trevor left for you out back?'

'Huh?' More awake now. 'The what?'

'The six-pack. Sounds like you found it.'

'I don't know — what?'

'He get your booze for you all the time?'

'I don't know what you're talking about. Did Angie tell you—' And then he cut himself off, still sober enough to know that he was letting the cat out of the bag.

'We're going to have a talk when I get home.'

Paul paused at the other end of the line. 'Do you have any idea when that might be?'

'Probably not for a few hours. I'm sort of working right now.'

'Because I'm really tired, and going to bed, so if you're going to ream me out, could you do it in the morning instead of when you get home?'

'Fine. We'll talk in the morning.'

'Okay. See ya, Dad.' And he hung up.

I shook my head as I hit the button to end my call. It was after eleven now. I tried Lawrence's cell a third time, without success.

Maybe he was already in position, down the street from the men's store. Maybe he'd gotten to the doughnut shop on time, waited a few minutes for me, and when I was a no-show, he'd left. After all, his responsibility was to Mr Brentwood, the owner of the men's shop, not me. He was doing me a favor letting me hang out with him; he didn't owe me any consideration.

So I walked out of the doughnut shop and headed in the direction of Brentwood's. I decided to leave the Virtue in the parking lot. Pulling up behind Lawrence's Buick might attract unwanted attention on the street. There was a hint of autumn chill in the air, and I pulled my shoulders up, as if that would somehow keep me warm.

I came around the corner onto Garvin, half a block down from the men's shop, and looked for Lawrence's aging Buick with the brand-new rear window, not that a brand-new window was something that stood out. A quick scan of both sides of Garvin turned up nothing. The street was lined with several parked cars, but there was almost no traffic, and there was a slight drizzle starting to come down. Within a couple of minutes the street was damp and shiny.

As I walked up the street, nearly to Brentwood's, I tried to think of other scenarios that could have delayed Lawrence. What if he wasn't planning to come at all? What if there'd been some arrest in the case, just in the last couple of hours, and Lawrence had gotten a call about it from his contacts in the police, so there was no point in staking out Brentwood's tonight?

Just then, a massive black SUV appeared at the top of the block. Its headlights, resting high atop the huge grill, cast a wide beam down the street.

'Jesus,' I whispered.

I sidled up against an unlit storefront, beneath an awning, as the SUV began to move slowly down the street. Then, inching along, I rolled myself around a corner and found myself in a three-foot-wide alley directly across the street from Brentwood's. The SUV glided past, as if moving through a tall, narrow frame. I poked my head out, watched as it went up the street, turned right at the next corner, and disappeared.

I got out my cell and tried Lawrence's cell again. Even before he'd finished his short message, I was shouting, but in a whispering kind of way, into my phone: 'Man, you gotta get here . . . It's going down . . . The bad guys are here . . . They've just gone by once and I think they're coming around again . . . I'm in an alley right across the street . . . Where the hell are you?'

I hit the button to end my call. Even in the cool night air, I felt myself breaking into a sweat.

The cops, I thought, maybe I should call the cops. Get them out here fast, because I had a feeling, I just had a feeling that the next time these guys came around in that Annihilator they'd—

I heard the roar of the engine for only a second, then a huge crash. The sound of shattering glass and crumbling brick and twisting metal.

I looked across the street and saw the tail end of the Annihilator. The front of it was, literally, in Brentwood's. The two back doors of the SUV flung open and two men dressed entirely in black, with black hoods or ski masks pulled down over their heads, were leaping out and charging through the destroyed storefront. The Annihilator was already backing out, then screeching to a halt, turning around and backing up to the shattered window. The rear tailgate rose automatically, and in the time it had taken for the driver to conduct this maneuver, the two guys inside had evidently cleared several racks of suits and were throwing them into the back of the SUV, then leaping back into the still-open rear doors, and now the Annihilator was back in gear and screeching up Garvin.

In another few seconds, the only sound was the alarm system, wailing irrelevantly, from inside Brentwood's.

'Lawrence,' I said softly under my breath, 'where the fuck are you, man?'

SEVENTEEN

I got out my cell and called 911 first.

'I'm calling to report a robbery,' I said.

'You've been robbed, sir?'

'No, I've witnessed a robbery.' I told her the name of the store, its location, and that a huge black SUV with at least three guys in it was screaming away from the scene. 'A black Annihilator, couldn't make out the plate, but it's heading east.'

'What is your name, sir?'

I ended the call. I knew they'd have my name sooner or later. Their call display system would have my number, and a check with my cell service would turn up my name. I'd be happy to talk to them – later.

I began running back, through the light rain, in the direction of the doughnut shop, to pick up my car and figure out what I should do next. What I didn't want to do, right now, was hang around at the scene, and be kept there all night by cops asking a lot of questions.

Not one to give up, I tried Lawrence's numbers again. As long as I'd had cell phones, I'd never figured out how to program in my most frequently called numbers. And I was learning right now that it was impossible to tap in numbers on a tiny keypad while jogging, so I stopped long enough, under the shelter of another store awning, to call. Still no answer at either number.

I decided, once I was back to the car, that I would go to Lawrence's apartment and try to find him there.

As I approached the doughnut shop, winded and damp, I could see that there was still no Buick there, but a taxi had pulled in next to my Virtue, I got out my key, slipped into the car, and turned the ignition.

Whir. And that was it. Nothing more.

'Shitfuckdamn . . .' I shouted, banging my fist into the steering wheel. I tried it again, then again, without success.

I went into the shop. There were customers at only three tables. A man and two boys in soccer jerseys, evidently coming home from a late game or practice, sat at one, a young man and woman whispering to one another were at another, and at the third, a fat, unshaven guy in a Celtics sweatshirt. He was drinking coffee from a paper cup, hovered, pencil in hand, over the crossword puzzle from *The Metropolitan*. He took a bite of his apple fritter.

'That your cab?' I asked.

He chewed slowly on his fritter, barely looking up from his paper. 'Yeah.'

'I need you to take me someplace.'

'I'll just be a couple of minutes.'

I breathed in and out twice. 'It's kind of an emergency.'

'I tell ya what,' he said. 'Answer me this. Five-letter word, last letter "h," and the clue is "Luke's pa." You tell me what that is, we leave right now.'

'Darth,' I said.

The cabby cocked his head, pursed his lips in surprise. He studied the puzzle. 'Shit, I think that's it. Oh yeah, right, Luke Skywalker's daddy. I shoulda been able to get that, but you know, sometimes, it's just not there.' He penciled in the answer I'd given him.

'Yeah.'

'Okay, where you headed?'

I told him, and he snapped the plastic lid back onto his coffee, then folded back the opening that would allow him to drink it while he drove. It was about a ten-minute ride, and my driver tried to engage me in conversation about some trades in the NHL, but my mind was elsewhere, and he quickly gave up.

We pulled up in front of the address from Lawrence's card, which turned out to be a single door fronting onto a sidewalk in a business district, sandwiched between a hairstyling place and a cheese store. Lawrence's apartment had to be over one of the shops.

'Stay here,' I said, handing the cabby a twenty.

'No problem,' he said. 'I'll work on my puzzle, save the hard ones for you when you get back.'

I got out of the back of the cab and rang the buzzer next to the door. I leaned on it for several seconds and then, after getting no answer, tried to open it myself. It was locked. I went back to the cabby and said, 'Don't go anywhere. I'm going round back, see if his car's here.'

I ran to the corner and down the cross street until I had reached the lane and parking lots behind the row of shops. When I figured I was behind the cheese store and beauty parlor, I looked for some familiar vehicles and spotted them right away. There was Lawrence's Jaguar and, parked next to it, his old Buick, rear window replaced. Both cars were locked and no one was inside either one of them, at least as far as I could tell. I couldn't exactly open the trunks.

That gives you an idea of how my mind was working. I was expecting to find something bad. There are times when you just know.

There was a fire escape at the back of the shops, and I mounted it as quickly as I could, which wasn't very fast. It was steep, and narrow, and the metal steps were slippery from the drizzle that continued to come down. I gripped the metal handrail to steady myself on the way up to the second floor, where there was a small landing outside a door. The window in the door was covered with a blind that kept me from seeing inside.

I knocked. I waited about ten seconds, then tried the door. It was unlocked.

I eased the door open, ran my hand up alongside the wall just inside, hunting for a light switch. I found one and flicked it up. 'Lawrence?' I was pretty sure I was in the apartment that also connected to the door that led in off the street. 'Hey, Lawrence . . . It's Zack. You home?'

I eased the door open wider, stepped in, and closed it behind me. The door to the fire escape was off the kitchen, which was compact and immaculate. The appliances appeared to date back to the late fifties, but looked as though they'd been delivered yesterday. There were new but retro gadgets tucked back on the counter, under the cabinets. A gleaming metal toaster, a Hamilton Beach mixer, a waffle iron that showed no signs of ever having any batter in it. The clutter-free countertop had a small stack of mail on it, a Visa bill, a phone bill, a couple of flyers.

There was a small corkboard next to a wall-mounted phone, with a few business cards pinned there, including mine, and a color photo, taken at the beach, of Lawrence and a male friend, arms looped around each other's necks playfully, grinning into the camera. White guy, brown hair, brown eyes. I wondered whether this might be his friend Kent, the restaurateur.

In the sink I saw a rinsed cup and a couple of spoons and an empty beer bottle, and atop the adjoining counter was a bowl filled with apples and bright yellow bananas. I reached over and touched one of the perfect-looking bananas, wondering whether it was wax. It was not.

Enough light spilled out from the kitchen to allow me a view of the living area, which included a small dining room table, couch, big TV in the corner and four small silver speakers on stands placed strategically around the room. Surround sound. Part of an entertainment system. On a set of shelves were hundreds of CDs – Erroll Garner, Stan Getz, Ella Fitzgerald, Oscar Peterson, every other great jazz artist who ever lived – and dozens of DVD cases.

'Lawrence?'

I crossed the room to the main door, the one that must open onto a set of stairs that led down to the door on the sidewalk. I flipped back the deadbolt and opened the door, confirming for myself that it did indeed open onto the flight of stairs leading downward.

There was a short hallway leading off to the right away from the main door. I flipped on a light switch, and now I could see there were three doors leading off it. The first was a bathroom. I flicked on the light, eased my head in, peered around the back of the door into an empty bathtub. Shampoos and soaps were perfectly arranged in a device that hung from the shower head. The shower curtain was as clean as the day it came out of the package, the tiled corners free of mildew. Lawrence was one mean neat freak.

The next room had to be Lawrence's study. It was not nearly so neat.

Filing drawers had been pulled out, papers tossed across the floor, books thrown off shelves. It didn't look as though someone had just searched this room. They'd torn through it in a fit of rage.

I felt my unease move up a notch. Especially when I glanced down and saw drops of blood in the blue carpeting that appeared to start near the study door and lead towards the third door in the hallway.

The blotches on the carpet grew larger as I neared the door. Whoever had lost blood was losing more of it as he moved along.

There was an inch of light between the door and the frame, and I pressed my palm up against the door and eased it open.

I went very cold. I had found Lawrence.

He was on the bed, stretched out from one corner to the other, on top of the covers, fully dressed in a sports jacket, slacks and black dress shoes. He was on his stomach, and his right arm was down by his side, his left stretched out awkwardly above his head.

The powder blue duvet was soaked red with blood.

He was not moving.

I stepped into the room. 'Lawrence,' I whispered. 'Oh man, Lawrence, what the hell did they do to you?'

I placed my hands, tentatively, on his back, not knowing what else to do. I knew I couldn't roll him over. I'd only been playing amateur private eye for a few hours, and hadn't expected to run into anything like this, but I knew enough from watching TV that I wasn't supposed to move the body.

Except I was sure I felt the body move, ever so slightly, under my hand.

Lawrence was breathing, just.

He was alive.

EIGHTEEN

I put my weight gently on the bed, careful not to jostle Lawrence, and leaned in close to his ear. 'Hang in, man, I'm getting help.' I had no way to know whether he understood what I saw saying or could even hear me.

There was a phone on his bedside table and I was about to snatch the receiver off its cradle when I thought, 'Don't touch anything.'

So I got out my cell and punched in the three emergency digits. Before the operator had a chance to get in a word, I barked out the address, then told her there was a man here, very seriously injured, who'd lost a lot of blood. I couldn't pry my eyes off Lawrence as I spoke. Looking at him, I couldn't see any signs that he was still alive. His breathing was too shallow to make his back rise and fall,

'How was the injury sustained?' the operator asked.

'I haven't turned him over. But someone's tried to kill him. He's been attacked. He might have been shot, he might have been stabbed, I just don't know. Is the ambulance already on its way?'

'Yes, sir. Don't try to do anything yourself. Wait for the paramedics.'

'Hey, don't worry. They may have a hard time finding this place. It's just a door between two shops. I'm gonna go down and—'

'Sir, please don't leave the phone—'

'I don't have to. I'm on a cell.' I held on to the phone, but didn't bother holding it to my ear as I ran out the apartment's main door and down the narrow stairwell, and turned back the deadbolt on the door that opened out to the sidewalk. The cabby was still sitting where I'd left him. I opened the front passenger door.

'You're running up quite a fare,' he said, only half glancing up from his crossword.

'I need you to stay here,' I sad. 'There's going to be an ambulance here any minute now, and when you see it, direct them to this door.'

'An ambulance? What's an ambulance—'

'Once they're here, you find me, I'll pay you what I owe you for the cab. I don't know if I've got enough cash, but if not, I've probably got a blank cab chit from *The Metropolitan* in my wallet.'

'Yeah, sure, but let me ask you this. What's a five-letter word for a dog? Starts with a "p."'

I turned and ran back up the stairs, leaving every door I went through wide open. I returned to the bedroom, found Lawrence exactly as I'd left him (like, maybe I was expecting him to be sitting up and making phone calls?), and put the cell back to my ear.

'I'm back.'

'Sir, you shouldn't have left—'

'Look, I'm assuming you're sending the police, too, because, in case I forgot to mention it, somebody tried to kill this guy.'

'Yes, sir, you did tell me that.'

I was so rattled I was repeating myself.

The operator wanted my name, and Lawrence's, and as I gave her all the information, I could hear the wail of a siren in the distance, getting louder with each passing second. And, a few seconds later, a commotion at the bottom of the stairs as the paramedics came charging up.

'Up here . . .' I shouted. I told the dispatcher help had arrived, hung up, and slipped the phone back into my jacket.

Two paramedics appeared almost simultaneously at the bedroom door.

'He's still breathing,' I said. 'At least he was five minutes ago.'

Said one, 'I'll have to ask you to move out to the living room, sir, so that we can do our job. But I would ask that you not leave the apartment, because the police are going to have to ask you some questions.'

I did as I was asked. In the living room, I looked at the CDs and books and DVDs on Lawrence's shelves, seeing them but not seeing them, while from Lawrence's bedroom I could hear the sounds of urgency and controlled chaos. Snippets of hurried conversation slipped out.

'Okay, turn.'

'Jesus.'

'Hand me that.'

'Hello, Mr Jones, just take it easy.'

Two uniformed cops came through the door, glancing around quickly, trying to assess the scene as rapidly as possible. One, a bulky six-footer with a thick mustache, focused on me while the other went down the hall to the bedroom.

Before he could ask his first question, the cabby was at the door.

'You need me anymore, man?' he asked.

My cop wheeled around. 'You're going to have to stick around, sir. If you'll just wait in your cab, I'll be down to speak to you shortly.'

The cabby rolled his eyes and retreated, but not before giving me a look that seemed to say, 'Thanks a heap, pal.'

'You called 911?' the cop asked me.

I admitted it. I told him who I was, and that I was doing a feature on Lawrence Jones for *The Metropolitan*—

The cop's eyes narrowed. 'You work for *The Metropolitan*?'

The paper has, over the years, been somewhat critical of the city's rank and file. 'That's right,' I said. The cop said nothing else and waited for me to continue. I told him how I'd joined Lawrence the last few nights on a stakeout in front of a men's store on Garvin, and when he hadn't shown up—

'Wait a minute,' the cop said. This habit of his, of interrupting me all the time, was getting annoying very quickly, but I didn't see that there'd be much to gain by complaining about it. 'Garvin? That's where that store was hit, within the last hour or so?'

'Yeah. I called that one in to 911, too.'

His eyes got even narrower. 'Any crime scenes you haven't been to tonight?'

They brought Lawrence out of the room on a stretcher, his face under one of those respirator masks, his eyes closed, blood everywhere. He didn't look anything like the tough, cool, unflappable guy I'd been hanging out with the last few days. They maneuvered him through the door and angled him delicately down the stairs.

'Which hospital?' I called out to them.

'Mercy General,' one of the paramedics grunted as he took the high end of Lawrence's stretcher down the stairs.

'I don't know who I should be calling,' I told the cop. 'I don't know about any of his family. All I know is, he's got a boyfriend . . . I'm trying to think.'

'He's gay?'

'Yeah.'

'And you?'

'What about me?'

'You gay?'

'I don't know, are you?'

'Hey, listen, if you want to be a smartass, I got all night for this, pal.'

'I just don't know what that has to do with anything. Lawrence is a friend, someone I'm doing a story on. But there's someone who should know, I think his name is Kent, runs a restaurant in the east end.'

'We can worry about that in a minute. Tell me how you got in here.'

He had several more questions, all of which I answered as honestly as possible. He slipped away a moment to talk to the other officer, who was standing outside the door to the bedroom. These guys were too low on the totem pole to start doing any real investigating. They'd be holding the fort until the crime scene guys and the detectives, the types they built glitzy TV shows around, showed up.

I wandered into the kitchen, glanced at the picture of Lawrence and the man I had assumed earlier was Kent. Then I remembered the name of the restaurant. Blaine's.

I grabbed a phone book tucked up against the wall under the cabinets and opened it to the B's. I ran my finger down the listings, found the one for the restaurant, and dialed it on my phone. Someone picked up on the second ring.

'Blaine's restaurant. I'm sorry, but we're just closing.'

'Is Kent there?' I asked.

'Who's calling?'

'My name's Zack Walker. But tell him it's a friend of Lawrence's.'

I leaned up against the kitchen counter and waited. Finally, 'Hello?'

'Is this Kent?'

'Yes.'

'Look, you don't know me, but I'm a friend of Lawrence's.'

'A friend?' Suspicious. I could almost imagine the eyebrow going up.

'Listen, not a close friend. But I don't know anything about Lawrence's next of kin, or who should be contacted, but he mentioned your name one time.'

'Next of kin?' Kent asked. The words were, I realized as soon as I'd said them to Kent, loaded. 'What are you talking about?'

'He's at Mercy General. You should probably get there.'

I went downstairs and stepped out onto the sidewalk, took in a deep breath of the cool night air.

As if there weren't enough cars at the curb, including the cab that brought me here, an unmarked black Ford with a whip antenna and mini-hubcaps screeched to a stop in front of Lawrence's door. A tall man with a mustache and short black hair, dressed in a black Burberry trench, got out from behind the wheel. It took a moment before I realized who he was. Detective Steve Trimble, from two nights before, who'd been investigating Miles Diamond's death-by-SUV at the men's store on Emmett.

He glanced at me as he strode by, no doubt thinking he recognized me from somewhere, then bounded up the stairs two at a time to Lawrence's apartment. In a matter of seconds he was back down, pointed in my direction, and said, 'With me.'

He started back to his car, turned to make sure I was following him, which I was. He motioned for me to go around to the other side and get in. I did.

'Who the fuck are you?' he asked. 'I know you from somewhere.'

I said, 'If I want to be spoken to like I'm a piece of shit, I can stay home. I've got teenagers.'

'Who are you?'

'Zack Walker. We met night before last. The thing on Emmett. Miles Diamond.'

Trimble squinted. 'You were with Lawrence.' It was almost a question.

'That's right.'

'And here you are again.' There was something about the way he said it, that this was some sort of cosmic coincidence.

'Yeah,' I said. 'I found him.'

'Isn't *that* interesting.'

'No more than his former partner showing up to find out who tried to kill him.'

He tried to conceal his surprise, but the flash in his eyes was there. 'Yeah, we used to work together. Lawrence told you that?'

'Yeah.'

'What else did he tell you?'

I said nothing for a moment. 'He told me a lot of things. Why don't you ask your questions.'

The flashing red lights from the other emergency vehicles burned shadows across Trimble's face.

When he didn't ask one right away, I said, 'He mentioned that you two worked together, plainclothes. That you went through some tough spots together.'

'Yeah, well, your paper did its best to make sure things didn't go easy for me.'

I honestly didn't know what my newspaper had written about that night when Trimble had frozen and Lawrence had shot that kid. That was back when I was working at home, writing science fiction novels, and not keeping up with the news the way I had to now. For a moment, I felt wistful.

'I'm afraid I don't know much about that,' I said. 'Before my time.'

'Who did that to Lawrence?' He motioned with his head in the direction of the apartment.

'I don't know.'

'He's in surgery now. The paramedics say he was stabbed. So far, none of the neighbors report hearing anything.'

I repeated for him everything I'd told the uniformed cop. About the store stakeout, the guys in the black Annihilator, how the night before, they'd followed us when we were in Lawrence's Buick.

'You think it was that bunch who tried to kill him?' Trimble asked.

'I don't know,' I said. 'I'm just telling you what I know. It's kind of convenient, though, getting him out of the way before they raid the men's shop.'

Trimble didn't say anything for a while.

I continued, 'Plus, someone was looking for something. The room he used for an office, it's been tossed.'

'Tossed?' Trimble said.

'Isn't that the word?' I said.

He reached for the radio hanging from the elaborate communications set-up in the center of the dashboard. 'Trimble here. We get anywhere tracking down the SUV that rammed in that store over on Garvin?'

'Negative,' a voice squawked back at him.

'If you get anything, let me know. That vehicle may also be wanted in connection with this thing here on Montgomery.' He replaced the handset and said to me, 'I guess you've got a real good story to write now, huh? Hanging out with a detective who ends up nearly getting killed doing his job. That's kind of lucky for you, right?'

I just shook my head. 'Let me guess,' I said. 'Next you'll say, "Anything to sell newspapers." You know what sells newspapers? The horoscope. Where do you get off saying shit like that?'

Trimble almost looked ashamed. 'Fuck,' he muttered under his breath.

'Look,' I said, 'I haven't known Lawrence as long as you, but I like the guy. We hit it off. And if you don't need me for anything else, it's been a very long night, and I'd like to go home.'

Trimble reached into his jacket and brought out a card, handed it to me. 'If you find out anything, hear anything, give me a call. My home number's on there, too. Look, Lawrence was my friend, too, he still is. I'm guessing . . .' He let the sentence trail off, like he didn't want to say what he was about to say. 'I'm guessing he told you that I let him down one time, a while back, and there's a lot of truth to that. I wasn't there for him that night, and I've got to live with that for the rest of my life. But if there's anything I can do now, to help him, to find out who did this to him, I'm going to do it. And I'd appreciate any help that you can give me.'

I nodded, took the card from his hand and slipped it into my jacket.

'Okay,' I said.

I got out of the cruiser and noticed that one of the uniformed cops was just finishing up with my cabby. As I approached the cab, my cell phone rang, and I jumped.

'Hey,' Sarah said.

'Hi,' I said.

'Listen, I'm sorry to call, I know you're on your stakeout now with Lawrence, but I wanted to give you a quick call.'

'Yeah,' I said, evenly. I felt very tired all of a sudden.

'I called home, talked to Paul. And he sounded, I don't know, I think he sounded drunk.'

'Uh-huh,' I said.

'I mean, he's sixteen, I'm not stupid, I was sixteen, too, once, but I just wondered what he was like when you left the house.'

'He was fine.'

'I asked Angie what he'd been up to, but she either didn't know or was covering up for him. She says she ran into you at the mall?'

'Yeah, that's right. Angie's home?'

'You were at the *mall*?'

I was trying to remember. It was true. I had been at the mall, but instead of just a few hours ago, it felt like days.

'Yeah, I guess I was. But when you talked to Angie, was she home?'

'Yeah, she said she'd just got in. Zack, what is it? You sound almost as weird as Paul did on the phone.'

'Listen, Sarah, I'm in a bit of a situation here at the moment. Why don't we talk in the morning?'

'Is something going on? Is everything okay?'

'Lawrence didn't make it to the stakeout tonight. He ran into a bit of trouble. I'm at his place now.'

'What kind of trouble?'

I wanted to tell her. Sarah was my rock. When I was down or hurting or scared, she was always there for me, even when I was being the jerk of the century. But I was tired, and too weary to handle the hundred questions she'd be entitled to ask.

'Honey, I've really got to go,' I said. 'I'll tell you all about it later.'

She could sense I was holding back. She needed to ask just one question. 'Are you okay?'

'Yeah,' I said. 'I'm okay.'

As I slipped the phone back into my jacket, I thought, *I am* so *not okay*. And I *so* did not want to go down this kind of road again. A road that led me, and those around me, to danger, and violence and heartache.

I asked the cabby to give me a lift back to the doughnut shop where I'd left my car.

'I got the word,' the cabby said as we drove through the night. 'It was "pooch".'

NINETEEN

Back at the doughnut place, once again behind the wheel of my car, it occurred to me that, as a staffer with the biggest newspaper in the city, I had some obligation to notify the city desk about what was going on.

I got hold of Dan, working late on the city copy desk, who generally feels that I am a total fucking idiot, stemming back to an incident before I joined the paper. Because he mostly worked nights, our paths had rarely crossed since I'd started my new job.

'Hey, Dan,' I said.

'Zack. Sarah's not here. She's at that retreat where all the management types went.'

'I know, Dan. She's my wife. She tells me things.'

'So, what can I do for you then? Pretend to fall down the stairs again?' Some things end up haunting you for a very long time.

'I thought you'd want to know that a *Metropolitan* employee, in the course of conducting his journalistic duties, found the subject of his feature nearly stabbed to death.'

I could hear Dan's breath intake. 'Which *Metropolitan* employee?'

'Me, Dan. Is there time to write anything for the replate?'

'It's like, ten minutes to deadline. Best I could do would be to get a brief in or something.'

'What do you think? I've got a hell of a story here, about a private detective by the name of Lawrence Jones, who's been investigating a series of robberies and ends up getting stabbed in his own apartment. I was doing a whole takeout on him.'

'You found him?'

'Yes.'

'And called the police?'

'Yes, Dan.'

'What's the address? At the very least, we can get a photog out there so we have crime scene pics to run with a story for tomorrow.'

The thing was, there wasn't that much we could print even if we'd had more time. Lawrence, it was clear, might already be dead on the operating table at Mercy General, and we couldn't go naming him in the paper before the police had made their attempts to contact members of his family. Nor could we say, with any certainty, that the smash-and-grab at Brentwood's was related to the assault on a man who lived above a hair salon. Nor would we want to say, in a two-paragraph story, that the injured man had been found by a *Metropolitan* reporter, thereby tipping the competition and undercutting that reporter's exclusive for the following day's paper.

So Dan decided the best thing to do would be to run a bare-bones item on the Metro page, tucked into the digest, that police were investigating a violent attack on an unnamed private investigator, but details were unavailable at press time.

'You'll have to come in tomorrow and write something major,' Dan said. 'I'll leave a note for dayside to expect you.'

I slipped the phone back into my jacket, feeling chilled and exhausted. It was only now, sitting in the Virtue, that it occurred to me that there was a chance that the car was not going to start. I prepared myself to dig my auto club emergency card out of my wallet. I slid the key in, turned it, and to my astonishment, the engine came on just like that.

'You are one unpredictable piece of shit,' I said, backing the Virtue out of the doughnut shop parking lot.

On the way home I detoured by Mercy General and went to the ER to find out how Lawrence was doing. There was a cop there, just standing around, who told me Mr Jones was still in surgery but he was either not at liberty to say anything more or simply didn't know.

A man who looked like the guy in the photo pinned to the bulletin board in Lawrence's was pacing in the waiting area and, when he heard me ask the cop about Lawrence, approached.

'Are you the one who phoned the restaurant?' he said.

I nodded. 'You must be Kent. I'm Zack.'

He extended a hand to me. 'Kent Aikens. Thanks for letting me know.'

'I didn't know who else to call. Has Lawrence got family?'

'Not local. I think his parents are dead, but he's got a sister named Letitia out in Denver, I think. I'm going to try to locate her, let her know. And when . . .' He hesitated, not sure whether the word he was looking for was 'if'. He composed himself and continued. 'When Lawrence wakes up, I can find out from him who else he wants me to call.'

'Sure,' I said. 'Have you spoken to the doctors?'

'They don't want to tell me much. I'm not, you know, family.' He shook his head angrily. 'I'm just the faggot friend, the only one who's even fucking here. But they did tell me that the knife punctured his lung, among other things. They said something about his lung filling up with blood. I spoke to him, like, yesterday. He phoned me. We were going to get together this Friday night, go to a club or something. He mentioned you, that you were some reporter?'

I nodded.

'And that you were hanging out with him. He had good things to say about you.'

I half smiled. 'He's a good guy.'

Kent swallowed, turned away so I wouldn't notice his chin quivering. I gave him one of my own business cards. 'If you need anything, or can let me know how Lawrence is doing, please let me know. That has my work and home numbers on it.'

Kent took the card without looking at it and slid it into the front pocket of his jeans. 'Okay,' he said. 'I thought, once he was through being a cop, there'd be less chance of this kind of thing happening. Working for himself, not chasing people down alleys, how could something like this happen?'

'It happened at his apartment,' I said. 'Someone came looking for him, most likely these people he'd been investigating. They killed another detective a couple of nights ago.'

Kent took that in, said nothing.

I said, 'You have any other idea who might have it in for him?'

He shook his head. 'It just doesn't make any sense. Lawrence is a good guy.'

173

The sliding glass doors to the ER parted and in strode Detective Trimble. Kent caught a glimpse of him and turned away, muttering, 'Oh, great. Our hero has arrived.'

'What?' I asked. 'You got problems with Trimble?'

'I know the history,' he said. 'Lawrence nearly died a few years ago because of that asshole. Look, if I find out anything, I'll give you a call, okay?' And he walked over to one of the vinyl and chrome waiting room chairs and took a seat, studying the pile of outdated magazines on the small table next to him.

Trimble strode past me, nodded, and kept walking in the direction of the operating rooms.

It was about one in the morning when I got home. The Camry was in the driveway, pulled up close to the garage. Angie had returned from Oakwood some time ago, I guessed, considering that Sarah had spoken to her when she phoned home from the retreat. I wondered whether my daughter might still be up, but when I came in and did a walkabout, it was clear that both she and her brother were asleep. All manner of interrogations could begin tomorrow, should I choose to conduct them.

I phoned Sarah from the kitchen phone.

'God, I've been waiting up for you, hoping you'd call,' she said from her hotel room. 'What's happening?'

'It's Lawrence,' I said 'Someone tried to kill him in his apartment. I found him. He's pretty bad. I don't know whether he's going to make it.'

Sarah waited a moment, and said, 'Tell me everything.'

I gave her the basics, that Lawrence's attacker was unknown, that it might or might not be related to the smash-and-grab at Brentwood's, that I had a major story to write first thing in the morning.

'Do you want me to come home?' she asked. 'I can bail on this thing. I don't have to stay. We won't be learning anything. It'll all be bullshit, the way these things always are.'

'No, no, it's okay, there's not much you could do if you came back.'

'I could be with you,' she said.

I felt a lump develop in my throat. God, it had been a long night.

'Really,' I said. 'I'm okay.'

'And the kids? Is everything okay there?' Sarah asked.

'Sure,' I lied, thinking about Trevor's surveillance of Angie, my surveillance of Trevor and Angie, Angie's mysterious visit to Trixie's, Paul's drinking binge.

'Everything's fine.'

TWENTY

I was tired enough to have slept for a week, yet I mostly tossed and turned during what was left of that night. I had a few things on my mind. There was my daughter, who was making secret visits to my dominatrix friend while being stalked all over town by a possibly unstable admirer. There was my son, who, at the age of sixteen, was getting into the booze, a behavior that put him in the company of most sixteen-year-old boys, and evidently my daughter's stalker was supplying him with the stuff. My new friend lay in the hospital after a near-fatal stabbing. I had impulsively spent $8,900 that we didn't have on a car that started only when it felt like it, plus another small fortune on a new wardrobe. And there was the fact that I was lying to my wife about just how serious things might be on the home front because it would involve disclosing that I was violating the privacy of a member of my own family.

At least I had those new clothes to wear.

By seven, I was sitting at the kitchen table, that morning's *Metropolitan* spread out on the table before me, reaching for my coffee and reading the headlines without registering them.

Paul showed up first, since he had to be at high school before Angie had to be at her first class at the university. He looked tired and bleary-eyed.

'Sit down,' I said.

'Just let me grab some juice,' he said.

'Sit down,' I said, using my Angry Father Voice.

He came over, pulled out a chair, and sat down across from me. He had that look of feigned bewilderment, as if to say, 'What could you possibly want to speak to me about?'

I said, 'You look a bit rough this morning.'

He swallowed. 'I'm good. Just a bit tired is all.'

'What did you do last night?'

'Hung out here. Had a couple of friends over.'

'What'd you do?'

Paul hesitated. 'Uh, just, I don't know, watched some movies, played video games.'

'What do you think the chances are, if I go look out back between the garage and the fence, that there's still a six-pack there?'

'Huh?'

'Shall we go look? I know it was there yesterday afternoon, and I have a pretty good idea who left it there, and I'm betting it's gone.'

Paul looked at the table. 'It's gone.'

'And I'll bet most of it's been thrown up or pissed away by now,' I said.

Paul swallowed again. No denials there.

'You got a fake ID?' I asked.

Paul feigned indignation. 'Oh my God. Don't you trust me?'

'Of course not. You're a teenager.' I took a shot in the dark. 'Let's see the ID.'

Paul sighed, took his wallet from his back pocket, opened it up, tossed a piece of plastic across the table at me. It was a reasonably good facsimile, as long as you didn't look too closely, of a driver's license, with Paul's picture on it. It would have to be pretty dark in a bar to fool anyone with.

'This says you're twenty-one,' I said. 'You're barely shaving.'

'I shaved two days ago.'

'Let me guess. You look too young to fool many people with this, so you get your older friends, Trevor Wylie included, to buy your beer for you.'

Paul said nothing. I slipped the fake ID into my pocket.

'Jeez, Dad, you know what I had to pay Trevor for that?'

'No, what?'

Paul decided it was better not saying. I said, 'Trevor's what, four or five years older than you? And he's your buddy?'

'He's okay.'

'That kid's using you, being nice to you, buying your beer for you, to get close to your sister.' I paused, got very serious. 'Don't let people use you to hurt your family.'

For a moment, Paul's eyes looked scared. 'He wouldn't hurt anybody. He just likes Ange, that's all.'

'You better hope so,' I said.

'And jeez, why are you coming down so hard on me about this? You didn't get this way with Angie.'

'Angie wasn't drinking when she was sixteen,' I said.

Now it was Paul's turn to smile. 'Yeah, right. I've got so much shit on her, you've got no idea.'

'What do you mean by that?' I asked, thinking maybe the comment had to do with more than just underage drinking. Maybe it had to do with Trixie. Paul and Angie confided in each other about a lot of things.

178

'She's no angel, Dad. I mean, she's okay, but if you think she's always been Little Miss Perfect or something, well, sorry.'

'Does this have anything to do with Oakwood?' I asked. 'With people out there?'

'Huh?' said Paul. 'Neither one of us want anything to do with that place again. Listen, I have to get ready or I'm going to be late.' And he got up from the table and walked out of the kitchen without even bothering to get his juice.

And Angie walked in.

'Hey,' she said. She gave me a once-over. 'Hey . . . You're not wearing any of your stuff from last night.' She sounded hurt.

'I'm sorry, honey. I got in real late, I think the bags are still in the car.'

'I don't believe it. You didn't even bring in your stuff?' She took a yogurt out of the fridge, peeled off the lid. 'Gee, good thing I helped you pick out a new wardrobe. You can't even bring it inside.'

'It's not like that,' I said. I told her about Lawrence.

'Are you kidding?' she said. 'Is he gonna make it?'

'I'm going to call the hospital in a little while. I'm guessing the first few hours will be pretty critical.'

She was still shaking her head in disbelief. 'Man, that's so freaky.'

'Yeah. Well, so,' I said, thinking that a lot of freaky things were going on around here lately. 'Where did you go after we split up last night?' Trying to make it sound like regular conversation, not an interrogation.

Angie shrugged. 'Just around. Did some studying with some friends.'

'Oh yeah.' I took a sip of my coffee. 'These friends taking the same courses you're taking?'

'Yep.'

'Uh-huh.' I watched Angie get out a slice of bread, drop it into the toaster, then root around in the fridge for some jam.

My daughter. Doing the small talk thing with Daddy. Making her breakfast. Talking about homework. Getting ready for class.

And a few hours earlier, she'd spent the evening with a dominatrix. Who was, I reminded myself, my friend.

I decided to try a different tack, come at things from another direction.

'So, have you thought any more about what you might want to do when you finish college?' I asked.

'I dunno. There's lots of time. I've got three more years.'

'Yeah, but, you know, you must have some ideas rattling around in your head. Lines of work you might want to get into.'

'There's lots of things,' Angie said. 'There's photography; sometimes I think advertising might be interesting. Or something where I'm working with people. I think I'd like working with people.'

I nodded. 'You'd like to work with people.'

'Yep.'

'What kind of work would you like to do for people?'

Another shrug. 'All kinds of things, I guess. Who knows? Why all the questions about my future?'

'Just interested, is all. I'd just like to see you get into a line of work you'd enjoy, that makes you happy, that offers lots of opportunities, that's financially rewarding, that's something that would make your mother and father proud.'

Angie looked up at that last one. 'Huh? What, you want me to become a doctor or something? Because I can tell you right now, I am not planning to become a doctor.'

'I'm not saying you have to become a doctor. All I'm saying is, you'll want to get some kind of job *you* can be proud of, and I'm sure if you're proud of it, your mother and I will be proud of it, too.'

Angie stirred her yogurt, getting the fruit down on the bottom mixed into the rest of it, and studied me for a moment. 'Dad,' she said.

'Yes, honey?'

'Are you, like, drifting into another one of your spells again?'

'Excuse me?'

'You know, when you start getting hyper-concerned about everything? Because, like, you're totally impossible when you're like that. I mean, I can understand you getting freaked out about Lawrence and all, but everything's fine here at home.'

'I don't know what you're talking about,' I said. 'Never mind, we won't talk about it, subject closed, conversation over.' I looked back down at my paper. 'We just want you to find a career that will make you happy.'

'Dad . . .'

'Okay, never mind. Forget it.' I decided to move to another subject. 'How's this thing with Trevor? He still bothering you?'

Angie sighed. 'He called me, late last night.'

'Oh yeah?'

'He says, we're meant to be together. That forces that might try to keep us apart are, what did he say, acting in vain.'

'You're kidding.'

'Weird, huh? He's so fucking intense, Says I remind him of that chick, the one in the *Matrix* movie, jumps around in slow motion kicking the crap out of guys. She is kind of pretty.'

'You know, there are things we can do. We could get, I don't know, a restraining order or something, or—'

'Dad.'

'We've got legal experts at the paper, I could ask one of them—'

'Dad.'

'They could probably give us a name. In fact, I met this police detective last night, he might even—'

'Dad . . .'

'Huh?'

'Dad, stop it. Okay? Trevor's a pain, but I'll deal with it. It's not like he's psycho or something.'

I wanted to tell her. That Trevor had been following her the night before, first to the coffee shop where she met the young man, then to the mall, then part of the way out to Oakwood. And I was working up to it, thinking, okay, she could get as mad as she wanted, but it was important that she—

'Jeez, Dad, maybe you should start snooping on him, like you did with—'

The Pool Boy.

I waved my hands in the air. 'Okay, okay, okay, never mind. I'm sorry.'

We didn't speak for a couple of minutes. She ate her toast across from me. I listened to every chew.

'There is something funny, though,' she said softly. 'Like, funny weird, not funny ha-ha.'

'What?'

'There were times last night, when I was driving around, when I had this feeling, I don't know. This is totally weird. Like I was being watched.'

'Really.'

'And I looked around, figuring it might be Trevor? You know? Because he's been so weird lately? But I didn't see him.'

'Huh.'

'Yeah. I'm probably just freaking out. This is what you've done to me. This is the kind of person you're turning me into.'

Angie rinsed her dish and put it in the dishwasher, then went into the front hall. She called to me, still sitting in the kitchen, 'Can I have the new car today?'

'I've got to get it looked at today. Half the time, it doesn't want to start.'

'Great.'

And then I heard the muffled sound of a cell phone, and I could hear her rustling through her bag. 'Hello?'

Then: 'Stop fucking phoning me, okay?'

I took the shopping bags out of the Virtue and put them up in my bedroom, then locked up the house and got into the car. It started, but I wanted to be sure the problem wasn't going to recur, so on the way into the office I stopped at Otto's Auto Repair, and found Otto under a Mustang that was up on the hoist. Otto had looked after our cars, off and on, for the last fifteen years.

'What's up?' he asked.

'I got myself a new car,' I explained, 'and I've been having a little trouble with it.'

'Let's have a look,' he said, and walked out the bay doors with me as I led him over to the Virtue.

'Whoa,' he said. 'This is one of those hybrid cars.'

'That's right.'

'Where's the extension cord?' And Otto started laughing.

'That's a good one, Otto,' I said.

'You really should have talked to me before you went out and bought one of these. I mean, they're good on gas and all, but they're a bit hinky in the electrical department. Sometimes they don't want to start.'

'Yeah, so I've discovered.'

Otto nodded, asked me to pull the lever inside that would pop the hood.

'Jesus,' he said. 'There's nothing here but a huge plastic cover. I got to get that off before I can see anything. Can you leave it with me? It might have something to do with the battery cells. It's got a shit-load of them. Loose wire, maybe. You could pick it up later in the afternoon.'

I grabbed a streetcar the rest of the way to work, and Nancy, the assignment editor who was filling in for Sarah while she was at her retreat, found me at my desk about five seconds after I'd sat down. She'd read Dan's turnover note and wanted to be brought up to speed. I gave her the short version of events, enough details that she could answer questions from any editors further up the food chain, including Magnuson, who could be assured, I said, that I was not involved in any shootouts.

'Shootouts?'

'You can just tell him, if he asks.'

'Write your story,' she said. 'Everything you've got. And figure out what likely follows you have.'

'If there are any follow-ups,' said Dick Colby, who had sneaked up behind Nancy, 'they're mine. This is my beat, you know.'

'I'm sorry, Dick,' I said. 'Next time I find a guy who's dying, I'll phone you so you can come down and call the ambulance.'

Nancy took a step back from Colby, trying to get some air.

'All I'm saying is,' Colby said, 'everyone should respect each other's territory. You don't see me writing science fiction stories.'

'You could do one,' I said, 'about a planet where no one bathes.'

'Oh fuck,' Nancy said under her breath.

'What did you say?' Colby asked me.

'Look,' said Nancy, who hated confrontation and wanted to defuse uncomfortable situations as quickly as possible, 'Dick, we can talk about this later, okay?'

Cheese Dick wandered off, grumbling.

'I can't believe you said that,' Nancy said.

'I can't believe we're still breathing,' I said.

My desk phone rang. I gave Nancy my 'I have to get this' smile, and put the receiver to my ear.

'Walker,' I said.

'Zack. It's Trixie.'

My stomach flipped,

'Hey,' I said. 'I was, uh, I was actually thinking of calling you today.'

'I heard, on the news, about Lawrence. Isn't this the guy you told me about on the phone?'

By now, Lawrence's name had been officially released by the police, and the story was on the radio. 'Yeah,' I said.

'Sounds terrible. How is he?'

'Not good.'

'Listen, you sound kind of preoccupied, so I can let you go. But what were you going to call me about?'

Think. The truth? Or something less than the truth?

'I don't know,' I said. 'I was just going to suggest getting a coffee sometime, maybe. How'd it go with that client? Your Girl Scout cookie fan?'

Trixie chuckled. 'Oh yeah. Later, after he'd left and I was getting changed, I found crumbs in my stockings.'

I thought about that for a moment, decided it wasn't worth trying to figure out the logistics.

'I think Paul got drunk last night.' As soon as I'd said it, I wondered why I'd done so. I guess I needed to talk about it with someone, and I hadn't broached it with Sarah yet. 'These teenage years, they're enough to kill you as a parent.'

'I don't envy you. Having kids, I don't think it's something I'd ever have been any good at.' There was an inexplicable sadness in Trixie's voice. But then she brightened. 'If only drinking had been the only thing I'd been into when I was sixteen.'

'And Angie,' I said, letting my daughter's name hang out there for a minute, 'she's growing up so fast, it's hard to keep up.'

'I'll bet,' said Trixie. There was a long pause. 'Zack, are you okay? You sound funny. Is everything all right?'

'There's a lot going on for me right now. I'm feeling a little, I don't know, overwhelmed.'

'I don't doubt it. Listen, if there's anything I can do, you call me, okay?'

'Sure,' I said, and we said our goodbyes.

★

186

I handed in my story by noon and told Nancy I was going to take a cab over to Brentwood's.

When I got there, I found the place cordoned off with yellow police tape, although there were some guys there, putting plywood sheets over where the windows used to be.

I ducked under the tape, went in through the front door, which was wide open, and found Arnett Brentwood with a list of stock in his hand, checking it against what was left on the hangers.

'Mr Brentwood?' I said. He was a small man, short and slight, but even in the aftermath of what had happened, was dressed meticulously in a black suit, white shirt and tie. We had met once before, but he did not immediately recognize me. I told him who I was, and where I was from, and that I had found Lawrence the night before in the bedroom of his apartment.

'I am very sorry for him,' Brentwood said. 'Sorry for his family. Please convey to them my sincerest concern and best wishes for his recovery.'

'I'll be sure to do that.'

'I would like to do it myself, but as you can see . . .' He opened his arms wide, gestured at the destruction inside his shop.

'I was the one who called it in,' I said, 'to 911. I was supposed to meet Lawrence here, and when he didn't show up, I went looking for him.'

'These people, the ones who broke into my store, these are the people who tried to kill Mr Jones?'

'It's possible,' I said.

'It's all over for me,' said Brentwood. 'I have been hit before. The insurance people, they say they won't cover me anymore. I can't do this anymore.'

And he looked away, thinking that I would not see the tear that was running down his cheek.

'You tell Mr Jones I am sorry,' he said. 'And you can tell him that I am finished.'

TWENTY-ONE

My next stop was the hospital. But not to give Lawrence the message from Mr Brentwood. I'm sure he felt bad enough without hearing that his client was being forced out of business. I'd been thinking of him all day, had called the hospital a couple of times and managed to get nothing more out of the nurses than 'critical but stable'.

With the Virtue still at Otto's, I grabbed a cab in front of the *Metro* building and asked to be taken to Mercy General. After inquiring at the front desk, I found out, not to my surprise, that Lawrence was in the intensive care ward. There was a sign outside the ward that told me ICU patients could only have two visitors at a time, and they had to be family. I found a nurse, told her who I was.

She reiterated what the sign said. 'I'm sure you're very concerned about Mr Jones, we all are, but it's family only.'

'Is there anyone with him right now?'

'I believe his sister's in there. She flew in from Denver.'

'I'll wait for her.'

I peered in through the window of the door to the ICU. There looked to be about a half dozen beds in there, and at one of the two far beds, which were up against the window that looked out onto the parking lot, a black woman was sitting in a chair. A curtain pulled partway around the bed kept me from seeing who was in it. All I could make out, under the pale blue hospital bedding, was the shape of legs and feet.

She was an attractive woman, in her late thirties I guessed, with gleaming black hair and a tailored blue suit, and every few seconds she dabbed at her eyes with a tissue. She reached out and held the patient's hand, leaned in a bit, cocked her head slightly to one side, as if she was trying to hear something the patient was saying. She tilted forwards out of her chair, and now I couldn't see her head as she disappeared behind the curtain.

I took a chair by the door and waited. About fifteen minutes later, the ICU door opened and she stepped out, walking slowly, her head hanging like she had a bag of rocks tied around her neck.

'Excuse me,' I said. 'Ms. Jones?'

'No,' she said. 'My name is Letitia McBride.'

'I'm sorry. But was your name Jones? Are you Lawrence's sister?'

She nodded, hesitantly. McBride was, I surmised, a married name.

I got up and introduced myself. 'Lawrence is a friend of mine. I came by to see him, but they won't let me in, not being a relative and all. I understand you flew in from Denver? The nurse told me.'

'That's right,' she said. 'Do you mind my asking you how you know my brother?'

Maybe, when your brother is gay, and a man you don't know approaches you and says he's his friend, you need a bit more information to understand the nature of the relationship. I obliged, telling her I was with *The Metropolitan* and had been doing a story on Lawrence, but that in the short time we'd hung out, we'd become friends. And that I had been the one who found him and called 911.

'Thank you,' she said, and reached out and touched my arm. 'The doctors said if he'd been found any later, he would have lost too much blood.'

'How is he?'

Letitia McBride's lips pursed out, she breathed in deeply through her nose, and her eyes moistened. 'He's hurt real bad,' she said. 'They say the next day is critical. He's a fighter, you know? And he's fighting now, more than he ever has before.' She blew her nose into a tissue. 'My baby brother.'

I tried to smile.

'Our mother, she drove a bus for the city, worked all kinds of shifts, some right through the night, and our dad, he wasn't home much because he was working two, three jobs, trying to make enough to support us. They loved us, we never doubted that, but we were on our own a lot, and I always looked out for him, making him dinner, making sure he got to bed on time. One day, this big dump truck smashes into our mother's bus, back end came right through the window, and we lost her. After that, Dad, he had to work even harder to support us, and I was looking after Lawrence all the time.'

'Is your father still alive?'

She shook her head. 'He passed on, oh, ten years ago now. Lawrence was never able to tell him.'

'Tell him?'

'About being different,' she said, looking at me cautiously.

'About his being gay.'

She nodded. 'Maybe, if it was now, attitudes are different, you know?'

I nodded.

'But even now, our dad probably wouldn't have understood. And you know what? Lawrence would never have held that against him. 'Cause he knew our father was such a good man, with a good heart. It wouldn't have been in our father to understand something like that. Lawrence would have accepted that, wouldn't even have bothered his father with it. Lawrence doesn't need anybody's acceptance. He's who he is.'

'I know,' I said.

She shook her head again, then appeared thoughtful for a moment, like she was trying to remember something. 'Mr Walker, what did you say your first name was?'

'Zack.'

'Oh my.'

'What?' I said.

'Lawrence, he's been kind of in and out, you know. They've got him on painkillers. But he's been asking for you. He's been saying your name.'

'Asking for me?'

'He keeps saying "Zack". And things that don't make sense.'

'Like what?'

'You should see him. You should come in.'

'I don't think they're going to believe I'm family,' I said.

She smiled at that, and it was a beautiful smile. Letitia glanced over at the nurses' station, didn't see anyone looking our way, and led me through the door into the ICU.

We slipped quietly past the other patients, who were in varying stages of disrepair, and when we got to the far side of the room, I could see around the curtain.

He looked bad.

There were tubes running in and out of him, monitors beside and above him, and I didn't understand what any of it meant. But you didn't have that much hardware hooked up to you unless it was pretty damn serious.

'Hey, man,' I said.

His eyes were closed, his head back on the pillow. Letitia moved in close to him. 'Larry,' she whispered. 'He's here. The man you were asking for. Zack. Zack is here.'

One eye half fluttered open, went closed again.

'It's okay,' I said. 'We should just let him rest.'

'No,' Letitia said to me. 'It sounded important, what he wanted to tell you.'

Now I leaned in a bit closer. 'Lawrence, it's Zack. Your sister says you wanted to give me some sort of a message. So, like, I'm here. But you take your time.'

The one eye fluttered open again, landed on me, tried to focus. Now the other eye struggled to open.

'Ohhhhh,' he said quietly.

'Yeah, you must be hurtin',' I said.

He grimaced, rolled his head back and forth on the pillow. 'Zack,' he said, barely more than a whisper.

'Yeah, I'm here. You kind of made a mess of my feature, you know? Getting yourself hurt this way, it kind of changed the angle. You shouldn't have gone and done that on me.'

'Watch,' he said.

'Huh? What did you say, Lawrence?'

'He said "watch",' Letitia said.

'Watch?' I shrugged. 'What do you mean, Lawrence? What watch? Somebody's watch?'

'Out,' he said, his eyes closing for a second.

'Watch out?' I said. 'Is that what you're trying to say? Watch out?' I glanced at Letitia.

Lawrence tried to swallow. Letitia held a straw that led down into a glass of water up to his mouth. A sip of water went down and he took a couple of breaths.

'After,' he said, looking at me now. 'You.'

'What are you saying, Lawrence?'

He closed his eyes again, exhausted.

'I think what he's saying,' Letitia said, 'is watch out, they're after you, too.'

That was kind of the way I'd read it, too.

TWENTY-TWO

'My best guess,' said Otto, 'is the battery cells.'

I'd grabbed another cab from the hospital back to the auto repair shop and was standing with Otto out in the parking lot next to the Virtue, which had spent quite a bit of time inside the shop during the day, but was now back outside.

'I tried and tried to get it to do what you said it did,' Otto said. 'There was only one time it wouldn't start, wouldn't do a damn thing. So I checked all the wiring to the cells, saw one I thought looked like it was loose, and fixed it. Couldn't get it to act up after that, so that may have done the trick, but shit, you should probably take this thing to a Virtue dealer where they got a better handle on this car than I got.'

'I'll consider that.'

Otto smiled, shoved a cigarette between his lips. 'I did a search on the net, too, where people talk about the cars they got? One guy, has one of these, had the same problem, and he'd jiggle the transmission shifter thing, like there might be a short in there, and sometimes that worked. I don't know. Try it out, if it doesn't start again, bring it back.'

'How will I bring it back if it doesn't start?' I asked Otto.

His eyes went to slits. 'That one of those chicken-and-egg questions?'

I got in the car, found the key in the ignition. The engine started on the first turn. 'That's a hopeful sign,' I said.

'I got your bill inside,' Otto reminded me, before I pulled away.

Driving back to the paper, I couldn't stop thinking about what Lawrence Jones had tried to tell me with the help of his sister. His suggestion, that I needed to watch out because 'they' were after me, too, was more than a tad unnerving.

Who would be after *me*?

I could imagine someone going after Lawrence. He was in a line of work where you encountered the odd bad guy. He'd been following those guys in the Annihilator. He'd probably pissed off a lot of people when he was a cop. Maybe somewhere along the line, as a private detective, he'd made life tough for some philandering husband he'd caught in the act.

But what did anyone have against me? Who would also have it in for Lawrence?

And I thought, back to those guys in the black SUV. What if they'd figured out Lawrence and I had been the ones following them that night? That those shots fired at their SUV had come from us?

Even if they'd had some way to trace the license plate on the Buick, Lawrence had told me he'd put bogus plates on the car, just to keep that kind of thing from happening. So how would they even have found him?

I thought of the specific words that Lawrence, lying in his hospital bed, hooked up to umpteen wires, had said.

Watch. Out. After. You.

When I got up to my desk in the *Metropolitan* news-room, I found Steve Trimble's card in my wallet and called his office phone. When I got his voicemail, I hung up and tried the cell number that was listed.

'Trimble.'

'Detective Trimble, Zack Walker here.'

'Yeah. What can I do for you?' His offer didn't sound particularly sincere.

'I'm doing a story on all this for tomorrow and wanted to make a last-minute check with you to see whether there's been any progress in the investigation, to find out who tried to kill Lawrence. You're in charge of the investigation, right?'

'Yeah.' Man of few words.

'So, has there been any progress in the investigation?'

'We're following up on a variety of leads at this time.' Strictly by the book, this guy was.

'Do you have any actual suspects?'

'Like I said, we're following up on a variety of leads at this time.'

'Does it look to you like this was the work of more than one person, or a single individual?'

Trimble paused. 'At this point I'd have to say there's nothing that specifically indicates more than one person, but there's nothing that specifically rules it out, either. What makes you ask?'

'Just asking,' I said.

'Look,' said Trimble, his tone softening a bit, 'I'm willing to work a two-way street here. You were there, you know Lawrence. If there's something you know that you think might be relevant, you share it with me, and anything I get, I give it to you first. We make an arrest, I call you.'

'Even before Dick Colby?'

Trimble actually laughed. 'Even before Dick Colby. I've given him lots of stuff in the past. Preferably over the phone, if you get my drift.'

'I do,' I said, feeling that maybe I'd broken the ice a bit with Trimble. If he was willing to make fun of Colby, he couldn't be all bad. 'If it's okay with you, I'd like to check in with you once a day, see if you've got anything. And if I've got something, I'll call you.'

'Anytime,' Trimble said. There was a pause. He added, 'Night or day.'

'Deal,' I said.

I'd barely replaced the receiver when the phone rang.

'Hey,' said Sarah. 'We're on a break here. This guy from the newspaper association is telling us how to *listen* to our reporters' concerns, to imagine how they *must feel* when their copy is chopped to ribbons, as a way of making a newsroom more harmonious. I want to feed this guy into a paper shredder. How's Lawrence doing?'

'Holding his own, I think. Not great, but not getting worse.'

'Have you seen him?'

'I went there this afternoon, a couple of hours ago.'

'How'd he look?'

'Bad.'

'Y'able to talk to him at all?'

I paused. 'Only a little. I did most of the talking. He's hooked up to a lot of machines and shit. Looks like a Borg.'

'Huh?' Sarah, not a *Star Trek* fan, missed the reference. 'I'm outa here tomorrow, after the morning session. Should be back home late afternoon, unless I decide to pop into the office first.'

'Don't bother. Just come home. We miss you.'

Maybe it was something about Letitia's story about looking after Lawrence when they were young, but more and more, I was appreciating that the only sure thing that protected us from the bad things out there were the people closest to us.

I wrote my story, let Nancy know it had been filed and updated with a call to Trimble, and left the building. The Virtue started for me just like that. Good ol' Otto. He knew what he was doing. I decided to stop on the way home for some groceries. Maybe, just maybe, there'd be a chance for me, Angie and Paul to have a meal together.

The cross street at the bottom of Crandall is a busy thoroughfare lined with shops, cafés, restaurants and a small theater that shows second-run stuff. It was a nice day, and the cafés had moved some tables and chairs out onto the sidewalks. I found a spot by the curb and went in Angelo's Fruit Market and bought the makings of a salad, then went next door, to the fresh pasta place, for some linguine and a tomato-Alfredo sauce, and as I was coming back out I glanced in the direction of the café two doors down, where there were half a dozen tables out front, and thought I recognized the person sitting with his back to me, fiddling with a laptop computer.

I came up behind him, this young man in a long black jacket, and peered over his shoulder. There was a map on the screen, which, at a glance, looked like our neighborhood. There was a small, pulsing dot moving across it.

'Lost Morpheus again?' I asked.

Startled, Trevor Wylie whirled around, reaching up with his right arm and easing shut the lid of his laptop at the same time.

'Mr Walker,' he said, taking off his sunglasses so he could see me more clearly.

'How are you, Trevor?' I said, moving around in front of him.

'Good, I'm good,' he said. 'Whatcha doing around here?'

'Just picking up some things for dinner. How about you?'

He motioned to the paper cup next to his computer. 'Having a coffee, doing a bit of surfing, homework.'

Across the street I noticed Trevor's black Chevy, sitting low in the back as though the rear springs were going. It was a hulking piece of Detroit machinery amidst smaller, newer, mostly imported cars. Black jacket, black car, the wandering black Annihilator. The forces of darkness were aligned against me.

'That really is an amazing program you've got there,' I said, resting my bags on the top of the table. 'If I ever get a dog, I guess I'll have to get something like that.'

'Sure.'

'What's your homework?'

'Just stuff. Nothing particularly interesting.' He looked around, thinking maybe, by the time he looked back, I'd be gone. But I was still there. 'How's Angie?' he asked.

'She's good, Trevor.'

'I think she might have something wrong with her cell phone,' he said. 'Sometimes, I try to call her, it doesn't go through.'

'You know how cells are. What were you calling her about? I could pass on a message.'

'College stuff. I was thinking I might try Mackenzie, I think they have a computer science program there, and that would be right up my alley, you know? And if my classes were around the same time as Angie's, we could share rides. I could drive one week, she could drive the next, that kind of thing. But I'll talk to her about it myself. You don't have to worry about it.'

'The thing is,' I said, 'I do worry.'

'What?'

'I worry. I'm kind of a worrier, Trevor. Ask anyone who knows me. I'm a bit over the top at times. Especially where members of my family are concerned. Like Angie. I worry about her. All fathers worry about their daughters.'

'Yeah, I guess they would.' Trevor slipped his shades back on. 'There's a lot of freaky people out there.'

'That's right,' I said. 'So I try to keep as close an eye on her as I can, you know? To make sure she's okay. Because if something ever happened to her, I don't know what I'd do.'

Trevor nodded in agreement. 'I can understand that. Totally.'

'I hope you do,' I said.

We didn't speak for a moment. Trevor broke the silence, 'So, you've written some SF.'

'Yeah,' I said. 'I've done a few sci-fi novels.'

'I like sci-fi. But as much as I like the scientific aspect of it, I find there's something mystical about it, too. There are forces other than those of nature at play. I don't think science rules everything in the universe.'

'Maybe not,' I said.

'And I believe, sometimes for reasons that we can't possibly understand, that certain things are meant to happen.'

'Okay.'

'And that there are people out there that we're destined to meet up with. That everyone has, from the moment they're born, a certain other person that they're supposed to hook up with for them to fulfill their destiny.'

'I don't know much about that,' I said. 'It's not the sort of thing I've written about. But it's one point of view.'

Trevor smiled knowingly, nodded slowly. 'It certainly is.'

I tilted my head in the direction of the black Chevy. 'That's your car, right?'

'Yeah.'

'You don't see a lot of those around,' I said. 'They haven't made that model for quite a few years, have they?'

'I don't suppose so.'

'And yet, with so few of them around, I saw one at the mall last night, at Midtown? Same color as yours, parked right by the doors.'

Trevor swallowed. 'Huh.'

'And then, I was heading out of town, towards Oakwood? And I saw another one, just like it, same color, everything.'

This time, Trevor didn't even have a 'huh' to offer.

'Isn't that a coincidence,' I said. 'That I'd see two cars exactly the same, in different places, in the same evening.'

I couldn't see his eyes behind the sunglasses. Couldn't tell whether he was looking away.

'Trevor, take your glasses off for a sec.' He sat rigidly, made no move to do what I'd asked. 'Trevor, just for a second.'

Slowly, making a ritual of it, he removed the glasses. I eyed him intently.

'I would never want anyone, ever, to hurt my daughter, or scare her, or cause her any trouble.'

'Of course not,' he said, not looking away.

'I just wanted to make myself clear about that.'

'Absolutely,' he said.

'So we understand each other,' I said.

'We do,' Trevor said. I nodded my farewell to him, and moved on.

'And don't buy my son booze anymore,' I added.

'Whatever you say.'

I turned and walked away.

I had two surprises shortly after that.

The first: As I walked by Trevor's Chevy on the way back to my car, there, asleep in the backseat, was Morpheus.

The second: After I got back in the Virtue, I turned onto Crandall. Looking up the street, I noticed the back end of a big black Annihilator SUV. Trolling past my house, slowly, then picking up speed as it headed north.

TWENTY-THREE

'Can we watch TV while we eat?' Paul asked, standing next to me in the kitchen.

I was putting linguine on three plates, and had put the salad in a glass bowl with a couple of tongs.

'I don't know,' I said. 'You know how your mother feels about having the TV on during dinner.'

'Yeah, but Mom's not here. And *The Simpsons* is on.'

This did raise an interesting question. Did we have to play by Sarah's rules if Sarah wasn't home? Especially when *The Simpsons* was on?

While I made up my mind, I said to Paul, 'Call your sister, tell her dinner is ready.'

Without moving an inch away from me, Paul shouted, loud enough to make the wine glasses on the kitchen shelf ring, 'Angie . . . Dinner . . .'

'Thanks,' I said.

She'd gotten home the same time as I had, headed straight up to her room and closed the door. I'd barely had a chance to ask whether she was dining with us, and she'd had only enough time to grunt 'Yes.'

Paul grabbed the TV remote as he took his plate to the table. We have a TV in the kitchen, which we often have tuned to the news. He turned it on, flipped through a few channels until he had the one he wanted.

'Oh . . .' said Paul. 'It's, the one where Homer's an astronaut.'

That was, I had to admit, a pretty good one. Particularly the part where he eats the potato chips, rotating in zero gravity in a parody of the space station docking maneuver in *2001: A Space Odyssey*. 'Okay,' I said, pulling up a chair.

And besides, I wanted something to take my mind off things, so that I'd stop obsessing about Trevor, Lawrence, what Angie was doing visiting Trixie and that Annihilator.

It wasn't like there was only one Annihilator in the city, or even one black one. Lots of people owned them. The sports editor had one, in yellow. There was a guy around the block had one, in green. And I'd seen plenty of black ones since they started coming onto the market a couple of years ago. It was probably the most popular color.

So a black Annihilator driving up my street was not reason to panic. A black Annihilator racing up the driveway, plowing through the front of the house, that would be reason to panic.

Half an hour earlier, when the SUV had made a left at the next cross street on Crandall, I had tromped on the accelerator. When the Virtue didn't take off with as much speed as I'd hoped, I literally leaned forward in the seat, as if rocking my own body would give the car some momentum. If I could get close enough to the truck, maybe I'd know for sure that it wasn't the one from the other night. For example, if I could read the license plate, that right there would be all the evidence I needed to relax. The plates on the one that had chased me and Lawrence, that rammed into Brentwood's, had been obscured.

And it had had deeply tinted windows. If the SUV that had driven up Crandall and past my house had regular windows, windows that allowed you to see who was driving and riding inside, that would be even more proof that it was not the same vehicle.

I got to the cross street, turned left. The SUV was gone.

I sped up to the next intersection, glanced both ways. They weren't hard to spot, these Annihilators, towering above all the other traffic as they did. But I didn't see one, not in either direction. So I drove home, slightly rattled, as always.

Once I'd put the linguine into a pot of boiling water, I went up to our bedroom and dumped the contents of the Gap bags I'd left there that morning onto the bed. I ripped off tags, put the shirts and 'loose fit' khakis on hangers.

Angie'd seemed a bit hurt in the morning that I hadn't been wearing any of my new purchases, so I stripped down, pulled on a new pair of boxers, buttoned up one of the new shirts, and stepped into a pair of tan khakis. Loose fit was right. Although they hugged my waist well enough with a belt, I had all this room in them, certainly compared to the jeans I'd been wearing. They were loose enough in the leg that I might be able to pull them on over shoes, a dressing routine I had abandoned around the same time I'd stopped making peanut butter and marshmallow Fluffernutter sandwiches. I admired myself briefly in the mirror, then went down to finish dinner preparations.

I was waiting for Angie to show before taking my first bite of dinner, and when Paul shoveled in a mouthful of pasta, I gave him a disapproving look.

'She could be forever,' he said. 'I think she's making herself look beautiful, and I can't wait that long.'

'What's she getting all dolled up for?'

'She's probably going out.'

I glanced at the fridge, where we've posted an oversize calendar and an erasable marker for keeping track of everyone's activities. For tonight, Angie had scribbled, 'Lecture.'

'She has a lecture tonight,' I said.

'Yeah, but I think she's going out after.'

I leaned in, as though we were conspirators. 'She seeing someone?'

'Hey, don't ask me. You want to know what she's up to, ask her. I know how this works. I squeal on her, then you'll be pumping her for information on what I'm doing.' He twirled some more linguine onto his fork. 'I'm going to eat this. I don't care that she's not here.'

'How about you?' I asked. 'You seeing someone?' Paul put the fork into his mouth, his cheek poking out on one side. I went on, 'What about, what was her name, Wendy?'

Paul shook his head. He chewed a few times, washed the linguine down with some water. 'I never went out with her. Besides, she has a butter face.'

'A butter face?'

'Yeah. Everything's great, but her face.'

Angie came in. She'd changed her clothes, refreshed her make-up, brushed her hair. She looked – and as her father, this gave me the usual sinking feeling – terrific.

'Oh sure,' she said, looking at her brother eat. 'Start without me, why don't you.'

'Hey, you owe me. Dad's asking me questions about your personal life, and I'm refusing to testify'

She glared at me. 'Is that true?'

'No,' I said.

'I need a car tonight,' Angie said, deciding that my attempt to pry information from her brother was too routine an occurrence to get worked up about. 'I've got an evening lecture. And I really want to take the Virtue. I want to drive down with the sunroof open.'

'I don't know, honey,' I said. 'Why don't I just give you a lift down? I could pick you up after.'

'I don't believe this. We have this huge discussion, about how we need a second car, about how you don't want me taking public transportation home late at night from school, and we get a second car, and you want to drive me down? When Mom isn't even here, and there's no one else who even needs the second car but me?'

Paul stopped chewing, looked at me, smiled. 'Yeah, Dad.'

How could I make my case, that it would be better if I drove her, if I couldn't bring forwards my evidence? Was I going to tell her that I'd spoken to Trevor a short while ago, had tried as best I could to intimidate him, suggested that he back off and leave her alone?

She'd kill me.

And what of this cryptic warning from Lawrence, that someone might be after me? Did that mean anything, really? And if it did, did it have anything to do with Angie? That seemed unlikely.

Okay, maybe I could tell her that I'd seen a black SUV cruising up the street, that it looked like a very mean SUV, just like the one used by those guys who—

I was going to sound like a crazy person.

'I guess you can have the car,' I said. 'I've just got a lot on my mind. It's this story I've been working on, and I guess it's got my danger radar working overtime.'

'Yeah, like we could tell the difference,' Angie said, sitting down. 'But Dad, everything is okay. Honestly. You just need to chill.'

'I took the car into Otto today,' I said. 'I think he's fixed the starting problem. I haven't had any trouble with it since he worked on it. But if you have any problems, *call me*.'

'Terrific,' Angie said. 'Oh, and I need five dollars for parking.'

'Hold on, pardner,' I said. 'There's no way you're getting parking money out of me. Not now that I know what I know.'

'Aw, come on, Dad. They may have closed off the walkway. I might actually need to pay to park this time.' Pleading.

'You showed Dad the secret way out?' Paul asked.

'I don't know what I was thinking,' Angie said.

'What a dope.'

I wasn't denying her the money on principle alone. By not giving her the five dollars, it was pretty much guaranteed that she'd sneak out of the Mackenzie grounds by using the route she'd showed me the day before. Which meant she'd be pulling out onto Edwards Street.

I could wait for her there.

If her lecture started at 8:30 p.m., as the note on the fridge calendar seemed to indicate, it would let out around 9:30. I could be in position, around 9:15, making sure, just one last time, that Trevor was no longer following her around.

And if he was, even after my chat with him, I'd have to think of something even more drastic. Maybe even a call to Detective Trimble.

'So, you doing anything after your lecture tonight?' I asked.

'Maybe,' said Angie. 'Might see some friends.'

'Hey,' I said, like I'd just remembered something, 'you ever keep in touch with any of your friends in Oakwood?'

Angie gave me a look that seemed to suggest a bad smell was coming off me. 'God, no. I don't keep in touch with anyone from out there.'

I nodded. 'I thought you kept in touch with some of your Oakwood friends. You did do two years of high school there.'

'No, Dad.'

'How about other than students? You keep in touch with anyone from out there?'

'Dad, when would I even get out there?'

'You don't actually have to go out there. You could talk, in one of your chat huts.'

Paul and Angie looked at each other. 'Chat huts?' they said.

'Rooms. Chat rooms. You know what I mean.'

This set them both off. Paul knocked on the table, said to Angie, 'Hello, may I come into your chat hut?'

Angie was laughing so hard she had tears in her eyes. 'Sorry, no, this is a chat *condo*.'

'Oh, excuse me . . .' He wanted to get off another line, but he was laughing too hard to do it.

'Okay, enough already,' I said.

Angie, pulling herself together, said, 'No, Dad, there's no one from Oakwood I keep in touch with through my chat huts.' Paul slid out of his chair and onto the floor, clutching his side.

Should I ask her flat out? Ask her why she'd been to visit Trixie? But if I asked her now, I'd have to come clean on the whole surveillance thing, and if I did *that* now, I wouldn't be able to take one last crack at it tonight, to see whether I'd scared off Trevor for good.

So I let it go.

'I've got stuff to do,' Angie said, taking her plate to the counter. Paul managed to get up and followed her out of the kitchen.

'I have to lie down,' he said, still laughing. 'I think I'm gonna die.'

Shortly before eight, Angie went downstairs, shouted, 'See ya . . .'

I scrambled out of my study, where I still tried writing books but more often built models of spaceships and other science fiction kitsch, like my recently completed models of the Green Hornet's Black Beauty, and Gort, the iconic robot from *The Day the Earth Stood Still*.

'Hey,' I yelled down to her. 'You be careful tonight, okay?'

'Oh . . .' Angie said. 'I just realized. I don't even have a key for the new car.'

'Two came with it,' I said. 'Hang on.' I'd left the second one in a dish where I keep spare change on top of my dresser. 'Come to the bottom of the stairs.' She did and I tossed it down to her.

'You look good, by the way,' Angie said, doing up the buttons on her blue coat.

'Huh?'

'Your clothes. I meant to say something at dinner, but got kind of distracted. They look good on you. Are you wearing new boxers?'

'Check it out,' I said, undoing my belt, turning around, and dropping my khakis halfway down my butt.

'Oooh . . . The ones with the chili peppers on them . . .' Angie said. 'You're hot, Dad, very hot. But please pull your pants back up.'

I obliged.

Angie had her set of keys out and was slipping the one for the Virtue onto her ring. She was having a bit of trouble with it, so I came down and got it onto the ring for her.

And then I gave her a hug. 'Remember, call me if you have a problem, and don't do anything stupid, okay?'

Angie smiled. 'You mean, don't do anything you might do?'

'Exactly.'

She gave me a hug back. 'I love you, Daddy.'

And then she was gone.

TWENTY-FOUR

I was keeping an eye on the clock. I figured I'd head out a little before nine, be down by the university twenty minutes after that, at the latest. Paul was up in his room doing, to my astonishment, some homework. I popped my head in, told him I'd be going out in a few minutes.

'Where?' he said, still looking at something he was writing on his computer screen.

'It's a work thing.'

'A work thing?'

'Yeah.'

He shook his head. 'I dunno. I think I need more details.'

I was heading down the hall when the phone rang. Paul grabbed the extension in his room, and when he didn't call me immediately, I figured it was for him. But by the time I was down to the kitchen, he shouted, 'Dad . . . Phone . . . It's Mom . . .'

I grabbed the kitchen extension. 'Hey,' I said.

'Isn't it awful about Stan?' Sarah said.

'What?' I said. 'What about Stan?' I assumed she was speaking of Stan Wannaker, the *Metropolitan* photographer. I don't think either of us knew any other Stans.

'Oh my God, you haven't heard? I'm up here, at this thing, and I hear about it, and you haven't?'

'Okay, you're connected. You're plugged in. What happened to Stan?'

'Okay, you're not going to believe this. He's dead.'

'What?'

'Stan. He's dead. I just found out like five minutes ago. We're all coming back home tonight. Nobody's in the mood for any more of this touchy-feely management bullshit after something like this has happened.'

'He did that thing with me yesterday,' I said, feeling very cold. 'That photo shoot at the car auction. What happened to him? Did he have an accident?'

'Someone beat him to death. Right behind the *Metropolitan* building, in the lot where the photogs park. Someone smashed his head in his car door.'

I didn't say anything. I was numb.

'I mean, the guy goes all over the world, Sarajevo, Afghanistan, fucking Iraq, and he gets killed in our parking lot.'

'There was that guy,' I said.

'What guy?'

'Remember, when I called you from the auction, and Stan got in a fight with this guy? Uh, I know his name, Cheese Dick told me.'

'How would Cheese Dick know anything about this?'

'He was looking at Stan's pics, the ones he took yesterday at the auction, and he said, he said, "Oh yeah," he said, "that's Barbie Bullock." That's what he said. That's what he said the guy's name was.'

'Barbie Bullock?'

'Yeah. Stan wasn't even taking a picture of him, I guess Bullock was just kind of in the picture, you know? And he tries to tear Stan's camera away from him.'

'Did he know who Stan was?'

'I mean, I don't know, it's possible. Stan did tell him he was a photog from *The Metropolitan*. Told him to back off.'

'Did Dick Colby say who this guy was, this Barbie guy?'

'He works for Lenny Indigo, that guy that got sent up? That name mean anything to you?'

'Sure. We ran the trial coverage. Sears covered it. He ran half the criminal operations in town.'

'That was the guy.'

'I'm calling Dick, telling him this. He'll be doing the story on it, he'll need this info, he can pass it on to the cops.'

'It doesn't make any sense,' I said. 'I mean, if it was Bullock, there's no way he'd be able to get the film back at this point. He'd have to know Stan would have turned it in by now. It's been a day and a half.'

'Maybe he didn't want the film,' Sarah said. 'Maybe he just wanted to get even.'

I glanced at the clock. It was after nine. I had to get going. 'Listen, Sarah, call Dick, tell him what I told you.'

'He may want to call you, get more details.'

'He'll have to call my cell. I'm going out.'

'Where? What do you have to do?'

'Look, I'll explain everything to you when you get home.'

It was the wrong thing to say. 'What do you mean, explain it to me when I get home? Whenever you say something like that, there's something I need to know right now.'

'Honestly, things are fine.'

'Is this about Paul?'

'No.'

'Then it's about Angie.'

'I didn't say that.'

'What's going on with Angie?'

I took a breath. 'First of all, I'm still worried about this Trevor Wylie. The guy's been following her around.'

'Look, so he runs into her once in a while. That doesn't make him a stalker.'

'No, Sarah, he's actually following her around. In his car. When Angie goes someplace, he follows her.'

'Oh God. Angie told you this?'

'No, she—' And I stopped myself.

'If she hasn't told you, then how do you know he's following her? Zack? Hello? Are you there?'

'It's a hunch,' I said.

Sarah got very quiet. 'No, not with you, it wouldn't be a hunch. Zack, how do you know Trevor's following her?'

'I might have seen him, you know, following her.'

'How did you see that? Good God, Zack, have you been *following* him?'

'No,' I said, emphatically. 'I have *not* been following him. Not exactly.'

'Then who have you been following?'

I said nothing.

'Zack? Tell me you're not following your own daughter.'

I guess I must have hesitated.

'Oh my God,' Sarah said. 'You're unfuckingbelievable.'

'It hasn't been to be nosy,' I explained. 'I just wanted to be sure she was okay. It wasn't like I was trying to invade her privacy, that was never my intention, you have to understand that.'

'Zack . . . Honest to God . . . I don't believe you . . . I mean, sure, we need to know what our kids are up to, but we don't trail them around like they're common criminals. Why don't we just put cameras in their rooms? Bug their phones? Open their mail? Get search warrants for their lockers at school?'

Actually, I thought there might be some merit in all those things, but didn't mention it.

'I never meant to do it, to follow her around. In fact, in some ways, I wish I'd never started this. There are some things you simply don't want to know.'

There was a long pause at the other end of the line. Finally, Sarah said, 'Like what?'

'No, no, never mind, you're right, it's a violation of Angie's privacy. Who she goes out with, who she goes to visit, that's entirely her business.'

'Who's she going out with? Who did she visit?'

'You hear yourself?'

'For fuck's sake, Zack, what's happening?'

What the hell, I thought. 'Do you have any idea why Angie would go out to Oakwood to visit Trixie? Late at night?'

'She's visiting *Trixie*? Trixie Snelling, of Whips and Chains Inc.?'

'Yeah. I don't remember them being friends when we lived out there.'

'No, neither do I. You were the only one, having coffee all the time, being all neighborly. It got to where I wondered if I should be checking you for rope burns.'

I ignored that. 'You think Angie's getting career counseling? Because, you know, if she were choosing between, I don't know, bank president and dominatrix, I'd probably go with bank president.'

'I have to get home.'

'Not a word to her about this,' I said. 'I don't know how to bring this up, not without letting her know that I've been following her around. Which reminds me, I have to get going.'

'Is that what you have to go do? You're going to follow her *tonight*?'

'Just to make sure Trevor's not on her tail anymore. I had a word with him today.'

'You spoke with him?'

'It was just a friendly conversation, that's all. Friendly, but firm. The kid's weird, Sarah. He's not as harmless as you think.'

'Go, then,' she said. 'Just go, let me know what you find out.'

'Okay. And tell Dick about this Barbie guy.'

'Why do they call him that, anyway?' Sarah asked. I told her about the thug's rumored collection. 'But doesn't a grown man who collects Barbie get teased a lot?' she asked.

'Sounds like you'd only do it once,' I said.

TWENTY-FIVE

I flew out the door, jumped into the Camry, and zoomed through four yellow lights on the way downtown to the Mackenzie campus. I approached the university from the north side, found Edwards Street, and drove along slowly until I found the covered walkway that came out by Galloway Hall.

It was dark, and I slunk down a bit in my seat, keeping my eye on Angie's secret exit. I didn't have to worry too much about her spotting the Camry. It was such a generic-looking car, and there were so many of them on the market, that it didn't attract any attention.

It was almost 9:30 p.m. As it turned out, I'd parked right in front of a diner, and I was craving a coffee. Was there time to run in? I decided to chance it, since I could keep an eye on the back of Galloway Hall from inside the diner.

I got out of the car, went up to the cash register that was at the head of the counter, and ordered coffee to go from a fat guy in a white apron. I had it in my hand and was back sitting in the Camry before there was any sign of Angie.

As I sat in the car my thoughts kept returning to Stan. It was unthinkable, that he could be dead. There was already so much going on inside my head, so much that had happened in the last twenty-four hours, so much that I had seen and found out, that I felt incapable of processing this latest information.

I was on overload.

Suddenly, bright light shone out of the walkway. It intensified, and then the Virtue emerged, tentatively, because the passageway was so narrow. It was like seeing the car come out of a sideways mail slot. I could barely see Angie behind the wheel, but I could make out the silhouette of a second person in the car, in the passenger seat. Was it a boy or a girl?

And then there was no need to guess. The passenger door opened, and the same boy I'd seen her with the night before got out and unhooked the chain that prevented Angie from driving over the curb and onto Edwards. Once Angie had pulled the Virtue through, the boy put the chain back in place and returned to the passenger seat.

But before Angie pulled away, her friend leaned over and kissed her on the cheek. And then she turned her face into his, and then their arms were around each others and I thought, Does she even have the car in park? Or is she making out while the vehicle's in drive, her foot pressed down on the brake?

I probably wouldn't tell Sarah about this part. I didn't think I'd ever tell anyone about this part.

Thankfully, they broke it up after a few seconds, and Angie drove west. I pulled in behind them, my coffee stowed in the cup holder, staying a few car lengths back. When I could, I let another car slip in between us, just so long as I could keep the Virtue in sight.

Angie had the roof open and waved her right hand out in the breeze. The boyfriend put both hands through the roof, and then, for a couple of seconds, there were four hands waving in the breeze.

'Jesus Christ, Angie . . . Keep your hands on the wheel . . .'

All parents, I decided right then, should spend some time following their teenagers who've recently acquired their driver's licenses. For sure, I was going to find a way to have a word with her about this.

The Virtue turned left, went a couple of blocks, turned right, then left, then straight on for a few miles. They wandered into the Heights, where the city's movers and shakers lived in their million-dollar homes. Then they double-backed down to the waterfront, then over by the university again. It didn't take long to figure out they were simply joyriding, taking a spin in the new wheels.

And when's the last time, Angie, you made a contribution for gas money? At least, in a hybrid, she was wasting less of it. But it galled me, how kids could drive around for hours without any thought whatsoever to who was footing the bill. And another thing—

Shut up, Zack. Like you never did anything like this when you were a teenager.

The important thing was, throughout this tour of the city, I hadn't seen Trevor Wylie or his dog Morpheus or his black Chevy once.

Maybe he'd tried. Maybe he'd followed her from home down to the university, and had been waiting for her at the main entrance, where you picked up your parking ticket. Maybe Angie'd outsmarted him by sneaking out the back way. I wish I knew. If he was still out there, but lost, it meant he'd probably be back at it tomorrow night. But if he'd packed it in, if he'd realized he was pushing a bit too hard, maybe I could let my guard down a bit.

My cell phone rang.

I struggled to drag it out of my jacket pocket and didn't have a chance to see who was calling before I hit the button and put the phone to my ear.

'Hello?'

'Dad?'

My heart skipped a beat. 'Angie,' I said. 'Hi, sweetheart.'

Ahead of me, I could see through the rear window of the Virtue that she had a phone to her ear.

'Where are you?'

'Huh?'

'I called home, got Paul, he said you were out.'

'Yeah, I'm just out doing a few things. What's up, honey?'

'Okay, you know how I told you I had this weird feeling, like maybe someone was following me?'

I felt a bit queasy. 'Uh-huh.'

'Like, I know it's nuts, but I've had this car following me for a while, and I'm starting to get that feeling again.'

'Okay. Uh, tell me more.'

'Yeah. It's some piece-of-crap car, sort of like our Camry? We've just been cruising around, trying out the new car, and I've noticed this car keeps showing up in my mirror.'

'Can you see that it's a guy?' I asked.

'Well, not exactly, I'm just assuming, you know? Like, how many female pervs drive around at night following people?'

'Okay,' I said. 'Don't panic. Maybe it's not the same car. Maybe you're just on edge or something. It's

222

probably my fault. I've freaked you out with all this talk about what happened to my friend Lawrence.'

'Maybe . . .' Angie didn't sound that sure.

'Is he following you right now?'

I saw Angie glance at her rearview mirror.

'Yeah, he's still there, Dad. I'm afraid to stop anywhere or anything, in case it's some creep and he jumps out or something.'

I eased up on the gas, hung a right down the first street I came to.

'Oh, hang on,' Angie said. 'False alarm. He's gone.'

'Are you sure?' I said. I'd wandered off into some industrial neighborhood. I had absolutely no idea where I was.

I could hear Angie let out a long breath. 'Yeah, yeah, he just turned off. I guess I was just imagining it, you know? Maybe I was thinking it was Trevor or something. It'd be just the sort of creepy thing he'd do.'

'Yeah,' I said. 'Pretty creepy.' I let out a long breath of my own as I pulled the car over to the side of the road and stopped. 'Maybe it's time for you to head home,' I suggested.

'I'll be home soon,' Angie said. 'We're just going to grab something to eat at McDonald's.'

'We?'

'Me and a friend.'

'Don't be *too* late, all right?'

'Dad, I'm eighteen, okay? Don't worry. Actually, I'm going to drop by the house in a bit. I have to grab a book for my friend, and then I'm going to give hi—'

'What was that, honey?'

'I said I'm going to drop by the house to pick up a book for my friend, and then I'm going to drive my friend home.'

'Yeah, well, you say hello to *him* for me,' I said.

'Dad, I never said, I mean, I didn't—'

There was a siren whoop behind me. I glanced in my mirror and saw the flashing red light of a police car.

'Honey,' I said, 'I'm going to have to go.'

'Okay.' She sounded relieved that I was ending our conversation. 'Talk to you later.' As we each disconnected, I rolled down my window for the approaching police officer.

'Good evening, Officer,' I said.

'License and registration, please,' he said.

'Sure, of course.' As I opened the glove compartment I said, 'Did I do something wrong, Officer?' Where the hell was the registration? The inside of the glove box looked like a wastebasket.

'You know you got a tail light out?' he asked.

Oh yeah.

'No,' I said. 'You're kidding. I had no idea. The car was just in for a service, probably a month ago.' I'd located a small plastic dealership binder. Surely the registration must be in there. I rifled through. Bingo . . .

'Whatcha doing around here?' the officer asked, using a flashlight to examine the registration paper I'd just handed him.

I didn't even know where 'here' was. 'I guess I'm a bit turned around,' I said.

'I'm waiting for your license,' he said, still hanging on to the registration. 'So, you're lost?'

'Yeah,' I said, shifting in my seat to get at the wallet in the back pocket of my new khakis. The pants were so new, it was hard to wriggle my wallet out. 'Maybe you can help me. I'm looking for the closest

McDonald's? Is there one near here?' I finally freed it and got my license out.

He told me where he thought I'd find the closest one, then started scribbling down some information from the two official bits of paper I'd handed him.

'I'm going to have to write you up,' he said. 'And you're going to have to get that brake light fixed. Tomorrow.'

'You bet,' I said.

He spent about another five minutes with me, handed me my ticket, and went back to his car. I turned the car around, hoping that a U-turn here wouldn't amount to another infraction, and drove back to the street where I'd lost track of Angie a few minutes earlier.

If I could drive past the McDonald's, I thought, see that she was okay, make sure that Trevor's car was nowhere to be seen, I'd pack it in. I'd head home.

The McDonald's was right where the cop said it would be, its golden arches visible nearly a mile away. It was on the left, and as I approached I put on my blinker, pulled into the turning lane. I figured I'd do a sweep through the parking lot, and if everything looked satisfactory, I'd call it a night.

I drove down the west side of the restaurant, the windows to my left, the cars parked on an angle to my right. And there was the Virtue, pulled in between a couple of small cars, neither of which was a black Chevy.

I swung around the back, where there were only a few cars parked, probably those belonging to employees, then down the east side, past more cars.

Everything looked okay.

There were two vehicles ahead of me, the first of which was turning left, across two lanes of traffic. I put on the brakes and waited to pull out.

I happened to glance left, and saw Angie and her boyfriend seated at a table, Angie's back to me, the boyfriend looking in my direction. I saw him raise his head as my car went by, saw him say something to Angie. As she turned to look outside, I was able to pull ahead another car length so she wouldn't be able to see my face.

Let's go, let's go, let's go, I thought, trying to will the car ahead of me to get moving.

And then, all of a sudden, he was at my window. Angie's boyfriend, banging on the glass.

'Hey . . .' he shouted. 'Hey, you . . .'

I wanted to pull ahead, but the car ahead of me was still in the way, and there was no place to go.

'I want to talk to you . . .' he shouted.

I was going to have to fess up, come clean. Admit to my daughter what I'd been up to. I hit the button, brought the window down.

'Why the fuck you following us around?' he demanded.

'Listen,' I said, trying to be calm. 'You don't understand. I'm actually—'

And then his fist was coming through the open window, so fast it was a blur, and then it was connecting with the side of my head.

TWENTY-SIX

I tried to avoid his fist, but it came through the window so quickly, I didn't have time to react. And when you're sitting in a car, seatbelted in, you don't have a whole lot of room to bob and weave. So Angie's boyfriend was able to strike the side of my cheek, just below the temple, bouncing my head sideways a foot or so, and it was like a rocket had exploded in front of my eyes.

He was still yelling at me, I'm not sure what, exactly. I heard 'pervert' in there somewhere, and 'fucking asshole', I believe, and somewhere off in the distance, a more familiar voice, screaming, 'Cam . . . What are you doing? Stop it . . .'

I figured the odds were that Angie had no inkling who her boyfriend Cam was punching out, and I now preferred to keep it that way, which precluded jumping out of the car and attempting to beat the shit out of Cam, who was probably twenty or more years younger than I and in a hell of a lot better shape, and would probably have beat the shit out of me, anyway.

So I hit the gas and swerved right, narrowly missing the bumper of the car in front of me, squeezed between it and a fence, and hung a hard right out of the parking lot, nearly cutting off a Corvette, whose driver had to slam on the brakes to avoid rear-ending me. The resulting squeal was no doubt heard a couple of blocks away.

I floored it. I wanted to put as much distance between me and that McDonald's as quickly as I could. So intent was I on making a fast getaway that I had yet to notice how much the side of my face was smarting.

My heart was doing a fair bit of pounding, too. Once I'd put a few blocks between myself and that McDonald's, I pulled into the parking lot of a 7-Eleven, swinging the car around so that I was facing the street, and turned off the ignition. I switched on the interior light and adjusted the mirror so I could get a look at the side of my face. It was already turning blue and puffing out.

I went inside and bought a small bag of ice, got back into the car and pressed the bag of cubes against the left side of my face. I wasn't sure which hurt more, the punch, the ice, or my pride, but it was all I could do not to scream as I held the bag against the bruise.

I hoped Cam wasn't the one Angie was thinking of spending her life with. This was not the best way to kick off a relationship with a future son-in-law.

Maybe, if I could keep the side of my face from swelling up too severely, Angie wouldn't even notice it the next time she saw me, which now probably wouldn't be until the next morning. I could go home, turn off the lights, and get into bed, an ice bag on my pillow. By morning, the swelling would be gone, although there was a good chance I might have a terminal case of freezer burn.

But if the bruise was still there, Angie would put it all together the moment she saw me. And there'd be so much explaining to do. Maybe it was better to come clean now, to wait up for her, to admit that I was an asshole, but that sometimes fathers worried about their daughters so much that they simply couldn't avoid being assholes. We're hardwired that way and—

'Fuck.' I was suddenly taken by the image of a black Chevy rumbling past the 7-Eleven, heading in the direction of the McDonald's.

I hadn't caught a good look at the driver, but the car was pretty unmistakable. Black, rusting out around the wheel wells, sitting low in the back.

I turned the key, reached down to the shift to put the car into reverse and back out of the spot. But I couldn't will my foot to move from the brake to the accelerator. Part of me was not prepared to continue the chase.

The fact was, I'd not been doing a very good job of this. My surveillance skills were rotten. I'd been busted three times. Twice by Angie – the first time at the mall, the second time when she phoned me while I was tailing her. And then, again, at the McDonald's. By Angie's friend, Cam.

I was not cut out for this kind of work.

It occurred to me that Angie would probably be fine as long as she had Cam with her. The guy was a better bodyguard than I. Maybe it would actually be a good thing if Trevor found Angie. Then he'd have to deal with Cam, whose powers of intimidation might exceed mine.

I pulled the ice away from my face, looked in the mirror. We're talking horror show.

I decided to swing by the paper on the way home.

I had to find out more about Stan Wannaker. There was this growing sense of connectedness between the events of the last forty-eight hours. Stan was dead. Stan had had a run-in with Bullock at the auction, which Lawrence and I had also attended. Lawrence was in the hospital, victim of a savage attack. There seemed to be these threads connecting one event to another, but I couldn't quite make them out, couldn't see how they joined.

The moment I stepped into the newsroom, I could feel the grief. There was none of the usual banter, people calling to one another across the desks asking if they wanted a coffee or to go across the street for an after-shift drink. Even though there were probably forty or more people in the room, it was hushed, only the sounds of computer keys being tapped to break the silence. There were small huddles of people, two over in this corner, three over here, talking in hushed tones.

Some people were crying.

I stopped at my desk, signed in on my computer to see whether I had any important messages, which I did not, then clicked over to the news basket where all the cityside stories were submitted and edited.

I was able to find the story the paper was running on Stan, in the next day's edition, on the front page above the fold, under the byline of Dick Colby:

Stan Wannaker, the *Metropolitan*'s award-winning photographer who faced danger in nearly every world hot spot, was found murdered in the newspaper's parking lot yesterday.

'It is a terrible loss,' said Bertrand Magnuson, the paper's managing editor. 'He was a wonderful, talented individual who embodied everything that the *Metropolitan* stands for.'

Wannaker, 44, started at the paper 27 years ago as a copy boy. Senior photo editor Ted Baines remembers how Wannaker spent a lot of time, as a kid, hanging around the photo desk. 'He wanted to be a shooter from the moment he walked through the doors. He was a natural from the beginning.'

In recent years, Wannaker had covered the fall of the Berlin Wall, the war in Yugoslavia, the U.S. invasion of Afghanistan and the war in Iraq.

'It's unbelievable,' said Mr Magnuson, 'that, after all he's been through, Stan would be a victim of violence outside our very building.'

Police say Wannaker's attacker, or attackers, did not appear to have been motivated by robbery. None of his cameras had been taken, and he still had his wallet and credit cards on him, as well as a sum of cash.

'It appears,' said a police spokesperson, 'that he was targeted for who he was, not what he might happen to be carrying.'

Police say Wannaker evidently was forced down onto his knees, then his car door was slammed on his head.

I looked up from the story, feeling as though I might be sick. Nancy, who was clearly putting in a very long day, was standing there.

'Hey,' she said. Her eyes were red.

'Hi,' I said. 'Sarah called me. She heard about it before I did. She's coming back tonight.'

Nancy nodded.

'They got any idea who did it?' I asked.

Nancy shook her head no. 'Colby's still making calls. He's out with the cops now. They think he was targeted, but it might still be just one of those crazy random things. Maybe some kids, high on something, they spotted him and went berserk.'

'I suppose.'

'I mean, it's not like some guy in Iraq or Afghanistan is going to come over here to settle some grudge.'

'Maybe it was someone closer to home,' I offered. Briefly, I told her about Stan's fight with the guy at the car auction the day before, and how Sarah was supposed to pass on what I'd told her to Colby.

'She did, I think. Colby said he might be giving you a call later.' She shook her head. Her chin quivered. 'A bunch of us are going across the street after the edition closes. Hoist a few to the memory of Stan. You want to come?'

'Yeah,' I said. 'I'd like to do that. Let me get a couple of other things out of the way.' I turned a bit in my chair, and it was then that Nancy noticed the side of my face. She reached out tentatively, like she was going to touch it, but stopped.

'What happened to you?' she asked.

'Wrong place at the wrong time,' I said.

I phoned Mercy General to see how Lawrence Jones was doing. Still critical, but he hadn't lost any ground. Even managed to say a couple of words, the nurse told me unofficially. I asked her to tell him Zack was asking about him, and that I would come by and see him tomorrow if they had him out of intensive care.

My story on Lawrence was in the Metro section. They'd cut about a third out of it. While it seemed like a big deal to me, Lawrence Jones was no house-hold name. Maybe if he'd still been a cop, and had been hurt while on duty, the story would have gotten better play. The thing was, at this point, I didn't give a rat's ass what they did with the story.

Eleven o'clock rolled around, and reporters and editors started slipping on their coats, moving almost in slow motion, as if they were off to Stan's funeral and not just a booze-up to remember him.

Someone called over to me. 'Zack, you joining us?'

I nodded, and was slipping my own jacket on when the cell phone in my pocket started ringing.

'Hey, Dad,' Angie said.

'Sweetheart,' I said. 'You okay?'

'Well, yeah, I'm fine, but the car isn't.'

'What's wrong?'

'I just dropped off my friend? We swung by the house, and I got this book, and then I had to go over to Eastland? To drop off my friend?'

'Okay, you said that.'

'And when I came back out to the car, it wouldn't start. You said to call if I had a problem.'

'Why did you have to turn off the car, if you were just dropping your friend off?' I asked.

A short pause. 'I just went up, just for a second, to my friend's apartment. And when I came back, it wouldn't start. It went kind of *ning, ning* but nothing happened after that.'

Nice going, Otto.

'Hang on a sec,' I said. I called over to Nancy, who was heading to the elevator, and told her I wouldn't be able to make it, that my daughter had car trouble. I was on my feet now, still talking to Angie, but headed for the back stairs, which would get me out to the car faster since they opened out onto the parking lot.

'I might fade in and out a bit,' I said, going down the concrete stairwell.

'You what?' Static, Angie's voice breaking up.

'Just hang on, I'll be out in the parking lot in a second.'

'The what? I can't hear you, Dad. You're breaking up.'

I went down the steps two at a time, burst through the metal door at the bottom and out into the lot.

'Hear me better now?' I said.

'Yeah, that's good.'

'So, where are you?'

'I'm on Eastland, a couple blocks up from that Dairy Queen? You know the one, where we'd stop sometimes after I had ballet lessons?'

I had an instant image of her, maybe ten years before, at one of her recitals, in pink tights and leotard, dancing across the stage. It had been a few years since Angie had taken ballet, but I knew the place where we would often stop for an ice cream or a chocolate shake on our way home.

'Okay, I think I know,' I said, getting out my keys and getting into the Camry. 'So, how far up?'

'There's a big apartment building, and some angled parking out front, and I'm pulled into one of those spots. On the right side, as you're coming up?'

'Okay. It should take me ten minutes, maybe, tops. You okay there?'

'I guess.'

'You all alone?'

'Yeah.'

'Just sit tight then, lock the doors. I'll be able to find you, and if I can't, I'll call you back. And if I can't get the car started, we'll call the auto club, get it towed to Otto's so he can have another look at it.'

'Okay. Can you still talk to me, Dad? Can you keep talking to me while you drive up?'

'Sure, sweetheart.'

'This person, that I gave a lift to?'

'Yeah?'

'Well, it was a guy.'

'You're kidding,' I said. 'I don't think I ever would have guessed.' I was out of the *Metropolitan* lot now, heading west. 'Someone from class?'

'Yeah, we've got a couple lectures together.'

'He got a name?'

'Cam. Cameron.'

'That's a pretty weird name. Cam Cameron.'

'Stop teasing, Dad. It's Cam, short for Cameron.'

'Oh. Okay. Nice guy?'

'I think so. This really weird thing happened, tonight. Like, he wanted to protect me.'

The side of my face throbbed. Did I really want to ask about this? It would seem strange for me not to. 'What happened?' I sounded very concerned, and realized, very shortly, I was going to have to explain the bruise on the side of my face.

'You know when I called earlier, and thought I was being followed by somebody, and then the car turned down another street?'

'Sure.'

'So Cam and I, we went into this McDonald's, and he sees the car go by the window, and he like freaks out, goes out after the guy.'

'You're kidding. You sure it was the same car?'

'I didn't even see it go by, but Cam, he's positive, he knows cars way better than I do, I can't tell one from another, and he goes out there and starts screaming at this guy, and hauls off and punches him right in the head.'

'Did you get a look at the guy?' I asked Angie. Not that it was going to matter for very much longer.

'No. I was just running outside when the car took off. But how many guys would do that for you. Huh? I mean, I couldn't believe he did that for me.'

'Sounds like an amazing guy.' Neither of us spoke for a moment as I sped down the road. 'You know, Angie, I think I should probably tell you—'

'Oh God, you're not going to believe this.'

'What?'

'It's him.'

I held my breath. 'Who? Who is it?'

Angie's voice became more distant. She was talking to someone else, not to me. 'Hey, Trevor. What are you doing here?'

'Hey,' I could hear him say. 'I was going by, saw you, thought I'd say hi. What are you doing way out here? You out here all alone? Because you shouldn't be out here at night all alone.'

'Just a sec, I'm talking to my dad. Dad, you hear that?'

'Trevor's there,' I said, getting a very large knot in the center of my chest.

'Yeah. Pretty amazing, huh? Hang on, I think he wants to talk to you.'

'Why does he want to talk to—'

There was some rustling as the cell phone changed hands. Trevor said, 'Hello, Mr Walker. How are you doing this evening?'

'Trevor, what are you doing there?' I eased my foot down a little harder on the accelerator.

'I saw Angie, out here all alone, and thought I should stop. It's not good for her to be out here all alone.'

'I'm on my way there right now, Trevor. So you don't have to worry about a thing.'

'I'll stay here with her until you get here.'

'Sure, Trevor. Give the phone back to Angie.'

More rustling. 'Hey, Dad.'

'You okay? He acting weird or anything? He's not threatening you or anything like that?'

'God no. He's just . . . hang on. Trevor, I have to talk to my dad.' There was a distant humming sound. 'I just put the window up. How does he fucking find me everywhere? He's so creepy, Dad. I've had it. Maybe you're right. Maybe we need to do something to keep him away from me. He's really freaking me out.'

'I know. I think we have to do something about him, honey. This kind of thing can't go on.'

'It's so, it's just so, I don't know. What the . . . Did you already call the auto club or something?'

'No. Why?'

'Some big truck or something's stopped behind me. He's got me boxed in. Well, not exactly. I mean, if the car doesn't work, I guess I can't really go anyplace.'

I swallowed hard. 'What kind of truck? Is it a tow truck or something?'

'No, hang on.' I could hear her shifting in her seat. 'It's like an SUV or something, a huge black one.'

'Angie, did you say a black SUV?'

'Yeah, but bigger than normal ones, you know?'

'Is it an Annihilator?'

'I don't know. I don't know what these things are called. Hang on, somebody's getting out, coming up to the window. Whoa, there's a couple guys getting out.'

'Angie, what do they look like?'

'Look like? I don't know. Just some guys in black jackets, that's all.'

'Angie, don't open the window, and lock the doors.'

'I think they just want to ask me some questions or something. What a hoot, if they think I can give them directions, what with my sense of direction—'

'Angie, don't put down the window . . .'

'Yeah?' I heard Angie say to someone.

Then I heard some muffled voices. And then Angie again: 'Hey, back off, man, I'm not getting out—'

'Angie . . .' I shouted into my cell.

'Get your fucking hands off me, ass—'

'Angie . . .'

Then I heard my daughter scream. And then the line went dead.

TWENTY-SEVEN

Immediately I phoned Angie's cell back. It rang four times, and then she answered.

'Hi, it's Angie.'

'Angie, Jesus, what's going—'

'I can't take your call right now, so feel free to leave a message.'

I figured I was at least another three or four minutes away, and I was driving the Camry in ways it was not designed for. I was taking the corners so quickly the car was drifting into four-wheel skids, and at least once the back wheel slammed into a curb before I was able to regain control.

The Dairy Queen where we used to stop after ballet class was up ahead. That was Eastland, and Angie had said the apartment building where she'd stopped was a few blocks up from there. I rounded the corner, heard a noise that sounded like a hubcap breaking free of the wheel and spinning off towards the sidewalk, and floored it.

It couldn't be the same guys. It didn't make any sense for it to be the same guys. What would those guys in the Annihilator, the ones who destroyed Brentwood's, the ones Lawrence and I chased through the Midtown Mall, want with Angie?

How did the lines cross? How did the dots connect? They didn't. They just didn't.

Maybe it wasn't even the same guys. Maybe it was a different bunch of guys, in a different black SUV.

But that didn't make the situation any better. Regardless of who they were, Angie sounded like she was in a lot of trouble.

And what about Trevor? Did he have something to do with this? He shows up, and all of a sudden this crew arrives? Had he set her up? Had he led them to her?

'Be okay,' I said aloud. 'Be okay, be okay, be okay.'

Up ahead, on the right, an apartment building. And cars parked, nose in, on an angle, out front. But the street out front was empty. No SUV. No guys. No Angie.

Wait. Someone was stumbling out beyond the back of the parked cars.

Trevor.

I slammed on the brakes, right behind our Virtue. Trevor was using the back of the car to support himself. I don't even remember putting the car in park or taking off my seat belt. But I was out, running around the front, headed for Trevor.

'Where is she?' I screamed. 'Where's Angie? What have you done with her?'

I lost it.

I grabbed Trevor by the lapels of his long black coat and swung him around, slamming him into the side of the Camry, shaking him violently, putting my face into his. I was consumed by rage and fear, and at that moment, I had only one thing in mind, which was to beat this kid to a pulp. Even the mild-mannered among us can, given the right set of circumstances, be overtaken by pure fury.

Why hadn't I stopped him earlier? I shouldn't have worried about Angie's feelings, about embarrassing her. I should have come down on this kid like a ton of bricks at the first hint of trouble. You trust what your gut tells you, Lawrence had advised me. And my gut had told me from the beginning that Trevor Wylie was trouble.

I felt a force traveling through me, into my arms, headed for my fists. I knew what I was about to do. I was going to destroy the face of this kid who'd somehow arranged for this terrible thing to happen to Angie.

I let go of his lapel with my right hand, still leaning up against him and holding him against the car, and brought my arm back, squeezed my fist, got ready for the first strike.

'No . . .' Trevor screamed. 'I didn't do this . . .'

There was something about his expression, the fear in his eyes that appeared to have already been there before I'd started throwing him around. There was no fight in him.

My fist was suspended in the air, still ready. 'Where is she?' I shouted. 'Where's Angie?'

If I have ever, in my entire life, seen anyone who looked more frightened, I don't remember when it was. For a moment, I thought he was in shock, his mouth open, his eyes frozen wide.

'Where is she?' I said again, not shouting this time. I brought my right arm down to my side.

'She's gone,' he whispered. 'They took her.'

I glanced over at the Virtue. The driver's door was open, Angie's keys in the ignition. I looked up at the apartment building, saw a few people come out onto their balconies, look through their windows, wondering what all the commotion was. Somewhere in that building, I figured, lived Angie's boyfriend Cam, but if his apartment wasn't on the side that faced the street, he wasn't going to be aware of what was happening out here.

I went back to Trevor. Only now did I notice that he had a dark gash on the side of his head. A patch of his hair was clotted with blood.

I put everything I had into trying to speak calmly.

'Trevor, who took Angie?'

'They, they were in this truck. They tried to start the car, and it wouldn't start, and then they took her.'

I was reaching into my jacket for my cell. I was getting ready to punch in 911.

'No . . .' Trevor screamed. Hysterically. 'No, no, don't call the police . . .' He was grabbing for my phone, trying to get it out of my hands.

'Trevor, I have to call the police. Let go of my phone.'

'No . . . They said they'd kill her . . . Don't call the police . . .' He was wide-eyed, grabbing me by the shoulders.

I was starting to reassess things. Not about calling the police. That was the only thing that made sense. I was reassessing Trevor. His panic was genuine. It was possible that he really had nothing to do with this.

'Trevor, you have to calm down. We have to get the police working on this right now, as fast as we—'

'They said they'd know.'

'What?'

'They said they'd know. That they have people in the police, people who tell them things, that if you call 911, if you call the cops, they'll know, and then they'll kill Angie.'

Kill Angie.

The world spun. For an instant, I had an image of Angie, sitting in a highchair, laughing, chocolate pudding on her nose.

'That's crazy,' I said, freeing the phone from Trevor's grasp. 'They're just bluffing.'

But I found myself hesitating, knowing I should punch in 911, but not quite able to do it.

'No.' Trevor shook his head violently. 'They weren't bluffing. I could tell. They said they'd know instantly.'

I swallowed. 'Trevor, tell me what happened. From the beginning.'

'They jumped out of a truck and they took her. They tried to start the car, but it wouldn't work, so they took Angie instead.'

'What do you mean? That doesn't make any sense.'

'Shut up . . . Just shut up . . . Let me try to explain.' There were tears running down his cheeks now, and when he went to wipe them away, his hand brushed his hair. When he saw the blood on his hand, he looked at it, baffled, then touched his head where his hair was black.

'We have to get you to a hospital,' I said.

'It's okay,' he said. 'I don't even feel it.' He sniffed, took a couple of breaths, tried to compose himself. 'I came over to say hi to Angie, and then this truck, this SUV pulls up.'

'Did you notice what kind it was?'

He blinked, tried to think. 'One of those army kinds of ones. An Annihilator, I think.'

'Tinted windows?'

'Uh, I, I guess. I think so.'

'Okay, go on.'

'So it stops behind Angie's car, they've got her blocked in, and they tell her to get out of the car, and she starts fighting with them.'

'Go on.'

For a moment, I thought maybe this wasn't happening, that it was a dream. That I wasn't here, in the middle of the night, on a street I rarely traveled, prying information out of some teenage stalker, whose motives I was still unsure of, about the whereabouts of my daughter. It simply couldn't be happening.

'And one of them, he gets in the car, but he can't get it to start, and he starts going nuts, banging on the steering wheel and swearing and everything. By now, there are people coming out, up there, on their balconies, and one of the other guys says they have to get out of there, they're attracting too much attention.'

'Okay.'

'So another one says, he says, "Grab the girl, we'll trade her for the car," and they drag Angie, right into the truck.'

Another flash. Angie, five years old, first day of kindergarten.

'But the one guy, I think the one who'd been driving, he comes up to me, he says, "You know the man owns this car?" And I said yes, and he says, "Is this his daughter?" and I said yes, and he says to tell you, he says, if you want your daughter back, get this car running and bring it to him, and he'll give you Angie back.'

'Take it to him? Where am I supposed to take it?'

'He didn't say.'

'He didn't say?' Now I had my hands on him again, ready to shake him until his head fell off. 'You didn't ask him where I'm supposed to fucking take the car?'

'He said he'd be in touch . . . Jesus . . .' Trevor pushed me away. 'He'd be in touch soon. And then he told me not to call the cops, to tell you not to call the cops, that they've got people in the force, that if you call the cops they'll know. And then' – he put his hand back to his blood-soaked hair, touched it tentatively – 'I guess, I think he hit me.'

'Why did they want the car?' I asked him. 'Why do they want this car?'

'I don't know . . .'

We were both quiet for a moment. I moved closer to Trevor, forced him up against the side of the Camry again. I leaned in.

'Trevor, I want you to be very straight with me. Did you have anything to do with this?'

'What?'

'Did you have anything to do with this? Because if you did, I swear to God . . .' I felt my fist forming again. 'Do you know who took Angie away?'

'Are you kidding? Are you out of your fucking mind? Do you have any idea what Angie means to me?'

'No,' I said. 'Suppose you tell me.'

Almost whispering. 'I love her. It's like I told you, about how certain people are meant to be together. That was supposed to be us. And I let them take her away . . . I wasn't able to do anything about it . . .' And he began to weep.

I took in a few breaths of night air, looked at the cell phone in my hand. Could I really believe this story, that if I called 911, somehow Angie's abductors would find out? Isn't that what any crook might say to keep you from doing the sensible thing? Come up with a bullshit story like that?

But then, what if it was true?

Either way, I was gambling with Angie's life. Wasn't it better to gamble with the cops on your side? Didn't that improve your odds?

'Don't do it,' Trevor said, seeing me stare at the phone and reading my mind. 'Don't do it, Mr Walker. They had me convinced. I don't want them to kill Angie.'

I looked up at the stars, as if hoping for some sort of divine guidance. 'Trevor, is there anything you're not telling me? Anything else I need to know?'

'I could help you,' he said. 'I could help you get the car to them. I could help you get Angie back.'

Somehow, I felt I'd benefit from more professional assistance.

'I don't think so, Trevor. You need to get out of here, go home, get someone to take care of that head of yours. You need to—'

And the cell phone in my hand rang.

I pressed the Send button. 'Yes?' I said.

'Hi, Daddy.' I could hear driving sounds in the background, tires humming on pavement.

'Angie . . . Angie, are you okay? Where are you?'

'Daddy, they want to talk to you.'

I heard the phone being moved about, then another voice.

'Mr Walker,' a man said.

'Yeah.'

The man coughed, cleared his throat. 'We need to arrange an exchange.'

TWENTY-EIGHT

'Whatever you want, it's yours,' I said. 'I just want my daughter back.'

'That's the spirit,' the man said. He coughed again, and hearing that, along with his voice, I was reminded of the man Stan had confronted at the auction.

'Looks like we can help each other out here,' he said. 'I'm guessing, given that you don't seem all that surprised to be hearing from me, that you've had a chance for that young lad to bring you up to speed.'

'I just got here, yeah. He's been filling me in. And he's hurt. His head is bleeding.'

'Gee, that's awful. If you could get me his name and address, I'll send him a card. I'm guessing he told you that calling the police would be a big mistake. Did he tell you that?'

'Yes.'

'And it looks to me like you took his advice, am I right?'

How could he know that, I wondered, unless it was true? That he did have contacts in the police?

'That's right,' I said. 'We don't need to involve the police in this. Not if it means you'll let go of my daughter.'

'That's what I like to hear. Cooperation. It's what makes the world go round. So, you know what it is we want?'

'You want the car.'

'That's right. That's one shitty car, I have to say. We could have been spared all this trouble if the fucking thing had only started.'

'It does that sometimes. I thought it was fixed.'

'You should have bought from a dealer. You'da got a warranty. Buying from these auctions, it's not the way to go.'

'Evidently not.' So he was the guy. From the auction. And, I was willing to bet, the guy who had slammed Stan Wannaker's head with a car door.

'If there hadn't been so many people gawking from their balconies, maybe we could have figured out a way to tow the thing, or get a truck, but people, they're awfully nosy, you know?'

'Sure. Can I talk to Angie?'

'Uh, no. You heard her a minute ago, you know she's fine. And as long as you do what I ask, and don't call the police –' he made a sickening throat-clearing noise that sounded like a toilet flushing '– she'll stay that way.'

'What do you want with this car? I'm guessing it's more than the gas mileage.'

'Hey, that's funny. That's good. Yeah, you're right, that's not the reason. Let's say it's carrying a shipment that we'd like to have. Shit, once we remove it, you can keep the fucking car. Only a candyass faggot would drive something like that around anyway.' He laughed, and then there was some other laughing in the background, and then he lapsed into a coughing fit.

'Hang on,' he said, almost apologetically. 'I need a sip of something.' I heard him smack his lips. 'I got kind of a tickly throat.'

I said, 'Once I get the car started, where do you want me to bring it?'

'I'll call you in an hour, let you know where. That should give you enough time to get that sucker running. Maybe it needs a jump.'

And he hung up.

'What did he say?' Trevor asked. 'How's Angie? Did you talk to Angie? Have they hurt Angie?'

'Shut up,' I said.

I got out my wallet, hunted for my auto club card, found it and punched in an 800 number.

'My car's dead,' I told the woman. 'This is a huge emergency. How long will it take someone to get here?' I gave her my location.

I could hear her clicking away on a computer. 'They should be there in no more than half an hour, sir.'

Too long, I thought. But I told them to come, anyway, and put the phone into my jacket.

'I can't wait,' I said, and got in behind the wheel of the Virtue and turned the key. I figured, sometimes it worked, sometimes it didn't. I might get lucky.

Nothing.

'Mr Walker,' Trevor said, 'why don't you let me—'

I turned on him. 'Go home.' I didn't even know whether Trevor had a home, but I knew he didn't belong here with me.

He shook his head. Quietly, he said, 'No, I'm not leaving. I can help.'

'I don't see how, Trevor.'

He paced briefly, then said, 'I'll be right back, I

have to go to my car, make sure Morpheus is okay.' He ran off. What a dipshit, I thought. My daughter's missing, and he's worried about his dog.

I got out of the car, put my hands on the roof, felt the cool metal on my palms. An idea began to form in my head. If the auto club got here soon enough, or if I could get the car going myself, there was another errand I was going to run before I got my next call from Angie's abductor, who was, it seemed clear now, Barbie Bullock.

The voice on the phone matched the bully from the auction, and Cheese Dick Colby had identified him from Stan's photos as Barbie Bullock, the man in charge of Lenny Indigo's operations ever since Lenny got sent away to cool his heels for a while.

So why would Bullock have been at the auction? Hadn't I noticed him looking at the Virtue around the time I first laid eyes on it? Was it possible he was there to buy it, that he was planning to bid on it, but pulled out after he'd attracted so much attention getting into a fight with Stan?

Who had this car belonged to before the feds had seized it?

And what was in it that the feds had missed, that Bullock figured he could obtain for himself by buying it?

I reached down below the driver's seat and pulled the lever that popped the trunk, I swung the trunk lid wide, scanned inside. It was clean. I lifted up the flooring, exposing the spare tire, a tire iron, and a jack. The painted metal was shiny under there, never having been exposed to the elements, and the spare tire was one of those mini ones that lasted only a few miles until you could get a proper replacement. The tread was jet black, never touched pavement.

I ran my fingers under the bottom side of the tire, looking for I didn't know what. But there was nothing there. I reached into other nooks and crannies, but couldn't find a thing. I opened the back door, reached into the seat crevices, got down on my knees and peered under the two front seats.

There was nothing to be found. Of course, if whatever I suspected was in this car had been in plain sight, then the feds would have found it before selling it to me and Lawrence, wouldn't they?

'What are you looking for?' It was Trevor.

'Whatever's in this car. There's got to be something in it somewhere.'

Trevor said, 'I bet they took her thataway.' He pointed west.

'Is that the way they drove off?'

He nodded. 'I'll bet, if we drove around, maybe we could find them.'

I was back on my feet again. 'Trevor, it's a big city. They could be anywhere. We're going to have to wait for their call. They'll tell us where to go.' I slammed the doors shut on the Virtue. 'If there's something in that car, I don't know where the hell it is.'

'Did you look in the rocker panels?' Trevor asked.

'The what?'

'I don't know what they are, but in *The French Connection?* That was where they hid all the bags of heroin. Down in the rocker panels.'

'I don't think I've got the equipment on me to start cutting through sheet metal,' I said, just as my cell phone went off in my jacket pocket. 'Hello?'

'Walker, Sarah left me a message, and Nancy says you may know something about this thing that happened to Stan.'

'Who is this?'

'It's Colby. The edition is gone, but I'm still working this thing. What did you have for me?'

'Nothing, Dick,' I said.

'What do you mean, nothing? I was told you had something that connected this thing that happened to Stan to this Bullock guy. Am I wrong about that?'

'I can't do this now, Dick.'

'Excuse me? One of your coworkers gets his head smashed in, and you're too busy to help us find out who did it? What kind of asshole are you?'

'The worst possible kind, Dick.' I hung up.

I decided to give the Virtue another try. I got behind the wheel again, turned the ignition.

Nothing.

What was it Otto had said? Something about a short in the transmission? I turned the key again, far enough that it allowed me to unlock the automatic transmission lever between the seats, and moved it from park, down through reverse and neutral and the lower gears, and back again. I did it a couple of times, then turned the key all the way forward in a bid to turn the engine over.

Bingo.

'Yes . . .' I shouted. 'Yes . . .'

The hell with the auto club. As long as the Virtue was running, I could keep it running. All I had to do now was move the Camry, which was parked behind the Virtue. I bailed out of the Virtue, jumped into the Camry, backed it up ten feet, effectively blocking in a couple of other people's cars, then got back into the Virtue.

I looked at my watch. It had been twelve minutes since Bullock's phone call. I still had better than forty-five minutes before he called again. I had at least one vital errand to run, and one important phone call to make.

'Where are you going?' Trevor asked me through the open window.

'I'm going to try to get my daughter back.'

'Let me come with you,' he said.

'I can't.'

Trevor's expression grew more frustrated. 'I might be able to help you. I, I might be able to figure out where they went.'

'Trevor, I'm going to ask you this one last time. Is there something you're not telling me?'

He pressed his lips together, looked one way and then another. 'No,' he said. 'No, there isn't.'

I put the car into reverse, and Trevor said, 'Give me your cell phone number. In case I find out anything, I can call you.' He had his own out and in his hand. I told him my number, which he immediately entered into his phone's memory bank. If I had a chance sometime, if we all got through this evening alive, I'd have to get him to show me how to do that.

'I have to go,' I said, backed out of the spot, and headed for Lawrence Jones's apartment.

As I drove I tried to put the pieces together. If Bullock wanted the Virtue back, how did he know where to find it? I hadn't even bought the car at the auction. Lawrence had handled everything. He'd done the bidding, he'd written the check, he'd filled out the forms—

Jesus.

And only a few hours later, someone had gone to see Lawrence Jones, torn his place apart, and left him for dead.

Probably after they'd found the check I'd written him, for the same exact amount as the check he'd written at the auction.

And the one I'd written him would have had my name and address on it.

Which explained why Lawrence, at the hospital, had tried to tell me that they were after me, too.

What were the odds that the kind of people who'd stab Lawrence for a name and an address were going to let me walk away with Angie once I'd let them search the Virtue for what they believed was hidden inside it?

This was not something I was going to be able to handle alone. I had to have help. I needed the police.

But if Bullock had his own people on the inside, or had members of the force on his payroll, how could I call the police and be confident they wouldn't pick up the phone and call Bullock?

The answer was not to call the police. The answer was to call a single policeman. A police detective. One who might feel he still owed Lawrence something, who might want to make up for a mistake he'd made in the past.

As I sped toward Lawrence's apartment, I dug into my back pocket and struggled once again to get out my wallet. In there, I found Steve Trimble's official business card. I let the wallet drop onto the passenger seat, glanced at the home number on the card, memorized it, and dropped the card next to my wallet. Now I dug out my phone and punched in the number with my thumb, keeping my other hand on the wheel.

'Hello?' A woman.

'Is Steve there?'

'May I tell him who's calling?'

I told her.

'Just a minute.'

I waited a good half minute. Finally, 'Walker, what do you want?'

'I haven't got a lot of time to explain this, Trimble, so listen carefully. Some people from Lenny Indigo's gang, one of them Barbie Bullock I think, have kidnapped my daughter. They've told me that if I call the police, they'll know and they'll kill her. They say they're willing to trade her for my car, which I bought yesterday at a police auction with Lawrence, and which I'm guessing has drugs hidden in it someplace. Am I going too fast?'

'I'm listening,' Trimble said.

I could see Lawrence Jones's building up ahead. I hung a right before I reached it, drove into the parking lot out back.

'They're calling me back in about half an hour, to tell me where I'm supposed to meet them. I don't think I can make this exchange alone. I need someone watching my back, and since I'm too scared to call 911 and tip these guys off, I'm calling you. And there's something else you should know.'

'What's that?'

'I think these are the people who tried to kill Lawrence.'

There was a pause at the other end of the line. 'Where will we meet?'

My mind raced. 'How fast can you get to Lawrence Jones's apartment?'

'Fast.'

'I'm in that part of town. I could meet you out front. I'll be in one of those Virtue hybrid cars. It's silver.'

'Ten minutes.'

'Okay.' I paused to catch my breath. 'I appreciate this.'

'Ten minutes,' he said again, and hung up.

I pulled up behind Lawrence's old Buick. I was hoping the cops, during their investigation of the attack on Lawrence, wouldn't have bothered to search this car. After all, it had bogus plates on it. There was a chance that if they'd rooted through any car, it would have been Lawrence's Jag, whose plates were legit.

I popped the Virtue trunk, left the engine running, walked around back and lifted up the cover I'd looked under only a few minutes earlier. I grasped the tire iron, walked over to the passenger side of the Buick, and smashed in the window.

I pulled up the lock button, opened the door, and reached for the handle to the glove box. It was locked. Using the thin end of the tire iron, I wedged open the glove box door.

I reached into the back, past the ownership manuals and tattered maps, and found the gun Lawrence had used to fire at the Annihilator two nights earlier. I took it out, and a roll of masking tape that was tucked in there. I knelt down next to the car and rolled up my right pant leg as far as my knee and taped the gun around my leg. I didn't much care what Bertrand Magnuson might think of this.

And if it hadn't been for Angie's suggestion that I go for ample-fit khakis, I wouldn't have been able to roll the pant leg back down over the gun so easily.

TWENTY-NINE

I waited around front, on the sidewalk, by the door to Lawrence Jones's apartment. I'd driven the Virtue around, left it running. Its excellent fuel economy was a major blessing now that I was afraid to turn the damn thing off.

Five minutes later, Trimble arrived in the same unmarked four-door Ford he'd shown up in the night before at this same location.

He put down his window, motioned me over. 'Have they called yet?' he asked.

I shook my head. 'Any moment now, I'm guessing.'

'You said these people are the same ones who tried to kill Lawrence,' Trimble said, his eyes narrowing.

'Yeah. I think that's how they got to me, they found my address on a check in Lawrence's apartment, maybe in his office or his wallet, I don't know. All this time, I've been worried about some kid following my daughter around, not knowing there was someone else out there a whole lot more dangerous.'

Trimble got out of the car. 'Are you going to be okay?'

I looked into his face. 'I'm not okay now, I can tell you that much. These people, what they did to Lawrence, you really think they're going to let me walk out of wherever they are, with Angie, alive?'

Trimble's face didn't move. He chose not to answer.

'Do you really think they've got cops on the inside?' I asked. 'Because maybe, if there are some you trust, we should get more help?'

'I've been thinking about that,' Trimble said. 'There've been rumors for a while that Lenny Indigo had people on his pad, in the force. But there's never been anything hard, nothing concrete. But more than once, we get ready to make a move on him, and he knows before we get there. We're lucky we finally nailed him a few months back, but his organization is still alive and kicking.'

'That's Bullock? This Barbie Bullock guy?'

'Yeah. His real name's Willy, or William. You'd think a nickname like Barbie would be hard to take, but if people are going to be calling you Willy, maybe it's not that much worse. He's dangerous, but not always a hundred per cent competent. He's been struggling lately to prove to Indigo that he's got what it takes to run the organization. And there's talk that he does have informants on the force. And I don't think right now would be the best time to test that theory, not if you want to get your daughter back in one piece.'

I didn't like his choice of words. They conjured up an image I had to push out of my mind.

'This Bullock, is he the kind of guy who'd kill Angie, even after I give him the car?'

'Look, let's just take this a step at a time. You got a paper, pen, ready for when they call? Because they're probably going to give you an address, where to make the trade.'

I patted my jacket, where I had my pen and the reporter's notebook. Almost as if my tapping had activated it, my cell phone rang inside my coat. I grabbed for it nervously, nearly dropping it as I pulled it from my pocket. I was sweating, and a drop had rolled down into my right eye, stinging and causing me to blink.

'Okay,' said Trimble. I had my thumb poised over the button, ready to take the call. It had now rung twice. 'Just take it easy. Listen carefully to what they have to say.' He eased his head up close to mine. 'I'm gonna listen in. Okay, go.'

I pressed the button and put the phone to my ear, tilting it out a bit so Trimble could hear the person on the other end.

'Hello,' I said, breathlessly and a little too fast.

'Hey,' said Sarah. 'Where the hell is everybody?'

I let out a breath. Trimble cocked his head to one side, looked at me, asking the question. I mouthed, 'My wife.'

'What?' I said. 'Are you home?'

Trimble had moved his head away. This was a call he didn't need to hear in detail, but he had some input just the same. He was shaking his head, indicating that he didn't want me to tell Sarah anything about what was going on.

The fact was, I didn't want to tell her anything. First of all, the longer we spoke, the greater chance there was I'd miss the call from Bullock. And second, I might not be able to persuade Sarah not to call the police. She had every right to know what was going on, but right now, I felt the fewer people who knew what was happening, the better the odds we'd get Angie back alive.

'I just got home. The drive coming back didn't seem all that long. Both the cars are gone, the only one here is Paul, and he says he doesn't know where anyone is.'

'We're out,' I said.

'Thanks very much, Captain Obvious. I figured that part out. Where are you? Where's Angie?'

I looked at my watch. The call could be coming any moment now. There would probably be a call-waiting beep. But would I be able to get to it fast enough? Would I press the wrong button and lose both calls, the way I usually did when I attempted to switch from one caller to another?

'I'm with Detective Trimble,' I said. Maybe I could include some elements of truth in my story. 'The one who's trying to find out who tried to kill Lawrence. He agreed to meet me, answer a few questions. Nancy wants me to do some follow-up, you know?'

'He's meeting you now? What is it, midnight?'

'You want to meet these people when they can see you, right?'

'And where's Angie? I tried her cell but couldn't raise her. You don't suppose she's gone out to see Trixie again, do you?'

And I was thinking that I would be thrilled, right about now, for Angie to be visiting with Trixie and being taught how to be the best goddamn dominatrix in the entire world. 'Uh, she called me earlier, said her battery was dying, but she was going to a late movie with some friends.'

'I can't stop thinking about why she might have gone to see Trixie. But I have a theory.'

The line beeped.

'Listen,' I said, hurriedly, 'go to bed I won't be home for a bit but if she's not home by the time I get there I'll wait up for her so don't worry about it I really have to go.'

The line beeped again.

'Okay,' said Sarah, who evidently hadn't detected the beep at her end. 'But don't you want to hear my theory about why—'

'Gotta go . . .' I said, hit the button, and said, 'Yeah?'

Trimble intuited that I'd taken another call. He leaned in again, and I tipped the phone toward him.

'Fuck, I was just about to hang up,' said Bullock on the other end. 'What, are you playing with yourself? This call not important enough to you?'

'I'm sorry. It was my wife. I practically had to hang up on her.'

'You tell her –' a short cough '– what's going on?'

'No. Of course not.'

'Because we don't want her calling the cops, do we?'

'No.' I swallowed. Trimble, in less than a whisper, said, 'Tell them to put your daughter on.' I said, 'Let me talk to Angie.'

'She's fine, don't worry about her.'

'If you want me to deliver this car,' I said, 'you'll put her on the line.'

Bullock sighed. 'Jesus, fine, whatever.' I could hear him say to someone else, 'Bring the girl over here, her dad wants to talk to her.' Then some phone fumbling.

Then: 'Daad.' It didn't sound like her. At least, it didn't sound like any Angie I knew.

'Angie, is that you?' I was trying, without much success, to keep the panic out of my voice.

'Hi, Daddy . . . I'm so tired.'

I could tell it was her now, but her words came out slowly, dreamily. 'Honey, what's wrong? Have they given you something?'

'I'm just really . . . really tired.'

'Have they hurt you?'

'Hmmm? No . . . Can you come and take me home? I want to go to bed. And I've got an essay to do, that's due tomorrow . . .'

'Honey, I'm coming to get you, I'm—'

'There,' said Bullock. 'You satisfied? She's fine.'

'What have you done to her? What the fuck is wrong with her?'

'Just relax. We just gave her a little something to calm her nerves, you know? Make her comfortable. Mellow her out. Sort of like Roofies.' The colloquial for the date rape drug. 'But we're honorable people. We wouldn't do anything improper.' He coughed, cleared his throat. It sounded as though he was taking a sip of water. 'So, you ready?'

'Yes.'

'We're at 32 Wyndham Lane. You know where that is?'

'No,' I said, but was writing down the address in my notebook.

'We're a few blocks south of the university, Mackenzie, down in there.' He gave me more detailed directions. It was, if I had my bearings right, a pretty nice part of town. Not quite the Heights, but filled with old, big homes.

'I can find it,' I said.

'Come up the drive, you'll see a three-car garage. Pull up to the center door.'

'All right.'

'And don't do anything dumb. No cops.'

'No cops,' I repeated. And Bullock broke off the call. I looked at Trimble. 'I guess this is it. You know

262

how to find this?' I showed him the address I'd written down, and he nodded.

Trimble said he would lead the way in his own car, but pull over a couple of blocks short of my destination, then hop into the Virtue with me. He moved pretty quickly in his souped-up unmarked car, and I struggled to keep up with him. He'd glance in his mirror, see that maybe he was losing me, and slow down a bit.

We entered a heavily treed residential area where the homes cost a hell of a lot more than they did on Crandall. Trimble found a spot to pull over, and I slowed and pulled up alongside so he could get in.

'We'll get a bit closer, then I'll get out before you pull in.'

I saw him check his gun in the holster that was belted to his waist, and I considered telling him that I had a weapon taped to my ankle, and then thought better of it. I knew what Trimble would say, that carrying a gun was best left to the professionals, and then he'd relieve me of it.

I didn't want that, although the tape I'd used to hold the gun in place pulled at the hairs on my calf, and smarted nearly every time I moved my leg.

We were on Wyndham now, and Trimble was reading house numbers. 'Okay, slow down, we should be almost there. Okay, stop.' He had his hand on the door handle and said, 'Try to stay cool. You may not think I'm around, but I'll be watching. Just do what they say, don't piss them off. We're going to get your daughter out of this.' He was looking me right in the eye. 'You believe me, right?'

'Yeah,' I said quietly. 'I believe you.'

'And I'd like to get the motherfuckers who put Lawrence in the hospital,' he said. 'Maybe we can all get what we want.'

And then he opened the door and ran up through the trees that shrouded the front lawn of a beautiful old Victorian house. In a moment, he was gone. I let my foot off the brake, slowly moved down the street, still looking for numbers, and then came upon 32. The number was visible below the light over the front door. Slowly, I turned into the drive, a cobblestone affair that rose from the street and wound down along the side of the two-story home, opening up around the back in front of a three-car garage that was separate from the house. There were two lights, one over the center garage door, and a second around the side over a regular door.

I brought the Virtue to a stop directly in front of the center garage, as asked, and found myself parked next to the black Annihilator, which was backed up to the garage on the right. The add-on bars that protected the front grill were scratched and bent out of shape, no doubt from being used to ram storefronts. Sitting there, engine and lights off, it was a fierce beast asleep.

I sat in the car, with the engine running, wondering what I should do next. Get out, go knock on a door?

But then, at the bottom of the door, a sliver of light appeared, and grew wider as the door slowly rose. Two sets of legs turned into full bodies as the door glided all the way up electrically. It was two men, neither of whom I recognized, dressed in black jeans and black leather jackets, dark sunglasses perched atop their noses like they were auditioning for bad guy parts in a Chuck Norris movie.

The one on the left looked at me and motioned me forwards with his index finger, the way the car wash guys do when they lead you onto the track. The two men stepped apart to allow me to drive the Virtue into the garage, and once the car was fully inside, I glanced into the rearview mirror and saw the garage door slowly slide back down.

THIRTY

One of the two guys in leather jackets – he was blond and lean and fit and kind of Swedish looking – approached my door. I put down the window and said, 'Should I turn it off? Once it's off, you never know whether it's going to start again.'

Blondie smiled. 'You can turn it off.'

I turned back the key, opened the door. It was a hell of a garage. You could have performed surgery in there. Banks of overhead lights, a spotless concrete floor. Across the back wall, cabinets and tools of the kind you might expect to see in an auto-repair shop. A machine that separated tires from rims, jacks you could push under cars, a broad counter where you could disassemble and fix things.

The Virtue was the only car in there. The right bay, which the Annihilator might have backed into if it weren't too tall for the door opening, was empty. And the left bay was filled, but not with any kind of vehicle. There had to be half a dozen long racks, the kind they push around the fashion district, of new suits, tags still attached. As you may have gathered, I am not particularly knowledgeable about matters related to fashion, but this looked like high-end stuff. Boss, Versace, Armani, apparently nothing from the Gap.

The other one, whose face looked like a relief map of the moon, littered with small round scars as though he'd barely survived chicken pox, came around the back of the car and up to the door. 'Keys inside?' Pockmark asked me.

'Yeah. In the ignition. Look, I'd like to see my daughter now.'

'I'll just bet you would,' he said. 'That's the boss's area. He'll be here in a minute.' To his blond friend, he said, 'You gonna pat him down?'

Something in my stomach did a somersault.

'Huh?' said Blondie. 'He's just some fucking doofus, not a cop or a detective or anything.'

'Yeah, well, check him anyway.'

I was sure, now, that the slight bulge at the bottom of my right pant leg was as obvious as a football. Maybe I could tell them it was a rare leg goiter. But when I glanced down, I realized it wasn't all that noticeable. Blondie came up behind me, told me to lift up my arms, patted under there without a great deal of enthusiasm, then reached into the inside pockets of my coat.

'Ooh,' he said to Pockmark. 'He's carrying a ball-point. He could have stabbed us to death. There's nothing else on him but a cell phone.'

'You should probably take that,' Pockmark said.

Blondie came around in front of me and held out his hand while I fished the cell out of my jacket and placed it in his palm. He took a few steps over to the counter and set it there. Pockmark had all the car doors open now, plus the trunk lid.

There was a crackly, staticky noise, and then a voice over a speaker. 'Hello?' It was Bullock. 'Is this thing working? Hello?'

Blondie walked over to a small intercom panel on the wall and pressed a button. 'Yeah?'

'Hello?'

'Don't press the button when I'm pressing the button, boss,' Blondie said.

'Okay, you there?'

'Yeah.'

'Don't press the button when I'm pressing the button,' Bullock said. 'This system is supposed to make things easier, asshole.'

'I know, I know.'

'I need one of you here to watch the girl,' Bullock said.

'I'll be right there,' Blondie said, taking his finger off the button and disappearing out the side door. A couple of minutes later, the door reopened, and in walked the man from the auction. Short, not much hair on top, but solid looking, like if you tried to push him over you'd need half a dozen other guys, or else you'd have to attach a bunch of ropes to him and pull him down like he was a Saddam Hussein statue. He was in another expensive-looking suit that didn't fit him all that well, bunched up around the tops of his shoes, the sleeves too long. I guessed he was one of those kinds of guys you couldn't fit off the rack, at least not the racks that were in that garage. He'd be wise to kidnap someone sometime who could do alterations.

He put his fist to his mouth, coughed and cleared his throat. In his other hand he carried a small glass bottle of juice, and took a sip.

'So, you must be Mr Walker,' he said, stepping closer to me but not extending his hand.

'And you must be Mr Bullock,' I said.

He looked surprised, and pleased. 'Hey, you know who I am. I guess the word's getting around, huh? You hear that?' He was talking to Pockmark now. 'He knows who I am.'

'That's great, boss.'

'I've been trying to enhance my reputation of late,' Bullock said to me. 'So you having heard about me, that's good.'

I was less sure. It might have been stupid, addressing him by his name. It was one more reason not to let us out of here alive. I knew who he was. Of course, I already knew where he lived, didn't I? Wasn't that enough knowledge to get me killed?

'I was at the auction, when you went ballistic on the photographer. Someone picked you out of those pictures later.'

Bullock shook his head, then waved his finger at me accusingly. 'That photographer was a very rude person. He disrespected me. And I can't afford that kind of thing right now, not from anybody.' He coughed, took another sip from the bottle.

'His name was Stan. I didn't know him real well, but he was a friend. He was a good guy.'

Bullock shrugged. 'It's not very nice to go around taking someone's picture without their permission. And the other thing is, he didn't turn out to be, in the end, a very good friend to you. Because if he hadn't been rude to me at that auction, and interfered with my business, chances are you wouldn't be here right now.'

I puzzled over that one a moment.

'It's simple,' Bullock said, noting my confusion. 'If we hadn't had that little scene and attracted so much attention, I could have hung around and bid on your car here myself, and believe me, I'd have outbid you no matter what. And then I'd have got the car, and had what I wanted from it by now. But when all that shit went down, I had to get out of there. You see, there tend to be a lot of feds around at a government auction.'

'I suppose so,' I said.

Bullock shook his head. 'Anyhoo, despite the odd setback, everything's coming together just as it should. We now have the car, that photographer's been taught a lesson, and soon we can all get on with our lives.'

Taught a lesson.

'So you've got the car,' I said, gesturing behind me. 'You've got what you wanted. Now let me and my daughter leave here.'

'Come along to the house,' Bullock said. To Pockmark, he said, 'With me.'

We walked out in single file, Bullock ahead of me, Pockmark behind. We went outside, walked about thirty feet to the house, entering through a back door that took us through an old but elegant kitchen and down a hall until we reached a heavy wood door. Bullock admitted us to what I guessed was his study or office.

I was not expecting to be nearly blinded by pink.

Three of the four walls were lined with shelves stocked with hundreds and hundreds of pink packages. Not stacked as they might be in a storage room, but on display, on parade. Tiny spotlights hanging from tracks bolted to the ceiling were strategically aimed at the boxes, and light shone off the clear plastic windows on the front of them. It was as though I had wandered into the Barbie aisle at Toys 'R' Us. There were hundreds of differently costumed Barbies, and Kens, and friends and associates of the Barbies and Kens, plus pink plastic houses and furniture and cars.

In the middle of the room, things were a bit more traditional. There was an oversize desk with a leather chair behind it, a couple more leather chairs and a leather couch up against one wall, just in front of one of the display shelves, and it was there that Angie sat, looking dazed. Bullock took a position behind his desk, nearly bare save for a phone, a small box that appeared to be the other end of the intercom system in the garage, and a bottle of water. Pockmark had taken a position next to Blondie, both of them by the open door, keeping an eye on me. I hadn't noticed this before, but he had a gun in his right hand, pointed, for the moment, at the blood-red carpeting.

'Sweetheart,' I said.

'Hey, Daddy,' Angie said tiredly.

I ran over to her, went to my knees, and took her into my arms. Feebly, she wrapped hers around me.

'Are you okay?' I asked her, holding her by the shoulders and looking into her weary eyes. She nodded slowly. 'I'm going to get you out of here as soon as possible, get you back home, okay?'

'Okay, Daddy.'

Bullock told Blondie to go back to the garage and start taking the car apart. I looked across the desk at him, but my eyes wandered. I couldn't help but look at the Barbies.

'I see you've noticed my little girls,' Bullock said, making a horrific phlegmy noise in his throat. He finished off the juice in the bottle, tossed it into a trash can by the desk, and reached for the water bottle.

'Yeah.'

'Your daughter and I, we were having a wonderful discussion about Barbies earlier,' he said. 'She said she sold most of hers at a garage sale.'

'A couple of years ago, I think.' I was about to say that she'd outgrown them, then thought better of it.

'Aww, that's really a shame. Terrible mistake. You should never sell off your childhood toys. You grow up, years later, you really regret it.' He sounded quite sincere.

'That's true,' I said, thinking, Would a guy engage you in conversation about his Barbie collection if he was planning to kill you?

'You agree?'

'I'm a bit of a collector myself. Not of Barbies, but science fiction memorabilia.'

'Oh . . .' said Barbie Bullock, all excited. 'You'll love this one.' He grabbed a pink box off one of the lower shelves. 'This is the *Star Trek* version of Ken and Barbie.'

He handed me the box. The dolls, still behind acetate and held in an upright position with small plastic twist-ties, were dressed for service aboard the USS *Enterprise*.

Ken was in a tan shirt and black pants, Barbie in a red minidress. 'From the original series,' I said. 'I recognize the get ups.'

'Yes, yes . . .' He took the box back from me, returned it to its spot on the shelf.

Angie shifted on the couch, rested her head on the arm. She was watching us like we were part of a dream she was having.

In addition to boxed dolls, there was the pink Barbie Volkswagen minibus, and a pink Beetle with an open roof for sliding Barbie and her friends in for a spin.

Barbie houses filled with Barbie furniture, Barbie cases, Barbie everything.

'Here are a few I'm most proud of,' Bullock said. I glanced at Pockmark, trying to judge from his expression whether he saw anything strange in all this. If he did, he was keeping it to himself.

'Here's Splashin' Barbie, with her own personal watercraft. And Winter Fantasy Barbie, Malibu Barbie of course, you couldn't not have a Malibu Barbie. And Cheerleader Flex Barbie, you can move her arms and legs better, so you can put her in all these cheering positions, which of course is never going to happen because I don't like to take the dolls out of the box.'

'Sure,' I said. 'Makes them more valuable that way.'

'Of course. It's nice, though, when you get the odd one that has been taken out of the box, so you don't feel restricted. You can handle it, play with it, that kind of thing. Here's my Barbie Romance Novel Gift Set, where she looks like one of those heroines on the front of a romance novel, not that I read those fucking things. And this here,' he held up a Barbie dressed in a skintight – or plastic-tight – black latex, wielding a whip, 'is Catwoman Barbie.'

Something for Trixie for Christmas, I thought.

'And check this out.' He handed me another box. Inside, Ken was dressed in a tuxedo, and Barbie's hair looked especially puffy and windswept. 'That's the James Bond 007 Ken and Barbie Gift Set.'

'I never knew,' I said. 'I simply had no idea.'

Bullock looked at me seriously. 'Can I ask you something?'

I wasn't in any position to say anything but 'Sure.'

'You think this makes me some kind of fag?'

'I really hadn't thought about it one way or another. As I said, I'm a collector myself, and so I try not to judge.' Fact was, I was not thinking 'fag'. I was thinking 'nut'.

'Well, I'm not a fag. I like pussy, ask anyone. Ain't that right?' he asked Pockmark.

'You bet,' said Pockmark. 'You love pussy.'

'That's right. You got time for a story?'

Slowly, I nodded.

'I had a sister growing up, she was two years older than me, my mom showered her with Barbies, you know? Kind of a shared interest. And when I was around six, and my sister, her name was Leanne, this would be when she was eight, she got hit by a car, you know. She died.'

'I'm sorry.'

'Yeah, so, this kind of cracked up my mom, she just kept on buying dolls and outfits and givin' them to me. And so I took them, built up a collection, to keep my mom happy. Like it was keeping my sister alive somehow, you know?'

'Where was your father?' I asked, genuinely wondering. It was hard to picture a dad standing by and watching this happen.

'Oh, him, he fucked off when I was like one. My mom raised me without that asshole. So my mom, she died a few years ago, too, she had cancer, but this collection, it's my way of keeping the memory of her and my sister alive.'

Pockmark said, 'Our boss here, he's sort of a tragic figure.'

Barbie Bullock nodded. 'Yeah, that's kind of what I am.'

'I can see that,' I said.

'The thing is, I've really kind of gotten into it over the years. It's good to have a hobby, right? Once, couple years back, we busted into a warehouse, thinking it was going to be full of stereos, and whaddya know, the place is jammed to the rafters with Barbie stuff. Must have been a shipment from Mattel to a toy store or something, it was like busting into Fort Knox by accident.'

He cleared his throat, like he was getting hoarse. He coughed twice, took a drink of water.

'Well,' I said, feeling the tape pull at the hairs on my leg. I was sure I'd put on enough to hold the gun in place. The last thing I wanted was for it to fall out of my pants. I didn't think there was a chance I could go for it, get it into my hand, before Pockmark had emptied his own gun into me.

My hope was that I wouldn't even need it. That Trimble would make an appearance at just the right moment.

'And there's my Wonder Woman Barbie. Check out her little magic lasso. And probably the neatest thing in my collection, Barbie and Ken dressed as Lily and Herman Munster, from that show in the sixties. You ever watch that?'

'Sure. And *The Addams Family*.'

'Oh, they have a set for that, too, but I'm still hunting for that one. I spotted one on eBay one time, but they wanted too much for it. And this here is Barbie's friend, Midge. See how her tummy's all big? She's pregnant, but the baby's just there with a magnet, you can take it off or put it back on again. Some nuts, they thought this doll was immoral, but I think it's perfectly natural, don't you?'

'Sure.' I paused. 'Do you think,' I said, gently, 'you might be good enough to let me and Angie walk out of here? I don't care anything about what you're up to here. Keep the car, I'll report it stolen, I don't care. I'm already pretty unpopular with my insurance company, so this shouldn't make things all that much worse.'

'As soon as we've had a look at the car,' Bullock said. 'As soon as we have what we're looking for. I'm guessing, when you bought that car, you had no idea what you were getting.'

'I still don't.'

'There's some fucking outstanding optional equipment on that car. A couple million in coke, to be exact. Tucked inside the door panels. When the feds arrested my boss, Mr Indigo, he'd recently brought that car across the border, hadn't had a chance to get his precious cargo out of it yet. And the feds, dumb fucks that they are, never even thought the car was used for smuggling. We'd have known had they found it, they would have entered the stuff into evidence, but they never did, so Mr Indigo, he gets a message to me, says get that car back, sell the stuff, because he's got a lot of lawyers to pay, you know? He's launching an appeal.'

He sipped his water.

'Tell you another story. Couple years ago, in California, guy goes to one of those government auctions, picks himself up a nice little car, real cheap, he's driving it for like six months, and he goes down to Mexico for the day, and he's crossing the border, coming home, they pull him over in some random search, and these drug dogs start sniffing, get a whiff of something. The fucking bumpers are loaded with coke, so they arrest the poor son of a bitch.' He laughed, which set off another short coughing fit. He took another sip. 'He tells 'em, "Hey, those aren't my drugs in the car, I bought it from the government, they left the drugs in the car." And the customs guys, they're laughing their balls off, you know? Like they hadn't heard that one before. So the guy, he goes to jail, he's suing the government now, fuck of a lot of good that's going to do him.'

'So you figured you'd buy the car at the auction, get the drugs, everything would be fine.'

Bullock nodded. 'The thing is, it's the greatest car for smuggling dope, you know? Little hybrid, environmentally responsible, you drive it, they think it's fucking Ralph Nader coming through customs. We sailed that car through, half a dozen times. When we weren't using it for that, Mrs Indigo liked to drive it around.'

'Uh-huh.'

'So, what with all that trouble with that cocksucking photographer, I bailed out. But we have a friend working at the auction place, and we checked with him later, found out who bought the car.'

Lawrence Jones.

'So we track down where the guy lives, and he's some kind of private detective. And we didn't find the car at his place, but guess what we did come across?'

Bullock reached into his pocket and pulled out a rumpled check. 'We look through his things, and we find a check, written to him, for the very same amount that he paid for the car. That's quite a coinky-dink, isn't it? And guess whose name was on that check?'

He tossed the check onto his desk, but I didn't have to look at it. 'And my address was on it, too,' I said.

'Bingo. So we take a few runs by your place, till we see the car, follow it, and you know the rest. But you want to know an even bigger coinky-dink?'

I said nothing.

'When we were looking for that car, around where this detective lives, we saw a car out back that looked awfully familiar to us. An old Buick. The night before, we were out conducting a bit of business, and this Buick starts tailing us, even started shooting at us. We got a pretty good idea it was this Jones fellow, although he had someone else in the car with him.'

I felt a bit weak in the knees. 'What kind of business?' I asked, playing dumb.

'We're also in the retail business. We sell suits. Nothing but the best. Like this,' he said, stepping out from behind the desk, raising his hands and turning around. 'Pretty nice merchandise, wouldn't you say? Armani.'

'The suits,' I said. 'I saw them in the garage. So you guys not only deal cocaine, you steal high-end designer clothing.'

Bullock smiled. 'We're diversified. That's the kind of economy we're dealing with these days. Can't put all your eggs in one basket.' He paused, said to Pockmark, 'I wonder how things are going in the garage?'

I wondered, too. Maybe Trimble was out there. Maybe he'd subdued Blondie, was on his way to take out his buddy and the Barbie collector.

Bullock pressed the intercom unit on his desk. 'Hey . . .' he shouted. 'How's it going out there? Hello?'

There was a bit of static and shouting as Bullock and Blondie tried to speak to each other at the same time. Bullock looked at me sadly, shook his head. 'I'm trying to run this place more professionally, and look at the problems I have.'

Finally, he and Blondie coordinated their button pushing, and Blondie's voice came through clearly. But he sounded very concerned.

'I think we may have a problem, Mr Bullock.'

Bullock frowned, glowered at the intercom. 'I don't want to hear that kind of shit . . . What do you mean, a problem?'

'There's nothing in this car. Not a fucking thing.'

THIRTY-ONE

'Nothing?' Bullock said.

'Everything I found, I tossed in a box, but it's definitely not what you were hoping for,' Blondie said over the speaker.

'Bring it here,' he said, and took his finger off the intercom. He looked first at Pockmark, then at me. 'What kind of shit you trying to pull here?' He was breathing pretty heavily now, which triggered a short coughing fit and prompted another sip of water.

'Believe me,' I said, 'if there's anyone here who wanted you to find what you wanted in that car, it's me.'

This was not a good development. Bullock not finding what he'd hoped to, his face flushed red with anger. Not a good development at all.

Unless, of course, it *was* a good development.

Maybe this would buy me and Angie some time. Maybe this would give Trimble time to do what he had to do. And speaking of Trimble, where the hell was he? Anytime he wanted to make an appearance and bring an end to these proceedings was okay by me.

Blondie strode through the door, holding a small cardboard box that had once held a dozen bottles of Ernest & Julio Gallo wine, set it on Bullock's desk, and took a step back, like he didn't want to be too close when his boss peered inside. The box definitely wasn't large enough to hold a shipment of coke, although I really had no idea how big a box you'd need for a shipment of coke.

Bullock peered over the edge of the box, looked at Blondie. 'Are you fucking kidding me?'

'That's it,' Blondie said, a hint of nervousness in his voice. I think he was worried he might be coming down with a case of 'shot messenger syndrome'. It couldn't be fun giving bad news to a guy like Bullock, who was still looking into the box, incredulous in his ill-fitting suit, still holding Barbie's pregnant friend Midge in his left hand.

'The fuck is this? An owner's manual, an apple juice, a box of Kleenex, is this some kind of joke? And whose cell phone is this?' He tossed Midge aside, picked up the phone, threw it back into the box.

Blondie nodded in my direction. 'It's his. I took it off him earlier, put it in the box with the other stuff.'

'You looked in the doors?'

'I looked in the doors, just where Mr Indigo said the stuff would be. There's nothing in the doors.'

'I gotta see this for myself.' He left the box on his desk, headed for the door. He told Pockmark to stay with Angie, and ordered me to come with him to the garage.

The tape around my ankle felt as though it was coming loose.

We entered the brilliantly lit garage, where my Virtue took center stage, hood, trunk and all four doors open. As I came around the car, I saw what a mess it was in. The panels on the insides of all four doors had been removed, exposing the skeletal sheet-metal work and side-impact beams.

'See for yourself,' Blondie said, which was the wrong thing to say, judging by the look Bullock gave him. Bullock looked inside all four doors, ran his hand inside where you couldn't see, but carefully, so as not to cut himself on the edge of the exposed metal.

'When I couldn't find it in the doors,' Blondie said, 'I took the mats and everything out of the trunk, and there was nothing there. I pulled out the backseat, see if there was anything under there, which there wasn't, so I put it back. I looked under the front seats, reached up into the springs. I'm tellin' ya, there's nothing in this goddamn car.'

Bullock began to pace, five steps one way, spinning around, five steps back. 'This is not good,' he said. 'This is not good.'

Blondie said, 'Maybe you should call Mr Indigo. We got that guard, he can get a message to him, ask whether the stuff might be someplace else and—'

'We are not calling Mr Indigo . . .' Bullock bellowed. 'That is the last fucking thing we are going to do, you understand?'

'Yeah, sure.'

'I'm not calling him, you're not calling him, no one is fucking calling him . . .'

'Okay, gotcha.'

'The last thing I need is him thinking I've fucked this up somehow . . . He's trusting me to run things, and if I can't do it, he can just as easily call someone in from the West Coast to do it instead, you understand?'

'I said yeah. Chill out, man.'

'Chill out? Is that what you said? You want me to chill out?' Bullock was in Blondie's face now, as best he could, being about six inches shorter. 'Getting this car back, recovering this shipment, this is a very important test not just for me, but for the three of us. That's why we're going to figure this out, find the coke, and Mr Indigo will know nothing more than that we did our fucking jobs. Is that clear?'

'Yeah, boss.'

I spoke up. 'What about in the rocker panels? Like in *The French Connection*. That's where they hid the stuff in the movie.'

'Shut up,' Bullock said.

He reached into his back pocket, pulled out a slender item, black in color, about six, seven inches long, pressed a button on it I couldn't see, and suddenly this item was twice as long, and half of it was very shiny. And then he began, slowly, to walk toward me.

'I think,' he said, waving the switchblade very slowly, 'that you're holding out on me.'

I took a step back towards the garage door. 'No,' I said. 'I'm not. If I knew where those drugs were, I'd go get them for you now. I have no idea why they aren't in that car.'

Bullock kept approaching, the knife kept waving. I thought, although I couldn't be sure, that I could see small traces of blood near the blade's base. I had a pretty good idea whose blood that might be.

I pressed myself up against the garage door, Bullock only inches from me now. He brought the knife close to my neck.

I thought I felt the gun sag just a bit against my ankle.

'That's a very kind offer,' he said. 'Makes me think you might already have an idea where those drugs might be.'

'I'm telling you, I don't. I swear on every one of your Barbies, I don't know.'

His eyes danced. Was my comment meant to convey sincerity, or was I mocking him, he wondered. And I wondered, Why is it, despite my best efforts, I keep saying and doing things that make me seem like an asshole?

Blondie said, 'It doesn't make much sense for him to have taken the drugs, boss. I mean, we were following the car for quite a while tonight, and would he be dumb enough to let his daughter drive it around if he knew there was drugs in it, or if he'd known there used to be drugs in it?'

Blondie was my new best friend.

'So what are you saying?' Bullock said.

'I'm saying that the drugs must never have been in the car. At least not since he bought it, or got it off that other guy who bought it at the auction.'

'You think that private detective knew, and he got the drugs out of the car?' Bullock asked.

'That's crazy,' I offered. 'Once we left the auction, I took the car. It's been with me from the moment we drove it out of the compound.'

Bullock thought about that. 'I don't know. Maybe we should go talk to him, this Mr Jones.' He smiled at me. 'I understand he ran into a little difficulty, but that he's still among the living. Maybe he'd be up to a few questions.'

'I'm telling you,' I said, 'I've had the car the whole time.'

Bullock considered that. 'Then that means the drugs were taken out of the car before it went up for auction. But we know the cops never found them, because they were never entered into evidence.'

'Which means someone else knew what was in the car, and got to it before we had a chance,' said Blondie.

Bullock's head went up and down, very slowly. 'I think we're going to need a little more help with this,' he said, and then took in a deep breath and shouted so loud it made my ears ring, 'Trimble . . .'

What?

There seemed no mistaking what Bullock had said. He hadn't exactly whispered it.

And then the side door to the garage opened, and Detective Steve Trimble stepped in. He strolled over to where Bullock and I were standing.

'You called,' he said to Bullock.

I had a feeling my situation had gone from bad to much, much worse.

THIRTY-TWO

'It's got to be Eddie Mayhew,' Trimble said.

'That's what I'm thinking,' Bullock said. 'Mayhew, that son of a bitch, and after all we've done for him.'

I thought back. The man I'd interviewed, for my feature on the government auction.

'Don't we pay him enough, that he shouldn't double-cross us?' Bullock asked.

'He knew you were interested in the car, right?' Trimble asked.

Bullock nodded. 'So if he knew we were interested, he had to suspect why, and he got into that car before it went up on the block.'

'And sold the stuff himself.'

'I'm betting the Jamaicans,' Bullock said.

'What an absolute moron,' Trimble said. 'First, crossing you; second, dealing with the Jamaicans. They're crazy. They can't be trusted.'

'Pay him a visit,' Bullock said. 'He either coughs up the stuff, or the money he got for selling it to someone else.'

'Even if he sold it, he won't have got for it what you would have,' the police detective said.

'Either way, bring him back here so that I might have a word with him,' Bullock said. 'And you know what, why don't you take your new friend along with you.' He nodded in my direction. 'Only a minute ago he offered to do whatever he could to help us get our goods back. As long as the girl's here, I don't think he's going to give you much trouble.'

Trimble shrugged. 'Sure,' he said, and turned to me. 'I love company.'

'You know where Eddie lives?' Bullock asked.

Trimble said he did, out in Delton, a town just beyond Oakwood.

'And call in,' Bullock told Trimble. 'Every half hour. I don't hear from you, then our friend here doesn't have to worry about coming back here for his daughter.'

I swallowed hard. And I wanted some clarification. 'You mean a half hour from now, which would be, like, 1:16 a.m., or every half hour on the 12 and the 6, which would be a lot easier to keep track of?'

Bullock stared at me, rolled his eyes. The kinds of decisions you had to make when you were in charge. 'On the 12 and the 6. First call, 1:30 a.m.'

'Okay,' I said. 'I just wanted to be sure. And can I say goodbye to Angie before we leave?'

Bullock shook his head. 'Would you just fucking go?'

'Come on,' Trimble said to me. 'The sooner we get this done, the sooner we get back.'

We walked down the cobblestone drive together, neither of us speaking, then hiked up Windham to where he'd left his unmarked cruiser. 'Ever get to drive a police car?' he asked. I said no. 'Here's your big chance.' He unlocked the car, and once I was behind the wheel and he was in the passenger seat, he tossed me the keys.

'You know the way to Delton?'

I nodded, turned the engine on, and started taking us in the direction of the expressway. It was dark in the car, the only light coming from the gauges on the dash and the streetlights as we passed under them. I suspected the gun was going to slip out of the bottom of my pants any time now, but the odds were that Trimble wouldn't notice. My foot, down by the accelerator, was shrouded in darkness, and the police communication system in the center of the dash further obscured the view.

'I guess you're thinking you'd have been better off calling 911,' Trimble said, turning slightly in the seat so he could watch me without getting a crick in his neck. I figured he wanted me behind the wheel so I wouldn't have my hands free to try anything.

'Yeah, in retrospect,' I said. 'Although it proves Bullock's no liar. He has someone on the inside.'

'Yeah, well, I doubt I'm the only one. Lenny Indigo was pretty resourceful that way, developing friends where he could best use them.'

'It didn't keep him out of jail.'

'Yeah,' Trimble said. 'Things finally caught up with him.' He paused. 'It happens sometimes.'

'I'm just gonna go out on a limb here and guess that, back on that night when you and Lawrence Jones were partners, and that kid took a shot at him, and you hesitated?'

I glanced over at Trimble. His eyes had become slits.

'I'm guessing you didn't just hesitate out of fear or anything. I'm guessing you recognized that kid. I remember Lawrence saying that he worked for Indigo's organization, and when you saw him, in the light, you recognized him. Maybe even knew him. And you also knew that he and you reported to the same guy, which

288

made you think that maybe it wouldn't be such a good idea to shoot him.'

Trimble's tongue was poking the inside of his cheek.

'So you didn't just freeze. You chose to protect a partner in crime instead of your partner on the force.'

'Just drive, okay?' Trimble said. 'If I want entertainment, I can turn on the radio.'

'Bullock's never going to let me and Angie walk away from this, is he?'

'I don't know that. We get his goods back, he might look a lot more favorably on your situation.'

'That's not how he dealt with Lawrence.'

I got onto the expressway ramp, gave the cruiser some more gas. It roared ahead. 'I don't suppose I could use the siren,' I said.

'No.'

'Did you know that Bullock did Lawrence? Did you know he was going to?'

'You don't have any proof that Bullock, or any of those clowns working with him, tried to kill Lawrence. I asked him about it, he says he didn't do it.'

I shook my head. 'And you believe that.'

'There's no reason for him to lie,' Trimble said, but with little conviction.

'Maybe Bullock thinks if you knew he killed your former partner, that might be too much of a test of your loyalty to him. And open your eyes, man. You deal in evidence. Bullock has my check. The one I gave to Lawrence. But that's not enough. This one goes into your cold-case file.'

'Someone'll take a fall for it.'

'Let me guess. You get that switchblade off Bullock, plant it on some punk who tries to resist arrest, or maybe some kid who dies of an arranged overdose, you plant the knife on him, they test the blood, figure out he did it. Something like that?'

'Sure, why not. Maybe I could even find it on you, or in your car.'

'Yeah,' I said. 'That would make sense. Feature writer stabs detective. What possible motive could I have? Who'd believe that?'

Trimble appeared to be giving it some serious thought. 'How about this? You two were having an affair. Getting it on. You'd been in the closet for years, decided to come out with him. Then Lawrence threatened to tell others, tell your wife, and you didn't want her to find out you're gay. That might work.'

'Excellent,' I said. 'Only problem is, Lawrence didn't die. I don't think he'll corroborate that story.'

Trimble smirked. 'I'll try to come up with something better. In the meantime, why don't you stop being such a smartass and be a bit more cooperative so I'm not pressed to think of scenarios that end up with you being dead.'

I glanced at the clock on the dash. A couple of minutes past one. I found myself looking at it every few seconds. I didn't want Trimble failing to check in with Bullock on time.

I couldn't see down by the gas pedal, but I had the feeling the barrel of the gun I'd taken from Lawrence's car was poking out below the hem of my Gap khakis. Even if I could get hold of my gun, was this the time to use it? Let's say I could somehow stop Trimble, would that get me any closer to rescuing Angie? Especially if it meant he couldn't make his check-in call? For all I cared, Trimble and Bullock and Blondie and Pockmark could all walk away free and clear, with their drugs or without, so long as I was able to take Angie home with me.

'The thing is,' Trimble said, after we'd driven several miles without saying a word to one another, 'I feel badly about Lawrence. I honestly do. He was a good cop, a good partner. But he was such a fucking idealist, so holier-than-thou. Always believed in playing by the rules, doing things by the book. Didn't seem to understand that no one else was playing by the rules, that cops get shafted from every corner. They send you out to clean up everybody's shit, put your life on the line, for a joke of a salary, and then you put your toe over that line the tiniest bit and they pull the rug out from under you. Lawrence didn't understand that you had to bend the rules, not a lot, just a bit, to make the job work in your favor. I still got a great record, I got loads of collars, I've got commendations. I've put a lot of bad people behind bars.'

'I'm moved,' I said.

I could feel the gun slip further from its flimsy masking-tape harness. Too bad Lawrence's glove compartment hadn't contained duct tape.

'Never mind,' Trimble said. 'Let's just do this.'

And we sat quietly for the next ten minutes. As signs appeared for Oakwood, Trimble said, 'It'll be coming up soon, just another couple of exits.'

Trimble told me where to get off. We drove through the so-called downtown of Delton, then north, through a neighborhood of small, post-Second World War houses. We came upon a two-story brick house, and even in the darkness, I could see the paint peeling off the window frames, the sag in the roof. There was an old Volvo in the driveway.

'Kill the lights before you turn into the drive,' Trimble said, and I did.

I stopped the car, turned the key back, and felt the gun slip from my ankle to the floor.

'We're going to go straight in,' Trimble said. 'Then right up the stairs, to his bedroom. I don't think he's got any kids. Don't see any tricycles or bikes around.'

'He doesn't have kids,' I said.

'How do you know that?'

'He told me. I interviewed him for a story.'

Trimble almost looked impressed. 'You're everywhere, aren't you? Okay, let's be very quiet.'

With my foot, I shifted the gun to the right of the accelerator, down behind the police communication equipment. If Trimble made me drive back, there was no chance he'd see it down there.

'Wait,' I said. 'It's 1:27. Depending on what happens once we get inside, you're not going to be able to call Bullock. So check in with him now.'

Trimble sighed, dug out his cell, punched in some numbers. 'It's me,' he said. 'Just checking in, everything's fine, we just got to Mayhew's place. I'll talk to you at two.' He looked at me as he slipped the phone back into his pocket. 'Satisfied?'

'Yeah. Thanks.'

'Out,' he said, and we opened our doors at the same time. I was afraid the inside dome light would make the gun visible, but it remained hidden in shadow. We walked towards the front door, gravel crunching under our shoes. Trimble mounted the steps to the front door ahead of me, opened the aluminum screen door, then tried the knob on the main door.

It turned.

'What an idiot,' Trimble whispered. 'These people move to the suburbs, they think they're going to be safe.'

He opened the door quietly. I held on to the screen door behind him, keeping it from slamming shut. It was about then it occurred to me that I was breaking and entering. Under some sort of duress, sure, but I was breaking and entering. With a cop, no less.

Once inside, I eased the screen door shut, and we waited a moment for our eyes to adjust. Just inside the door, on the right, was a set of stairs. We both held our breath, and upstairs, we could hear snoring.

Trimble smiled devilishly at me and pointed up. He had his gun out now and was taking the carpeted steps one at a time. I let him get a couple of steps ahead of me before I began to follow.

The stairs turned at a landing, and as we reached it, the snoring grew louder. These were loud, rumbling snores. We could have stomped our way up these stairs and not wakened Mayhew.

Once we reached the upstairs hallway, Trimble paused again, making sure he could tell which room the snores were coming from. He crept ahead of me to the doorway of the bedroom on the left, where, from the soft beam of moonlight that was coming through the window, we could make out a shape under the covers, which were pulled up so far you couldn't see any more of the person than what appeared to be a few tufts of hair. I didn't remember Mayhew having that much hair.

Trimble pointed to the lamp on the bedside table and whispered, 'Get ready to turn that on.'

I slipped my hand under the shade, found the small grooved knob, and held it between my thumb and forefinger as the snores continued to echo through the room. Trimble gripped his weapon with both hands and held the muzzle to within a couple of inches of Mayhew's head. He nodded to me.

I turned on the light.

Trimble shouted, 'Wakey wakey, Eddie . . .'

And Mayhew stirred suddenly, reached up an arm to pull the covers down, and, upon seeing the muzzle only inches away, screamed.

Only it wasn't Mayhew screaming. It was a woman.

'Jesus . . .' Trimble shouted, moving the gun away. But that didn't stop the woman from continuing to scream.

'Shut up . . .' Trimble shouted. More screaming. 'Shut up . . . Shut the fuck up . . .'

Screaming back at her wasn't working, so he brought the gun back into play, putting the barrel right up to her nose. Trimble said, 'Shut. Up.'

She managed to compose herself. She struggled to sit up in the bed, and I could now see that what I'd thought were tufts of hair were rollers. She had a good dozen of them on her gray-haired head, pinned into position. She was wearing an off-white, heavy flannel, full-sleeved nightgown, and it was fair to say that we had not caught her at her best.

'Who are you?' she asked.

'Where's Eddie?' Trimble asked.

'I just, I don't, what do you want?'

'I just asked you, I want to know where Eddie is. He's your husband, right?'

'Yes, he is. What do you want with Edward?'

'We want to know where he is.'

'I don't know. I really don't know. I wish I did know. If he was going to be late, he should have called me. He's supposed to call, but sometimes he doesn't.'

Trimble looked very tired. 'Is there anyone else in the house?'

'What? No, there's no one else. Unless Edward's downstairs.'

Trimble sat on the edge of the bed, brought the gun down so that it was still in his hand, but lying on the covers. 'Mrs Mayhew,' he said softly. 'It's very important that we find your husband.'

'Is he in some kind of trouble? Because if he is, I have to tell you, I'm not all that surprised, the bastard.'

'If we can find him in time, maybe we can keep him out of any trouble.'

'Are you the police?'

'We are,' Trimble said slowly, 'a branch of the police, but we work a little under the radar, if you get my understanding.'

Mrs Mayhew nodded. She was starting to look a little relieved now that maybe we weren't bad guys, as she'd first thought.

'Because your husband works for the government,' he said, 'he's been able to assist us in our investigation, working somewhat undercover himself.'

'Edward? Working undercover? He's certainly never mentioned anything to me. But of course, he hardly talks to me about anything. I ask him, "How was your day? What happened? Who did you see?' And you know what he says? He says absolutely nothing.'

'That's good. That's good, that he didn't tell you. A lot of times, you figure, even when you tell someone not to tell anyone what they're doing, you figure they're still going to tell their wives, you know?'

She nodded.

'But now we're into a situation where we've lost track of Eddie and need to locate him.'

'It's like I said in the beginning. I don't know where he is. Did you look downstairs? Maybe he's just watching TV. Sometimes he sits down there all night, staring at the tube, for hours and hours and hours. And I call down, and ask doesn't he want to come up to bed with me, and still he sits there, watching his stupid shows.'

'There was no one downstairs watching TV,' Trimble said, and walked over to the closet, opened the door. 'Come over here,' he said to Mrs Mayhew. She slipped out from under the covers, a bit hesitant at first because she was in a nightgown, but it did an excellent job of covering everything and I was betting Trimble was no more turned on by acres of flannel than I. Still, you couldn't blame her for being worried, what with two strange men in her bedroom at two in the morning.

She looked in the closet.

'Are all your husband's clothes here?' Trimble asked.

'Uh, gee, let me see.' She moved some hangers around, looked down at the floor. 'His extra pair of jeans is gone, and I don't think all his shirts . . . I don't see his . . . That's gone, too . . . That's really odd.'

'Take a look in the drawer,' Trimble said.

She did, opening the second drawer down in the dresser. 'My God. All his socks are gone,' she said. 'And his boxers. I did the laundry yesterday and put everything in here. But it's not here now.'

Without being asked, she went out of the bedroom and into the bathroom, flicking on the light as she entered. She opened the vanity, turned and looked at the two of us, her hand up over her mouth. 'His toothbrush,' she said. 'His toothbrush is gone.'

'When's the last time you saw your husband?' Trimble asked.

'At, at breakfast. Actually, now that I think about it, he did say he had stuff to do after work tonight, and that he'd be home late. So I went to bed without him. But he never said anything about going away anywhere, about having to pack his boxers and a toothbrush. Did he have to go away on secret government business?'

Trimble said, 'Your husband got a cell phone?'

She nodded. Trimble told her to call. She went downstairs to the kitchen, flicking lights on along the way, and sat down at the kitchen table, where the phone sat. She tapped in a number, held the receiver to her ear. 'It says the number's not in service. Why would it say the number's not in service? That doesn't make any sense at all. Maybe he's in a bad area.'

Trimble had a look at the phone. 'This is one of those new ones,' he said. 'It shows who's called you recently.'

'That's right. Edward said we should get that, but I don't think it's worth the extra money.'

'And you can call up the last ten numbers that have been dialed.'

'I didn't know that,' Mrs Mayhew said.

Trimble took a chair across from her, swung the phone around so that it was in front of him. 'I'm going to call out some numbers to you and you tell me if you know what they are.'

He did the first one.

'That's my sister Cleo, in Milwaukee. I called her this evening, to see if she was still coming to visit in

April. We're very close, but we don't get together as often as we'd like. She married this man, he's not very nice, he doesn't like to travel.'

Trimble gave her another number. 'That's Edward's work,' she said. 'I called him around three, but he was out.'

Then another. Mrs Mayhew shook her head. 'That one doesn't ring a bell.'

Trimble hit the button that would immediately connect him to the number, waited, and then said, 'Oh, hello. I was wondering, which Ramada is this? Uh-huh. Okay. I'm trying to track down a friend of mine, we're supposed to have breakfast together. Do you have an Edward Mayhew registered there?' He nodded. 'That's great. And what room is he in? Thanks very much.'

He hung up the phone, looked at me. 'Eddie's at the Ramada. The one by the airport. I'm guessing he's booked on a morning flight.'

'What?' said Mrs Mayhew. 'No no, you must have that wrong. Eddie's not going away . . . We don't take separate vacations . . . We certainly never have . . . What does he think he's doing? He's up at the Ramada, you say? He's going to get a piece of my mind . . .'

'Mrs Mayhew, I'm afraid I can't have you getting in touch with Eddie right now.'

'That's ridiculous. Give me that phone.'

Trimble sighed. 'Mrs Mayhew, let's go back upstairs.'

'What? You can't stop me from calling my husband.'

'Listen,' I said. I almost said, 'Listen, Trimble,' but felt using names in front of Mrs Mayhew might not be advisable. 'Let's just head out there, it won't take that long.'

'We can't have her warning him,' Trimble said.

'What do you mean, warning him?' Mrs Mayhew demanded to know. 'And just who are you people, anyway? I think it's high time that you answered a few of my questions for a change.'

'Upstairs,' Trimble said, the gentleness gone from his voice. He grabbed Mrs Mayhew by the arm and started dragging her out of the kitchen.

'Hang on . . .' I said. 'What are you going to do?'

'Yeah, what are you going to do?' Mrs Mayhew asked as Trimble ushered her up the stairs, his gun out and poking her in the side.

I couldn't stand by and let him kill her, if that was what he planned, although I didn't know how I'd stop him. The gun I'd borrowed for the evening was out in the car.

I grabbed at his shoulder. 'Can't you just tie her up or something, till you can get to the hotel?'

He looked at me, weighing things. I could see he didn't want to kill Mrs Mayhew, but there was a risk in letting her live. Trimble knew Eddie Mayhew would likely be dead by morning, and a police investigation would lead to Mrs Mayhew and her tale of two night-time visitors.

'Shit,' he said quietly to himself. He pushed Mrs Mayhew ahead, back into the bedroom, and went over to the dresser. He rummaged through the drawers and tossed out a couple of pairs of pantyhose onto the bed. He whirled around, looked at me, pointed the gun, and said, 'Do it.'

'What?'

'Tie her up.' Mrs Mayhew's eyes were darting back and forth between us.

'I hardly know her,' I said.

'Would you rather I shot her?'

Mrs Mayhew looked back at me. 'I'd rather not be shot,' she said, and I proceeded to do as I was asked, tying her wrists together and securing them to the headboard.

Trimble, not trusting my handiwork, double-checked that Mrs Mayhew was secure, then grabbed the second pair of pantyhose and gagged her.

'Fuck,' he grumbled. 'Let's take a drive.'

THIRTY-THREE

'Trimble . . .' I said as we stepped out the door. I had just glanced at my watch. It was one minute past two. 'You have to call in . . . Right now . . .'

'Let's get on the road first, then I'll call.'

'No,' I said, with more forcefulness than I knew I had. 'Now.'

'Fine,' he said, and got out his phone. 'This is a huge pain. Now that Barbie's got to prove himself, he's got all these little plans and procedures. Fucking intercoms and phone-ins and—'

Someone picked up. 'Yeah, it's me, checking in, talk to you in thirty.'

As we walked back to the car he said, 'Mayhew must have already made his deal. He's got his money, and he's getting out of the country.'

'Am I still driving?' I asked, sounding positive, like I was happy to help, but mostly wanting to make sure Trimble didn't see the gun down by the accelerator pedal.

'Yeah, sure,' he said, waving his hand.

Once we were both in the car and back on the road, Trimble shook his head. 'Man oh man, things are not unfolding the way they should.'

'What?'

He kept shaking his head, made a fist and pounded it repeatedly on the top of the dashboard. I hoped he wouldn't set off the passenger-side airbag. 'We made a big mistake back there. I should have killed her.'

'No, you shouldn't have killed her.'

'Oh man,' he said, putting his fist back to his mouth. 'I've really fucked up this time.'

'You couldn't kill her. There was no way you could kill her.'

'Don't you see how this is going to play out? Eddie, he's on borrowed time, it's all over once Bullock's had a chance to talk to him. And then when the cops come to interview her, you think she's not going to talk? That she's not going to be able to provide a description of me?'

I swallowed. 'And me.'

Trimble waved his hand dismissively. At first, I thought that simply meant he cared more about his own skin than mine. But then I realized it was more likely that my being picked out of a line up by Mrs Mayhew was never going to happen. I was as unlikely to see the sun come up as Eddie.

'Fuck,' he whispered under his breath. 'Fuck.'

'You've never had to kill anyone for Bullock, have you?' I asked. 'You've done lots for him, but never that.'

His silence was as good as a yes.

'So there's at least one line you have trouble crossing,' I said. 'But if you're not willing to kill for him, how can you stand by and let him kill others? Because that's what he's going to do. To Eddie. To me. And to Angie.'

'That's not for sure.'

I almost laughed. 'Well, that's comforting.'

'I shouldn't have left her alive back there.'

'I'm not turning around,' I said. 'If you tell me to turn around and take you back there so you can kill that woman, I'll run us off a bridge. I'll floor it and run us into a tree. But I won't go back.'

'What about your daughter?' Trimble asked. Not in a threatening way, more like he was just interested.

'I don't know. Maybe I'll try to smash your side of the car, so you're dead, and I survive, long enough to call the cops, the *good* ones, see if *they* can save Angie.'

'Oh, that's a good plan,' Trimble said. 'A carefully engineered car wreck.'

He shook his head a couple more times, stared straight ahead out the window. 'God,' he said under his breath. 'This is one very deep hole to crawl out of.'

We got back onto the expressway, but instead of driving all the way back into the city, took the highway that skirted the city's north side and went past the airport.

'Let me ask you this,' I said. 'All that shit about his dead sister and weird mother aside, what kind of guy has a Barbie collection like that?'

Trimble must have waited a good ten seconds before he responded. 'Fucking nutjob, that's what,' he said.

We drove awhile longer, neither of us saying anything. Then Trimble said, 'Have you been to see Lawrence, in the hospital?'

'Yeah.'

Trimble paused. 'How is he?'

'He's bad.'

And then the car went quiet again.

★

Nearly half an hour after we left the Mayhew house, we pulled into the parking lot of the airport Ramada. I pointed out the time to Trimble, and he put in a call to Bullock as required to protect Angie. The hotel was dead, no cars going in or out, no one in the lobby. We parked around the side, but it was after midnight, and every access was locked except the main doors out front.

'Just walk in like you own the place, like you're a guest here,' Trimble said. 'Head straight for the elevators.'

We walked through the lobby, the two employees behind the desk paying no attention to us. Once we were at the bank of elevators, we were out of their sight, and Trimble said, 'He's in room 1023. At least he better be.'

The doors opened and we stepped inside. Trimble found the button marked '10' and tapped it with his index finger. The doors parted, and Trimble scanned the markers indicating where the rooms were. Suites 1020 to 1034 were down the left hall, so we bore left.

We stood in front of 1023 and Trimble rapped on the door. 'Mr Mayhew?' he called out, friendly like. He rapped a bit harder. 'Mr Mayhew?' He stood right up close to the door, so if Eddie looked through the peephole, he'd wouldn't see much more than a couple of nostrils.

We heard some stirring inside, then a muffled voice at the door. 'Hello?'

'Mr Mayhew?'

'Yes? Yes? Who is it? Yes?'

'I'm from the front desk. We thought we should tell you, there were some suspicious-looking men asking for you, and we thought you should know.'

'Oh God, oh my God, oh, oh, oh my God,' he said.

'We don't like to see our guests have any trouble, so we told them you'd already checked out.'

'Oh God, really? You really did that? Oh, thank you so much. Thank you. Oh God, thank you so much.'

'No problem, sir.'

'What did they look like? Did you see them? Did you see what they looked like? I mean, I guess you did, if they were here. You saw them?'

Trimble looked me up and down, glanced at himself. 'Two men, white, one in a suit, the other more casually dressed.'

'And they left? They're gone? They've gone away?'

'Yes, sir.'

'Oh my God, that's good. That's good. Listen, stay there a moment, I'd like to give you something. Just stay there a sec, I'm getting you a tip.'

'Oh, really, that's not necessary,' Trimble said.

'No no, just give me a minute, I'll get you something for your trouble, you did a wonderful thing, a terrific thing,' he said, his voice fading back into the room. Trimble got ready. He took a step back from the door, so he'd be able to take a run at it. Then we heard the deadbolt slip back, the chain slide off its track, and then the door began to open.

'And if they come back, there's more where this came from—'

Trimble hit the door like a freight train, propelling Eddie back into the room and onto the floor. The door must have caught his toes, at least on one foot, because he was already holding them in both hands, screaming, as we came in.

Trimble had his gun out and pressed up against Eddie's forehead. 'Stop your whimpering.'

'My toes, man . . . Oh my God, my toes . . . They're all broken . . . You've broken my toes . . .'

'We'll call a toe truck,' Trimble said, glancing at me and grinning. 'I haven't used that joke since I was six.'

Eddie's eyes were squeezed shut, and he was rocking back and forth on his butt, still holding on to his foot. He was wearing nothing but a pair of green boxers with a tear in the crotch, and I looked away, not really interested in a peek at his luggage. He was thin and kind of bony, his back was splattered with pimples and blotches, and his short, curly hair was wet, like he'd been in the shower recently.

'Come on, Eddie, pull it together,' Trimble said. 'We got a lot to talk about.'

He opened his eyes, looked at Trimble, then at me. He recognized me, but couldn't remember exactly who I was.

I helped him out. 'We met yesterday, at the auction.'

Mayhew could figure out why Trimble was here, but my presence was a mystery. 'What, what are you doing here? Why are you here?' he asked.

'I'm doing a feature on a day in the life of a bad cop, and Detective Trimble here kindly allowed me to tag along.'

'Get up,' Trimble said, grabbing Eddie under the arm and hauling him onto the bed. It was a nice-size room, with a sitting area and a set of sliding glass doors that led out to a balcony.

'I don't think I can walk,' Eddie said. 'You've crippled me. You've crippled me for life.'

'I think that's the least of your problems,' said Trimble, walking around the room. On top of the dresser, next to the television, he found a small folder. 'What's this, Eddie? These look like airplane tickets.' He took them out of their folder. 'Let's have a look here. Rio? You're going to Rio? Now, here's something interesting. There's no return ticket here. That's really dumb, Eddie. That just makes people suspicious. Even if you aren't planning to come back, you buy a return ticket.'

'I just wanted to get away, just for a few days, a little break, get some sun, you know, just a little break.' He looked pitiful sitting in the middle of the king-size bed. 'I wasn't sure exactly what day I was coming back, you know, like maybe Wednesday, but maybe Thursday, could be Saturday, you know, depends.'

'I see. And you're going alone? No ticket for the missus?'

'We like to take separate vacations sometimes. It's good for a marriage, you know? Kind of heats things up, once you get back.' He tried to smile, force a laugh. I tried to picture things heating up between Eddie and Mrs Mayhew.

Trimble pulled up a chair, sat down by the foot of the bed. 'Have any idea why I'm here, Eddie?'

He shrugged, smiled. 'Honestly, for the life of me, I can't begin to guess. You've got me. I'm absolutely dumfounded. This is a total bafflement to me.'

'Barbie Bullock sent me.'

Eddie's grin evaporated. When he swallowed, his Adam's apple bobbed. 'Really? He sent you to find me? What for? Why would a guy like that want anything to do with me?'

'He got a big surprise tonight. He was tearing apart that car, the one he told you he was interested in, the one you gave him the address for, of the guy who bought it at the auction?'

'Sure, yeah, I remember. It's sort of coming back to me. I was just a bit fuzzy there for a minute. Was there a problem? Car not start or something?'

Now Trimble chuckled. 'There was nothing in the car, Eddie. Nothing at all.'

Absolute astonishment. 'Are you serious?' Eddie, still holding on to his toes, shook his head in wonderment. 'That's crazy, totally crazy, unbelievable, totally totally unbelievable.'

'The stuff's missing,' Trimble said. 'And then, what do you know, here you are in a hotel, ready to fly off to Rio with a one-way ticket, your closet cleaned out at home, and your wife has no idea that you were planning a little getaway.'

'You talked to Rita? You didn't talk to Rita, did you?'

Trimble nodded. 'She's very upset. I think she'd like to take a vacation, too. Maybe to visit her sister in Milwaukee.'

'I was going to have her come down and join me in a couple days. Soon as I find us a nice spot. I was going to give her a call.'

Trimble nodded, like it all made sense. 'That's what I always do when I go to a foreign country, Eddie. Try to find my accommodation once I get there.'

I said, 'Eddie, here's the deal. Bullock has my daughter. If we don't come back with the drugs, or the money you got for the drugs, then I'm guessing he's going to kill her. And if that happens, all the bad cops in the world couldn't do as much to you as I will.'

'I don't know anything about any money,' Eddie Mayhew said quietly.

Trimble got up, grabbed the over-the-shoulder bag that was sitting on a chair, and dumped it onto the bed. Socks, underwear, a belt, some sundries, tumbled out. And a thick white envelope.

Trimble opened it, thumbed a thick stack of cash. 'That looks like three thousand or so right there.' He slipped it into his jacket, walked over to the closet, and took out Eddie's coat. Seconds later, he had another thick envelope in his hand. 'That looks like another three or four. Where else you got it hidden?'

Eddie hung his head, unwrapped his hands from around his foot. The toes were red and bloody. He began to cry.

'Eddie,' Trimble said.

'I'm sorry,' he whimpered. 'I'm really sorry. So so sorry. You have no idea how sorry I am. Tell Mr Bullock I'm sorry about this, I'll make it all up to him.'

'Eddie, who'd you sell to?'

Eddie just looked at him, his eyes moistening.

'Eddie?'

'The Jamaicans.'

'It's a wonder you're still alive. What did you get?'

'One-fifty.'

'What?'

'One-fifty. A hundred and fifty thousand.'

'Tell me you're kidding,' Trimble said, slapping Eddie across the face. 'Tell me you're fucking kidding.'

'A hundred and fifty could last me a long time. Long time. I watch my pennies.'

'You should have got half a mill, easy, maybe more. Mr Bullock was going to make a couple million out of that.'

Eddie, his cheek red, looked up as a tear ran down his cheek. 'I didn't want to get greedy,' he said.

'So you got the stuff out of the car before it went to auction, cut a deal behind Bullock's back, figured you'd pocket the cash yourself. So we've got about six, seven thousand in the room here. Where's the rest of it?'

'I mailed it.'

Now Trimble's face was red, without being slapped. He went very quiet. 'Eddie, you what?'

'I mailed it, to Rio. Some of it I mailed, some of it I FedExed, to different hotels, to be held in care of. You know, in care of me. When I get there, I ask at the front desk, they got any mail for me, I pick it up.'

'You put more than $140,000 in the mail?'

'I didn't want them to find all that on me if they did a search when I was getting on the plane.'

I had a sinking feeling. We were going to be returning to Bullock's place with very bad news.

'Can't you tell Mr Bullock I'm sorry? I'll make this right. I'll go to Rio, go to all the hotels where I sent the money, and I'll send it all back. I can put all the cash in a bank, then send him a certified check.'

Trimble looked at me, shook his head, then tossed a pair of pants at Eddie's face. 'You're going to have to explain this to Mr Bullock yourself. Get dressed.'

Eddie eased himself off the bed, winced when he put his foot on the carpet. 'I really do think all my toes are broken,' he said. 'Could we stop at the hospital on the way, get somebody to look at this? Or, I know, I know. Listen, couldn't you tell him you couldn't find me? You do that, and I'll send you the money. You can have it all. Mr Bullock doesn't ever have to know. You could come to Rio with me, I'll take you to the hotels. They're all five-star, we could hang out awhile, at each one. Get ourselves some girls, have a party. But it's all yours, you don't want to pay for my room, that's cool, that's okay, I understand. I mean, if you could spare me a couple thou, that'd be great, but the rest, it would be yours.' To me, he said, 'You can have some, too, I mean, if that's okay with Detective Trimble.'

And back to Trimble: 'You know what Bullock is going to do to me. You can't just let that happen. You can't take me back there. You know what he'll do to me. He won't be at all understanding. You know he'll kill me.'

Trimble closed his eyes a moment in frustration. 'Get dressed, Eddie. We're going for a ride.'

He turned away from Eddie, pulled me aside. 'This is gonna be ugly. We've got no drugs, we've got no money, and he—'

Eddie was running for the sliding glass door to the balcony. He hobbled a bit, trying to keep the weight off his bad foot, flung the door open, and in a second his hands were on the railing, and he was over it like it was a vaulting horse.

And I thought, for a moment, how odd it was, that a guy, knowing his life was going to be over in a few seconds, would still favor his bad foot so it wouldn't hurt him too much.

THIRTY-FOUR

We both ran to the balcony, but Trimble edged in front of me to get out there first. I noticed he was careful not to touch the railing as he peered over, so I followed his lead. Ten floors down, the lower half of Eddie Mayhew was sprawled across the short hood of a minivan, and the rest of him had gone through the windshield. The van's alarm system had kicked in and was whooping.

'Terrific,' said Trimble, going back into the room. He took the case off a pillow and wiped down the back of the chair he'd grabbed, the handles of the over-the-shoulder bag. 'Did you touch anything?' he asked me.

'We didn't kill him,' I said. 'You didn't kill him. He jumped.'

'Yeah, well, I had every reason to have tossed him off the balcony, so I might as well have. Did you touch anything?'

'No. I don't think so.' I honestly wasn't certain, shaken as I was by what I'd just seen.

To be sure, Trimble used the pillowcase to wipe down the doorknobs, and the last thing he did was open the door with it, then tossed the case back into the room. 'Put it back on the pillow,' he told me, and I did.

And then we were in the hall, heading for the elevator. But Trimble shouldered open a door under an Exit sign and we were in the stairwell. 'I don't want anyone downstairs seeing an elevator come up to ten,' he said. He was running down the steps, taking two at a time. We did about a flight every five seconds, and about a minute later, we were back on the first floor, going down a hallway and out a side entrance that wasn't locked from the inside.

I had thought we'd be hearing sirens by the time we went outside, but there was only the distant wailing of the van's alarm from around the other side of the building. As if reading my mind, Trimble said, 'No one pays any attention to those things.'

It was true. Anytime I hear an alarm go off, I figure someone's hit the wrong button on their remote key by mistake.

We got into Trimble's car, me behind the wheel again. I could still see the gun down by the pedal. 'Drive out slow,' he said. 'We don't want anyone thinking this is a getaway vehicle.'

I glanced at the dashboard clock. It was time for another call to home base.

Trimble got out his cell, entered the number. 'Can't get a signal,' he said.

'What?'

'I can't get a signal. It's says No Service. Let me try again.' He entered Bullock's number again, put the phone to his ear. 'Cut out. Fucking cells.'

I went to reach for mine, then realized it was in a cardboard box on Bullock's desk. 'Try again . . .' I said.

'Okay, hang on, it's ringing.' A pause. 'Hey, it's me. Checking in . . . Yeah, I was having trouble getting a signal. Everything okay there?' Another pause. 'We're on our way back, actually . . . We had a visit with Eddie . . . No, listen, let me tell you about it when we get back . . . Yeah, bye.'

Trimble cleared his throat. 'I think Bullock could sense that things didn't go as well as they might have.'

I had us on the highway to downtown. Trimble seemed contemplative.

'Imagine what that must have been like, huh?' he said. 'Ten floors down. Then splat.'

'Imagine,' I said, 'thinking that was preferable to being taken back to see Bullock.'

As we got closer to downtown I asked Trimble what was on his mind.

'I was thinking about when you have a scarf, or a shirt maybe, and you get a tear at one end, say, and the threads start coming apart. And you try to tidy up the edges, you snip off the loose strings, but then, after another day or so, there are more loose threads. And you realize that the thing is just going to keep unraveling and there isn't a fucking thing you can do about it.'

I slowed for a red light.

'You know how many people have to die tonight for things to not unravel?' Trimble asked. I thought it was more a rhetorical question, so I didn't say anything. 'You, of course. And your daughter. And Eddie would have had to, if he hadn't taken care of that himself. And his wife, of course. That one's going to haunt me forever. There's enough witnesses to fill a streetcar.'

'Some have died already,' I said. 'There's a photographer at my paper. His name was Stan Wannaker, and your friend Bullock smashed his head in a car door earlier this evening. Not to get anything from him. Just to settle a score. And Lawrence is still probably iffy. It's only luck that's kept him alive. When Bullock left him, he had to believe he was leaving him for dead.'

Trimble said nothing. I guess he didn't have the energy this time to defend Bullock on that one. He was staring out the window. It was odd. He seemed at peace somehow, like maybe he'd arrived at some kind of a decision.

'One time,' he said, letting out a small chuckle, 'Lawrence and I, back when we were in uniform, we got partnered up one time, years before we'd end up together as detectives, and we get a call, a jumper, a hotel like the Ramada, must have been thirty floors or so. And there's a guy hanging off the other side of the balcony, the railing behind him, you know, leaning forward, holding on from behind?'

'I think I see it,' I said.

'So Lawrence and I – never Larry, right? – go into the room where the balcony is, and the guy says to stand back, or he'll let go if we come out there. So I stand back in the room and Lawrence gets into the room next door and goes out onto that balcony so he can talk to the guy without getting too close. And Lawrence looks down, and he tells the guy that his balcony, the one Lawrence is standing on, is way better to jump from than the one the guy is on.'

'Why?'

'Lawrence is looking down, and he says to the guy, "If you jump from your balcony, you might catch the edge of the pool, maybe hit the water, and you'll probably just bust your spine or something, and you'll be in a wheelchair the rest of your life sucking your meals through a straw. But if you come around to the next room, and jump off this balcony, you'll catch the parking lot, and you'll be dead in a second."'

'So the guy starts thinking about it, thinks maybe Lawrence is onto something, so he comes in off the balcony, and he's walking through the room and he says to me, "Your partner says I have to jump off the other balcony,' and I say okay, and escort him next door, and then together, Lawrence and I subdue this guy till the psycho ward arrives."' Trimble smiled to himself. 'Saved that dumbass's life. We pissed ourselves laughing all night over that.'

'That's kind of amazing. Smart, too.'

'Oh, he was good, Lawrence was. He always had a good feel for people, good judge of character.'

Neither of us said anything for a few seconds.

'Maybe he made a mistake in my case,' Trimble said.

'You can still make this right,' I said. 'Maybe you can't undo all the mistakes you've made, but maybe you can keep any more big ones from happening.'

Trimble shook his head, bemused. He looked over at me. 'Sometimes you just have to play the hand you're dealt.'

I didn't know what he meant by that.

We were heading down Wyndham, Bullock's house half a block away. 'What about it, Trimble?' I asked. 'How's this going to play out? I'd kind of like to have some idea before we go in there.'

'Yeah, me too,' he said. His gun appeared in his lap, gripped tightly in his right hand. 'Park the car and get out.'

We opened the doors at the same time, and I was half out of the front seat as Trimble was coming around the back of the car.

'Shit,' I said. 'I dropped my wallet.'

And I leaned back into the car, reached up by the accelerator, and slipped my hand around the cold metal of the gun grip. Quickly, before Trimble was around my side of the car, I slipped the gun into the pocket of my jacket. I'd already been patted down once. The odds were that I wouldn't be again.

Together, we walked into the house.

THIRTY-FIVE

Angie was still on the couch, but, I was relieved to see, more alert this time. As I entered the Hall of Barbies she jumped up and ran to me and I took her into my arms and hugged her, burying my face in her hair.

'Hey,' I said softly, patting her back. 'You okay?'

She looked up at me, her eyes red, and nodded. 'They haven't hurt you?' I asked. She shook her head.

'What about you?' she asked, reaching up to touch the left side of my face, which I'd forgotten had a good-size lump on it from much earlier that evening. 'Did they hit you?'

'No,' I said, not able to keep myself from smiling. 'That was from someone else.'

Angie blinked, like maybe she had an inkling for an instant, then dismissed the idea.

'She's been a perfect guest,' Bullock said, standing behind his desk as Blondie and Pockmark took up positions just inside the door. 'Your Angie was telling me that one Christmas when she was a little girl you assembled her a Barbie house. With a little swing attached to one side, and a spiral staircase on the other?'

'I remember,' I said. 'It took me hours.'

'I have that one,' Bullock said. 'But not here. It's a little too big for the shelves.'

I squeezed Angie into me. 'We're going to be okay,' I whispered to her. 'I promise you.'

Bullock snorted, smiled. Trimble stepped around me and Angie so he could face Bullock head-on.

'Where's Eddie?' Bullock asked. 'You said on the phone that you didn't have him with you. I specifically told you to bring him back here. I'm running this show now, so when I say jump, you're supposed to jump. Isn't that right?'

'That's right, boss,' said Pockmark. 'You're the man.'

Bullock looked at his underling with the bad complexion and said, 'Why don't you go outside, do a walk of the place, make sure there's no one around.'

Pockmark, almost cheerful, said, 'Yeah, sure, I could do that.'

'Eddie was unable to join us,' Trimble said. 'He figured he'd get treated better taking a leap down ten stories, rather than come here and face you.'

Bullock was stone-faced. 'What are you telling me?'

'He jumped. He's dead.'

Bullock leaned forward. 'Jesus Christ on a saltine, are you shitting me?'

'No.'

'But you got the stuff, right? Before he jumped? You got the stuff?'

'There is no stuff. He sold it.'

Bullock was starting to hyperventilate, which sent him into a coughing fit. He drank a few sips from the nearly empty water bottle.

'Then you got the money. Tell me you got the fucking money.'

Trimble said, 'Not exactly. He sold the shipment for

a handful of magic beans to the Jamaicans. A hundred and fifty thou.'

'A hundred fifty?' Bullock was stone-faced no more. He was stunned. 'He sold that for a hundred fifty? That would have kept half the junkies in this city happy for a year. A hundred fifty?'

'Yeah.'

Bullock made a fist and slammed it so hard onto the table that we all jumped, even Blondie. A pink display box featuring Malibu Barbie slipped off the shelf and hit the floor.

'Fuck . . .' Bullock screamed. And that set off yet another coughing fit. When he was done, he finished off the water bottle and tossed it into the garbage. Another guy who didn't know how to recycle.

Somewhat calmed now, he said to Trimble, 'So, you came back with the hundred fifty?'

Trimble paused. 'No. I came back with around seven thousand, maybe not even that. I haven't had a chance to count it yet.' He dug the envelope out of his pocket and tossed it onto Bullock's desk.

Bullock stared at Trimble, apparently unable to believe what he was hearing. 'Where's the rest of it?'

'He put it in envelopes and mailed it to Rio. Some in the regular mail, some by courier.'

'He put the cash in the mail,' Bullock said. Even Blondie looked surprised.

Trimble nodded. 'I guess he had a lot of faith in the postal system. Sent it to a bunch of five-star hotels in Rio, planned to go down there and pick it up. At least it could have been worse.'

Bullock cocked his head. 'How do you think it could be worse?'

'Could have been you who paid nearly nine grand for that car at auction. At least it was Walker's money that did that.' He glanced over at me, like maybe he thought he was scoring me a brownie point.

It didn't appear as though Bullock saw this as any sort of silver lining. He didn't look at me or Angie, but settled himself into his chair behind the desk, then glanced down and saw the Barbie box on the floor. He eyed it curiously, as if seeing it for the first time.

'I'm guessing Mr Indigo's not going to be very pleased about this,' Trimble said.

'Not pleased,' Bullock repeated. 'Not pleased, you say? That's very astute of you. Not pleased. Mr Indigo will be disappointed, perhaps even miffed. But you know what he'll be mostly?'

Trimble's eyebrows went up a notch.

'He'll be fucking apoplectic, that's what he'll be . . . And he'll have someone else running this organization before daylight, that's what he'll do.'

Bullock shook his head with rage, and then his eyes landed on the Barbie box that had dropped to the floor. 'Steve,' he said to Detective Trimble, his voice dripping with politeness, 'would you please put that Barbie back up where it belongs?'

'Excuse me?' Trimble said.

'My Barbie box. Would you please put it back up on the shelf? I guess it fell when I lost my temper a moment ago.'

'You want me to put your Barbie back on the shelf.'

'That's correct. I want to see if you're good for anything this evening.'

I held on to Angie. This had a very bad feel to it.

'I think you're closer,' Trimble told him. 'Why don't you do it.'

Blondie was looking very ill at ease, and wanted to try to defuse the situation. 'I'll get it,' he said.

'No . . .' Bullock shouted, and Blondie jumped back. 'Did I ask you?'

'I was just trying to help.'

Pockmark strolled back into the room, quipped, 'All quiet,' and, spotting the Malibu Barbie on the floor, quickly scooped it up and put it back on the shelf before Bullock could scream at him not to.

'Fuck,' said Bullock, and Pockmark looked at him, baffled, wondering why his action hadn't rated a thank you.

'What do you want from me?' Trimble said. 'I help you out, I tip you off to things, I run your fucking errands. And you've done right by me, I'll grant you that. And I've even stood by and done nothing when I find out you put my old partner in the hospital,'

'Who told you that?' Bullock demanded, 'I've been over this with you,'

Trimble didn't think that was worthy of a response. He continued, 'Who was it talked Eddie into helping you out? It wasn't me, I didn't pick him, and I wouldn't have, either. That was your decision. I've known him long enough to know he's not the sharpest knife in the drawer. So he double-crossed you. That's too bad, but I don't see how that's my fault.'

I felt the weight of the gun in my jacket pocket. I didn't know where this was going, this set of hostilities between Trimble and Bullock. And I didn't know whether it was going to afford me any sort of advantage.

'I'll tell you what,' Trimble said. 'Let Walker here, and his daughter, take a walk.' Bullock eyed the cop suspiciously, wondering what kind of game he was up to. Trimble continued, 'They don't have anything to do with this. He made the mistake of buying the wrong car, his daughter made the mistake of driving it. They've never done you any harm, they didn't rip you off.'

Bullock stared at Trimble as though he'd never seen him before. 'Have you lost your fucking mind? You're suggesting we let them walk out of here. After they know what we've been up to, about that smartass photographer, about Eddie, where I live and conduct my business. You think, we let them walk out of here, they'll just forget any of that stuff ever happened? You think that maybe all we have to do is ask them real nice?'

Even I was thinking Trimble had lost his mind. If I were Bullock, I'd kill us, too. Angie clutched me more tightly.

'I'm just saying,' Trimble said, 'that maybe it's time to lay low for a bit. You start piling up corpses, it has a way of attracting attention.'

Bullock suddenly looked contemplative, as though he might actually be considering what Trimble had to say. 'You make some interesting points, Steve. I'd like to think on them a moment, perhaps discuss a couple of things with Mr Walker here. Would you mind waiting out in the garage while I did that?'

Trimble eyed Bullock warily. None of this felt right.

'Sure,' Trimble said, then turned and walked out of the room, but not before looking over at me. He did something funny with the corner of his mouth that seemed to say, 'Hey, I gave it a shot. Good luck.'

Once Trimble was out of the room, Bullock walked over to Blondie and said, in a loud enough whisper that I could hear it, 'Do him.'

Blondie turned, but I was taking a step in his direction, and shouting, 'Trim—'

Pockmark was behind me, grabbing me at the top of my jacket and tossing me onto the couch. Angie screamed as I tumbled onto the cushions. Pockmark had his gun out and pointed at me as Blondie went out the door and pulled it shut behind him.

'You're not going to kill him,' I said.

Bullock said, 'He's been a pain in the ass for a while. You start seeing the signs, that he's starting to get some crisis of conscience or something. There's nothing worse than a cop with a conscience.'

'He wasn't bullshitting you,' I said. 'You let us walk out of here, we'll forget everything.'

'Sure,' Bullock said. 'Sure. That's exactly what I'd do, if I was you.'

Outside, there was a popping noise. One lone shot in the night, followed by silence. Not enough to make anyone go to their phone and put in a call to the cops. You hear one shot, you listen for another, to confirm your suspicions that something's amiss. When you don't hear it, you go back to sleep. Just like car alarms.

Angie heard it, and she looked at me. There wasn't much hope in her eyes.

'I mean it,' I said. 'We walk out of here, you never hear from us again.' Desperate for any way to sweeten the offer, I said, 'You can even keep the car.'

I guess that struck Bullock as pretty funny, because he started to laugh.

'I'm serious. You can probably sell it for what I paid for it. I'll sign it over to you.'

'Oh, that's too much,' Bullock said, and laughed again.

As I'd seen so often before, the laughter sent him into a coughing fit. There was one loud, hoarse cough, and when he inhaled to catch his breath, it set off another. He began to make some awful hacking noises in his throat, like maybe he was going to cough up a hairball or something.

Bullock went to grab for the water bottle, then remembered that he'd finished it and tossed the empty into the trash. He glanced around, then peered into the cardboard box still sitting on his desk, the one Blondie had brought in from the garage, containing everything he'd found in my car.

I remembered that my cell phone was in there, but something else had caught Bullock's eye.

He reached in and came out with a full bottle of Snapple apple juice. And I wondered, just for a moment, where that had come from. I hadn't bought any bottle of apple juice.

And then I realized it was the bottle I'd picked out of my own recycling basket, the one I'd taken with me when I went out for my first surveillance job to track Angie's stalker, Trevor.

What a trivial problem he seemed now.

And I remembered how, once I'd filled that bottle myself, I'd tucked it into the pouch behind the passenger seat to keep it from rolling around.

And I remembered that it was, of course, not apple juice.

Bullock uncapped the bottle and moved it towards his mouth.

I thought back to that discussion Lawrence had had with me, about the robbery he'd interrupted, the guy with the ragweed allergy. How Lawrence had said you had to wait for your moment when you were in a tense situation, and that when it had arrived, you'd know it.

I had a feeling, that if there was ever going to be a moment, this was going to be it.

THIRTY-SIX

I slipped my hand into my jacket pocket, wrapped it around the cold metal of the gun's grip, got my body ready to launch off the couch in a hurry.

Bullock didn't just sip from the bottle. He took a long swig, which meant my day-old urine was already hitting the back of his throat before he had a chance to realize that it was not, in fact, apple juice. Already I was thinking that being over on the couch, away from the desk and off to one side, was a good place to be, because I was expecting, any second, something of an eruption from Bullock.

I was not disappointed.

It all took less than a second or two, but if you could have slowed down time, broken it down into milliseconds, you'd have seen his eyes bug out first. Then the cheeks puffed out, the body lunged forwards, and then he spewed. The contents of his mouth sprayed out across his desk and onto the carpeting beyond. There was a lot of noise that went along with this. It was as if you went into a recording studio to combine screams of anguish, retching and intense vulgarity. Somewhere, in the midst of perhaps the most disgusting sound I'd ever heard, Bullock managed to let loose with a loud, gargly 'Shit . . .'

I felt no compunction to point out to Bullock that while he had that wrong, he was closer than he knew.

Pockmark thought, and had every reason to believe, that his boss must be dying. He rushed across the room at the first signs of Bullock's distress, then dodged as Bullock spewed across his desk, hitting the box and phone and intercom and the envelopes of cash Trimble had taken off Eddie Mayhew.

'What?' Pockmark said. 'Is the juice bad?'

He'd totally forgotten about me, and his gun hung down at his side as he went to save his boss, who was now spitting repeatedly, and not particularly fussy about where any of it landed.

Angie's mouth was hanging open in shock. And I was on my feet, taking the gun out of my pocket and, gripping it with both hands, pointing it at Pockmark, then Bullock, then back at Pockmark, not having to waver too much, because the two of them were now pretty much shoulder to shoulder.

'Ewww,' said Pockmark.

'Fuck . . .' Bullock said, spitting onto the top of his desk. 'What the fuck is this?' He glanced at the bottle, put it up to his nose, and turned his head away, disgusted.

I didn't have a lot of time to think about what I was going to say, so I said the first thing that came to mind, and that was 'Freeze . . .' I was close to saying 'Freeze, motherfuckers . . .' but it struck me as even more of a cliché, and besides, my daughter was standing right there.

Bullock and Pockmark looked at me, stupidly at first, a kind of 'Huh?' expression on both their faces. Bullock wiped the back of his left sleeve across his mouth. When Pockmark saw the gun in my hand, he went to raise his and I shouted at him, 'Freeze, motherfucker . . .'

I couldn't help myself. I could always apologize to Angie later. And the thing was, it worked this time.

Pockmark froze.

Angie, who two seconds earlier had been reeling from Bullock's explosive performance, now looked at me with further astonishment, wondering, perhaps, what I had done with her real father.

'I want you to put that gun on the floor,' I said, pointing my gun now directly at Pockmark.

'I thought you dumbfucks searched him,' Bullock said.

'We did . . . He had nothing on him . . .'

'You call that nothing?'

'I asked you to put that gun down,' I said, stepping around in front of Angie to shield her in case Pockmark decided to try something stupid.

But he still wouldn't drop it. It hung there at the end of his arm, still pointing down. He glared at me, as if we were engaged in a staring contest, that he would no more drop his gun than look away.

I didn't see this situation getting any better if something wasn't done about it right away. Blondie was still out there somewhere, probably coming back soon. At the moment, I only had two of them to deal with, and it wasn't going to get any easier with three.

So I shot Pockmark.

For a second, I couldn't believe I'd done it. No one was more surprised than I. Well, maybe Pockmark. And Angie seemed a bit taken aback as well, because she screamed. From where she stood, slightly behind and to the side of me, she didn't know for a moment who'd actually pulled the trigger. And in that room, the shot sounded like a cannon going off.

I'd aimed a bit low when I squeezed the trigger, not wanting to actually shoot Pockmark in the head or chest, even though I realized that if you want to bring someone down, you aim for the biggest part of his body, the torso. Aiming for someone's leg and actually hitting it was not something you could count on, so I guess you could say I got lucky. Certainly luckier than Pockmark.

'Jesus . . .' he yelped, and the gun hit the floor. He stumbled over to a chair, both hands pressed over a growing shiny patch on his black jeans. 'Jesus Christ.'

There was a time when I might have apologized for something like this, but not tonight.

Bullock said nothing. He kept glaring at me.

'Angie, sweetheart,' I said.

From behind me, she said, 'Yes, Daddy?'

'Do you think you could go over and pick up that gun? Very carefully, by the handle?'

'Okay.'

She came around me, and I noticed that she was still a bit unsteady on her feet. When she bent over to pick up the gun, I thought she might fall over, but she steadied herself, grabbed it gingerly, found it a bit heavier than she'd anticipated, I think, and handed it to me. I slipped it into my other pocket.

Now all we had to do was get out of there. Get to the Virtue, hope it would start, get Angie to a hospital to make sure she was okay. But Blondie was still out there someplace. In the house, maybe out in the garage. And, as thick as the walls seemed to be in this old house, he might still have heard the shot, or Angie's scream, and be on his way back to investigate.

To Bullock, I said, 'Take out your knife.'

'I don't have a knife.' Didn't even blink.

'The one in your back pocket, the one you put to my neck when we were in the garage.'

'I don't have it now,' he said.

'Okay,' I said. 'You can either toss out your knife, or Barbie and Ken get it.'

Bullock suddenly looked alarmed. 'What? What did you say?'

'Toss it, or the dolls die,' I said.

Bullock almost smiled. 'You're absolutely out of your mind. Whaddya gonna do, take one of them hostage?'

That was a plan I could keep in reserve. For now, I was happy to play executioner. I turned the gun toward the shelves of pink packages. I didn't really have to aim. I could fire anywhere and hit something.

So I did.

I caught the Munsters version of Ken and Barbie. The box spun on the shelf, hit the back wall, and bounced back onto the floor. The bullet had torn through the packaging and caught Ken in the neck, knocking his Frankenstein-like head clean off.

'My God . . .' Bullock said. 'What have you done? You some kind of fucking animal?'

'Toss out the knife,' I said.

'That's Munster Barbie . . . It took me five years to find that . . .'

I fired again, putting a hole through the door of Barbie's pink Volkswagen minibus.

It then occurred to me that I'd fired three bullets. I had no idea how many I had left, and there was no sense using them all on defenseless pieces of plastic.

'Stop it . . .' Bullock screamed. 'Stop it . . .'

He reached into his back pocket and threw the switchblade, closed, across the room.

'What's wrong with you?' he asked. 'Are you insane?'

Pockmark, leaning into his chair and still holding his wounded leg, looked at Bullock and said, 'So *now* he's insane. He shoots me in the fucking leg, you got nothing to say.'

I was ready to move out. Bullock and Pockmark, to the best of my knowledge, were disarmed. But I had to get myself and Angie down the hall, out the door, to the garage, get the door open, get us into the Virtue, get it started (fingers crossed) and drive away. Once I was out of this room and no longer able to keep a gun on Bullock, he'd probably come after us.

And Blondie was still out there.

A phone rang.

I looked at Bullock, who looked at me. The ringing was coming from inside the cardboard box where he'd found the Snapple bottle.

It was my cell phone.

Tentatively, I moved closer to the desk, still holding the gun on Bullock, and reached in with my left hand for the phone. The phone was damp, but there wasn't time to be squeamish about picking it up. I pressed the button after the third ring and put the phone up to my left ear, half expecting it to be Bertrand Magnuson, checking in with me to make sure I wasn't using a weapon in the performance of my duties as a

Metropolitan staff member. No, I could say honestly, I was only shooting people in my off-time.

'Hello,' I said evenly.

'Mr Walker? It's Trevor.'

Jesus. Just what I needed.

'This isn't really a good time, Trevor. I've kind of got my hands full.'

'Okay, listen, I'm sorry, but I wanted to know how it was going, because if you haven't found Angie, I think I can tell you where she is.'

'I know where she is, Trevor. She's here with me.'

'So you're at the house on Wyndham Lane?'

I felt blood pounding in my temples. 'That's right, Trevor. We're in a house on Wyndham Lane.'

'Excellent.'

'Trevor, where are you?'

'Well, I'm sort of in the bushes, by the house. I didn't think you were here, because I didn't see your car or anything. But that big black SUV? The one they used to take away Angie? It's here. But if you're with Angie, I'm assuming everything's okay, right?'

'Not entirely, Trevor. There are still a few things to work out. How, exactly, did you know where to find us?'

'Okay, I'll tell you, but you're gonna be pissed.'

THIRTY-SEVEN

'Go ahead,' I said to Trevor, trying to keep my voice even. 'I won't get mad. I promise.'

Angie was feeling a bit unsteady on her feet and plopped back onto the couch while I continued to hold a gun on Bullock. Pockmark had lost a fair bit of blood, and his head hung down onto his chest as he gripped his thigh. The guy needed to get to a hospital.

'This was the thing I was going to tell you a while ago,' Trevor said, 'but I couldn't think of a way to do it, but I've been thinking about it and decided the best thing to do is help Angie, no matter what.'

'Okay, Trevor. I'd be real grateful if you can move this story along and just tell me.'

'I know what I've done, some people might call inappropriate. But I wasn't doing it for my own purposes alone. I think there's a larger issue at stake here, a point to be made about how we're all being monitored in one way or another, that Big Brother is watching our every move, and that we need to take a stand against this kind of dehumanization that threatens to rob us of our—'

'Trevor . . .'

'Okay. You know that day you found me at your place, and I had my computer with me, and I was looking for my dog?'

'The tracking thing,' I said. 'Let me guess.'

'Yeah,' he said. 'Right.'

'You've been tracking Angie's whereabouts, with the same kind of gizmo you clipped onto your dog's collar.'

'You don't have to thank me now,' Trevor said. 'When I ran into Angie the other day at Starbucks, I was helping her with her coat and I sort of slipped it into one of the inside pockets where I figured she'd never look.'

I glanced over at Angie, and at her coat, draped over the end of the couch.

'Hold on a second, Trevor,' I said. To Angie, I said, 'Honey?'

'Yes, Dad?'

'Take a look in the inside pockets of your coat, see if you find anything in there.'

'Like what?'

'Sort of like a button or something.'

She pulled the coat over onto her lap, started rifling through the pockets, and came out with a small silver disc. 'This?' she said.

I went back onto the phone. 'We found it, Trevor.'

'What is this?' Angie asked.

'It's a tracking thing,' I told her. 'Trevor put it in your pocket, that's how he's been following you all over town, showing up where you least expected him.'

Even slightly out of it, Angie went red with anger. 'Is that him on the phone? Give it to me. I want to talk to him.'

'Later, hon,' I said.

At the other end of the line, Trevor said, 'She sounds a bit pissed.'

'Trevor, what can you see from where you are?'

'Huh? Uh, like I say, I'm just in the bushes, looking at the house. I've got Morpheus with me.'

'Where's your car?'

'It's about six blocks back. I didn't want anyone to see it, so I walked down, but I've got my laptop with me.'

'Jeez, I think I'm dying,' Pockmark said. I had a look at him. He didn't look to me like he was dying, but there was no question he needed some medical attention.

'Shut up,' Bullock said. 'If you'd frisked him better, we wouldn't be in this mess now. Wait'll I tell Mr Indigo.'

'I can't wait to hear that myself,' Pockmark said. 'How you gonna explain all this?'

'What's going on?' Trevor said.

'Nothing,' I said. 'Just some other people in the room here havin' a chat. We need a ride out of here, Trevor, but we don't have time for you to run back to your Chevy. Also, there's another man outside or around the garage somewhere, and he isn't going to want us to leave.'

'I saw a guy a minute ago. I think he'd just dumped something into the back of the SUV.'

Trimble's body, I figured.

'And then he went back into the garage.'

I thought for a moment. If we could get Blondie back out of the garage, then Trevor could go in, open the door, get the Virtue running and out into the driveway, and all Angie and I had to do was run out, hop in, and go.

'Hang on, Trevor, okay?'

'Yeah.'

To Bullock, I said, 'You can talk to the garage with that thing there, right?' I pointed to the intercom. He nodded. 'Tell your guy to come on back here.'

'And if I don't?'

'Then I take a shot at Wonder Woman Barbie.'

He didn't have to think long about that. He pressed the button, shouted, 'Hey . . .' He waited a second for a response, tried again. 'Hey, are you—'

'Hello?'

'Take your finger off the button . . .'

'Hello? Go ahead . . .'

'Fuck,' Bullock said under his breath, waited a beat, then pressed the button again. 'Are you there?'

'Yup.'

'You get that job done?'

'Yeah. Stevie's loaded up and ready to go. We can take a drive, unload him somewhere. I know where there's a wood chipper. You want to do the others at the same time?'

I had a chill, knowing now what was in store for us.

'First thing I need you to do is come back here. It's these others we have to deal with.'

'Yeah, sure, just be a sec.'

'You,' I said to Pockmark. I wanted him out of the chair. If he stayed there, he'd be visible the moment Blondie opened the door. He forced himself out of the chair, dragged his leg to the other side of the room, and sat down on the floor. I motioned for Angie to get off the couch, and handed her the gun I'd taken from Pockmark.

'Think you can manage this?' I said to her. 'I want you to keep it on Mr Barbie here.'

337

She nodded. Tiredly, but she was more awake every minute.

I spoke into the cell. 'Trevor, you there?'

'Yeah,' he whispered.

'Has that guy left the garage yet?'

'No.'

'The moment he walks out and heads for the house, you let me know.'

'Okay. Nothing yet. Maybe he's – Hang on, the side door's opening up. He's coming out . . . He's going into the house.'

'Is he holding a gun?'

'Uh, I don't, I don't think so . . .'

I figured it wouldn't take him any more than ten or fifteen seconds to get from the house door to the room we were in now. I positioned myself against the wall, by the doorframe. I could hear Blondie's steps coming down the hall, stop, then the knob turned and the door began to open.

'I was—' he started to say, but then he felt the cold ring of metal against his temple.

'Don't move,' I said.

'No problem,' he said.

'Come in very slowly.'

He quickly took in the scene, assessed it. His partner on the floor, bleeding. Bullock not moving, standing behind a very damp desk. Angie standing on the other side of the door, her gun trained on Bullock.

'Nice frisking job,' Bullock said to him.

'Where's your gun?' I asked.

'Tucked into the back of my pants,' he said. I looked around, saw it, couldn't help but think that he had a butt sticking out of his butt. Funny how the mind works.

I moved slightly behind him, keeping the gun close to his head, then took the gun from the back of his pants with my left hand. Now that I'd given Pockmark's weapon to Angie, I could slip this new one into my now empty left pocket.

'Now step into the room and lie face down on the floor,' I said.

Blondie did as he was asked.

I got back on the phone. 'Trevor, go into the garage.'

'Gotcha.'

I could hear him running across the property, then the sound of a door opening and closing.

'See my car?'

'Yeah. Shit, it's all in pieces.'

'It's mostly the inside door panels. Don't worry about that. See if the keys are in it.'

'Hang on, yeah, they're here.'

'See if it'll start.'

I listened. The Virtue was so quiet, I wasn't sure I'd hear it come on even if it did. 'No, it won't.'

I could hear my heart pounding in my temples. 'Turn the key ahead, move the shifter back and forth a couple times, try it again.'

I heard some noise in the background. 'Okay, it's on. You're a genius.'

I let out a breath. 'Just leave it running. There should be a button somewhere that opens that middle garage door.'

'Just a minute. Okay, yeah, I think this is it. Yep, the garage door is going up.'

'I want you to back the Virtue out, get it turned around in the driveway, leave the engine running. Leave the driver's door open, you get in the back. Have the back door open that faces the house. When I come out, I'm going to put Angie in the back with you so you can look after her. She's a bit woozy.'

'You don't want me to drive?'

'I'll drive. Can you do everything I've asked?'

'Yeah, sure. I'll leave my phone on but put it in my pocket for a sec. Stay on the line.'

'Okay.' To Angie, I said, 'We're leaving, honey. We're getting out of here in just a few seconds.'

'Okay, Daddy,' she said. 'Did I hear right, is Trevor out there?'

'Yeah.'

'That little weasel, putting that fucking thing in my coat.'

'Why don't we get angry with him about it later, after he saves our lives?'

'I suppose.' She grabbed her coat, slinging it over her arm so she could still keep the gun on Bullock.

'Mr Walker?'

I held the phone back up to my ear. 'Yeah.'

'I'm all set to go here. Run out, hop in the driver's seat, and we're off.'

'Good man,' I said. 'We'll be right out.' I slipped the phone into my jacket. 'We're going to be on our way, guys.' I pointed to Pockmark, the dark stain on his trousers getting even larger. 'I think you should see about getting this one to a doctor.'

I motioned Angie towards the door. 'You go first,' I said. 'Get in the car.'

She slid by me and out the door. I heard her run down the hall, through the kitchen, then a door open and close.

'Get under the desk,' I said to Bullock. He scrunched down and got under. Then I told Blondie to do the

340

same. He had some difficulty jamming himself under there with his boss.

Then I ran.

I was out the house door in a second. The Virtue was sitting there, right where it was supposed to be, Trevor and Angie in the back, plus Morpheus, jumping around the backseat and into the front. The driver's door was left open, and I hopped in, threw the car into drive, and pressed the accelerator, knocking Morpheus, who was without doubt one of the ugliest dogs I'd ever seen, off his feet and into the back of the front bucket. The car jerked to a start, and we were flying down the sloped driveway so quickly the car's front underpan slammed into the street as we turned onto it.

I caught a glimpse of Trevor, the strap of his laptop case looped over his shoulder, in my mirror and saw that he was turned around, looking behind us.

'They're coming . . .' he said. 'Two of them . . . They're running to the SUV . . .'

'I think I'm going to be sick,' Angie said as I swerved to avoid hitting a station wagon I'd just cut off.

'It's okay,' Trevor said to her softly. 'It's going to be okay.' Morpheus bounded into the backseat and licked Trevor in the face.

We were nearing the end of Wyndham, and in my mirror I saw headlights sweeping down to the end of the Bullock house driveway. The Annihilator burst into view, straightened, started coming after us like the enormous beast it was.

I glanced back. Angie looked pale. 'I really need some air,' she said. 'I gotta put down a window or I'm gonna be sick. Oh crap, there's no buttons or anything to put the window down.'

It was true. When they'd taken the inside door panels off to search for drugs, they'd removed the power window controls. But there was still a button on the dash for the sunroof, and I opened it. 'How's that?' I asked.

'Better,' she said.

'Trevor,' I said. 'Call 911.'

'Yeah.' He had his phone out and was about to punch in the numbers when I hung a hard right at an intersection, tossing my passengers – human and canine – about. 'You might try to get your seat belts on if you get a chance,' I advised.

'Here,' Trevor said to Angie, 'I'll get yours.' And he leaned across, grabbed the belt from above her shoulder, and secured it. Then he did his own. 'I'm calling them now,' he said. Morpheus was in Angie's lap now, looking like maybe he was going to have a nap.

I didn't have a destination in mind. I just wanted to get away.

The Annihilator cut that last corner short, riding up over one curb and down another. As far back as it was, I could still hear its engine roar with the Virtue sunroof open.

Trevor, craning his head around every few seconds, said, 'They're gaining.'

I leaned on the gas, but the hybrid didn't take off the way I might have hoped. The SUV was closing the distance.

'Is this the police?' Trevor said into his phone. 'We're being chased by some people who want to kill us . . . Uh, we're in a silver Virtue, going north on—' He looked around. 'Where are we?' he shouted.

I wasn't sure. I knew about as much as Trevor did, that we were heading north.

'I'm not sure. But look for a silver car being chased by a black SUV. There's two men in it and they're—'

We were hit from behind. The Annihilator, its shoulder-high headlamps filling the Virtue with light, had nudged the back bumper. Morpheus sprung up from his short nap, put his paws on the back window ledge, and began barking and slobbering. I swung the wheel to the right, then the left, crossing the middle lane and then back again. At least this time they weren't shooting at us. I'd taken guns off both of Bullock's men and—

And then they were shooting at us.

'He's got a gun . . .' Trevor shouted. 'Like a machine gun or something . . .'

'Get down . . .' I shouted, and Trevor threw his arm around Angie and forced her head below the bottom of the rear window.

'It's going to be okay,' he told her again. 'I'm going to take care of you. I'll always take care of you.' There were more shots, a *pop-pop-pop-pop*. All our windows were still intact, but I thought I'd heard at least one bullet strike the trunk or back bumper.

I rounded a corner, the tires shifting and slipping on some streetcar tracks. Up ahead, a late-night streetcar taking people home after the bars had closed was rolling along. I swung out to the left, passing it in the opposite lane. I glanced in my mirror and the Annihilator was gone, but once I'd passed the streetcar, it appeared on my right side. It had passed the streetcar on the inside and was now getting ready to ram us from the side.

I hit the brakes. The Annihilator, as big and as heavy as it was, couldn't stop in as short a distance. I turned left down a narrow residential street. In seconds, I saw the headlights behind me again. I zigzagged my way through the neighborhood's streets, a right, another right, a left, a right. I'd completely lost my bearings, but I hadn't lost the Annihilator.

The thing was, my car was no match for it, not unless Bullock and Blondie ran out of gas. Driving the vehicle that got better mileage didn't count for much at the moment. It wasn't like I could take this chase off the streets. Off-road I'd have even less chance of getting away from that four-wheel-drive monster.

Ahead, I saw some familiar buildings. I was starting to get my bearings. We were coming up on Mackenzie University and its historic, grand structures.

I blasted past the gate, where you picked up your parking ticket when entering the grounds. The university streets were nearly deserted, hardly any cars parked along the lanes, no students walking around.

The Annihilator came in after me, barreling like a locomotive.

Angie raised her head enough to see where we were.

'Get back down,' Trevor said.

'Wait,' Angie said, looking around. 'Dad, I've got an idea.'

'Me too,' I said, my hands wet with sweat as I gripped the wheel.

It was going to be tricky, that was for sure. But for all the car's faults, its steering was tight and precise.

I slowed a bit, let the Annihilator gain on us. It only took a second. The SUV's massive grill loomed over our trunk, its lights like fire, its engine roaring as if it were about to devour us.

Morpheus barked incessantly.

I sped through the grounds, looking for Galloway Hall. There it was, up ahead. And there, around the building's far side, Angie's shortcut. The pedestrian pathway.

I waited until the last possible second, then cranked the wheel hard to the right, gripping it with both hands, and aimed the car for the center of the opening, this low-ceilinged pathway that Angie used to sneak out of Mackenzie without paying for her parking.

The Annihilator was no more than a couple of feet behind us.

We'd only been in the tunnel a thousandth of a second when we heard it. An ear-splitting noise. Metal meeting brick. Glass shattering. Sheet metal tearing.

I'd have looked back, but I had to keep my eyes straight ahead to make sure neither fender caught the brick walls. But I was able to catch a glimpse of the fireball in the rearview mirror. I didn't slow down. I didn't know how much of the Annihilator might be left to follow us in.

As it turned out, what was left of the truck only went about thirty or forty feet, but I couldn't bring myself to let up on the gas until we were out the other end. Only then did I stop the car, a couple of feet shy of the chain that kept us from driving out onto Edwards Street.

I unbuckled and, along with Angie and Trevor and Morpheus, got out of the Virtue and looked back.

The brick archway had caught the Annihilator at the base of the windshield. Bullock and Blondie would have been thrown forwards from the force of the collision, but only in the instant before the brick archway sliced the entire top of the vehicle, and in all likelihood their heads, clean off.

THIRTY-EIGHT

There was a lot of explaining to be done.

Before the cops began with their onslaught of questions, I told them, standing by the Virtue and holding a shaken Angie in my arms, that there were a few things they needed to know about immediately. There was the matter of a tied-up woman in a house out in the suburbs. And the fact that her husband had taken a header off a balcony at the airport Ramada, and that the odds were she didn't know a thing about it yet.

Also, there was a guy with a bullet in his leg in a house on Wyndham Lane. Assuming he was still there, and hadn't already hobbled his way down to the closest emergency room.

It was pretty likely they were going to find, in the back of that disintegrated Annihilator, a dead police detective. And further investigation by their forensic folks would show that he hadn't died in the accident.

And last, but far from least, there was my daughter Angie. She seemed okay, but as I explained to one of the officers, she'd been drugged with something earlier in the evening and should be checked out at a hospital immediately. There were already ambulances at the scene, waiting for the folks from the fire department to see who or what they could recover from the wreckage of the SUV, so a couple of paramedics rushed over to see how she was.

'I'm going to have to answer a whole lot of questions,' I said as they loaded her into the back of the ambulance, an anxious Trevor moving from one foot to another as he cautioned the paramedics to be careful with her. 'I'll give your mother a call, send her to the hospital to wait with you. After they've checked you out, made sure you're okay, the cops are going to have a lot of questions for you, too.'

Angie nodded tiredly and slipped her arms around my neck. 'You look nice in your new clothes, Daddy,' she said.

'Thanks, honey.'

'Promise me you'll have them check that bump on the side of your head?'

I smiled. 'I think it's fine. It might even have knocked some sense into me.'

She was puzzled by that, but let it go. 'You were something,' she said. 'You were really something.' And then her mouth dropped open, as though she'd suddenly remembered something.

'What?' I said.

'Shit,' she said. 'I've got an essay due in the morning.'

I smiled. 'I think being kidnapped and narrowly escaping death is an even better excuse than having your dog eat your homework. I'm sure the paramedics will write you a note. Which course is it?'

'My psych course. I had all the research done. All I had to do was write it up, which I was gonna do last night.'

'Don't worry about it,' I said. 'Your professor will understand. What was it about, anyway?'

She smiled. 'Man and masochism,' she said. 'Trying to figure out why some guys get turned on by pain.'

My eyebrows went up. 'This is what they're teaching you in school?'

'College, Dad.'

Tumblers started falling into place. 'So, what kind of research did you have to do for a paper like that?'

'I read all kinds of stuff, and I even talked to Trixie.'

'Oh yeah,' I said, like I was trying to remember. 'Our old neighbor.'

'She's hardly old. She's pretty dynamite looking, actually.'

'You know what I meant.'

'Yeah. Like, it's no secret anymore what she does for a living, so I gave her a call, she gave me all kinds of great quotes. I made her promise not to tell you, 'cause I knew you and Mom would freak if you knew I was going out to see her.'

'No,' I said defensively, 'we'd have understood.'

'She's actually a very nice person,' Angie said.

'Yeah, for sure. She is.'

'It's not the sort of thing I'd like to do for a living, though, you know?'

I nodded. 'Well, I don't like to judge.'

Angie smiled. 'I hope you're not pissed.'

It was my turn to smile. 'I'll get over it. Listen, you really should get checked out.'

She turned and there was Trevor, trying hard to look nonchalant in his long black coat, but you could see it in his eyes, that he was rattled, that he'd been through a night like no other. Morpheus seemed a bit drained, too, standing at Trevor's side, leaning into him, his long tongue hanging in front of him.

Angie approached Trevor, smiled. 'Thank you,' she said. She leaned in and gave him a light kiss on the cheek. 'Thanks for being there. I guess I'll give you shit later about how you happened to know where we were.'

He said, 'Nothing I ever did was meant to hurt you. It was meant to protect you.'

'Yeah, well, I think you got lucky on that one.'

'I wasn't the only one,' he said, as if to remind her that her good fortune was linked to him in some small way. 'I think this is one of those defining moments.'

'What?' Angie said.

'A moment that defines who you and I are, what we mean to each other. We've been caught together in a confluence. I don't see how either one of us can ignore that.'

The attendants were closing the ambulance door, leaving Angie with nothing else to say, but she waved her fingers at me and mouthed, 'I love you.' I waved back and watched her face through the window as the ambulance pulled away.

I got out my cell and phoned home. It was going to be hard to explain to Sarah that Angie being at the hospital, in the overall scheme of things, was actually the best news I'd had to share all evening.

'Hello?' she said tiredly.

'It's me,' I said.

'Hey, what time is it? Oh my God, do you know what time it is?'

'It's late, yeah, sorry.'

'It's the middle of the night. Wait, I'm going to see if Angie's back.'

'Just listen a sec. The first thing I have to tell you is, everybody's fine, we're all okay.'

You just know, when someone starts off the conversation that way, everything you're about to hear is going to be bad.

The cops kept me, and Trevor, for hours. I guess they had others interviewing Trevor, but me they put in a car so that we could all take a trip to Bullock's place, where I showed them the haul from the Brentwood's heist, the room where Angie'd been held, Pockmark and the Barbies shot. Pockmark wasn't there, but was picked up early in the morning in the ER at Mercy General. There was blood on the garage floor, presumably from where Blondie had shot Trimble before putting his body into the Annihilator.

I told them Bullock, or possibly one of his two henchmen, had put Lawrence Jones into the hospital and killed the *Metropolitan* photographer Stan Wannaker. Not to get back his film, but to get even for the incident at the auction.

I told them about how I'd bought a car at a government auction that had supposedly, at one time, been loaded with drugs, and how Eddie Mayhew had hoped to pull a fast one on Lenny Indigo's people by sneaking the drugs out and selling them to a rival organization. About how the only cop I felt I could trust was the last one in the world I should have called, and how Trimble's apparent moves toward redemption had come too late to make a difference.

There were lots of other details to fill in, but I gave them the broad strokes. And then I called the city desk and said that, after I'd gone home and had a bit of sleep, I'd be coming in.

I had a story to write.

A couple of days later, we had a few people over to the house. Sarah made a chocolate cake. A Betty Crocker mix, with icing out of the can. Angie's favorite. I wore some more of my new clothes.

Trixie drove in from Oakwood. A few of the people from the paper, friends of Stan's, came by. Bertrand Magnuson even dropped by, briefly, and took me aside.

'If it'd been me,' he said, 'I'd have shot that fucker in the nuts instead of the leg.' A detective I'd spent several hours explaining everything to dropped in for a short visit, long enough to grab a piece of cake. It was a low-key affair, no speeches, no toasts, just a chance to celebrate quietly that Angie was okay and that this whole mess with Barbie Bullock and his gang was behind us.

Trevor Wylie was there, wearing his shades in the house, shadowing Angie as much as she'd allow it. At one point, when they were both in the kitchen, I heard him pressing her to take a short walk with him, to get some air. 'Maybe later,' Angie told him.

What I learned was, she was expecting some special company. 'I've invited Cameron to come by,' Angie said while Trevor was out of earshot. She sidled up next to me as I used one of our carving knives to cut a piece of cake for a guest. I knew we had a pastry knife and lifter somewhere, but that was the kind of thing only Sarah would be able to find.

'That's great,' I said.

'He's been really worried about me, after all that happened, so I asked him to come over. It'll give you a chance to meet him. He's really a nice guy, and

I'm ready to introduce you, provided you don't go wandering around his house late at night when I'm already upstairs asleep.'

'That'd be nice,' I said, trying to suppress a smirk. 'I'm sure he'll be interested to meet me, too.'

Trevor interrupted us. 'Can I get you anything, Angie?' he asked.

'No, I'm good.'

'You want to catch some air now? Because there are some things I'd like to talk to you about.'

Angie glanced at me, the back of her head to Trevor, and her eyes rolled. 'I can't just walk out now, Trev, not with all these people here, okay?'

I'll be around,' he said, slipping out of the kitchen.

Quietly, Angie said to me, 'I know he was there for me, for us, at the right time, but honestly, he's freaking me out. But there's like some Chinese or Indian tradition or something going on here, that he feels he's obligated to watch out for me forever now. You save someone's life, you have to hound them till the day they die.'

'I know,' I said. 'It's awkward, isn't it? Considering.'

'Yeah. You know what he told me?' I leaned in. 'He said we're linked cosmically. At first, I thought he said "comically", and so I laughed, and that was definitely the wrong thing to do. He tells me, if he's not with me, he won't ever be with anyone. It was like he wanted to add I wouldn't ever be with anyone else either.'

'Let me think about a way to handle it,' I said. Angie gave me a look. 'I'll talk to your mom. I won't do anything crazy. How you doing, otherwise?'

'I don't know if it's all hit me yet. It's hard to believe it all really happened. Like maybe it was just a bad dream.'

'That's kind of how I feel,' I said, and kissed her on the forehead before Angie went back to talk to our guests.

There was a knock at the door. I opened it and came face-to-face with my attacker: Angie's boyfriend Cameron. I'd never had a good look at him, and he was a good-looking boy, about my height, trying to grow a bit of hair on his face and not having a lot of luck with it.

He eyed me curiously, leaned back to double-check the number above the front door.

'Uh, are you Angie's dad?'

I admitted it.

'I came by to see her? She said there was sort of a thing going on?'

'Sure,' I said, and when I turned to open the door wider, he was able to see what was left of the bruise on the left side of my face. He stopped in mid-step.

'Do I . . . don't I know . . .' And then, as the realization sunk in, he muttered, 'Holy shit,' and his body seemed to collapse in on itself.

I extended my hand. 'I think we've met, but we didn't have time for proper introductions the other night at McDonald's.'

He shook my hand limply. 'Oh shit,' he said again. 'I'm really sorry. I had no idea . . .'

'I know. And you were just looking out for Angie, and that makes you okay in my book, so why don't you come in.'

I led him down the hall, and when Angie saw him she put down her cake and walked briskly across the room, throwing her arms around his neck and giving him a kiss. And not on the cheek, either. He glanced back nervously at me and, pointing my way, whispered something to Angie. She looked at me, opened her mouth as if in shock, then slowly a smile developed as she put it together. She shook her head at me, as if to say 'What next?' and then turned back to Cameron to give him another kiss.

Trevor was at the far end of the living room, watching Angie and Cameron locked in their embrace, and even through his sunglasses, you could almost see the hurt in his eyes.

He stood and watched them for a moment, then turned and walked out of the room. I went after him, figuring a couple of words were in order, but he'd slipped through the kitchen and, apparently, out of the house.

An hour or so later, after everyone had cleared out, and Sarah and Paul were out front making some farewell chitchat with our friends, the phone rang. I grabbed it in the kitchen and looked at the sliver of cake still sitting on the table. I was stuffed, but that didn't mean I wouldn't have more.

'Hello?' I said.

'Hey.' Even though the voice was tired and a bit weak, I recognized it immediately.

'Lawrence . . .' I said. 'Is it ever nice to hear your voice. How are you?'

'Well enough to make a phone call, anyway. Cops were by, filled me in a bit on all your news.'

'I tried to call yesterday, but the nurse said you were still pretty out of it.'

'Painkillers, man. Gotta love 'em.'

I told him my own version of the events of the last few days, filling in a few gaps that had been overlooked by the cops.

Angie appeared in the kitchen doorway for a moment, and she'd been cornered by Trevor. Cameron, I gathered, had already left, along with most of our guests. I was trying to hear what they were saying at the same time as I was listening to Lawrence. Trevor was, I think, asking her again for a moment alone to speak to her.

'Fine, okay,' Angie said.

'Hang on,' I said to Lawrence, and then to Trevor, 'You off, man?'

'Yeah,' he said. 'Thanks.'

'We're just gonna walk down the street a bit,' Angie told me. 'I'll be back soon to help you and Mom clean up. And,' she said, looking scornful, 'to discuss what happened the other night at McDonald's.'

'Sure, hon,' I said.

Back to Lawrence. He said, 'I guess this is the last time you take advice from me on where to get a good deal on a car. Next time, try a dealer.'

'Barbie Bullock said the same thing. Might be the only advice he ever gave that was worth paying attention to.'

'Yeah, well, shit, sorry. I feel terrible about all this, like it was my fault.'

'It's okay. I've still got the car. Got the door panels back, just need a little body work on the back to patch some bullet holes.' I paused. 'There any satisfaction in knowing that the guy who did this to you is no longer with us?'

'I'll tell you this much,' Lawrence said. 'If Bullock had lived, I don't know that they'd ever have convicted him for what he did to me.'

'What do you mean?'

'I'd have made a pretty bad witness. I never really got a look at him. He got me as I was coming down the hall, going into my study, the lights were off, all of a sudden there's this searing pain in my gut as he drives in the knife, and then he's gone. I managed to drag myself into the bedroom, and the next thing I know I'm waking up in a hospital.'

'Yeah, well, maybe things have a way of working out, you know.'

'I wanted to call you to say thanks, for being there, calling 911 and getting me to a hospital, but also, I never had a chance to get back to you about that Trevor Wylie kid.'

'Oh yeah,' I said, only now remembering that Lawrence had promised to give me some information about the teenager when we met that night on our Brentwood's stakeout. Only problem was, Lawrence and I never had that meeting.

'It hardly matters now,' I said.

'Why?'

'Well, he's a bit strange, no question, but I might not be talking to you now if it weren't for him being in the right place at the right time. He's kind of latching himself onto Angie, and she's going to have to hurt his feelings, I suspect, but I imagine she'll be as nice about it as she can.'

'Well,' Lawrence said, 'you know, just 'cause a kid does something right doesn't mean he's still not screwed up. Stalking someone, that's not normal behavior.'

Lawrence couldn't see my shrug at the other end of the phone. I mean, he was right, but it all seemed a bit moot now.

'The thing is,' Lawrence said, 'I'd done some checking

on him that day, after our run-in with him at your place, when we found him back of the garage, and I got in touch with a few people I know who'll tell me things that they're not supposed to, mental health types, and they faxed me some stuff, told me some other things, and I'd made some notes.'

'Yeah?' I said, slightly curious, my eyes still drifting back to the cake.

'This Wylie kid's got a long psychiatric history. Violent outbursts, obsessive compulsive behavior. Slightly delusional behavior. And there's something about a sister.'

'Yeah?'

'The reason he's here, living without his parents, is, he attacked this sister, maybe even tried to kill her. No charges were ever laid, the family had enough money to make sure that didn't happen, they kept the authorities out of it, but they ended up kicking the kid out, he was scaring the shit out of them.'

I felt very cold. 'You're not making this up, are you, Lawrence?'

'There's more, Zack. I was checking out his car, that Chevy of his. This was shortly after I left your place. It was unlocked, and down there between the seats, I find all these snapshots of Angie. He'd been taking pictures of her, making a collection. And I grabbed those, nearly lost my hand to the fucking dog when I did it, too. He was dozing in the backseat, woke up quick.'

'Jesus,' I said. That cold feeling had turned into a shiver. And I thought back to a few nights earlier, when I'd been riding behind Trevor's Chevy, on the way out to Oakwood, and he'd become distracted by

357

something between the seats. That must have been when he'd discovered the pictures were missing.

'But here's the really creepy thing. I put those photos in a folder, with the other stuff I'd found, in my study, and I sent Kent – you met Kent, right?'

'Sure. That night, at the hospital. Nice guy.'

'Yeah, he's really been there for me these last few days. Him, and my sister Letitia, who's heading back to Denver tomorrow. Anyway, I sent Kent back to my place to get this stuff, so I could give you more details over the phone, but he couldn't find the folder anyplace.'

'Go on,' I said slowly.

'The place had been totally torn apart, and the folder was gone, and the pics along with it.'

'But that was Bullock and his crew,' I said. 'I saw your office that night. It was a complete mess. They were tearing apart your place, trying to find anything that would tell them what happened to the Virtue. They found the check I wrote you, for the same amount you'd paid the people at the auction, and that's what led them to me.'

'They didn't have to tear apart my place to find that check,' Lawrence said. 'It was sitting right on the counter, in the kitchen, on top of some mail. I'd left it there so I'd remember to deposit it. They couldn't miss it. It would have been the first thing they found.'

'Then why would they tear apart your office?' I asked. 'And why would they want your folder on Trevor Wylie?'

But even as I said it, I knew Bullock and his crew would have had no use for the folder on Trevor Wylie.

But Trevor might have been interested in it.

And if Trevor knew that Lawrence Jones was investigating him, and had gone to get any incriminating evidence himself . . . After he'd turned back early on that drive out to Oakwood, he'd have had time to go to Lawrence's before the detective and I were supposed to meet at Brentwood's . . .

I looked at the cake and noticed that the carving knife I'd been using to cut slices was not there.

'Lawrence,' I said, 'could Trevor have known that you were asking around about him?'

'I might have fucked up,' he said. 'As I was walking away from the car, he was coming the other way, saw me. And then, if he noticed at some point the pictures were missing, well, he might have put it together.'

'And he knew where you lived,' I said. 'Remember you gave him your card, told him to shove it up his ass when we found him in my backyard.'

'Yeah, that was mature.'

'Jesus, Lawrence, do you think it's possible it wasn't Bullock who tried to kill you that night in your apartment? I mean, Bullock said he didn't do it, but at the time I didn't think a denial from him meant much, but he wasn't afraid to admit killing Stan, or . . .'

'Or what?' Lawrence said.

And I thought: Angie's with him. She's with him right now. She's with the guy who attacked Lawrence and left him for dead.

'He tells me, if he's not with me, he won't ever be with anyone. It was like he wanted to add I wouldn't ever be with anyone else either.'

THIRTY-NINE

I dropped the phone and flew out the front door and down the steps of the porch. Sarah and Paul were standing in the driveway, the last of our guests gone, Paul making some derisive comments about the Virtue.

I must have appeared pretty alarmed, because Sarah, at the sight of me, looked horrified. 'What?' she said.

'Which way did Angie and Trevor go?'

Paul pointed south. 'That way,' he said. 'What's going on?'

I was running. Both Sarah and Paul were starting after me, and I shouted back to Sarah, 'Call the police . . .' Sarah, bless her, didn't ask questions, but ran straight into the house as Paul hung in with me.

We went past Trevor's black Chevy, parked at the curb, Morpheus's snout sticking out the half-rolled-down window. He jammed his entire head out, slobber dripping from his jowls, the sudden commotion of us running by sending him into a barking fit. He snapped at me and Paul as we ran by, scratched frantically at the windows with his long-nailed paws.

My eyes followed the sidewalk all the way down to the busy cross street, and there was no sign of either of them. I hadn't gone all that far before I started feeling winded, but I wasn't slowing down. Paul was keeping pace, and could easily have outrun me, but he didn't know what, exactly, the mission was.

'What is it, Dad?' he asked.

'It's Trevor,' I said, my arms and legs pumping.

'What about him?'

'It's him. He's the one who tried to kill Lawrence Jones.'

You could see it in his face, the flash of betrayal, how he'd accepted favors from someone who now presented a very real threat to our family.

'I'll bet they're at one of the cafés,' Paul said, and started to pull away from me. He got to the corner about ten seconds before I did, standing there, looking both ways, hoping for a glimpse of either of them. Not only was Paul younger and faster than I, but he had better eyesight, too. If anyone could spot Angie and Trevor, it would be him.

'There . . .' he said to me. 'Come on . . .'

I followed him up the sidewalk, in and around people strolling and coming in and out of shops and cafés. And then we were upon them, Angie and Trevor standing outside a coffee shop, his hand on her elbow, trying to motion her inside, Angie pulling away, resisting.

'I don't want to talk anymore, Trevor,' she said. 'That's it.'

'No, you listen . . .' Trevor said. 'I've got things to say to—'

He glanced to his left, saw me and Paul standing there. 'Daddy,' Angie said, and moved to join us, and Trevor yanked on her arm, dragging her back.

'Let her go, Trevor,' I said.

'Let go of my sister . . .' Paul shouted. I'd never heard him speak like that in his entire life.

'Shut up . . .' Trevor said. 'Everybody just shut up . . .'

People who had been passing on the sidewalk quickly sensed there was an 'incident' going on, and gave us a wide berth. Some had stopped to watch, but were hanging back.

With his free hand, he reached down into the pocket of his black coat and pulled out the knife that had gone missing from the kitchen. It was flecked with cake crumbs and frosting.

'Keep the fuck away . . .' he shouted, waving the knife in the air. Angie's eyes were wide with fear.

Paul went to move forwards, and I put my arm out, holding him back.

'Trevor,' I said, trying to be very calm, 'put that knife away, and we'll talk about things.'

He was moving his head slowly back and forth, looking at Angie, then at us and back to Angie. He spoke to her, the knife suspended in the air, none of us able to take a breath.

'I loved you,' he said. 'I loved you so much.'

'Sure,' Angie whispered, a tear trailing down one cheek. 'You're a great guy, Trevor.'

'I don't want to be some *guy* . . . Don't you understand what we are to each other? Don't you realize, every day now, every day that you live, you can thank me? I'd be entitled to take your life, because every day you get since that night is a gift from me.'

'Trevor,' I said.

He paid no attention to me. 'I couldn't believe it, you with that other guy. *Cameron.* Did he save your life? Has he been watching out for you, for weeks, keeping track of you, making sure you're okay? Has he done

362

for you what I've done? Do you understand anything about gratitude, or about how much you owe me?'

'Trevor,' I said again, softly. 'Put down the knife.'

He shook his head angrily.

'Nothing really serious has happened so far,' I said. I hesitated, then added, 'Even Mr Jones is going to make it. I was just talking to him on the phone. He's a hell of a lot better. So, right now, as of this moment, you're in less trouble than you might think.'

Trevor's cheeks turned crimson. 'He was going to say bad things about me,' he said to me. 'He took my pictures . . . He stole them right out of my car . . . He had no right to do that . . . And when I found them, he had all these notes written about me.'

'All anyone wants to do is help you, Trevor,' I said. 'But you have to put down the knife and—'

Something brushed past my leg, and suddenly Morpheus was running up to Trevor, wagging his tail, leaping up with his paws, catching Trevor right in the stomach. He didn't want to stab his own dog, so rather than push him off with his knife hand, Trevor released his grip on Angie's arm to shove Morpheus's head aside.

Angie bolted. Paul and I moved.

I went for the arm holding the knife, grabbing it with both hands as Paul grabbed Trevor around the middle, nearly trampling Morpheus in the process, the two of us slamming Trevor up against the brick wall. With Paul holding his body, Trevor had no leverage in his arm, and I slammed it once, twice, three times against the brick until the knife slipped from his hand and clattered to the sidewalk. Paul, who had gone into some kind of rage, had freed a fist and was pounding it into Trevor, a word accompanying each punch. 'Leave . . . My . . . Sister . . . Alone . . .'

There was a siren.

Morpheus had gone berserk, ripping into Paul's and my legs, getting his teeth into the denim and shaking his head back and forth. As we held Trevor against the wall, we kicked back, trying to get the dog off us before he tore through the jeans and was into flesh.

Someone, I don't even know who, managed to haul the dog off us, and as I felt Trevor give up his struggling, I said to Paul, who was still punching, 'It's okay, it's okay, calm down, it's okay. Stop. You can stop.'

And he did, and there were tears in his eyes, and his sister had her hands on his shoulders, and then she was folding her arms around her brother as the cops came running up the sidewalk.

FORTY

I was sitting in one of the wicker chairs on the front porch. It was a little past dinner, and the temperature was starting to drop. We were heading into fall, and I was debating whether to keep sitting out there, head inside, or head inside for a sweater and come back out.

The door opened and Sarah came out, a pad of paper and our checkbook in her hand. She took the wicker chair next to mine.

'How is she?' I asked.

'She's good,' Sarah said. 'You know she's got a lecture tonight, and I gave her lots of choices. I said she could stay home if she wanted to, or you or I could drive her down to Mackenzie, wait for her until her lecture is over and bring her home.'

It had been a week. We insisted Angie take a break from classes. Sarah spoke to the registrar, explained all that Angie had been through, and was told that she could take as long as she needed to get back on her feet. After a couple of days, she was getting antsy, and now, seven days later, she was sick of hanging around the house and wanted to get back to her regular routine.

'What did she decide?' I asked.

'She said she wants the car. She's going to drive herself to her lecture tonight, drive herself home.'

'Oh,' I said. Angie might be ready for that, but were Sarah and I?

'Yeah,' Sarah said. 'Oh.'

'How do you feel about that?'

'I'd like to keep her home for the rest of her life,' Sarah said. 'How do you feel?'

'I think your position is a reasonable one.'

We were both quiet for a moment. Sarah broke the silence. 'I think we should let her.'

'I guess. But I think she should take the Camry. Until we're absolutely sure that starting problem is fixed on the Virtue.'

'Agreed.'

'And you know,' I said, going slowly, 'if you're worried, we could sort of follow her along, make sure she got down to the university okay.'

Sarah eyed me. 'Follow her.' It was a question, not a command.

'It was just a thought. I was trying to think of a way to make this easier for you.'

Sarah thought about it. 'It's not that I'm not tempted,' she said, 'but I don't think so.' She turned her attention to the checkbook, which she was leafing through, frowning.

'Speaking of the Virtue,' she said. 'We're going to be paying it off for quite a while. If we put, say, $300 a month down on the line of credit, it's going to take us nearly thirty months or so to pay it off.'

'Uh-huh,' I said.

'We don't really have another $300 a month at the moment,' Sarah said. 'Not with all of Angie's college expenses, and we need to be socking money away now for Paul, he's going to want to go someplace.'

'The car seemed like a good idea at the time,' I said. 'It seemed like such a good deal.'

We were quiet again for a while as Sarah scribbled away at some figures. She's always done the finances in our house. I worry about everything else. All the time.

'You know,' I said, 'it's just occurred to me now, I can't believe I forgot about this, but I know a place where there's a lot of money just sitting around.'

Sarah's pen paused over the notepad. 'What are you talking about?'

'It never came up, all the questions I had to answer for the police, I never even thought to mention it.'

'What?'

'There's mail, some very thick envelopes I'd imagine, waiting to be claimed at several five-star hotels down in Rio de Janeiro. If you could find all the places they were sent to, you'd have yourself $140,000 in cash.'

Sarah put down her pen. 'Excuse me?'

'The money Eddie Mayhew got from the Jamaicans for the drugs he took out of our car. He sent it down there, he was going to go down and collect it, live high for a while.'

'So it's just sitting down there now,' Sarah said.

I nodded. 'And here's the interesting thing. I might just be the only person who knows about it.'

Sarah set aside her notepad. 'How's that?'

'Eddie told Trimble, and then when Trimble and I went back to Bullock's place, he told Bullock and the guy I thought of as Blondie. The other guy, the one I shot, he wasn't in the room at the time.'

'And all of those people . . .' Sarah said slowly.

'Are no longer with us,' I said.

'So if somebody were to go down to Rio, start going around to various hotels, and said he was Eddie Mayhew, they'd hand over the money to him.'

'I guess,' I said.

We watched some people walk past on the sidewalk. They waved, we waved back.

'It's dirty money, of course,' I said.

'That's for sure,' Sarah said. 'Although . . . it was made from selling something that was in *our* car.'

'But it wasn't yet our car when the stuff was removed from our car.'

'That's true,' Sarah said.

A car drove by. Somewhere in the distance, a siren.

'And whoever tried to claim those envelopes would need some sort of identification,' Sarah said.

'Oh sure, a fake ID, you'd have to have one of those. I don't even know where a person would begin to find one of those,' I said, and thought of Paul and his underage drinking friends.

I guess a full minute went by where we said nothing. Sarah started doing some more scribbling on her notepad, adding up some numbers. I was afraid to look over and see what sort of figures she might be playing with.

'The thing is,' I said, 'I could never pull it off.'

'Did somebody suggest you should?' Sarah said, almost defensively. 'I didn't say a word.'

'You know how I am. I'm too nervous. I'd break into a sweat at the hotel counter. I'd start stammering. They'd call the police. I'd crack before the interrogation even began. I don't hold up well under pressure, you know.'

'Sure,' Sarah said. 'That's why it's totally out of the question. It's just something to talk about, that's all.'

'That's right,' I said. 'Just something to talk about.'

'Yeah,' said Sarah, a bit dreamily. 'Just something to talk about.'

Another car went by. A couple of kids rode by on bicycles, laughing.

'I'll bet, though,' Sarah said, 'and I'm just thinking out loud here, but I'll bet if you made an appointment to see Harley, told him you needed something to calm you down, I'll bet you he could give you something.'

She kept her head down, focused on her notepad, afraid to look at me.

I got up from the chair. 'I'm gonna go see if we have any Scotch,' I said, and went into the house.

Read on for an extract from the next darkly
humourous and twist-filled novel in the
Zack Walker series

BAD LUCK

from bestselling author

LINWOOD BARCLAY

ONE

Trixie Snelling seemed to be working up to something over lunch this particular Tuesday, and really just killing time talking about scouring costume stores to find forehead ridges to please a client who liked to be dominated by a Klingon, but she never got to it because I had to take a call on my cell that my father had been eaten by a bear.

'There were those two Klingon chicks in the series where the bald guy was the captain, right?' Trixie asked me, because she knew that I was something of an authority when it came to matters related to science fiction.

'Yeah,' I said. 'Lursa and B'Etor Duras. They were sisters. They tried to overthrow the Gowron leadership of the Klingon High Council.' I paused, then added, 'Lots of leather and cleavage.'

'I'm okay there,' Trixie said, shaking her head at the useless information I had stored in my head. I wondered sometimes what important stuff gets crowded out when your brain is filled with trivia.

'My closet's so full of leather,' Trixie continued, 'I'm afraid it's all going to congeal back into a cow. I should show you sometime.' Even though Trixie was dressed, at the moment, in a dark blue pullover sweater

371

and fashionable jeans over high-heeled boots, it wasn't difficult to imagine her in full dominatrix regalia. I had seen her that way once – and not as a client – back in the days when we were neighbors. We'd kept in touch after Sarah and I and the kids had moved away, and even though we were just friends, and met regularly for lunch or a coffee, I never quite got over the novelty of what she did for a living.

She continued, 'But getting these ridges onto my forehead, making them blend in with the rest of my head, then there's the makeup that makes me look like I've fallen asleep at the tanning salon, I mean, getting ready for this guy is a major production. Where are the guys who just want to be whipped by the girl next door? Plus, he wants me to torment him without wrinkling his Starfleet uniform.'

'He wears a Starfleet uniform,' I said. 'What rank is he?'

'Captain,' Trixie said. 'There's these little gold dots on his collar that supposedly denote rank, but he just tells me to call him Captain, so that's fine. He's paying for it. I'm just glad he doesn't want me to call him Rear Admiral. Imagine what that might entail.'

'I imagine that you are well compensated for your efforts.'

Trixie gave me a half smile. 'Absolutely.' The smile disappeared as quickly as it had appeared. Trixie picked at her spinach salad as I twirled some fettuccine carbonara onto my fork.

'What's on your mind?' I asked.

She shook her head. 'Nothing.' She picked at her salad some more. 'What's going on with you? Things working out with Sarah as your boss?'

I shrugged, then nodded. I'd been working as a feature writer at *The Metropolitan* for more than a year now, having accepted the fact that I could not make a go of it staying home and writing science fiction novels. I'd been assigned to Sarah, whose responsibilities at the city desk included overseeing a number of feature writers, some neurotic, some egotistical, some neurotically egotistical, and then there was me, her obsessive, often pain-in-the-ass, husband.

'Oh sure,' I said. 'I mean, she wants to kill me, but other than that, the relationship is working well.' I had a bite of pasta. 'I'm on the newsroom safety committee.'

'There's a surprise,' Trixie said.

'It's no joke. We've got air quality issues, radiation off the computer screens, there's—'

'Let me see if I understand this. You work for a major daily newspaper, where they send reporters off to Iraq and Iran and Afghanistan and God knows where else, and they expose murderous biker gangs and do first-person stories about what it's like to be a skyscraper window washer, and you're worried about air quality and computer radiation?'

'You make it sound kind of weenie-like,' I said.

Again, Trixie gave me the half smile. 'Sarah okay with you and me being friends?'

I nodded. 'I were you, I'd be more worried about my own reputation, hanging out with a writer for *The Metropolitan*.'

'And how was your trip? Didn't you guys go someplace?'

'That was months ago,' I said. 'A little trip to Rio.'

'Good time?'

I shrugged. 'I found it a bit stressful.' I paused, then added, 'I'm not a good traveler.'

'How's Angie?' Trixie asked. My daughter was nineteen now, in her second year at Mackenzie University.

'Good,' I said. 'Paul's good, too. He's seventeen now, finishing up high school.'

'They're good kids.' Trixie's eyes seemed to mist when she said it, and then she seemed to be looking off to one side, at nothing in particular.

'I keep getting this vibe that there's something on your mind,' I said. 'Talk to me.'

Trixie said nothing, breathed in slowly through her nose. If she needed time to work up to something, I could wait.

'Well,' she said, 'you know the local paper in Oakwood? *The Suburban*? There's this—'

And then the cell phone inside my jacket began to ring.

'Hang on,' I said to Trixie. I got out the phone, flipped it open, put it to my ear. 'Yeah?'

'Zack?'

'Hi, Sarah.'

'Where are you?'

'I'm having lunch with Trixie. Remember I said?'

'So you're not driving or anything?'

'No. I'm sitting down.' My mind flashed to Paul and Angie. When you have teenagers, and someone's about to give you some sort of bad news, you know it's probably going to be about them. 'Has something happened with the kids?' I asked.

'No no,' Sarah said quickly. 'Kids are fine, far as I know.'

I let out a breath.

'So anyway,' Sarah said, 'there's this stringer I use sometimes, Tracy McAvoy? Up in the Fifty Lakes District? She does the odd feature, breaking news when it happens up there and we can't get a staffer there fast enough. Remember she did the piece about that seaplane crash, the hunters that died, last year?'

I didn't, but I said, 'Sure.' However, I could recall seeing the byline, occasionally, in the paper. Fifty Lakes is about a ninety-minute drive north of the city, lots of lakes (well, about fifty) and hills, cabins and boating and fishing, that kind of thing. A lot of city people had cottages up there. My father, for one.

'I just got off the phone with her,' Sarah said. 'She's got this story about a possible bear attack. Pretty vicious.'

I could guess where this was going. Tracy was an okay reporter, she could file a basic story, but the city desk was wanting something more, some color, maybe a piece for the weekend paper. The sort of thing I was born to do. 'Sarah, just get to it.'

'Would you shut up and listen? It was in Braynor, well, in the woods outside Braynor.'

'Yeah, okay. Braynor's where my dad's camp is.'

'I know. Well, here's the thing. They found this body, this man, and I guess there wasn't a whole lot of him left to identify, and they found him right by Crystal Lake.'

That was the lake where Dad ran his fishing camp. A handful of cabins, rental boats. I mentioned that to Sarah.

'I know, Zack. That's where they found the body. In the woods by your father's place.'

'Jesus,' I said. 'I guess I should give him a call.' I paused. 'I can't even remember the last time I talked to him. It's been a while.'

'Here's the thing,' Sarah said, hesitating. 'Nobody's seen your dad for a while. And they haven't identified this body yet.'

A chill ran through me.

'I phoned your dad's place,' Sarah added. 'But there wasn't any answer.'

I slipped the phone back into my jacket and said apologetically to Trixie, 'Hold that thought. Something's sort of come up.'

Order your copy of *Bad Luck* today!